Andrew Alexander Blair

The Chemical Analysis of Iron

A complete account of all the best known methods for the analysis of iron, steel,

pig-iron, iron ore, limestone, slag, clay, sand, coal, coke, and furnace and producer

gases

Andrew Alexander Blair

The Chemical Analysis of Iron
A complete account of all the best known methods for the analysis of iron, steel, pig-iron, iron ore, limestone, slag, clay, sand, coal, coke, and furnace and producer gases

ISBN/EAN: 9783337652623

Printed in Europe, USA, Canada, Australia, Japan

Cover: Foto ©Andreas Hilbeck / pixelio.de

More available books at **www.hansebooks.com**

THE

CHEMICAL ANALYSIS OF IRON.

A COMPLETE ACCOUNT OF ALL THE BEST KNOWN METHODS

FOR THE

Analysis of Iron, Steel, Pig-Iron, Iron Ore, Limestone, Slag, Clay, Sand, Coal, Coke, and Furnace and Producer Gases.

BY

ANDREW ALEXANDER BLAIR,

Graduate United States Naval Academy, 1866; Chief Chemist United States Board appointed to Test Iron, Steel, and other Metals, 1875; Chief Chemist United States Geological Survey and Tenth Census, 1880; Member American Philosophical Society, etc.

SECOND EDITION.

PHILADELPHIA:

J. B. LIPPINCOTT COMPANY.

1891.

TO MY WIFE,

WITHOUT WHOSE ASSISTANCE IT WOULD NEVER HAVE
BEEN WRITTEN,

THIS VOLUME

IS DEDICATED.

PREFACE TO THE SECOND EDITION.

In preparing the second edition of this book I have tried to correct the mistakes that were apparent in the first edition, and to add such matter as the advance in analytical chemistry seemed to justify. In effecting the first of the objects I have been aided by such kindly criticism as the profession and reviews offered me, and in the second by the advice and assistance of many of my fellow-workers. Among others my thanks are due to Messrs. Maunsel White and A. L. Colby, of the Bethlehem Iron Company, Mr. Clemens Jones, of the Thomas Iron Company, Mr. E. F. Wood, of the Homestead Steel-Works, Mr. T. T. Morrell, of the Cambria Iron Company, Mr. H. C. Babbitt, of the Wellman Steel Company, Prof. F. W. Clarke, Chief Chemist U.S. Geological Survey, Mr. J. E. Stead, of Middlesborough, England, and Mr. J. Edward Whitfield, of Philadelphia.

It will be seen that the "Table of Atomic Weights" has been revised ; the latest and most reliable values for the elements are given, and the "Table of Factors" has been changed to correspond to these values.

LABORATORY OF BOOTH, GARRETT & BLAIR,
PHILADELPHIA, June, 1891.

CONTENTS.

THE CHEMICAL ANALYSIS OF IRON.

APPARATUS.

THE speed and facility with which results may be obtained, and often the accuracy of these results, are dependent upon various mechanical appliances as well as upon the skill of the analyst. These appliances will be considered under separate heads.

APPARATUS FOR THE PREPARATION OF THE SAMPLES.

For crushing iron ores, a mortar and pestle, such as are ordinarily used, have caused much trouble. In breaking up hard ores the wear, especially on the pestle, is considerable, and the particles of cast iron may cause the sample to yield too high a result in the determination of metallic iron. Of course in non-magnetic ores these particles may be removed with a magnet, but in the case of magnetic or partly magnetic ores this cannot be done, and a hardened steel mortar and pestle should be used. The sample should be broken to about pea size, well mixed, and quartered, this quarter broken still finer, and mixed and quartered in the same way until the resulting portion is small enough to be bottled. The final grinding can be best made on a chilled-iron plate with a hardened steel muller. Except with unusually refractory ores, further grinding is unnecessary, but with such ores the final grinding must be in an agate mortar. In large laboratories and where many ores are analyzed, arrangements such as are shown in the accompanying sketches will prove very useful. Fig. 1 shows a steel mortar, the pestle worked by power, and a chilled plate and muller. A is the mortar; B, a wooden stem in which the pestle fits. The cams H fit on the shaft and raise the pestle by means of the tappets *a*, which are faced with raw hide. An iron hoop shrunk on the mortar has a ring, in which is fastened the lower block of the pulley D; the upper block is attached to a traveller, E. When in use the mortar is covered with a leather cap, which prevents the pieces of ore from flying out of the mortar. To transfer the powdered ore to

FIG. 1.

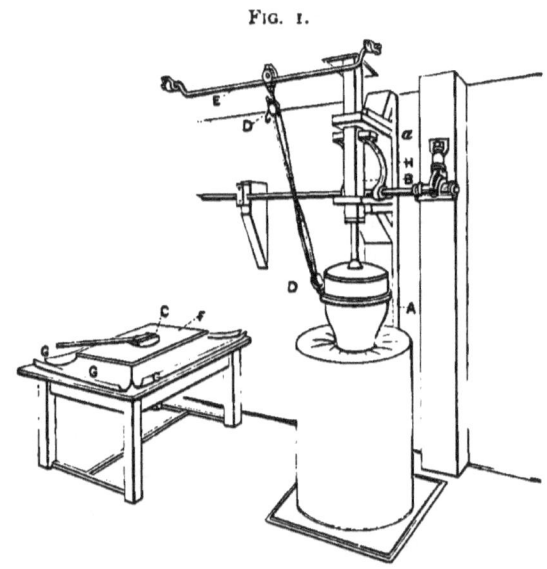

the chilled plate F, remove the leather cap, raise the pestle clear of the mortar, and fasten it up by a hook from the framework to the tappet *a*. Raise the mortar by pulling the fall from the upper block and fastening the hook in its end into a ring at the lower block. By means of the traveller, run the mortar over the plate and turn the ore out. After quartering the sample down, finish the grinding on the chilled plate with the muller C. The sheet-iron troughs G serve to catch any ore that falls from the plate. In some laboratories a small Blake crusher is used for crushing the ore, but it is more liable to get out of order, and is not so easily cleaned as the mortar and pestle. Fig. 2 shows an arrangement for facilitating the final grinding in the agate mortar, in which the pestle is rotated by a Stow flexible shaft.

FIG. 2.

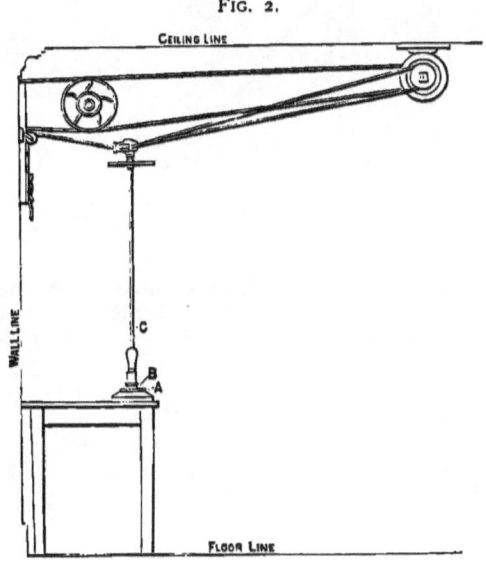

The apparatus shown in Fig. 3, designed by Mr. Maunsel White, has been in use several years at the chemical laboratory of the Bethlehem Iron Company, and has worked very satisfactorily. The power is applied from an overhead countershaft not shown in the cut. The lower portion of the vertical shaft carries two horizontal pulleys, A and B; these pulleys are connected, as shown, with the spindle carrying the pestle and with the circular box D, in which the mortar is securely fastened by four claw-bolts, which may be seen in the drawing.

The piece D is made with a spindle which extends down into a bearing in the supporting piece H. The piece H, which may be called a lever, is secured to the frame F by a bolt which passes through it, and around which it can be turned through an angle sufficient to permit of the easy emptying of the mortar without displacing the belt.

A groove at the farther end of H, as shown, carries a weighted rod which supplies the pressure of the mortar against the pestle. The weights are made movable so that the pressure can be varied for special cases.

FIG. 3.

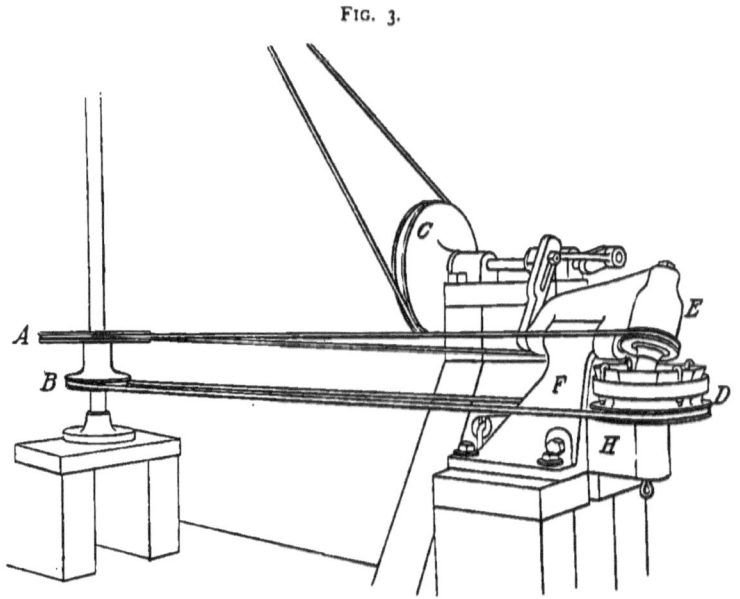

The agate pestle is secured in a brass spindle with a grooved collar for carrying the belt; this spindle revolves in a bored socket in the piece E, and is secured from dropping out by means of a small nut, shown at the top of the piece. The piece E is connected to the frame F by a circular bolt, the end of which is supplied with an arm for rocking the piece E; this obtains by fastening the bolt with dowel-pins where it passes through the piece E while free to move in the frame F. The pulley C is run from the countershaft, and revolves a small shaft whose end carries a crank connected by a short rod to the bolt-arm of the piece E, and supplies the power and means for the rocking motion.

It will now be seen that while the mortar revolves, the pestle, revolving more rapidly, sweeps across the face of the mortar by the rocking motion of the piece E, thus constantly changing the material between the grinding surfaces.

In taking samples of iron or steel, a perfectly clean dry drill should be used, and the utmost care taken to prevent grease, oil, or dirt of any kind from getting in the sample. With bar-iron or steel the scale on the

FIG. 4.

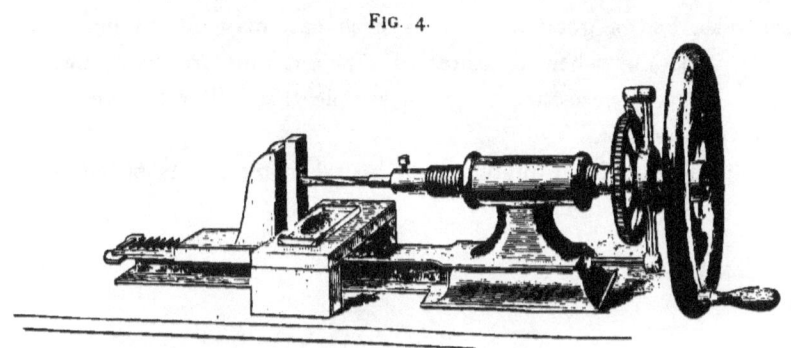

outside of the piece should be removed as carefully as possible, the first drillings from each hole thrown away, and the remainder thoroughly mixed and placed in a perfectly clean dry bottle. Fig. 4 shows a convenient form of drill-press for the purpose. A half-inch Morse twist-drill is the best for general use. In taking samples of pig-iron, the loose sand should be carefully removed from the outside of the pig and a piece of stout paper wrapped around it to prevent the sand and slag from the outside getting mixed with the clean drillings, which are received on a piece of glazed paper turned up at the edges (Fig. 4). Drillings from pig-iron can be best mixed by

FIG. 5.

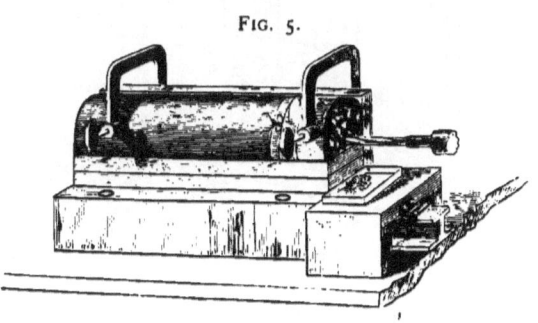

rubbing them up in a small porcelain mortar. At blast-furnaces, to save the trouble of breaking pieces from the pigs the arrangement shown in

Fig. 5 is very convenient, as half a pig can be placed in the press. The framework is securely bolted to the table on which the press stands, and the pig is secured by means of the iron clamps. By removing the pieces of wood under the pig it is lowered so that two or three holes can be bored in different parts of the face of the pig to get an average. By taking one pig from the first bed, one from the last, and one from an intermediate bed, a good average of each cast may be obtained. When the ore varies, or when mixtures of different ores are used, these precautions are very necessary to get a sample that will really represent an average of the cast.

Drillings from large ingots must be taken by means of an ordinary brace.

FIG. 6.

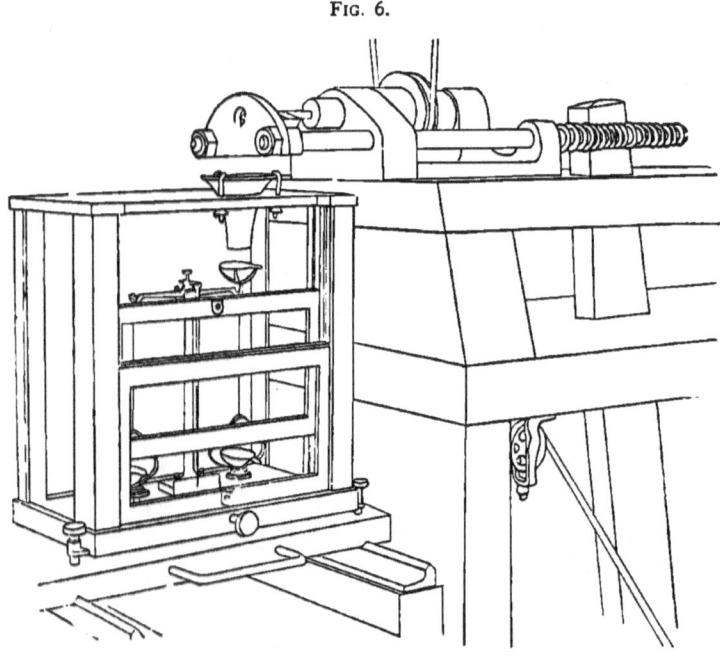

Fig. 6 shows an apparatus for the drilling and weighing of samples of steel for colorimetric carbon or other rapid determinations, designed by Mr. Maunsel White, and in use at the laboratory of the Bethlehem Iron

Company. The drill is mounted above the balance, the point of the drill directly overhanging the balance-pan. The piece to be drilled is placed against the semicircular plate carried by the two rods that pass through the drill-frame; on the rear end of each rod is a coiled spring which supplies the pressure necessary for drilling. The rear ends of the rods are held together by a tie-piece, which is connected to a lever operated by the foot, so that the rods and plate can be forced forward for the reception of the piece to be drilled.

The balance is supplied with an overhead pan which receives the drillings guided to it through the funnel fixed in the top of the balance-case for this purpose. When the pan falls, showing that sufficient sample has been drilled, pressure is applied to the lever by the foot and the piece taken out. The balance-case rests upon an iron plate grooved on the bottom; these grooves engage with guides screwed to the table and permit the balance-case to be pulled forward, which facilitates the cleaning of the funnel from all clinging particles. This operation is done with a camel-hair brush or a feather. A magnet is run around in the lower pans to guard against the chance of falling particles interfering with the accuracy of the weights. The upper door of the balance-case is then lowered into the position shown in Fig. 6, which gives free access to the upper pan containing the sample. The sample is now accurately weighed, the pan lifted out, and the drillings transferred to the test-tube.

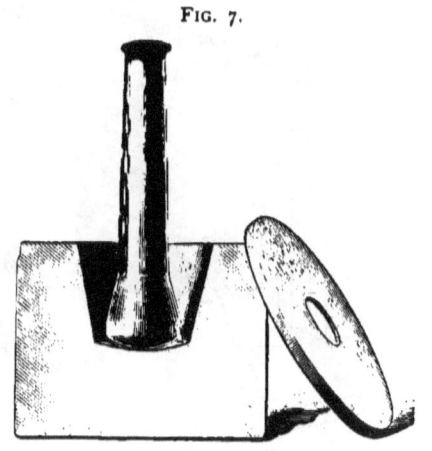

FIG. 7.

The use of a ¼-inch twist-drill has been adopted and found to give good results. The pans and funnel are aluminium and the bearings agate; the beam is short, 5½ inches in length, in consequence of which the weighing is done rapidly.

In taking samples of spiegel or of white-iron, small clean pieces from a number of pigs should be taken and powdered in a hardened steel mortar. The mortar shown in the sketch (Fig. 7) is forged from high carbon steel, hardened, and the temper drawn from the outside. This makes the mortar both hard and tough. The sheet-iron cover prevents the pieces from flying. The face of the pestle is very hard, and the handle comparatively soft, so that it will not break when struck by the hammer.

In taking samples for analysis, when the method used requires the sample to be in a fine state of subdivision, the very fine part of the sample should never be separated from the coarser particles by a sieve or screen, but the sample should be mixed thoroughly, and a portion, fine and coarse together, taken and powdered, so that all may pass through the sieve.

FIG. 8.

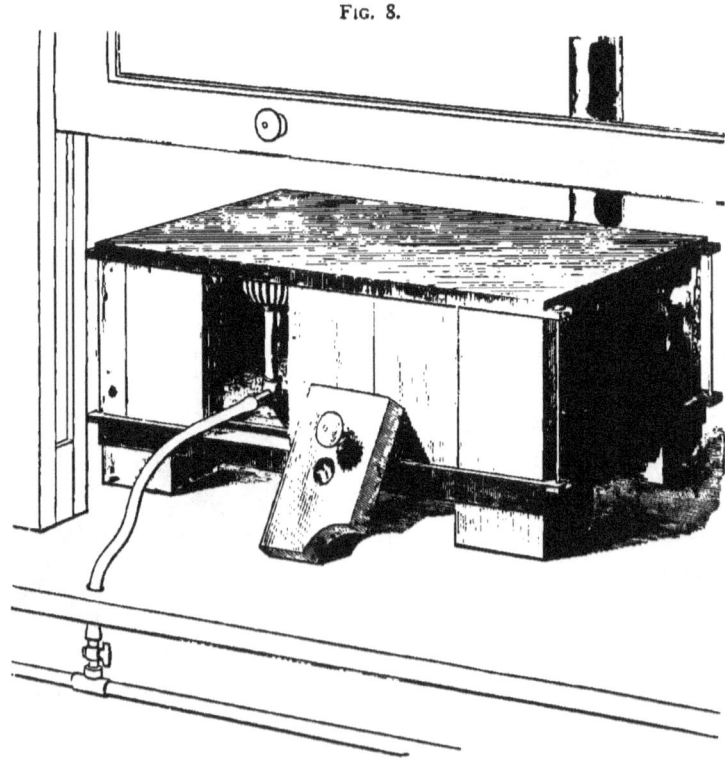

GENERAL LABORATORY APPARATUS.

Sand-Bath and Air-Bath.

Fig. 8 shows a very convenient form of sand-bath, and Fig. 9 an air-bath. This air-bath is made from an ordinary cast-iron sink, which is supported on fire-bricks. The top is of asbestos board, with a piece

FIG. 9.

of sheet-iron underneath to strengthen it. The holes are large enough to take the largest-sized beakers, while the smaller beakers are supported by asbestos rings. An ordinary gas-regulator or governor, which supplies the gas at a constant pressure, keeps the temperature sufficiently uniform. Evaporations may thus be effected with great saving of time and with little danger of loss by spirting. The products of combustion of the gas are carried off by a separate flue, and the H_2SO_4 formed does not come in contact with the solutions in the baths.

Instead of sand-bath the term hot plate is generally used for this piece of apparatus, the surface of the iron being kept clean and free from rust by an occasional coat of stove-polish. Evaporations on the hot plate may be hastened by standing the beaker containing the solution inside another beaker with the bottom cut off. Beakers may be readily

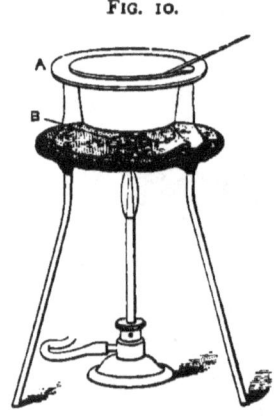

FIG. 10.

cut in this way by starting a crack and leading it around with a red-hot iron or glass rod. For evaporating solutions in capsules or dishes a beaker cut off in this way and placed on a tripod covered with wire gauze, as shown in Fig. 10, may be used with great advantage. The capsule is supported on an asbestos ring, A, the bottom being about ½ inch (12 mm.) from the wire gauze. A piece of thin asbestos board, B, about ¾ inch (18 mm.) in diameter, rests on the gauze and covers the point of the flame of the Bunsen burner, and, by throwing the heat more on the sides of the capsule, tends to prevent spirting when the solution in the capsule gets thick and pasty.

Apparatus for Hastening Evaporations.

The little piece of apparatus shown in Fig. 11 was designed by Mr. J. E. Whitfield, and is most useful in hastening evaporations. It consists of a platinum tube $\frac{3}{16}$ of an inch in diameter, coiled above the burner to present more heating surface, through which passes a blast of air. As the platinum tube and Bunsen burner are both supported on the arm of the stand, the level of the tube may be made to accommodate itself to a crucible on a stand, to a capsule on a tripod (Fig. 10), or to a beaker on the air-bath. In the treatment of the insoluble residues from ores by hydrofluoric and sulphuric acids it is quite invaluable, as it not only hastens the evaporation but prevents loss by spirting.

FIG. 11.

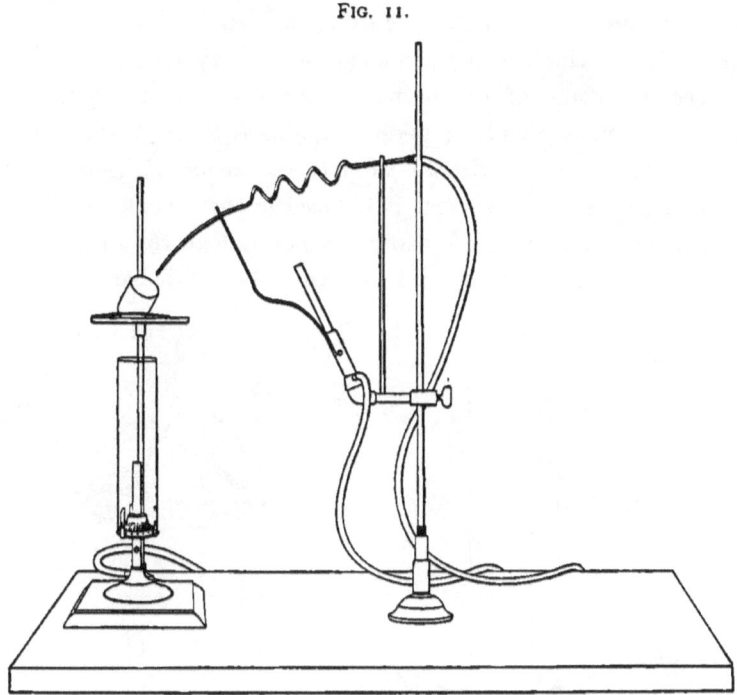

The blast of hot air breaks the bubbles on the surface of the liquid, and when properly directed it gives the liquid a rotary motion that tends to throw onto the sides of the crucible any particles of the liquid thrown up by the bubbles. The amount of heat that can be applied to a crucible under these circumstances, without causing loss, is really surprising. It is equally useful when evaporating solutions in beakers on the air-bath or hot plate. In laboratories where a blast of air is always at command, the principle may be applied in many ways for hastening evaporations

Even a cold blast of air from a drawn-out glass tube directed on the surface of a liquid hastens the evaporation very materially.

Igniting Precipitates.

For ignitions, a Bunsen burner with a ring to regulate the supply of air, provided with an ordinary glass chimney, as shown in Fig. 12, is most convenient. By shutting off the air entirely a very low heat may be obtained, which is not rendered variable by air-currents, and the heat of the full flame of the burner is increased by the greater draft caused by the chimney and the perfect steadiness of the flame. By using a small platinum rod or wire to support the cover of the crucible, as shown in Fig. 12, a gentle current is induced in the crucible, which, while it greatly facilitates burning off carbon, is not sufficiently strong to cause loss by carrying off even the lightest ash. The crucible may also be

FIG. 12.

FIG. 13.

FIG. 14.

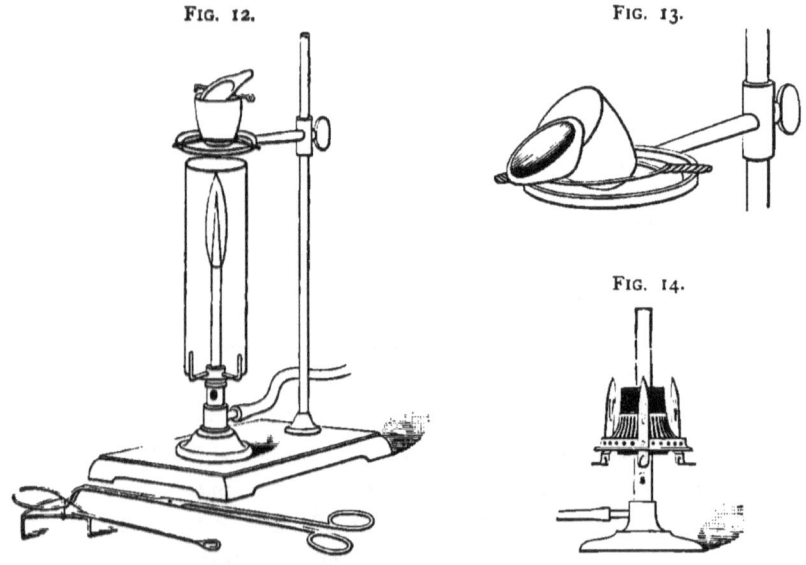

inclined on its side, as in Fig. 13, the heat in this case being applied near the top of the crucible. Fig. 14 shows an easy method of fitting a chimney to a Bunsen burner by means of a cork and an ordinary Argand chimney-holder. When a higher temperature than that obtainable by a Bunsen burner is required, a blast-lamp, worked by a foot-bellows, by a water-blast, or by a small blower, is used.

Tripods.

The most convenient arrangement for heating liquids in beakers, flasks, etc., is the iron tripod (Fig. 15). It consists of a cast-iron ring with three legs of heavy iron wire ¼ inch (6 mm.) in diameter. The ring is covered with brass wire gauze, 40 meshes to the inch, which can be replaced when it is burned out, but which lasts a long time. The vertical height of the tripod is about 7½ inches (191 mm.). A very convenient form of burner is the Finkner ratchet-burner, as the flame can be raised or lowered by means of the ratchet on the burner, thus avoiding the necessity of reaching back over the table to the gas-cock. As the air and gas are both turned off at once, there is less danger of the flame blowing out when it is turned very low.

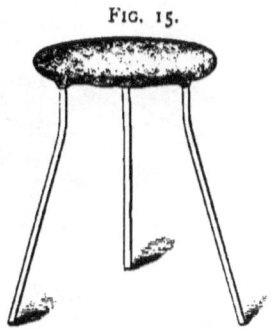

FIG. 15.

Filter-Pumps.

The use of filter-pumps for Bunsen's method of rapid filtration is now very general, and greatly facilitates many operations. The kind of pump is usually determined by the water-supply. With a good pressure of water, the most convenient form of pump is the injector. Fig. 16 shows the Richards' injector united with a blast-cylinder, by the use of which a good air-pressure for use with the blast-lamp may be obtained. When the pump is used for filtering strong solutions of HNO_3 a glass injector may be used, and the water allowed to flow at once into the sink or waste-pipe. When the pressure of water is not great enough for an injector the Bunsen pump may be used, the vacuum obtained of course depending on the amount of fall. A tank with a ball-cock attachment makes this form of pump most convenient.

An ordinary air-pump may also be used for many purposes, but of course is unsuitable for filtering corrosive liquids, such as HNO_3, unless a wash-bottle containing a caustic alkali is interposed between the flask and

the air-pump. The apparatus shown in Fig. 17 will give a very good idea
of an arrangement which is very convenient when a water-supply is not

FIG. 16.

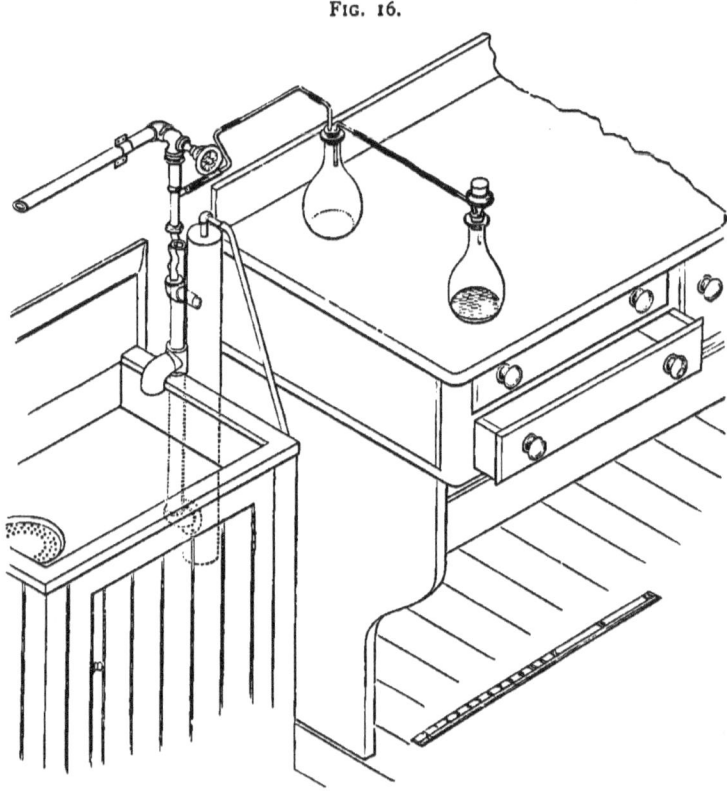

available. The jug, which may be of three or five gallons capacity, serves
as a reservoir. It connects directly with the air-pump.

Bunsen's Method of Rapid Filtration.

This method is too widely known to make a detailed description necessary, but some hints in regard to the details may be useful. In the first
place, it is very difficult to get good 60° funnels, so that the little perforated
cones of platinum to support the point of the filter, which are sold by chemical dealers, rarely fit the funnel, and when they do not fit, the filters are

apt to tear. The small funnel of platinum foil, as recommended by Bunsen, can be made to fit the funnel better, but the edges sometimes cut the filter.

FIG. 17.

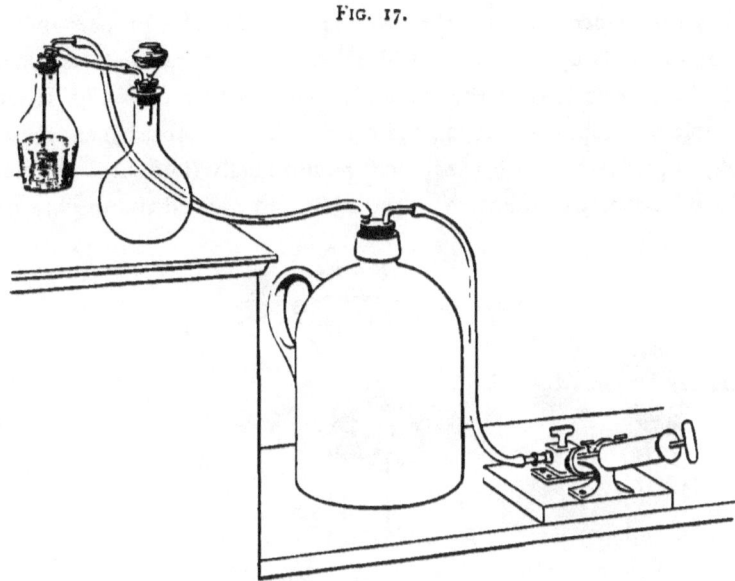

A small funnel of parchment pricked full of pin-holes, and of the size and shape of the platinum-foil funnel, works very well. It is a mistake to use too great a pressure, especially at first, and the filter should be kept full. The filtering flask should always be connected, not with the vacuum-pipe directly, but with another flask fitted with a little Bunsen valve, which allows the air to pass into the vacuum-pipe, but, in case of a sudden stoppage in the pump, prevents the back pressure from entering the filtering-flask and blowing out the contents of the funnel.

FIG. 18.

Fig. 18 shows an arrangement for filtering into a beaker instead of into a flask. It is necessary to have a glass cover over the beaker, as shown in the sketch, on account of the tendency the solution has to spatter, particles of the solution being carried out of the beaker in the current of air flowing into the vacuum-pipe.

Gooch's Method of Rapid Filtration.

The pierced crucible and cone, with asbestos felt, devised by Gooch,* are almost indispensable to the iron analyst for the proper and rapid execution of many operations, as will be seen by the frequent references to them in the descriptions of the methods given farther on. Fig. 19 shows the crucible and cap, and Fig. 20 the cone. The asbestos, which should be of a soft, silky, flexible fibre, is scraped longitudinally (not cut) to a fine, soft down, and purified by boiling in strong HCl, and washed thoroughly on the

FIG. 19.   FIG. 20.   FIG. 21.

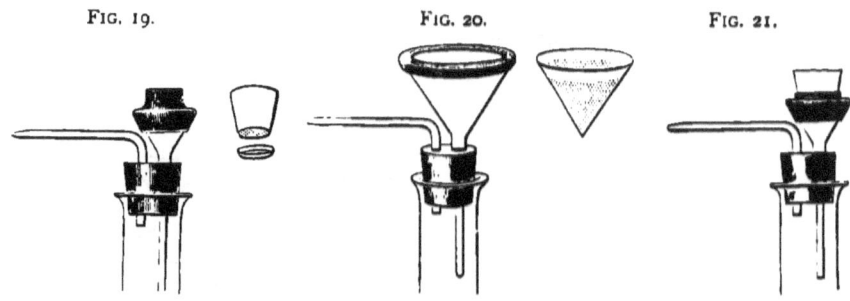

cone. It may be dried and kept in a bottle. The perforated crucible is placed in one end of a piece of soft rubber tubing, the other end of which is stretched over the top of a funnel, as shown in Figs. 19 and 21. The neck of the funnel passes through the stopper of a vacuum-flask. To prepare the felt, pour a little of the prepared asbestos suspended in water into the crucible and attach the pump. The asbestos at once assumes the condition of a firm, compact layer, which is washed with ease under the pressure of the pump. After washing the felt, suck it dry on the pump, remove the crucible, detach any little pieces of fibre that may be on the outside of the bottom of the crucible, slip on the little cap, dry, ignite, and weigh. Remove the cap, place the crucible in the rubber holder, start the pump and pour the liquid and precipitate to be filtered into the crucible, wash, dry, ignite, if required, cool, and weigh as before. The cone is fitted to a funnel by means of a rubber band stretched over the top of the funnel.

---

* Proceedings Am. Acad. Arts and Sciences, 1878, p. 342; Chem. News, xxxvii. 181.

The pressure of the pump pulls the cone down so that the overlapping part of the band forms a tight joint between the cone and the upper part of the funnel (Fig. 22). The felt is prepared in the same manner as in the crucible. Fill the cone with the asbestos suspended in water, start the pump, press down the cone into the funnel, and, if necessary, pour in more of the asbestos, letting it run all around from the upper edge of the cone so as to fill all the holes and make a firm, cohesive layer all over the inside of the perforated portion of the cone. Wash it well with water and suck it dry. It will then be ready for use. The cone is not intended for use when the precipitate is to be weighed, but, as it

FIG. 22.

presents a very large filtering surface, it is most useful for such precipitates as MnO_2 precipitated by Ford's method, etc. In this case, when the precipitate has been washed and sucked dry, by removing the cone from the funnel and carefully separating the felt from the sides of the cone with a little piece of flattened platinum wire, it may be removed from the cone with the precipitate enclosed in it, and the whole mass transferred to a beaker or flask for resolution. The cones may be of various sizes ; for ordinary use, a cone 1¾ inches (45 mm.) in diameter is very convenient. They may also be used with a paper filter. In both the crucibles and cones the holes should be very small, and drilled (not punched) as closely together as possible.

Counterpoised Filters.

The Gooch crucible and felt are most useful for weighing precipitates which are to be dried and not ignited, as in the direct weighing of the phospho-molybdate of ammonium. When they are not available, however, recourse must be had to counterpoised filters. The best method for preparing and using them is as follows : Take two washed filters of the same size and about the same thickness, fold them as if about to fit them in funnels, and, by cutting from the upper edge of the heavier of the two with a pair of scissors, make them nearly balance. Place them between a pair of watch-glasses, as shown in Fig. 23, dry them at 100° C., and allow them to cool in a desiccator. Place one in each pan of the balance, and, handling them with a pair of forceps, clip them until they balance exactly.   Place each filter in a funnel, filter the precipitate

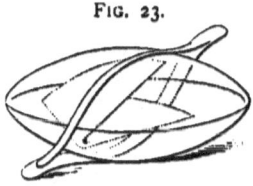

FIG. 23.

on one of them, pass the *clear* filtrate (not the washings) through the other, and wash them both in the same manner.   Remove them from the funnels, turning over the top edges of the filter containing the precipitate to prevent any of the latter from falling out, place them in a watch-glass, dry them at 100° C. (or at the required temperature, whatever it may be), cover them with the other watch-glass, cool in a desiccator, place them on opposite pans of the balance, and the weight added to the pan containing the empty filter, to make them balance, is the weight of the precipitate.

Filter-Paper.

All filter-paper contains more or less inorganic matter, which remains, after burning the paper, as a white or brownish ash.   The Swedish paper with the water-mark J. H. Munktell leaves the smallest amount of ash, and this ash contains from 35 to 65 per cent. silica, besides ferric oxide, alumina, lime, and magnesia in varying proportions.

Schleicher & Schull prepare some very pure filters by washing them with HCl and HFl, and these should always be used for very accurate work unless the analyst prepares ashless papers for himself.   The commoner kinds of German paper contain much larger amounts of inorganic matter than the Swedish paper, and it usually consists principally of carbonate of calcium, but sometimes contains appreciable amounts of phosphates.

Filters of this kind should always be washed with HCl before they are used.   They may be washed by fitting them in a funnel, pouring on hot HCl and water (1 part acid to 3 parts water), and washing thoroughly with hot water.   They may also be washed in the apparatus shown in Fig. 24.   It consists of a bottle of the proper size with the bottom cut off with a hot iron.   It contains a disk of wood cut to fit the shape of the bottle and perforated with a number of gimlet-holes.   Fill the bottle half full of cut filters, pour on a mixture of HCl and water (1–3), allow them to stand about half an hour, and wash thoroughly with distilled water. The bottle may be attached to the vacuum-pump and washed under pressure. Dry the filters at a temperature below 100° C. For preparing ashless filters the apparatus shown in Fig. 25 is used. It is of spun copper, lined with platinum throughout. Over the vertical tube is a perforated platinum disk countersunk to the level of the bottom of the

FIG. 24.

FIG. 25.

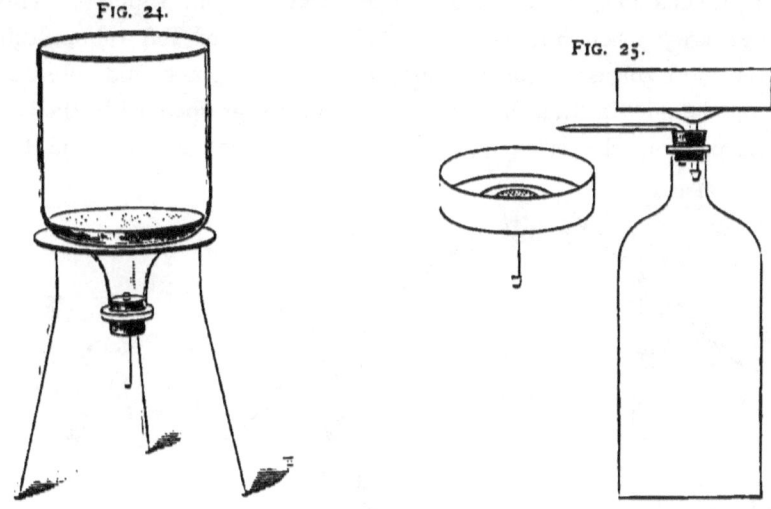

dish. It is attached to the pump, and the filters are washed first with HCl and water (1–3), then with water to remove the lime, then with HFl and water (1–3) to dissolve the silica, and finally with distilled water. Swedish filters washed in this way are practically ashless, the ash from five filters, each 3 inches (75 mm.) in diameter, weighing less than $\frac{1}{10}$ mg. Filters may be cut out, using tin disks of the proper diameter as patterns; they may be bought ready cut, or they can be cut out at shops where circular labels are cut at very small cost. The best way is to buy Swedish paper and a good tough German paper, by the ream, have the paper cut into filters of the proper sizes, say 5½ inches (140 mm.), 4¼ inches (108 mm.), and 3 inches (76 mm.) in diameter, and wash the Swedish with HCl and HFl and the German with HCl. The ashless filters can be used for final filtrations when the precipitate is to be ignited and weighed, and the German for all other work.

Washing-Bottles.

Figs. 26, 27, and 28 represent different forms of washing-bottles. For ordinary use that represented in Fig. 26 is the best. The neck is wrapped with thin asbestos board, covered with a piece of wash-leather or chamois, which is sewed to keep it from slipping. This is very necessary when hot water is used. A piece of soft rubber tubing at A is more pleasant for the mouth than the glass, and after compressing the air in the flask the tube can be grasped with the teeth, thus keeping up the stream of water for some time without effort. It

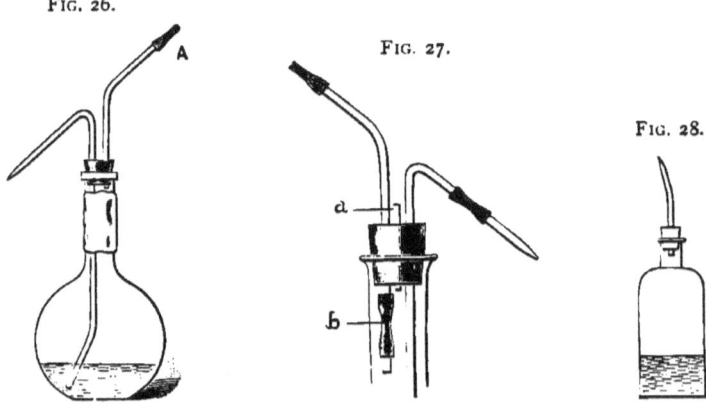

FIG. 26.   FIG. 27.   FIG. 28.

also prevents the lips from being scalded when using very hot water. Fig. 27 shows a movable tip, which allows the stream of water to be directed by means of the finger. The form of flask shown in Fig. 27 is very convenient to use with ammonia-water, etc. The tube *a* is closed with the index finger, while the Bunsen valve *b* closing as soon as the air is compressed in the flask prevents the vapors from coming back into the mouth, and the stream of liquid is stopped instantly by removing the finger from *a*. Fig. 28 shows the Berzelius form, which is sometimes very useful. The air is compressed by blowing into the bottle through the jet, and by quickly inverting the bottle the stream of liquid is forced out until the equilibrium is restored. It requires a little practice to use this form of bottle easily, but when the art is once acquired it can be used with ammonia-water as well as pure water, and the facility with which it can be moved and pointed in any direction with the hand makes it most convenient for some purposes.

Removing Precipitates. from Beakers.

A feather trimmed in the way shown in Fig. 29 may be used to remove particles of adhering precipitates from beakers, evaporating-dishes, etc. A piece of soft rubber tubing on the end of a piece of glass rod or sealed glass tube is much more effective and convenient in most cases.

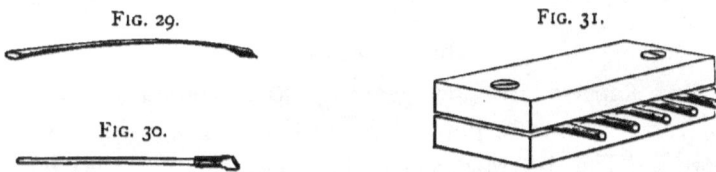

FIG. 29.   FIG. 31.

FIG. 30.

It is made by taking a short length of rubber tubing, placing a little pure caoutchouc dissolved in chloroform or naphtha in one end, squeezing the sides together between two pieces of board (Fig. 31), and allowing it to remain for at least twenty-four hours. It may then be trimmed down and placed on the end of a piece of glass rod or on the end of a piece of glass tubing having the ends fused together (Fig. 30). This little instrument has acquired the name of "policeman."

Measuring-Glasses.

In adding reagents to a sample or to a solution, measured amounts should nearly always be used, and, as it is generally well under all circumstances to avoid adding them from the bottle direct, little beakers of the form shown in Fig. 32 are very useful. They can be graduated and marked by covering the side with a thin coating of paraffine, measuring in water from a burette, marking the levels and amounts in the paraffine with a sharp-pointed instrument, and etching them in the glass by filling the marks

FIG. 32

with HFl. After standing a few minutes the HFl may be washed off under the hydrant and the paraffine removed with hot water. As the amounts are intended to be only approximate, no great degree of care need be exercised in the graduation.

Caps for Reagent-Bottles.

The stoppers and lips of reagent-bottles are very apt to become covered with chloride of ammonium, dust, etc., when exposed in the laboratory, and especially such as are not in constant use, volumetric solutions, stock-bottles, etc. It is well to keep them always covered with caps, which may be bought from the dealers, or with cracked beakers, which answer the purpose nearly as well in most cases.

Rubber Stoppers.

Rubber stoppers are now generally used instead of cork. Solid stoppers should always be purchased, and the holes cut with the ordinary cork-borers. This is readily done by moistening the cork-borer with water or alcohol. A little practice will enable any one to do this with great ease.

Desiccators.

Crucibles should always be cooled before weighing in desiccators.

FIG. 33.

The form shown in Fig. 33 is most convenient. The desiccator should contain fused chloride of calcium. The crucible rests on a small triangle, which may be made of copper wire, each side being covered by winding a thin strip of platinum foil around it to prevent the crucible from coming in contact with the copper, which may become more or less corroded.

PLATINUM APPARATUS.

Crucibles.

The shape of the crucible is of considerable importance as regards its wearing properties. Fig. 34 shows the best form for general use.

A crucible 1½ inches (38 mm.) high, 1$\frac{5}{16}$ inches (33½ mm.) wide at the top, with a capacity of 20 c.c., and weighing with the lid about 25 grammes, is well adapted for weighing the usual precipi-tates found in the course of iron analysis. For fusions a much larger crucible is necessary: one 1$\frac{13}{16}$ inches (46 mm.) high, 1$\frac{13}{16}$ inches (46 mm.) wide on top, with a capa-city of 55 cc., and weighing about 60 grammes, will be found convenient and serviceable. Pure platinum is the

Fig. 34.

best metal for crucibles. The iridium alloy, at one time so popular, has not been found to wear well. It is stiffer than the pure metal, but much more liable to crack. The endurance of a crucible depends very much upon the treatment it receives. The salts of easily reduced metals fusing at a low temperature, such as lead, tin, bismuth, antimony, etc., should never be ignited in platinum; besides these, the phosphoric acid in some phosphates is occasionally partly reduced, rendering the platinum very brittle. A platinum crucible should never be bent out of shape when it can be avoided, and a wooden plug exactly the shape of the crucible (Fig. 35) is very useful to straighten it on when it has been bent. It should always be carefully cleaned before use: the precipitate last ignited should be dissolved in acid if possible, and the crucible washed out with water, dried, ignited, and cooled in a desiccator before weighing. A precipitate of Fe_2O_3 will sometimes stain a crucible very badly; this stain may be removed by allowing the crucible to stand with cold HCl for twelve hours, and then warming it for a short time. Stains that are not removed by HCl may be removed by

Fig. 35.

fusing $KHSO_4$ in the crucible, or by fusing Na_2CO_3 in it, dissolving in water, and then treating the crucible with HCl. Whenever a crucible begins to look dull and tarnished it should be cleaned inside and out with very fine sea-sand (not sharp sand) by moistening the finger, dip-ping it in the sand, and rubbing the crucible with it. This method of cleaning decreases the weight of the crucible very slightly, the sea-sand burnishing without cutting the crucible. It is very convenient to have each crucible and its cover marked with a number, as shown in Fig. 34.

Dishes.

Fig. 36 shows a very convenient form of dish for the determination of Si in pig-iron, SiO_2 in iron ores, etc. It is $3\frac{1}{4}$ inches (83 mm.) in diameter and $2\frac{1}{4}$ inches (57 mm.) high.

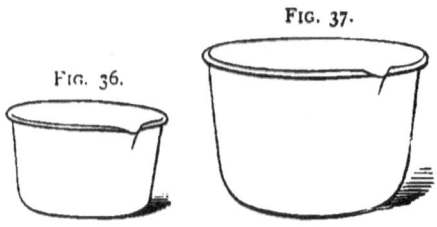

FIG. 37.

FIG. 36.

Fig. 37, for such work as precipitation of Fe_2O_3, etc. It is 5 inches (127 mm.) in diameter and $3\frac{5}{16}$ inches (84 mm.) high. The wire which is fused into the top of the dish makes it much stiffer than it would otherwise be, and consequently it may be made lighter and cheaper than would be possible without the wire. The wire is hammered out and helps to form the lip. A platinum stirring-rod, formed from a piece of seamless tubing, rounded and fused together at the ends, is useful for many purposes. It may be from $5\frac{1}{2}$ to 7 inches (140 to 179 mm.) long, $\frac{1}{4}$ inch (6 mm.) in diameter, weighing from 7.5 to 11 grammes.

Spatula.

Fig. 38 shows a very convenient and useful form of spatula. The blade, which is made of the platinum-iridium alloy, is fused into a tube of the same alloy which forms the handle. The weight of the spatula shown in the sketch is 14 grammes, length $6\frac{1}{2}$ inches (165 mm.).

FIG. 38.

Triangles and Tripods.

The triangles for supporting the crucibles during the ignition are shown in Figs. 12 and 13, as are also tripods for holding the lids, etc. These are made from wire about $\frac{1}{16}$ inch (1.6 mm.) diameter, the ends are fused, and the wire, where it is twisted, has the parts in contact fused together almost to the inside of the triangle, which makes it much stiffer. The triangles should be attached to the iron rings of the supports with a few turns of fine platinum wire.

Crucible-Tongs.

Fig. 39 shows the best form of crucible-tongs. The part from *a* to *b* is of platinum, the straight part from *a* to *c* fitting over the end of the iron. The surfaces at *d* are in contact when the tongs are closed, and with this portion the lid can be handled, and the crucible is clasped by the curved ends, which hold it firmly without any danger of bending the crucible.

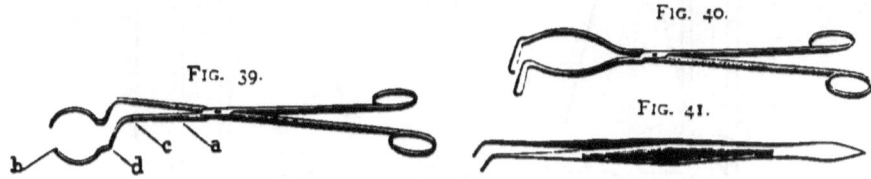

FIG. 40.

FIG. 39.

FIG. 41.

They are especially useful in handling a crucible containing a liquid fusion. Another form, shown in Fig. 40, is generally of brass, the points and bend being lined with platinum. A small pair of forceps (Fig. 41) is useful for taking the crucible from the desiccator and placing it on the balance, the lid of the crucible being slipped a little to one side to allow one of the points of the forceps to go inside the crucible.

Balances.

The balance is one of the most important things in the equipment of a laboratory, and a cheap balance is nearly always a very poor investment. The quality of balances has improved greatly in the last few years, and it is now possible to get a most admirable instrument of this kind at a comparatively low price. Fig. 42 shows a balance which for sensitiveness and quickness is unsurpassed. It is made to carry up to 200 grammes in each pan. The beam is of aluminium, as are also the pans. The stirrups are of nickel, the knife-edges and bearings of agate, while the arrangement for carrying the riders (Fig. 43) is most ingenious and effective. It is of course very convenient to have one balance for weighing crucibles, etc., and another for weighing samples for analysis. The balance for the latter purpose may be much smaller than the balance for the former, and should be

FIG. 42.

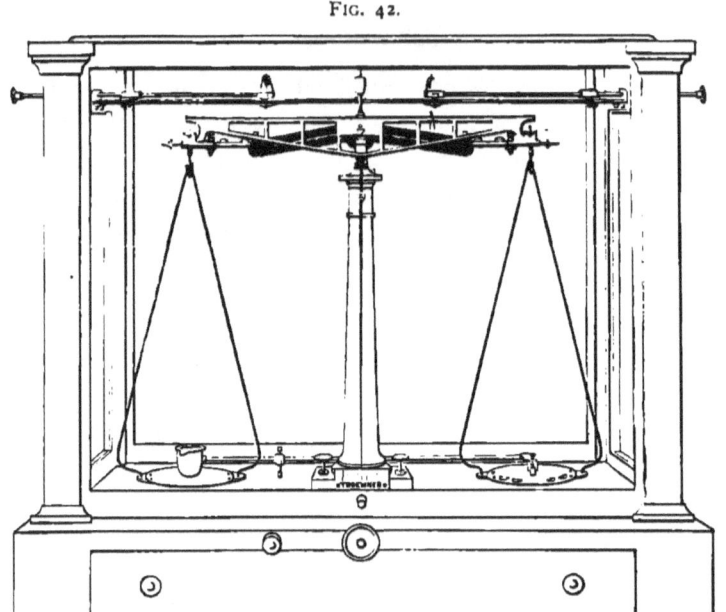

provided with a small aluminium pan with a spout (Fig. 44), to facilitate

FIG. 43.

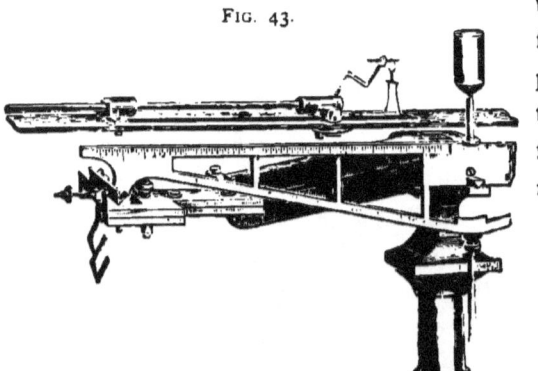

the transfer of samples to flasks, test-tubes, etc. This pan should have a counterpoise. A pair of small forceps, slightly magnetized, may be used to advantage

FIG. 44.

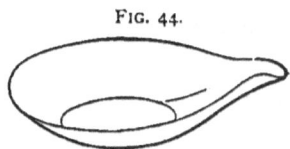

in getting exact weights of steel drillings, and a camel's-hair brush is necessary to detach small particles of ores, etc., from the aluminium pan or balanced watch-glasses.

Factor Weights.

The use of factor weights is in many cases extremely convenient, as it does away with all calculation, and is to that extent time-saving and valuable in avoiding one source of error. Thus, in determining carbon by combustion in steel, using 2.7273 grammes of the steel, 0.1 milligramme of carbonic acid is equal to 0.001 per cent. of carbon in the steel. For determining silicon in pig-iron the $\frac{1}{4}$ factor weight, or 1.1755 grammes, is very convenient. When the weight of SiO_2 is multiplied by 4, one milligramme is equal to 0.01 per cent. of silicon. Or, for rapid silicon determinations, the $\frac{1}{10}$ factor weight, 0.4702 gramme, is used.

REAGENTS.

Distilled Water.

When only a small amount of distilled water is needed, a tin-lined copper still and condenser, such as are furnished by all dealers, may be

FIG. 45.

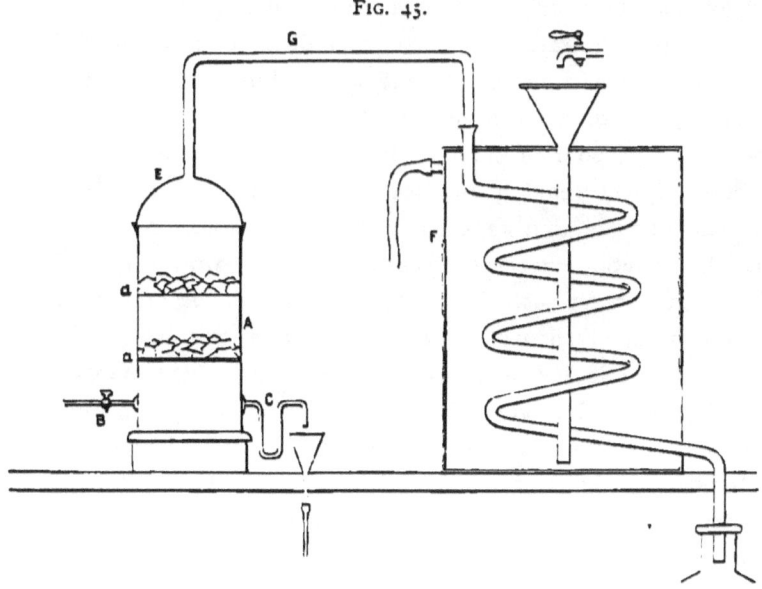

used, but where there is a supply of steam, an arrangement like that shown in Fig. 45 will be found most useful. A is a tin-lined copper cylinder, with a dome-shaped top, E, fitted to A by the joint shown in the sketch, which may be made tight by paper or a linen rag. Two perforated shelves, *a, a*, support layers of clean quartz-gravel or pieces of block-tin, which wash the steam and prevent dirt from being carried over mechanically. The steam enters at B, and the water condensed in the cylinder A passes off through the pipe C. The washed steam passes up through the block-tin pipe G, and is condensed in the worm-tub F. A glass worm should never be used, as the water condensed in it dissolves notable amounts of glass.

ACIDS AND HALOGENS.

Hydrochloric Acid. HCl. Sp. gr. 1.2.

Chemically pure hydrochloric acid is readily obtained. It should be free from chlorine, sulphuric and sulphurous acid, arsenic, and fixed salts. To test for sulphuric and sulphurous acid, evaporate 100 c.c. to dryness with a little pure nitrate of potassium, redissolve in water with a few drops of HCl, filter, if necessary, and add chloride of barium. To test for arsenic, put into a clean dry test-tube a few centigrammes of pure stannous chloride, pour in carefully 6 or 8 c.c. HCl, and gradually 2 or 3 c.c. pure H_2SO_4, shaking the test-tube gently. If the HCl is free from arsenic the solution remains clear and colorless, but if arsenic is present the solution becomes yellowish, then brownish, and finally metallic arsenic is deposited. The test-tube should be gently warmed if no reaction occurs at first. To test for chlorine, pour some of the acid into a solution of iodide of potassium containing a little starch solution. A blue coloration indicates chlorine or ferric chloride. To test for metallic salts, neutralize about 100 c.c. of the acid with ammonia and add sulphide of ammonium. To test for salts of the alkalies, evaporate about 100 c.c. of the acid to dryness, and test any residue which may remain.

Nitric Acid. HNO₃. Sp. gr. 1.41.

Nitric acid should be free from nitrous acid, the presence of which may be known by the yellowish color it produces. It may be freed from this gas by passing a current of air through the acid until it becomes colorless. To test for HCl or Cl, dilute largely and add a solution of nitrate of silver. To test for fixed salts, evaporate about 100 c.c. to dryness. The ordinary acid diluted with an equal volume of water gives the acid of 1.2 sp. gr. used to dissolve steel for the color carbon test. It should be carefully tested for Cl or HCl.

Sulphuric Acid. H₂SO₄. Sp. gr. 1.84.

Sulphuric acid should be colorless. To test for oxides of nitrogen, Warington* suggests placing about two pounds of the acid in a bottle, which it half fills, and shaking violently. The air washes the gases out of the acid, and the presence of the oxides of nitrogen may be detected by placing in the mouth of the bottle a piece of filter-paper saturated with iodide of potassium and starch solution, which is colored blue when any of these oxides are present. To test for lead, supersaturate some of the acid with ammonia and add sulphide of ammonium.

Hydrofluoric Acid. HFl.

The use of Ceresine bottles, suggested by Prof. Edward Hart, of Lafayette College, has made it quite possible to obtain pure hydrofluoric acid, but the crude acid may be redistilled in the laboratory into platinum bottles. The crude acid, which may be purchased from glass engravers and etchers, is distilled from

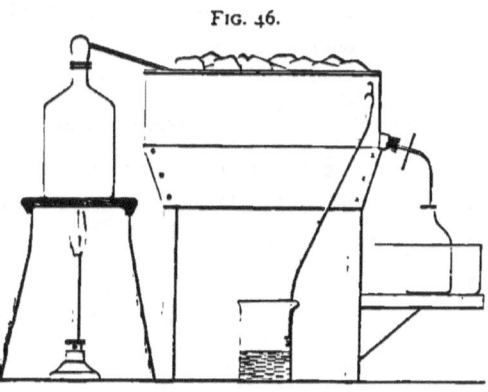

FIG. 46.

a platinum, silver, or lead still, as shown in Fig. 46. The head of the still

---

* Crookes's Select Methods, 2d ed., p. 494.

and condensing-tube is of platinum. The condensing-tube runs through
a copper box filled with. ice, and a platinum bottle receives the condensed
acid. Where the tube comes through the lower part of the box it is
secured by a rubber stopper, and a small bit of paper around the tube
prevents any condensed moisture on the outside of the tube from running
into the bottle. Before distilling the acid, put into it a few crystals of
permanganate of potassium and a few c.c. of H_2SO_4. The redistilled acid
should leave no residue upon evaporation.

Acetic Acid. $H,C_2H_3O_2$. Sp. gr. 1.04.

Acetic acid of the strength given above is the best for use in iron analysis. It should give no residue on evaporation, and no precipitate upon neutralization with ammonia and the addition of sulphide of ammonium. It
should be free from phosphoric acid. To test it for phosphoric acid, evaporate 100 c.c. nearly to dryness, add a little magnesium mixture and a large
excess of ammonia, cool in ice-water, and stir vigorously. When phosphoric acid is present, a precipitate of ammonium magnesium phosphate
will be obtained.

Citric Acid. $H_3,C_6H_5O_7,H_2O$.

Citric acid is easily obtained in a state of purity in the form of crystals having the above composition. It should be kept in the solid condition, and dissolved as needed. It is soluble in ¾ part of water at 15° C.

Tartaric Acid. $H_2,C_4H_4O_6$.

Tartaric acid is also easily obtained sufficiently pure for use in iron
analysis. The crystals should be dissolved only as needed. The only
impurity is a small amount of lime. It is soluble in ½ part of water at
15° C.

Oxalic Acid. H_2,C_2O_4.

Oxalic acid crystallizes from its aqueous solution as $H_2,C_2O_4,2H_2O$,
soluble in 8.7 parts of water at 15° C. It loses its water of hydration very
easily even at the ordinary temperature in dry air, and very quickly at
100° C.

Bromine. Br.

Bromine is easily obtained in a condition sufficiently pure for use as a reagent. It is a dark brown, extremely corrosive liquid, of sp. gr. 2.97. It is soluble in about 30 parts of water at 15° C. It is best kept in a glass-stoppered bottle with a ground cap. As the aqueous solution is generally used, it is convenient to put only a small amount, say 20 or 30 c.c., in the bottle, fill the bottle nearly full of cold distilled water, shake it up well, and pour off the saturated solution as required. There usually remains in the bottom of the bottle a small amount of impurity, which is insoluble in water.

Iodine. I.

Iodine is a metallic-looking crystalline solid, of sp. gr. 4.95. Resublimed iodine is not sufficiently pure for use, and must be redistilled with great care, unless it is used as iodine dissolved in iodide of iron, and filtered. To distil it, place about ½ kilo. in a large glass retort of about 2 litres capacity connected with an adapter about 18 inches (456 mm.) long and 3 inches (75 mm.) in diameter at the largest part. The heat from a Bunsen burner turned quite low will cause the violet vapors of iodine to pass rapidly into the adapter, where they will condense without any means being taken to cool it. By gently warming the outside of the adapter after the distillation has been finished, the iodine may readily be detached in large masses and removed. It should be kept in a wide-mouth, glass-stoppered bottle.

Chlorine. Cl.

Chlorine is a yellowish gas about two and one-half times heavier than air. It is sparingly soluble in water. When required it must be made. The details are given under " Determination of Silicon in Iron and Steel."

Sulphurous Acid. H_2SO_3.

To make sulphurous acid gas, mix powdered charcoal and strong sulphuric acid until a thin paste is formed, heat the paste in a flask, very gently at first, and pass the gas through a washing-bottle containing a little water. The reaction is $C + 2H_2SO_4 = CO_2 + 2SO_2 + 2H_2O$. The tube leading from the flask into the washing-bottle should have a bulb in it to prevent the reflux of water into the flask in case of sudden cooling. Clippings of sheet copper, or copper turnings, may be used instead of charcoal, and are generally to be preferred. The aqueous solution of the gas is made by passing the washed gas into distilled water. The gas, SO_2, has a specific gravity of 2.21 (air $= 1$). 1 c.c. of water at 15° C. dissolves 0.1353 gramme of SO_2.

Chromic Acid. CrO_3.

Chromic anhydride as a red powder or in the form of scarlet crystals is easily obtained in a state of purity. It is deliquescent, and dissolves in a small quantity of water, forming a dark brownish-colored liquid. It may be made by pouring 1 volume of a saturated solution of bichromate of potassium into 1½ volumes of strong sulphuric acid, stirring constantly. The liquid on cooling deposits needles of chromic anhydride, which must be separated from the mother-liquid and purified by recrystallization.

GASES.

Carbonic Acid Gas. CO_2.

The best form of generator is shown in Fig. 47. It was first suggested by Casamajor.* It consists of a large tubulated bottle, the bottom of which is covered to the depth of about 1 inch (25 mm.) with buckshot, on top of which rest lumps of marble. Dilute hydrochloric acid (1 acid to 5 water) is admitted through the tube which enters at the tubulure at the bottom of the bottle, bending down so as to reach the bottom of the bottle. The wash-bottle A contains water. By blowing in the rubber tube attached to the acid-bottle the acid passes over into the tubulated bottle. When the stopcock K is closed, the pressure in

---

* American Chemist, vi. 209

the tubulated bottle forces the acid back into the acid-bottle. When the acid becomes exhausted and remains in the tubulated bottle, pour a little strong HCl into the acid-bottle and blow it over into the tubulated bottle. The generated gas will force the liquid back into the acid-bottle, when it can be replaced by fresh acid. A slightly different form is shown in Fig. 50.

Sulphuretted Hydrogen Gas. H_2S.

The same form of apparatus is used for generating H_2S. Ferrous sulphide is substituted for marble, but HCl is used instead of H_2SO_4, as is generally advised, for the ferrous sulphate formed crystallizes out and clogs the apparatus.

Hydrogen. H.

The same form of apparatus as that used for CO_2 and H_2S can be used to advantage for generating hydrogen gas. Pieces of zinc, which may be obtained by melting the zinc and pouring it in a sheet about $\frac{1}{4}$ inch (6 mm.) thick, so that it can be easily broken, are to be used, and not granulated zinc. Hydrochloric acid is better than sulphuric.

Oxygen Gas. O.

Oxygen compressed in cylinders can be obtained from most dealers in chemicals, but it should always be carefully tested before being used for the determination of carbon in steel or iron, as the cylinders are sometimes filled with coal-gas, and a cylinder which has once held coal-gas is rarely free from hydrocarbons.

The gas may be made on a small scale in the laboratory by carefully mixing in a porcelain mortar 100 grammes chlorate of potassium and 5 grammes powdered binoxide of manganese, transferring to a retort, which the mixture should not more than half fill, and heating carefully over a Bunsen burner. The evolved gas may be collected in a gasholder or in an india-rubber bag. The latter is not to be recommended for use for carbon determinations, as rubber is very liable to give off hydrocarbons.

ALKALIES AND ALKALINE SALTS.
Ammonia. NH₄HO.

The solution of ammonia gas (NH_3) commonly used is of sp. gr. 0.88, and contains about 30 to 35 per cent. of ammonia. It should be kept in glass-stoppered bottles and in a cool place, as the gas passes off very rapidly even at the ordinary temperature when open to the air. It should be colorless, leave no residue upon evaporation, be free from chlorides and sulphates, and give no precipitate with H_2S.

Bisulphite of Ammonium. NH₄HSO₃.

Bisulphite of ammonium is made by passing sulphurous acid gas into strong ammonia until the solution becomes yellowish in color and smells strongly of sulphurous acid. By the first method of manufacture of SO_2 given on page 42, a large amount of CO_2 is formed at the same time, which is absorbed by the ammonia. This is gradually displaced by the SO_2, and if the solution is kept cool, white crystals of the neutral sulphite, $(NH_4)_2SO_3H_2O$, are deposited. These are gradually dissolved by the excess of SO_2 until the solution becomes quite clear, assuming a yellowish tint. When copper is used instead of charcoal, no CO_2 is evolved and no carbonate of ammonium is formed. By exposure to air bisulphite of ammonium is gradually oxidized to sulphate. Old bisulphite of ammonium always contains a small amount of hyposulphite, which occasions a precipitate of sulphur when deoxidizing solutions of ferric salts. It is not now difficult to purchase pure bisulphite of ammonium, but bisulphite of sodium is very apt to contain phosphoric acid. When made from strong ammonia-water, 18 c.c. of bisulphite will deoxidize a solution of 10 grammes of iron or steel.

Sulphide of Ammonium. (NH₄)₂S.

Sulphide of ammonium is made by saturating strong ammonia with H_2S and adding an equal volume of ammonia. The reactions are

$$NH_4HO + H_2S = NH_4HS + H_2O \text{ and }$$
$$NH_4HS + NH_4HO = (NH_4)_2S + H_2O.$$

The solution becomes yellow by age or by exposure to the air.

Chloride of Ammonium. NH₄Cl.

Chloride of ammonium is a white, crystalline, anhydrous salt, soluble in about its own weight of water at 100° C., and in 2.7 parts of water at 18° C. It is volatilized when heated without previous fusion. The salt is usually purified by sublimation. It generally contains a little iron, but is free from other impurities. To prepare chloride of ammonium for use in J. Lawrence Smith's method for decomposition of silicates, dissolve it in boiling water and evaporate down on a water-bath or air-bath. When the salt begins to crystallize out, stir vigorously. The crystals formed will be very small. Drain off the liquid and dry. The salt can then be readily powdered.

Nitrate of Ammonium. NH₄NO₃.

Nitrate of ammonium is a white, crystalline salt, soluble in one-half its weight of water at 18° C., and in much less at 100° C. When dissolved in water it produces great cold. By evaporation it loses ammonia and becomes acid. When heated it fuses at 108° C., and is decomposed between 230° C. and 250° C. into water and nitrous oxide, $NH_4NO_3 = 2H_2O + N_2O$. It should leave no residue when volatilized.

Fluoride of Ammonium. NH₄Fl.

Fluoride of ammonium may be made by saturating hydrofluoric acid by ammonia. The salt crystallizes when left to evaporate over quicklime. It is slightly deliquescent, and therefore difficult to keep, as the solution attacks glass.

Acetate of Ammonium. NH₄C₂H₃O₂.

Acetate of ammonium is best made by slightly acidulating ammonia by acetic acid. One volume of strong ammonia-water requires about 2 volumes of acetic acid, 1.04 sp. gr., to neutralize it. It is best to make it as needed, as it decomposes when kept.

Oxalate of Ammonium. (NH₄)₂C₂O₄ + H₂O.

Oxalate of ammonium is a white salt, crystallizing in long prisms united in tufts. It is soluble in 3 parts of water at 18° C.

Caustic Soda. NaHO.

Fused sodic hydrate purified by alcohol is sufficiently pure for ordinary purposes. It forms white opaque masses, having a strong affinity for water. It dissolves in water with evolution of heat. Pure sodic hydrate is prepared by allowing metallic sodium to decompose water in a platinum dish. It must be kept in a silver or platinum bottle, as the solution acts very rapidly on glass.

Phosphate of Sodium and Ammonium. $NaNH_4HPO_4,4H_2O$.

Phosphate of sodium and ammonium (microcosmic salt) is a white, crystalline salt, soluble in 6 parts of cold and 1 part of hot water. It should not be kept in solution for any great length of time, as it attacks glass very readily. It loses its water of crystallization very easily, and when heated gives off its ammonia, leaving pure metaphosphate of sodium, which in the fused condition dissolves metallic oxides in many cases with the production of characteristic colors, which makes it a valuable reagent for blow-pipe analysis. It is easily obtained in a state of purity.

Carbonate of Sodium. Na_2CO_3.

Carbonate of sodium is never quite pure. It always contains small amounts of silica, alumina, lime, and magnesia, besides sulphuric acid. It may generally be obtained quite free from phosphoric acid. Every lot should be carefully examined for all the above impurities, and the amount per gramme noted, so that the proper subtraction may be made in each analysis. It is used in solution only for the neutralization of solutions, as in the determination of manganese by the acetate method, and, as the solution attacks glass very rapidly, it is best to dissolve the salt only as it is needed.

Nitrate of Sodium. $NaNO_3$.

Nitrate of sodium is used occasionally instead of nitrate of potassium in making fusions of ores containing titanic acid. It may be prepared by acidulating a strong solution of carbonate of sodium with nitric acid, heating until the water and excess of nitric acid are driven off, and powdering the dry salt.

Hyposulphite of Sodium. Thiosulphate of Sodium. $Na_2S_2O_3 + 5H_2O$.

Hyposulphite of sodium is very soluble in water, but decomposes even in tightly-stoppered bottles, sulphate of sodium being formed and sulphur precipitated. It should, therefore, be dissolved only as used. The ordinary salt of commerce is sufficiently pure for use.

Acetate of Sodium. $NaC_2H_3O_2 + 3H_2O$.

Crystallized acetate of sodium dissolves in 3.9 parts of water at 6° C. It is rarely quite pure, containing, usually, calcium and iron salts, but it may be used after solution and filtration for partial analyses, as in the determination of manganese by the acetate method, etc. In complete analyses it is better to use acetate of ammonium. When the use of acetate of sodium is unavoidable, it can be made by dissolving C. P. carbonate of sodium in acetic acid, boiling off the liberated carbonic acid, and adding acetic acid to slight acid reaction.

Caustic Potassa. KHO.

Caustic potassa purified by solution in alcohol, filtration, and subsequent evaporation to dryness and fusion, is quite pure enough for all the ordinary purposes of iron analysis. An aqueous solution of 1.27 sp. gr. is used to absorb carbonic acid in the determination of carbon in iron and steel, in the determination of carbonic acid in ores, etc. 300 grammes of fused KHO dissolved in 1 litre of water will give a solution of about this strength.

Nitrite of Potassium. KNO_2.

Nitrite of potassium is used to separate nickel and cobalt. It is very difficult to buy the pure salt, but it is easily made as follows: Heat 1 part of nitrate of potassium in an iron dish until it is just fused, then add, with constant stirring, 2 parts of metallic lead. Raise the heat slightly to complete the oxidation of the lead, and allow the mass to cool. Treat the mass with water, filter from the oxide of lead, pass CO_2 through the solution to precipitate the greater part of the dissolved lead, and filter. To the filtrate add a little sulphide of ammonium to precipitate the last traces of lead, filter, evaporate to dryness, and fuse in a platinum dish to decompose any hyposulphite that may have been formed, and preserve the fused salt for use. Nitrite of potassium is deliquescent.

Nitrate of Potassium. KNO_3.

Nitrate of potassium is a white, crystalline salt, anhydrous, and soluble in 7½ parts of water at 0° C., and in 0.4 part of water at 100° C. It melts below a red heat to a colorless liquid, and at a red heat gives off oxygen gas more or less contaminated by nitrogen, being converted into nitrite and oxide of potassium. The salt may be purchased in a sufficient state of purity for all purposes of iron analysis, but, as it may contain small amounts of sulphuric acid, the amount should always be determined and the proper allowance made when it is to be used for the estimation of sulphur in ores.

Sulphide of Potassium. K_2S.

Sulphide of potassium is made by passing H_2S into a solution of caustic potassa and filtering from any precipitated alumina or sulphide of iron. It is used instead of the corresponding ammonia-salt when the solution contains copper, as sulphide of copper is slightly soluble in sulphide of ammonium.

Bichromate of Potassium. $K_2Cr_2O_7$.

Bichromate of potassium is an orange-colored, anhydrous, crystalline salt, soluble in 20 parts of water at 0° C., and in 1 part of water at 100° C. It melts below a red heat to a transparent red liquid, crumbling to powder upon cooling. Heated with strong H_2SO_4 it gives off about one-sixth its weight of oxygen gas, the reaction being $K_2Cr_2O_7 + 4H_2SO_4 = Cr_2K_2(SO_4)_4 + 4H_2O + 3O$. It is readily obtained in a state of purity, but should always be fused to destroy any organic matter before being used to determine carbon in iron or in ores.

Chlorate of Potassium. $KClO_3$.

Chlorate of potassium is a white, crystalline, anhydrous salt. It is soluble in about 30 parts of water at 0° C., and in about 2 parts at 100° C.

It is readily decomposed by heat, first into a mixture of chloride and perchlorate of potassium, a portion of the oxygen being set free, and at a higher temperature the perchlorate is decomposed, the remaining oxygen is given off and chloride of potassium alone remains. It is easily obtained in a sufficient state of purity for use in iron analysis. Heated with nitric acid it yields nitrate and perchlorate of potassium, water, chlorine, and oxygen, thus:

$$8KClO_3 + 6HNO_3 = 6KNO_3 - 2KClO_4 + 6Cl - 13O + 3H_2O.$$

Heated with hydrochloric acid it gives chloride of potassium, water, and a mixture of peroxide of chlorine and chlorine, called *euchlorine*, thus:

$$4KClO_3 + 12HCl = 4KCl - 6H_2O - 3ClO_2 - 9Cl.$$

Bisulphate of Potassium. KHSO₄.

Bisulphate of potassium is a white, crystalline salt, soluble in about one-half its weight of boiling water. A large amount of water decomposes it into sulphate of potassium and free sulphuric acid; even in the presence of a large excess of sulphuric acid the neutral salt crystallizes out, leaving free sulphuric acid in the solution. Bisulphate of potassium melts at 197° C.; at higher temperatures it gives off water, leaving the anhydrous salt, and at a red heat it gives off sulphuric acid, leaving the neutral sulphate. It is difficult to obtain it very pure, but it may be made as follows: Dissolve bicarbonate of potassium in water, filter, and from a graduated vessel add H_2SO_4 until, after boiling off the liberated CO_2, the solution is neutral, or but very faintly alkaline to test-paper. Filter, if necessary, and to the filtrate add as much H_2SO_4 as was added in the first place to neutralize the bicarbonate. Boil the solution down, and finally fuse the mass in a platinum dish. Cool it, and when it is almost ready to solidify pour it into another dish. Break it up, and preserve it in glass-stoppered bottles.

Iodide of Potassium. KI.

Iodide of potassium is a white, crystalline, anhydrous salt, very soluble in water, and in dissolving it causes a fall of temperature in the solution. It is soluble in about 0.8 part of water at 0° C., and in 0.5 part of

4

water at 100° C. It is soluble in 6 parts of alcohol at the ordinary temperature, and, when dissolved, the addition of HCl does not turn it brown if it is free from iodate. A solution of 1 part of iodide of potassium in 2 parts of water will dissolve 2 parts of iodine, but upon dilution some of the iodine is precipitated.

Permanganate of Potassium. $KMnO_4$.

Permanganate of potassium is a dark purple-red, anhydrous salt, crystallizing in long needles. It is soluble in 16 parts of water at 15° C. It is easily obtained very pure, but the solution should always be filtered through ignited asbestos, as paper has a strong reducing action on it.

Ferrocyanide of Potassium. $K_4Fe_2Cy_6 + 3H_2O$.

Ferrocyanide of potassium is a yellow, crystalline salt, soluble in 4 parts of water at 0° C., and in 2 parts of water at 100° C. It is used as a reagent to show the presence of ferric salts, which produce a blue coloration, caused by the formation of ferrocyanide of iron (Prussian blue).

Ferricyanide of Potassium. $K_3Fe_2Cy_6$.

Ferricyanide of potassium is a blood-red, anhydrous, crystalline salt, soluble in about 3.1 parts of water at 0° C., and in 1.3 parts of water at 100° C. The dilute solution, like that of the ferrocyanide, is yellow in color. Ferrous salts added to the solution give a blue coloration, due to the formation of ferrous ferricyanide, while ferric salts produce no change of color. The ferricyanide should never be kept in solution.

SALTS OF THE ALKALINE EARTHS.

Carbonate of Barium. $BaCO_3$.

Carbonate of barium prepared by precipitation is a soft white powder. It is difficult to obtain it in a state of purity, but it is easily prepared by adding a solution of carbonate of ammonium to a clear boiling solution of chloride of barium, washing the precipitated carbonate of barium with hot water, first by decantation and afterwards on a filter. The carbonate of ammonium should, of course, be free from sulphate. The thoroughly washed carbonate of barium should be transferred to a bottle and shaken up with water, in which condition it is ready for use. Carbonate of barium is very slightly soluble in water, requiring, according to the different authorities, from 4,000 to 25,000 parts of water to dissolve it. It is poisonous.

Acetate of Barium. $Ba(C_2H_3O_2)_2$.

Acetate of barium may be prepared by dissolving pure carbonate of barium in acetic acid. It crystallizes with 1 or 3 molecules of water, but dried at 0° C., or exposed to the air, it effloresces and yields the anhydrous salt as a white powder. It is very soluble in water, dissolving in about 2 parts of water at 0° C., and in about 1 part at 100° C. When heated it decomposes into acetone and carbonate of barium, thus:

$$Ba(C_2H_3O_2)_2 = C_3H_6O + BaCO_3.$$

Chloride of Barium. $BaCl_2, 2H_2O$.

Chloride of barium is a white, crystalline salt, soluble in about 3 parts of water at 15° C., and in about 1½ parts at 100° C. Heated to 100° C. it loses its water of crystallization, yielding the anhydride as a white mass, which melts at a full red heat. Chloride of barium is almost insoluble in strong HCl. It is used almost exclusively for the determination of sulphuric acid, and may be kept in solution for this purpose. 100 grammes of the crystallized salt dissolved in 1 litre of water is a good proportion to use. Of this solution 10 c.c. will precipitate 1.16 grammes of $BaSO_4$, equal to 0.4 gramme SO_3 or 0.16 gramme S.

Caustic Baryta. Hydrate of Barium. $BaH_2O_2, 8H_2O$.

Hydrate of barium is a white, crystalline salt, soluble in 20 parts of water at 15° C., and in 3 parts of water at 100° C. The anhydride may be prepared by heating nitrate of barium to redness in a platinum crucible, raising the heat gradually at first to avoid loss from frothing. It attacks platinum, however, at a high temperature. The solution has a strong affinity for carbonic acid, absorbing it readily from the air, the carbonate of barium so formed causing a scum on the surface of the solution. The solution attacks glass very strongly.

Chloride of Calcium. $CaCl_2$.

Crystallized chloride of calcium loses all its water of crystallization at 200° C., yielding the white porous anhydrous chloride, which is very deliquescent. The anhydrous salt fuses at a low red heat, but is partly changed to oxide. For this reason the fused salt should never be used for drying CO_2 in the determination of this gas, as some of it is taken up by the oxide of calcium. A solution of chloride of calcium containing 59 parts of the anhydrous salt to 100 parts of water boils at 115° C., a saturated solution at 179.5° C.

Carbonate of Calcium. $CaCO_3$.

Pure carbonate of calcium, for use in Prof. J. Lawrence Smith's method for the determination of alkalies in silicates, is prepared as follows: Dissolve marble or calcite, free from magnesia, in dilute HCl, add an excess of powdered marble, heat the solution, and add some milk of lime to precipitate magnesia, phosphate of calcium, etc. Filter, heat the solution almost to boiling, and precipitate by carbonate of ammonium. The carbonate of calcium formed will be a very dense powder, which will settle readily and be easily washed. Wash thoroughly, dry, and preserve for use.

METALS AND METALLIC SALTS.

Metallic Copper.

Metallic copper absorbs chlorine gas at ordinary temperatures, and is used in iron analysis to absorb any chlorine that may be given off during the combustion of the carbonaceous matter liberated by the action of solvents on iron and steel. It is used in the form of drillings, which should be taken with a perfectly dry drill, and which should be free from oil and grease. The drillings should be kept in a stoppered bottle, and may be used as long as they are perfectly bright and clean.

Sulphate of Copper. $CuSO_4,5H_2O$.

Sulphate of copper is a blue, crystalline salt, soluble in 2.7 parts of water at 18° C., and in 0.55 part of water at 100° C. The aqueous solution of the neutral salt is strongly acid to litmus-paper. The crystals of sulphate of copper effloresce on the surface when exposed to the air; heated to 100° C. they lose 4 molecules of water, and when heated to 200° C. they lose the remaining molecule. The anhydrous salt is a white saline mass, which is decomposed at a bright-red heat, giving off sulphurous acid and oxygen and leaving cupric oxide. The anhydrous salt has a strong affinity for water, and also for hydrochloric acid gas. A solution of sulphate of copper dissolves metallic iron, the copper being precipitated from the solution at the same time in a spongy mass.

Anhydrous Sulphate of Copper.

The property anhydrous sulphate of copper possesses of absorbing hydrochloric acid gas makes it useful in the determination of carbon by combustion, and it is best prepared for this purpose as follows: Heat crystals of sulphate of copper, about the size of a coffee bean, in a porcelain dish until the blue color of the crystals disappears and they become white. Transfer while still hot to a dry, glass-stoppered bottle.

Anhydrous Cuprous Chloride. $CuCl$.

To prepare the granulated salt for use as an absorbent of hydrochloric acid and chlorine in carbon determinations, moisten the ordinary powdered salt of commerce in a porcelain dish and rub it up with a glass rod into little lumps about the size of a coffee bean. Heat it gradually until the water is expelled and the lumps, which will be dark brown in color, harden. Transfer to a glass-stoppered bottle.

Cupric Chloride. $CuCl_2 + Aq$.

To prepare cupric chloride for use in dissolving iron or steel for the determination of carbon, grind up equal weights of sulphate of copper and common salt in a porcelain mortar, and pour over the mixture a small amount of water heated to 50°–60° C. The liquid becomes emerald-green in color, and deposits upon evaporation sulphate of sodium. Decant from the deposited salt and evaporate again until the solution is reduced to a very small bulk. Cool, and decant from the remainder of the sulphate of sodium and the excess of chloride of sodium. By further evaporation and cooling the cupric chloride may be obtained in the form of green crystals. These crystals are deliquescent. The solution should be diluted and filtered through asbestos.

Double Chloride of Copper and Ammonium. $2(NH_4Cl),CuCl_2,2H_2O.$

Double Chloride of Copper and Potassium. $2(KCl),CuCl_2,2H_2O.$

The double chloride of copper and ammonium is a bluish-green crystalline salt, quite soluble in water.

The double chloride of copper and potassium is bluish-green likewise and more soluble than the ammonium salt. The recent experiments of the American members of the International Steel Standards Committee have shown that the double chloride of copper and ammonium is nearly always impure, from the presence of hydrocarbons in the chloride of ammonium, derived probably from the gas liquor from which ammonia salts are distilled. These hydrocarbons unite with the carbonaceous residue liberated from steel and iron in the process of determining carbon, and of course vitiate the results. Several recrystallizations free the salt to a certain extent from this impurity. The use of the potassium salt is not open to this objection.

To prepare these salts proceed as follows: Dissolve 107 parts of chloride of ammonium or 149.1 parts of chloride of potassium and 170.3 parts of crystallized cupric chloride $(CuCl_2,2H_2O)$ in water and crystallize out the double salt. Dissolve about 300 grammes of the double salt in 1 litre of water, filter through ignited asbestos, and preserve for use in glass-stoppered bottles.

Oxide of Copper. CuO.

Oxide of copper, both fine and coarse, for combustions is easily obtained. It may be prepared as follows: Dissolve metallic copper in nitric acid, evaporate to dryness in a porcelain dish, transfer it to a Hessian crucible, and heat it in a furnace until no more nitrous fumes are given off. Keep the crucible well covered to prevent any coal getting into it, and avoid raising the heat too high, or the mass will fuse. Stir it from time to time, and when finished the oxide on top will be in a fine powder, while that in the bottom of the crucible will have sintered. Rub it up in a mortar and pass through a fine metal sieve. Keep the two kinds, fine and coarse, separate in glass-stoppered bottles, carefully covered to preserve them from dust.

Iron Wire.

Very fine soft piano-forte wire is the best form of iron to use when standardizing solutions of permanganate or bichromate of potassium by metallic iron. Wrap one end of a piece of wire, about 2 feet (610 mm.) long, around a lead-pencil, and, using this as a handle, draw the wire several times through a piece of fine emery-cloth, then through a fold of dry filter-paper, then, holding the wire with the paper, wrap it around the pencil. Cut off the end that has not been cleaned, and the little spiral of wire will be in a convenient form for weighing.

Ferrous Sulphate. $FeSO_4.7H_2O.$

Ferrous sulphate (green vitriol, or copperas) is a bluish-green crystalline salt, soluble in 1.64 parts of water at 10° C., and in 0.3 part at 100° C. It is insoluble in alcohol. The crystals lose 6 molecules of water when heated to 114° C., but retain the last molecule even at 280° C. Heated to a red heat the anhydrous sulphate is decomposed, giving off sulphurous acid and leaving a basic ferric sulphate, which at a higher temperature is entirely decomposed, leaving only ferric oxide. To prepare the crystals for use in volumetric analysis, add alcohol to the aqueous solution of the ferrous sulphate, when the salt is precipitated as a bluish-white powder. Filter, wash with alcohol, dry thoroughly, and preserve in glass-stoppered bottles. The salt prepared in this way remains unaltered for a long time.

Double Sulphate of Iron and Ammonium. $FeSO_4(NH_4)_2SO_4.6H_2O.$

The double sulphate of iron and ammonium is a light green crystalline salt, soluble in 2.8 parts of water at 16.5° C. It may be prepared as

follows : Dissolve 276 grammes of crystallized ferrous sulphate in water,
filter, and add to the filtrate a clear solution of sulphate of ammonium
($(NH_4)_2SO_4$, Glauber's Sal Secretum), evaporate down, and allow the
double salt to crystallize out.   Drain the crystals, wash slightly with cold
water, and dry on blotting-paper.   When perfectly dry, preserve in a
glass-stoppered bottle.   The crystals remain unaltered for a long time
even in moist air.   They contain exactly $\frac{1}{4}$ their weight of metallic iron.

Mercurous Nitrate. $HgNO_3,H_2O.$

To prepare this salt, pour cold, moderately strong HNO_3 on an excess
of metallic mercury, and when the violent action has subsided, pour off
the acid and allow the salt to crystallize out by the cooling of the acid.
The salt is soluble in a small amount of water, but a large amount decomposes it into a basic salt and free acid.

Mercuric Oxide. $HgO.$

Mercuric oxide is a light orange-yellow substance when prepared by
precipitation from a mercuric salt.   To a dilute solution of mercuric
chloride add a slight excess of caustic potassa, allow the precipitate to
settle, wash it thoroughly by decantation with hot water, and finally wash
it into a glass-stoppered bottle.   It is used shaken up with water.

Chromate of Lead. $PbCrO_4.$

Fused chromate of lead is a dark brown mass showing a radiated
structure, and when powdered it is dark yellow in color, very heavy,
and slightly hygroscopic.   It is easily obtained very pure, but may be
made as follows: Dissolve acetate of lead in water, add a little acetic
acid, filter, and precipitate by a solution of bichromate of potassium.
Wash by decantation, and finally on linen, dry, and heat in a Hessian
crucible until the mass is just fused.   Pour on a polished iron slab, grind
in a clean mortar, and preserve the powder in glass-stoppered bottles,
covered to exclude dust.   Chromate of lead heated to a full red heat
gives off oxygen and is reduced to a mixture of basic chromate of lead
and oxide of chromium.

Peroxide of Lead. PbO$_2$.

Peroxide of lead is rather difficult to obtain in a state of purity; it is liable to contain nitrate of lead and oxide of manganese. The latter element interferes materially with its use as a reagent in the determination of manganese by the color test. It should always be carefully examined by boiling with dilute nitric acid, and, if it imparts any color to the solution, must be promptly rejected. It may be readily prepared by digesting red oxide of lead in dilute nitric acid, decanting off the nitrate of lead, and washing the residue thoroughly with hot water. Red oxide of lead by this treatment is decomposed into protoxide of lead, which dissolves in the nitric acid, and peroxide, which remains insoluble. Peroxide of lead is a heavy brown powder, which, when heated, gives off oxygen and is converted into red lead or protoxide of lead.

Oxide of Lead dissolved in Caustic Potassa.

Pour a cold solution of nitrate of lead into caustic potassa, 1.27 sp. gr., stirring constantly to dissolve the oxide of lead, which precipitates. Add the nitrate of lead until a permanent precipitate is produced. Allow this to settle, and siphon the clear liquid into a glass-stoppered bottle. It is well to coat the stopper with a little paraffine, to prevent its sticking.

Platinic Chloride Solution.

Dissolve platinum-foil in HCl, adding HNO$_3$ from time to time, evaporate to dryness on the water-bath, redissolve in HCl, and evaporate again to drive off the HNO$_3$. Redissolve in water with the addition of a few drops of HCl, filter, and preserve in a bottle the stopper and neck of which are protected by a ground-glass cap to prevent any access of ammonia to the solution.

Metallic Zinc.

Melt zinc, which should be as free as possible from lead and iron, in a Hessian crucible, and pour it in a thin stream from a height of four or five feet into a bucket of cold water, giving the crucible a circular motion to prevent the zinc from falling in exactly the same place all the time. Pour off the water, dry the granulated zinc, and preserve it in bottles for use.

Oxide of Zinc in Water.

Emmerton* suggests the following method of preparing this reagent: Dissolve ordinary zinc white in HCl, add the zinc white until there is an excess which will not dissolve, then add a little bromine-water, heat the solution, filter, and precipitate the oxide of zinc by ammonia, being careful to avoid an excess. Wash thoroughly by decantation, and then wash into a bottle. Shake the bottle well, to diffuse the oxide through the water, before using.

REAGENTS FOR DETERMINING PHOSPHORUS.
Magnesia Mixture.

Dissolve 110 grammes of crystallized chloride of magnesium ($MgCl_2 + 6H_2O$) or 50 grammes of the anhydrous salt in water, and filter. Dissolve 28 grammes of chloride of ammonium in water, add a little bromine-water and a slight excess of ammonia, and filter. Add this solution to the solution of chloride of magnesium, add enough ammonia to make the solution smell decidedly of ammonia, dilute to about 2 litres, transfer to a bottle, shake vigorously from time to time, allow to stand for several days, and filter into a small bottle as required for use. 10 c.c. of this solution will precipitate about 0.15 gramme P_2O_5.

Molybdate Solution.

Dissolve 100 grammes of molybdic acid in 422 c.c. of ammonia, 0.95 sp. gr., then add, with constant stirring, 1250 c.c. of nitric acid, 1.2 sp. gr. Or to 123 grammes of crystallized molybdate of ammonium add 333 c.c. of ammonia, 0.95 sp. gr., and 62 c.c. of water. To this solution add 1250 c.c. of nitric acid, 1.2 sp. gr., with constant stirring. Allow the molybdate solution to stand for several days, and siphon off the clear liquid for use.

* Trans. Am. Inst. Min. Engineers, vol. x. p. 201.

METHODS FOR THE ANALYSIS

OF

PIG-IRON, BAR-IRON, AND STEEL.

DETERMINATION OF SULPHUR.

By Evolution as H₂S.

KARSTEN was the first to suggest dissolving iron or steel in HCl, or dilute H_2SO_4, and collecting the evolved H_2S by absorbing it in a solution of a metallic salt. He recommended $CuCl_2$.

Absorption by Alkaline Solution of Nitrate of Lead.

The apparatus, Fig. 47, shows the usual arrangement for carrying out the process, with the addition of the generating-bottles for supplying hydrogen gas. This is the apparatus described under the head of "Apparatus for Generating CO_2," page 42. The wash-bottle A contains an alkaline solution of nitrate of lead, and is connected with the funnel-tube by the rubber tube B, and a small piece of glass tubing, C, turned at a right angle with one end drawn down and covered with a short piece of rubber tubing. This fits in the neck of the bulb of the funnel-tube and makes a tight joint. The analytical process is conducted as follows: Description of the apparatus.

Weigh 10 grammes of borings or drillings, free from lumps, into the previously dried flask D, and close it with the rubber stopper fitted with a funnel-tube and a delivery-tube. The Description of the process.

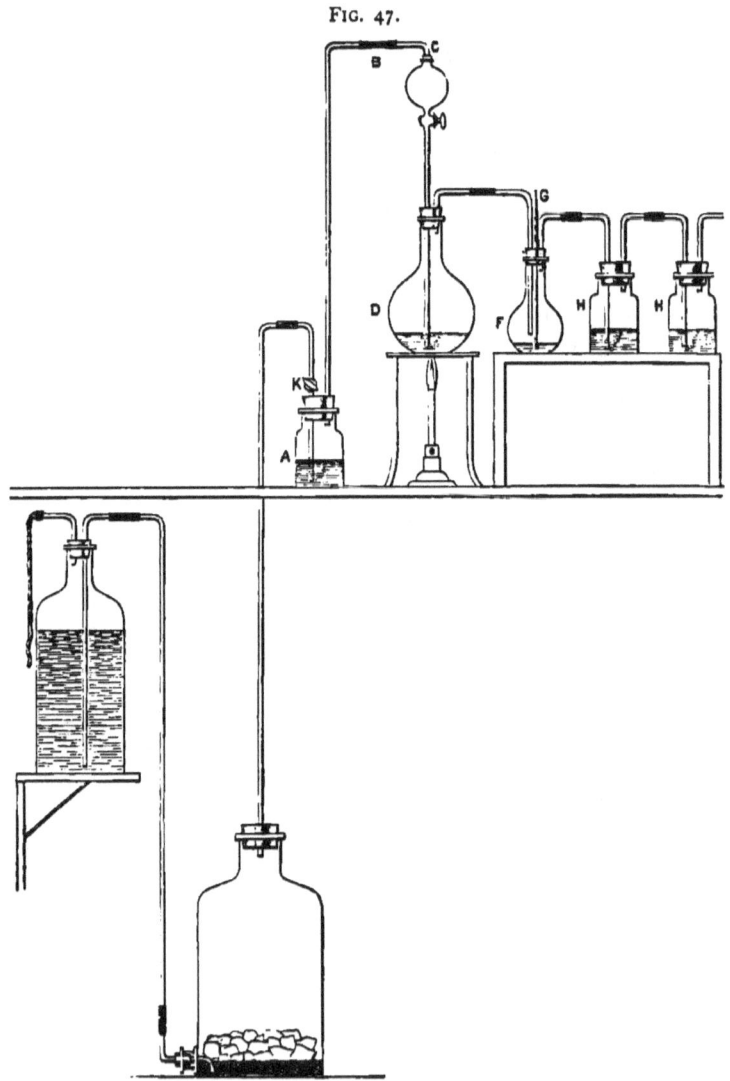

FIG. 47.

small flask F serves as a condenser, and is fitted with an inlet-tube reaching almost to the surface of a small amount of water in the bottom of the flask, a safety-tube, G, dipping just below the surface of the water, and an exit-tube connected with the first of the two wide-mouth bottles H. In each of the bottles H are poured about 20 or 30 c.c. of potassium hydrate solution of nitrate of lead* and enough water to fill them two-thirds full. Connect the apparatus, and run a slow stream of hydrogen through until all the air is expelled, then close the glass stopcock of the funnel-tube, and shut off the supply of hydrogen by closing the small glass stopcock K. If the connections are all tight, the water in the safety-tube G will keep its level. When this is assured, disconnect the tube C, and fill the bulb—which should be of about 100 c.c. capacity—with a mixture of 50 c.c. strong HCl and 50 c.c. water. Replace the tube C, turn on the hydrogen, and open the stopcock of the funnel-tube, so as to allow the acid to flow drop by drop into the flask D. When the acid has all run into the flask, regulate the flow of the hydrogen so that the gas will continue to pass through the solutions in the bottles H, H, at the rate of 6 or 8 bubbles a second, and heat the flask D very cautiously. When the solution in the flask D has boiled for a few minutes, and all the metal has dissolved, remove the source of heat and continue the current of hydrogen for about ten minutes, regulating its flow by means of the stopcock K, to prevent any reflux of the liquid in H, which might be caused by the cooling of the flask D. Shut off the hydrogen, disconnect the apparatus, and wash the contents of the bottle H into a No. 2 Griffin's beaker. Unless a precipitate of sulphide of lead appears in the second bottle H, it need not be emptied, but the same solution can be used over again for the next analysis. Collect the precipitate in a small filter, wash it once or twice

----

* See page 57.

with hot water, and, while still moist, throw the filter and precipitate back into the beaker, in which have been placed just
the instant before some powdered $KClO_3$ and from 5 to 20 c.c.
strong HCl, according to the amount of the precipitate of lead
sulphide. Allow it to stand in a cool place until the fumes
shall have partly passed off, then add about twice its volume of
hot water, and filter into a No. 1 beaker. Wash with hot
water, heat the filtrate to boiling, and add NH_4HO until the
solution is slightly alkaline to litmus-paper. Acidulate with a
few drops of HCl, add 5 to 10 c.c. $BaCl_2$ solution,* boil for a
few minutes, and stand aside in a warm place overnight. Filter

Precipita-
tion as
$BaSO_4$.

the precipitate of $BaSO_4$, preferably on a Gooch perforated
crucible, wash with hot water, ignite, and weigh as $BaSO_4$,
which contains 13.75 per cent. S. It is always well to test the
alkaline filtrate from the lead sulphide with a few drops of the
lead solution, for it might happen that all the lead would be
precipitated from the solution as sulphide, and an excess of
H_2S remain in the solution as sulphide of potassium.

Absorption by Ammoniacal Solution of Sulphate of Cadmium.

Precipita-
tion as
CdS.

T. T. Morrell† passes the evolved gas into an ammoniacal
solution of sulphate of cadmium. Prepare a solution of sulphate
of cadmium of convenient strength, and add enough ammonia to
redissolve the precipitate and give a clear solution. Place this
solution in the bottles H, H, and proceed as usual. Filter the
precipitate of sulphide of cadmium in a counterpoised filter, wash
with water containing a little ammonia, dry at 100° C., and
weigh as CdS, which contains 22.25 per cent. of S.

Absorption by Ammoniacal Solution of Nitrate of Silver.

Berzelius proposed the use of a dilute solution of nitrate of
silver made alkaline by ammonia. The method of procedure is

---

* See page 51.   † Chem. News, xxviii. 229.

as follows: Dissolve 1 gramme of $AgNO_3$ in a small quantity of water, and make it strongly alkaline with NH_4HO; pour about two-thirds of the solution into the first of the bottles H, and the remainder into the second, and fill up to the proper level with water. Proceed exactly as described above until the sulphide of silver has been filtered off and washed. Dry this precipitate carefully at a low temperature, say 100° C., and brush it carefully into a small, dry beaker, returning the filter to the funnel. Pour into the bottles H, should any of the sulphide remain adhering to the sides, 20 or 30 c.c. strong HNO_3, and when it is all dissolved, pour the acid in the filter, allowing it to run into the beaker containing the sulphide of silver, and wash out the bottles with a little HNO_3, allowing this to run over the filter also. Digest the sulphide of silver until it is all dissolved, then dilute with hot water, add an excess of HCl, and filter off the chloride of silver. Add a small amount of carbonate of sodium, and evaporate nearly dry, dilute, add a few drops of HCl, filter if necessary, and precipitate as before by chloride of barium. Even when the sample contains no sulphur a slight precipitate of carbide of silver may be thrown down by the carburetted hydrogen evolved from the iron or steel by the action of the acid.

Preparation of the ammoniacal solution of nitrate of silver.

Details of the method.

Absorption and Oxidation by Bromine and HCl.

Fresenius * suggested passing the evolved gases through a solution of bromine in HCl, which has the advantage of oxidizing the sulphuretted hydrogen at once, but the disadvantage of filling the room with bromine-fumes unless the apparatus is placed under a hood with a good draft. It is necessary when using this method to avoid bringing the bromine-fumes in contact with rubber stoppers. Instead of the bottles H, attach to the exit-tube a bulb-tube of the shape shown in Fig. 48, containing 3 to 5

Advantage of this method.

Disadvantage.

Description of apparatus.

---

* Fresenius, Zeitschrift, xiii. 37.

c.c. of bromine and enough HCl to fill the bulb-tube to the
marks shown in the cut. When the operation is finished, wash

the contents of the bulb-tube out into
a beaker, heat until the bromine is all
driven off, neutralize by NH_4HO, and
precipitate the sulphuric acid exactly as
described on page 62. Instead of neutralizing by NH_4HO, the HCl solution
may be evaporated down nearly to dryness after adding a little carbonate of
sodium or the solution of chloride of
barium; but repeated experiments have
shown that sulphate of barium is prac-
tically insoluble in chloride of ammonium, so that the plan of
neutralizing by NH_4HO, being the shorter and less troublesome,
is to be preferred.

Details of the method.

FIG. 48.

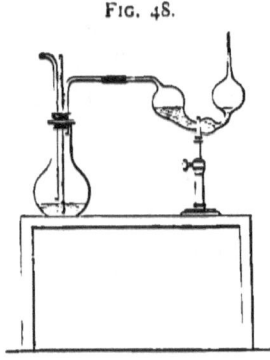

Insolubility of $BaSO_4$ in NH_4Cl.

Absorption and Oxidation by Permanganate of Potassium.

Drown * suggested the use of permanganate of potassium solution as an absorbent and oxidizer; the process being carried out
as follows: Make a solution of permanganate of potassium, 5
grammes to the litre of water, and fill the bottles H to their
proper height with this liquid, using three bottles, however, instead
of two, and proceed with the operation as before described, being
careful to avoid a rapid evolution of the gas. Wash the contents of the bottles H into a clean beaker, dissolve any oxide
of manganese that may adhere to the sides of the bottles in HCl,
add this to the solution in the beaker, and then add enough HCl
to decompose the permanganate entirely. Boil until the solution is colorless, filter if necessary, and precipitate by chloride
of barium. Allow it to stand overnight, filter, wash, ignite, and
weigh the $BaSO_4$.

Details of the pro-cess.

Avoid rapid evolution of gas.

---

* Journal Inst. Min. Engineers, ii. 224.

Absorption and Oxidation by Peroxide of Hydrogen.

Craig * suggested the use of ammoniacal solution of peroxide of hydrogen in the absorbing-bottles. Attach to the exit-tube of the flask D (Fig. 47) a nitrogen-bulb of the usual form (Fig. 48), in which have been placed 4 c.c. of peroxide of hydrogen and 16 c.c. of ammonia, and proceed as before directed. When the operation is finished, wash the contents of the nitrogen-bulb into a small beaker, acidulate slightly with HCl, boil, add chloride of barium, and determine the amount of $BaSO_4$ as usual. As peroxide of hydrogen always contains sulphuric acid, the amount must be carefully determined in each fresh lot of the H_2O_2, and the proper correction made for the volume used.

Necessity noted for determining amount of sulphuric acid in peroxide of hydrogen.

By Oxidation and Solution.

Many chemists still prefer the old method of oxidizing and dissolving the metal and precipitating the sulphuric acid in the solution by chloride of barium. The details are as follows: Treat 5 grammes of drillings in a No. 4 Griffin's beaker, covered by a watch-glass with 40 c.c. of strong HNO_3. This requires care, for drillings of bar-iron and low steel are often acted on so violently, even by strong HNO_3, as to cause the solution to boil over. In this case it is best to place the beaker in a dish containing a little cold water and to add the acid gradually. When all the acid has been added and the action has ceased, some small particles generally remain undissolved, and their solution is effected by heating the beaker on the sand-bath and finally by adding a few drops of HCl. With pig-iron and steel there is usually no action in the cold, and in this case heat the beaker carefully until the action begins, then stand the beaker in a cooler place, and if the action becomes very violent, stand the beaker in cold water until it moderates. Very high carbon steels

This method preferred by many chemists.

Precautions necessary in dissolving iron or steel in HNO_3

---

* Chem. News, xlvi. 199.

dissolve with great difficulty even in boiling acid; but the solution may be hastened by adding a few drops of HCl from time to time. When solution is complete and only particles of graphite and silica remain undissolved, which is shown by the residue being entirely flotant, remove the cover, add a little carbonate of sodium, and evaporate the solution to dryness in the air-bath. The addition of the carbonate of sodium is to prevent any possible loss of sulphuric acid, which might otherwise occur by the decomposition of the sulphate of iron at a

Further details. high temperature. Remove the beaker from the air-bath, and when cold add 30 c.c. HCl, and heat until the oxide of iron is dissolved, evaporate again to dryness to render the silica insoluble, redissolve in as little HCl as possible, dilute, and filter. Heat the filtrate to boiling, add 5–10 c.c. solution of chloride of barium, and allow it to stand in a warm place overnight.

When ignited precipitate contains iron it is to be fused with Na_2CO_3. Filter, wash with a little dilute HCl, and finally with hot water; dry, ignite, and weigh as $BaSO_4$. If this ignited precipitate is reddish in color, it shows that Fe_2O_3 has been precipitated with the $BaSO_4$. In this case fuse with Na_2CO_3, dissolve in water, filter, acidulate the filtrate, and precipitate as before.

Special Precautions in the Determination of Sulphur in Pig-Iron.

Residue from HCl solution of pig-iron contains S. Although it sometimes happens that the carbonaceous residue left after treating pig-iron with HCl contains no sulphur, as a rule it contains enough to affect seriously the accuracy of the analysis. It is not only in the case of cupriferous pig-irons that this occurs, but sometimes in pig-irons quite free from copper, and nearly always in those containing titanium. When an accurate determination of sulphur in pig-iron is required, *the examination of the carbonaceous residue should never be neglected when the evolution method has been used.*

Transfer the residue and solution from the flask D, page 61.

to a clean beaker, and filter, using the pump and cone,* with a strong filter-paper, and wash thoroughly, first with a little dilute HCl, and then with water. Dry the residue on a filter, brush it into a small porcelain mortar, rejecting the filter, and grind it up with 10 grammes dry Na_2CO_3 and 5 grammes KNO_3. Transfer it to a large platinum crucible, and heat it gradually until it is fused. Run the fused mass well up on the sides of the crucible, allow it to cool, fill the crucible nearly full with hot water, and stand it over a very low light for a few minutes. If the crucible is large enough, the fusion will dissolve completely; if not, decant the liquid into a beaker, fill the crucible with hot water again, and repeat the operation until the crucible is quite clean. It will usually be stained somewhat; but this is of no importance, and the stain can be removed afterwards by a little HCl. Filter the aqueous solution, wash the beaker and filter a few times with hot water, acidulate the filtrate carefully with HCl, and evaporate to dryness in the air-bath. Redissolve in hot water with a little HCl, filter, heat the filtrate to boiling, precipitate by $BaCl_2$ solution, allow to stand in a warm place overnight, filter, and weigh the $BaSO_4$. As it is impossible to get Na_2CO_3 and KNO_3 absolutely free from sulphur, a blank determination should be made for each new lot of these reagents, and the amount of $BaSO_4$ found subtracted from the amount obtained by the fusion of the residue, the remainder being calculated to S and added to the amount evolved as H_2S. Instead of fusing the carbonaceous residue, it may, after drying, be brushed into a small, clean beaker and treated with aqua regia, evaporated to dryness, redissolved in a little water and a few drops of HCl, filtered, and the sulphuric acid precipitated by $BaCl_2$ solution, with the usual precautions. The fusion method is, however, to be preferred.

Examination by fusion with Na_2CO_3 and KNO_3.

Necessity noted for testing Na_2CO_3 and KNO_3 for S.

Treatment of residue with aqua regia.

---

* See page 26.

RAPID METHOD.

Volumetric Determination by Iodine.

This method, suggested by Elliott,* involves the evolution of the sulphur as H_2S, its absorption in a solution of sodium hydrate, and titration by iodine in iodide of potassium. It requires a standard solution of iodine, a standard solution of hyposulphite of sodium, a starch solution, and a standard solution of bichromate of potassium.

Iodine Solution.

Dissolve 6.5 grammes pure iodine in water with 9 grammes iodide of potassium, and dilute to 1 litre.

Hyposulphite of Sodium Solution.

Dissolve 25 grammes hyposulphite of sodium in water, add 2 grammes carbonate of ammonium, and dilute to 1 litre. The carbonate of ammonium retards the decomposition of the hyposulphite of sodium.

Starch Solution.

Weigh out into a porcelain or Wedgwood mortar 1 gramme pure wheat starch, and rub it to a thin cream with water. Pour it into 150 c.c. boiling water, allow it to stand until cold, and decant the clear solution. The addition of 10 or 15 c.c. glycerine makes the solution keep better. It is better, however, to make a fresh starch solution every few days.

Bichromate of Potassium Solution.

Dissolve 5 grammes pure bichromate of potassium in water, and dilute to 1 litre.

---

* Chem. News. xxiii. 61.

All these solutions should be placed in glass-stoppered bottles and kept in a dark place.

Standardizing the Solutions.

Standardize the bichromate solution as directed in the "Analysis of Iron Ores." When bichromate of potassium is added to iodide of potassium in presence of free HCl, iodine is liberated, in accordance with the formula $K_2Cr_2O_7 + 6KI + 14HCl = 8KCl + Cr_2Cl_6 + 7H_2O + 6I$, or 1 equivalent of $K_2Cr_2O_7 = 294.5$ liberates 6 equivalents of iodine $= 761.1$. Therefore, by adding to a solution of iodide of potassium in the presence of HCl a known amount of bichromate, we can calculate the absolute amount of iodine liberated, and by titrating this solution by the hyposulphite solution we can accurately standardize the latter. The reaction which takes place when a solution of hyposulphite (thiosulphate) of sodium is acted on by iodine is $2NaHS_2O_3 + 2I = 2HI + Na_2S_4O_6$, or 2 equivalents of thiosulphate unite with 2 equivalents of iodine to form hydriodic acid and tetrathionate of sodium. By adding a few drops of starch solution to a solution containing iodine, blue iodide of starch is formed, and colors the solution as long as it contains free iodine. When enough hyposulphite is added to a solution of this kind to combine exactly with the iodine, the blue color disappears. Conversely, upon adding a solution of iodine to a solution containing hyposulphite of sodium and a little starch, the sensitive blue color of the iodide of starch will disappear as fast as formed until all the thiosulphate has been changed to tetrathionate, and then the first drop of iodine in excess will change the solution to a permanent blue. The same thing holds true as regards a solution containing free H_2S, the reaction being $H_2S + 2I = 2HI + S$. Proceed therefore as follows: Dissolve about 1 gramme of pure iodide of potassium in 300 c.c. water, add 5 c.c. HCl. and then 25 c.c. of the bichromate solution, which will liberate a known amount of iodine. Drop in

Standard-
izing the
hyposul-
phite solu-
tion.
now the hyposulphite solution from a burette until the iodine
nearly disappears, add a few drops of starch solution, and continue the hyposulphite until the blue color fades out entirely.
The amount of iodine being known, the value of the hyposulphite solution is calculated from the reading of the burette. Now

Standard-
izing the
iodide so-
lution.
measure into a beaker with a carefully graduated pipette 25 c.c.
of the hyposulphite solution, dilute to 300 c.c., add a few
drops of the starch solution, and drop, from a burette, standard
iodine solution until the blue color is permanent. The value
of the hyposulphite solution being known, that of the iodine
solution is readily calculated. An example will illustrate this:

Illustration
of the cal-
culation of
the values
of the so-
lutions.
Suppose we find by titration that 1 c.c. of our bichromate solution is equal to .00566 gramme metallic iron; then, as the
reaction is $6FeCl_2 + K_2Cr_2O_7 + 14HCl = 3Fe_2Cl_6 + 2KCl + Cr_2Cl_6 + 7H_2O$, 1 equivalent of $K_2Cr_2O_7 = 294.5$ is equal to 6 equivalents of $Fe = 336$. Hence $336 : 294.5 = .00566 : .004961$, or 1
c.c. of the bichromate solution contains .004961 gramme $K_2Cr_2O_7$,
and consequently 25 c.c. contain .124025 gramme $K_2Cr_2O_7$. Then,
as we saw by the formula that 294.5 parts bichromate liberate
761.1 parts iodine, we have $294.5 : 761.1 = .124025 : .32052$, or 25
c.c. bichromate solution liberate .32052 gramme iodine. We
now find that it requires 25.3 c.c. of the hyposulphite solution
to decolorize the solution made by adding 25 c.c. bichromate
solution to the iodide of potassium; consequently each c.c. of
the hyposulphite contains enough $NaHS_2O_3$ to react with .01267
gramme iodine. We now measure out 10 c.c. of the hyposulphite solution, dilute it to 300 c.c., add a few drops of starch
solution, and find that it requires 20.1 c.c. of the iodide solution to
give the permanent blue color. Hence 20.1 c.c. $= .1267$ gramme
iodine, or 1 c.c. iodide solution contains .006303 gramme iodine.
As the reaction with H_2S is $H_2S + 2I = 2HI + S$, it requires 2
equivalents of iodine to decompose 1 equivalent of H_2S, and the
proportion is $2I : S :: 253.7 : 32.06 :: .006303 : .000796$, or 1 c.c.
iodine is equal to .000796 gramme sulphur.

The standard solutions once ready, the actual determination of sulphur in a sample is very simple. Measure 50 c.c. of a solution of caustic soda, 1.1 sp. gr., free from sulphur, into the first of the bottles D. The second need not be used, but it is a good plan to keep a caustic potassa solution of nitrate of lead in it, and attach it after the other, to be certain that no H_2S escapes the caustic soda solution. Proceed with the determination as directed on page 61, and when finished wash the contents of the bottle D into a beaker, dilute to 500 c.c., acidulate with HCl, add a few drops of starch solution, and titrate with the iodide solution. See exactly how much HCl is required to acidulate strongly 50 c.c. of the caustic soda solution, and this amount can be added at once, so that no time need be lost in testing the solution with litmus before titrating.

Mr. E. F. Wood,* of the Homestead Steel-Works, modifies the method as follows: Pass the evolved gas into an ammoniacal solution of sulphate of cadmium instead of caustic soda. Filter, place the filter containing the precipitate of sulphide of cadmium in a beaker containing cold water, add enough hydrochloric acid to dissolve the precipitate, and titrate with iodine solution as above described.

Mr. Wood thinks that this method has several advantages over that in which caustic soda is used to absorb the H_2S. The hydrocarbon gases absorbed by the alkaline solution are gotten rid of, and the error which their presence may produce is avoided; the bulk of the precipitate is an indication of the amount of sulphur and a guide to the proper amount of hydrochloric acid to use for its solution; and when the sulphide of cadmium is filtered off, only a small amount of hydrochloric acid is required, and the generation of heat from the neutralization of the alkali is avoided.

Details of the method.

Wood's modification.

---

* Communicated to the author.

DETERMINATION OF SILICON.

By Solution in HNO_3 and HCl.

Dissolve 5 grammes of drillings in 40 c.c. HNO_3 with the precautions mentioned on page 65 ; although when silicon *alone* is to be determined, HNO_3 of 1.2 sp. gr. may be used, when, in most cases, the solution of the drillings will be more rapid. Remove the cover, evaporate the solution to dryness in the air-bath, replace the cover, and raise the temperature of the bath until the nitrate of iron is decomposed. Remove the beaker from the air-bath, allow it to cool, add 30 c.c. HCl, and heat gradually until all the ferric oxide is dissolved. Remove the cover, and evaporate again to dryness in the air-bath, redissolve in 30 c.c. HCl, dilute to about 150 c.c., and filter on an ashless filter. Detach any adhering silica from the sides and bottom of the beaker with a "policeman," and wash it out with cold water. Wash the filter first with dilute HCl, and finally with water. Dry, and ignite in a platinum crucible until all the carbon is burned, weigh the residue in the crucible, moisten it with water, add 1–10 drops H_2SO_4, and enough HFl to dissolve it completely, evaporate to dryness, ignite, and weigh. The difference between the two weights is SiO_2, which contains 47.02 per cent. of Si. In the absence of HFl, unless the SiO_2 is perfectly white, fuse with 5 or 6 times the weight of Na_2CO_3, dissolve in water, acidulate with HCl, evaporate to dryness (in a platinum or porcelain dish, with the arrangement shown on page 20), redissolve in HCl and water, dilute, filter, wash, ignite, and weigh. When the weight of Na_2CO_3 taken does not exceed 2 or 3 grammes, allow the crucible to cool after fusion, and then add to it gradually an excess of strong H_2SO_4, heating very slowly, until the mass is quite liquid and fumes of SO_3 come off. Allow it to cool, dissolve in water, filter, wash well, ignite, and weigh.

Side notes:

Best strength of HNO_3 for solution.

Testing purity of SiO_2 with HFl.

By fusion with Na_2CO_3 and evaporation with HCl.

By treating fusion in crucible with H_2SO_4.

By Solution in HNO₃ and H₂SO₄.

Drown * has suggested a method which, for pig-irons, has come into very general use, and which is much more rapid than the other method, and quite as exact. Treat 1 gramme of borings in a platinum or porcelain dish with 20 c.c. HNO_3, 1.2 sp. gr. When all action has ceased, add 20 c.c. of H_2SO_4 (equal parts acid and water), and evaporate—using the arrangement shown on page 20—until copious fumes of SO_3 are given off. Allow to cool, and dilute with 150 c.c. water; heat carefully until all the sulphate of iron has dissolved, filter hot, wash first with dilute HCl, 1.1 sp. gr., and then with hot water, ignite, and weigh. Treat the contents of the crucible with H_2SO_4 and HFl, evaporate to dryness, ignite, and weigh again. The difference between the two weights is SiO_2.

By Volatilization in a Current of Chlorine Gas.

As almost all steels and irons contain slags of various com- positions, it must be understood that the SiO_2 obtained by the methods above given is the total SiO_2, comprising any SiO_2 that may be present in the admixed slag, as well as that formed from the Si present in the metal. The volatilization method separates the two. The process suggested by Drown,† and worked out independently two years later by Watts,‡ is as fol- lows: Fig. 49 shows the general arrangement of the apparatus. The large flask contains binoxide of manganese in lumps. The bottle above it contains strong common HCl, which runs into the flask through a siphon-tube extending almost to the bottom. The flask stands in a dish containing water, which can be heated by the burner under the tripod. The evolution-tube from the flask has a stopcock, and connects with the three bulb-tubes on the stand, the first containing water, the second

---

* Jour. Inst. Min. Engineers, vii. 346.   † Ibid., viii. 508.
‡ Chem. News, xlv. 279.

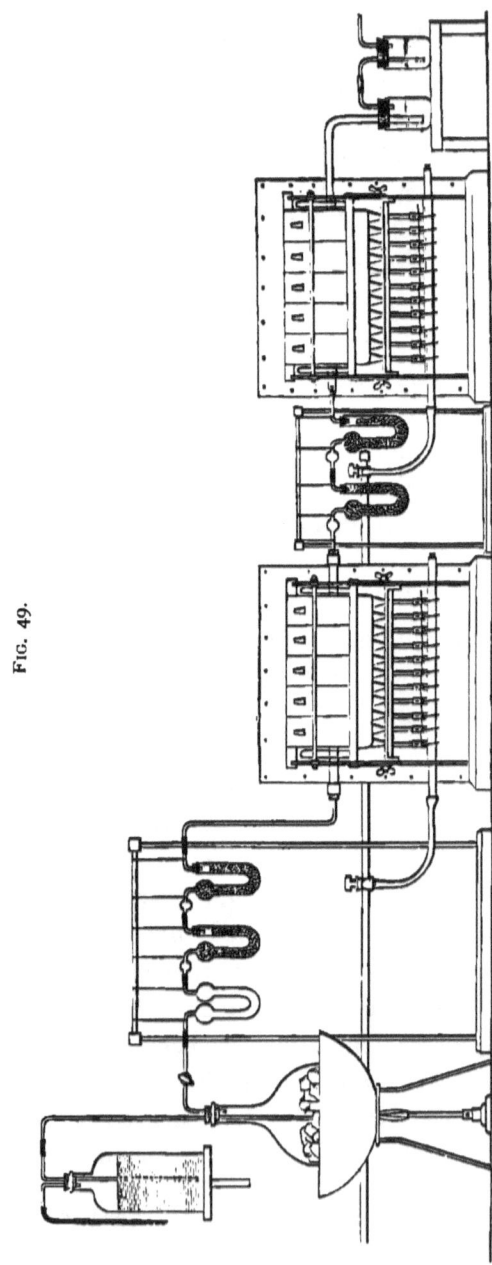

FIG. 49.

pumice-stone, and the third pumice saturated with strong H_2SO_4. The outlet-tube from the latter leads into the porcelain or glass tube in the furnace. This tube contains small lumps of char- Purification of the Cl from O. coal or gas carbon, kept in position by loosely-fitting plugs of asbestos, and occupying about 8 inches (200 mm.) in the middle of the tube. The outlet-tube from this connects with the drying-tubes on the second stand, which contain pumice moistened with strong H_2SO_4. The outlet from the second drying-tube connects with the glass combustion-tube, which leads through the second furnace, and is bent at a right angle where it is connected with the large tubes, half filled with water. The apparatus being in order,* start a slow current of chlorine Details of the method. through the apparatus by blowing HCl from the bottle into the flask and filling the dish in which the latter stands with water. Light a low light under the dish, and open the stopcock wide enough to allow a very slow current to bubble through the bulbs. Light the burners of the first furnace so that the tube is heated to dull redness. When the apparatus is full of chlorine, weigh 1 gramme of pig-iron, or 3 grammes of steel, into a porcelain boat about 3 inches long, distributing the drillings evenly along the bottom of the boat. Remove the stopper at the rear end of the second tube and insert the boat to about the centre. Replace the stopper, and continue the current of chlorine in the cold for ten or fifteen minutes to make sure that no oxygen remains in the tube, then light the burner under the forward end of the boat. The heat must be just sufficient to Volatilization of the Fe₂Cl₆. volatilize the ferric chloride, which should condense in the cooler part of the tube, and the current of gas should be slow enough to prevent any ferric chloride from being carried forward into the water-tubes or any loss of carbon from the boat.

---

* All the stoppers used should be of rubber coated with paraffine on the ends, or of asbestos, and where glass tubes are joined together with rubber the ends of the glass tubes should be brought into close contact.

When the fumes of ferric chloride begin to come off more slowly, light the next burner, and continue until all the burners under the boat are lighted, maintaining the heat until the fumes of ferric chloride cease. The tube for the entire length occupied by the boat should be at a dull red heat. Should the condensed ferric chloride at any time choke the tube so as to prevent the passage of the gas, heat that part of the tube gently with a spirit-lamp, so as to drive the ferric chloride a little farther along the tube. When the fumes of ferric chloride are no longer given off from the boat, the operation may be considered finished. Turn out the lights under the tube containing the boat, remove the stopper, and draw out the boat, which now contains the carbon, the slag, and the greater part of the manganese (as

Residue in boat available for determination of C or slag.

$MnCl_2$) which were contained in the iron or steel. This residue may be used for the determination of the carbon or the slag, as will be shown farther on. If another determination is to be made, another tube may be substituted for the one which contained the boat, and the analysis carried out in the manner described above. If not, put out all the lights, close the stopcock, and withdraw the combustion-tube with the water-tubes. Remove the stoppers from the latter, and pour the contents of these tubes into a platinum dish containing a small amount of an aqueous solution of sulphurous acid, to prevent the chlorine in the solutions from acting on the platinum. Rinse the tubes into the dish, and if any silica has separated out and adheres to the water-tubes or to the end of the combustion-tube, loosen it with a "policeman" and wash it into the dish. Add 5 c.c. strong H_2SO_4, evaporate to dryness, and heat until fumes of SO_3 are given off. Allow the dish to cool, add 100 c.c. cold water, and filter off on a small ashless filter any SiO_2, which burn and weigh as such. Calculate to Si. The

Separation from TiO_2.

filtrate from the SiO_2 will contain any TiO_2 which may have been in the metal and which can be determined, as will be shown farther on. Silicon and titanium are volatilized as chlorides, $SiCl_4$ and $TiCl_4$, under the conditions shown above, and decomposed by water thus: $SiCl_4 + 2H_2O = 4HCl + SiO_2$ and $TiCl_4 + 2H_2O = 4HCl + TiO_2$.

Volatilization of $SiCl_4$ and $TiCl_4$. Decomposition by H_2O.

Rapid Method for Determination of Silicon. (S. Alfred Ford.*)

At the Edgar Thomson Steel-Works the molten pig-metal is taken directly from the furnaces to the converters, and it is generally necessary to determine the amount of silicon in the pig-iron as a guide in blowing the metal. To get the sample for analysis, a small ladle is dipped into the iron as it runs from the furnace, and a small quantity of molten iron is taken. The ladle is then held about three feet above a bucket of water, and the molten metal drooped into the water, at the same time giving the ladle a circular motion over the bucket. This will cause the iron to form in globules, more or less round according to the amount of silicon contained in the iron. Thus, with iron which contains 2 per cent. of silicon or more, the globules will be almost perfectly round, concave on the upper surface, and generally from $\frac{1}{4}$ inch (6 mm.) to $\frac{3}{8}$ inch (9 mm.) in diameter; while if the iron be low in silicon, the shot or drops will be very small, flat, and irregular in shape, and if the iron be very low in silicon, as is the case with spiegel and ferromanganese, the shot will be elongated and have tails sometimes $\frac{1}{4}$ inch (6 mm.) in length. In fact, a close observer can soon judge very closely as to the amount of silicon from the condition of these shot or drops. The next step in the process is to take the shot from the bucket and place them for a minute in the ladle which has been used to dip up the molten iron. The ladle, being hot, will dry the shot almost instantly. The shot are then placed in a large steel mortar (Fig. 7, page 17) and crushed. The crushed shot are then sifted with a fine sieve, and .5 gramme

Method of taking sample.

Appearance of shot depending on amount of Si.

Pulverizing the sample.

* Prepared by Mr. Ford for this volume.

Determina-
tion of the
Si.

of the fine siftings are placed in a platinum evaporating-dish, 10 c.c. HCl, 1.2 sp. gr., are then added, and the dish covered with a watch-glass. The dish is then placed over a light, and the iron dissolved; as soon as solution takes place, which requires about one minute, as the particles of iron are so small, the watch-glass is removed and the solution evaporated to dryness as rapidly as possible over a naked light; as soon as dry, not even waiting for the dish to cool, dilute HCl is dropped on the chloride of iron, and as soon as all the sesquioxide of iron (which may have been formed by the decomposition of the chloride) is dissolved, water is added. The contents of the dish are then poured on a filter, to which is attached a pump, filtered, and washed. The filter and its contents are then placed in a

Burning C
in stream
of O.

weighed platinum crucible, placed over a blast-lamp; as soon as the filter-paper is burned off, the crucible is turned on its side, the lid removed, and a small jet of oxygen is driven very gently into the crucible. As soon as what little carbon there is in the precipitate is burned off, the crucible is cooled and weighed, and the amount of silicon calculated from the weight of the silica in the crucible.

Time re-
quired for
determi-
nation
of Si.

By this method the amount of silicon in a pig-iron can be determined in twelve minutes from the time the ladle is put into the molten iron, and it gives results close enough for practical purposes.

DETERMINATION OF SLAG AND OXIDES.

Presence of
slag in iron
and steel.

A certain amount of slag and oxide of iron is always present in puddled iron as a mechanical admixture. It is also found, as a general thing, in basic steel, and the presence of slag in steel made by the acid process, as well as in pig-iron, is not unusual. The easiest method for the determination of these substances is by solution in iodine, as suggested by Eggertz.

By Solution in Iodine.

Weigh 5 grammes of borings free from lumps into a No. 2 Details of the method.
Griffin's beaker. Stand the beaker, carefully covered with a
watch-glass, in a dish filled with scraped ice or snow, so that the
bottom and sides of the beaker half-way up shall be in contact
with it. Pour over the iron in the beaker 25 c.c. of ice-cold
boiled water, and stir until all the air in the borings has escaped.
Add gradually 28 or 30 grammes of resublimed iodine,* stirring
occasionally, until all the iodine has dissolved. Keep the beaker
constantly surrounded by ice, and add the iodine slowly enough
to prevent any rise in the temperature of the solution. Stir the
solution frequently until the iron is perfectly dissolved, which
will take several hours; then add 100 c.c. cold boiled water,
allow the insoluble matter to settle, and decant the supernatant
fluid on a small ashless filter. Wash the insoluble matter several
times, by decantation, with cold water, then add to it a little Insuring total solu- tion of Fe.
water, with a few drops of HCl, and observe whether any hydro-
gen is disengaged. If none can be perceived, the metallic iron
may be considered entirely dissolved; but if gas is given off,
the opposite is the case. In either event, quickly decant the
acidulated water on the filter, and if any metallic iron remains,
add a very little water and some iodine to dissolve the iron
entirely. Then transfer the insoluble matter, consisting of
graphite, carbonaceous matter, slag, oxide of iron, and some Separation of SiO₂.
silica, to the filter, wash the filter once with very dilute HCl
(1 acid to 20 water), and finally with cold water, until the filtrate
is free from iron. Unfold the filter, and with a fine jet wash
the insoluble matter off into a small platinum or silver dish.
Evaporate almost to dryness, add 50 c.c. solution of caustic
potassa, sp. gr. 1.1, and boil five or ten minutes. Decant the
liquid on a very small ashless filter, repeat the boiling with

---

* Page 41.

fresh caustic potassa, transfer the insoluble matter to the filter, and wash well with hot water. Wash once with dilute HCl (1 acid to 20 water), and finally with hot water, until the filtrate gives no precipitate with a solution of nitrate of silver. Dry, ignite, and weigh as Slag and Oxide of Iron.

Instead of using iodine directly for the solution of the iron, a solution of iodine in iodide of iron, as suggested by Eggertz,[*] may be used to great advantage, as it affords a ready method for getting rid of the impurities usually present in resublimed iodine. Treat 5 grammes of iron (as free as possible from silicon) with 25 grammes of iodine, and, when the solution is complete, add 30 grammes more of iodine, which will dissolve in the iodide of iron in a few minutes. Dilute to 50 c.c. with cold boiled water and filter through a washed filter. Add the filtrate at once to 5 grammes of the weighed sample, and, after solution is complete, proceed as directed above.

Use of iodine in iodide of iron as a solvent.

By Volatilization in a Current of Chlorine Gas.

Proceed exactly as in the method for the determination of silicon (pages 74 *et seq.*) until the boat is withdrawn from the combustion-tube. Wash the contents of the boat into a small beaker with a jet of cold water, and filter on a small ashless filter. The water dissolves any soluble metallic chlorides, $MnCl_2$, $CaCl_2$, etc., which are not volatile at a low red heat, and the insoluble matter in the filter consists of slag and carbon. Burn off the carbon and weigh the residue as Slag and Oxides. Or, if the carbon has been determined by another operation, filter the carbon and slag on a counterpoised filter[†] or on a Gooch crucible, dry at 100° C., and weigh as Carbon, Slag, and Oxides; by subtracting the weight of the carbon the difference is Slag and Oxides.

Washing out soluble chlorides.

Using counterpoised filters.

---

[*] Jern-Kontorets Annaler, 1881, p. 301, and Chem. News, xliv. 173.

[†] See page 27.

DETERMINATION OF PHOSPHORUS.

For the determination of phosphorus in iron and steel but two methods are in general use, either of which, properly carried out, will give extremely accurate results. Some chemists prefer one method, some the other, while a combination of the two is sometimes used. The two general methods are known respectively as the *Acetate Method* and the *Molybdate Method*. There are innumerable variations in the details, especially of the latter method, but any departure from what might be termed the standard instructions should never be attempted by any but a very experienced analyst.

Methods in general use.

The Acetate Method.

The essential parts of this method were suggested by Fresenius,* the changes and improvements in details being the work of many chemists.†

Dissolve 5 grammes of drillings in a No. 4 Griffin's beaker in 40 c.c. strong HNO_3, with the precautions detailed on page 65. Evaporate the solution to dryness in the air-bath, replace the cover, and heat until the nitrate of iron is nearly all decomposed. Cool, add 30 c.c. HCl, heat gradually until the oxide of iron is dissolved, and evaporate to dryness again in the air-bath. Cool, dissolve in 30 c.c. HCl, dilute, and, in steels or puddled iron, when silicon is to be determined, filter, and treat the insoluble matter as directed for the determination of Si, page 72.

Details of the acetate method.

When Si is to be determined.

In the case of pig-irons which may contain titanium, filter, and keep the residue of graphite, silica, etc., for treatment, as directed farther on, "when titanium is present."

When Ti is present.

In the case of steels, when silicon is not to be determined in this portion, the solution need not be filtered at all, but may be diluted at once to about 250 c.c.

When Si is not to be determined.

---

* Jour. für Pr. Ch., xlv. 258.

† Tenth Census of the U. S., vol. xv. "Iron Ores of the U. S.," p. 523.

In any case, heat the filtered or unfiltered HCl solution nearly to boiling, remove the beaker from the light, and add gradually from a small beaker a mixture of 10 c.c. NH_4HSO_3* and 20 c.c. NH_4HO, stirring constantly. The precipitate, which forms at first, redissolves, and when all but about 2 or 3 c.c. of the NH_4HSO_3 solution has been added, replace the beaker

Deoxidizing the solution. over the light. If at any time while adding the NH_4HSO_3 solution the precipitate formed will not redissolve even after vigorous stirring, add a few drops of HCl, and, when the solution clears, continue the addition, very slowly, of the NH_4HSO_3. After replacing the beaker on the light, add to the solution (which should smell quite strongly of SO_2) NH_4HO, drop by drop, until the solution is quite decolorized, and until finally a *slight* greenish precipitate remains undissolved even after vigorous stirring. Now add the remaining 2 or 3 c.c. of the NH_4HSO_3 solution, which should throw down a white precipitate, which usually redissolves, leaving the solution quite clear and almost perfectly decolorized. Should any precipitate remain undissolved, however, add HCl, drop by drop, until the solution clears, when it should smell perceptibly of SO_2. If the reagents are used in exactly the proportions indicated, the reactions will take place as described, and the operations will be readily and quickly carried out. If the solution of NH_4HSO_3 is weaker than it should be, of course the ferric chloride will not be reduced, and the solution, at the end of the operation described above, will not be decolorized and will not smell of SO_2. In this case add more of the NH_4HSO_3 (without the addition of NH_4HO) until the solution smells strongly of SO_2, then add NH_4HO until the slight permanent precipitate appears, and redissolve it in as few drops of HCl as possible. The solution being now very nearly neutral, the iron in the ferrous condition, and an excess of SO_2 being present, add to the solution 5 c.c.

---

* See page 44.

of HCl to make it decidedly acid and to insure the complete decomposition of any excess of the NH_4HSO_3 which may be present. Boil the solution,* while a stream of CO_2 passes through it, until every trace of SO_2 is expelled, then pass a current of H_2S through it for about fifteen minutes to precipi-

Boiling off excess of SO_2.

FIG. 50.

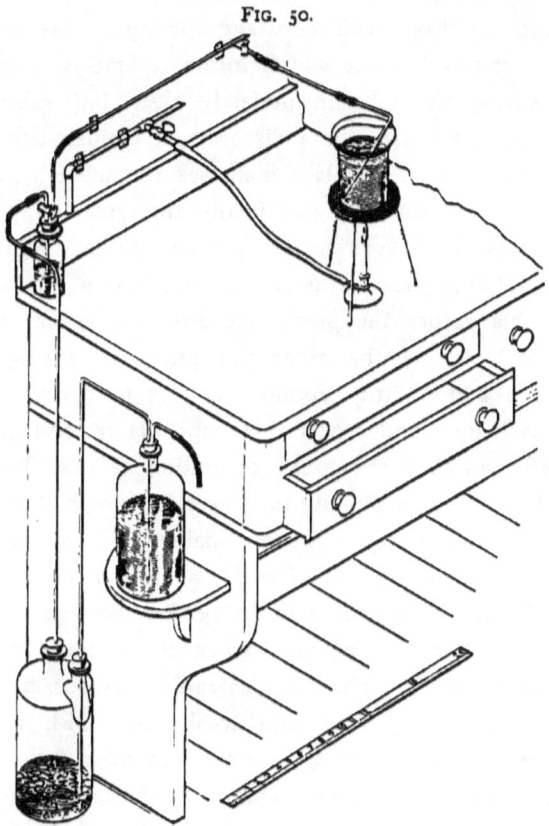

tate any arsenic which may be present, and finally allow the solution to stand in a warm place until the smell of H_2S has disappeared, or, better, pass a current of CO_2 through the

Precipitating the As.

---

* By passing a current of CO_2 through the boiling solution the SO_2 is soon expelled, and the operation requires no watching.

solution, which will expel the H_2S in a few minutes. The arrangement, Fig. 50, is convenient for this purpose. Filter from any As_2S_3, CuS, S, etc., into a No. 5 beaker, wash with cold water, and to the filtrate add a few drops of bromine-water, and cool it by placing the beaker in cold water. To the cold solution add NH_4HO from a small beaker very slowly, and

Precipitat-
ing the
ferric
phosphate
and hy-
drate.

finally drop by drop, with constant stirring. The green precipitate of ferrous hydrate which forms at first is dissolved by stirring, leaving the solution perfectly clear, but subsequently, although the green precipitate dissolves, a whitish one remains, and the next drop of NH_4HO increases the whitish precipitate or gives it a reddish tint, and finally the greenish precipitate remains undissolved even after vigorous stirring, and another drop of NH_4HO makes the whole precipitate appear green. If before this occurs the precipitate does not appear decidedly red in color, dissolve the green precipitate by a drop or two of HCl, and add a little bromine-water (1 or 2 c.c.), then add NH_4HO as before, and repeat this until the reddish precipitate is obtained, and then the green coloration as described above. Dissolve this green precipitate in a very few drops of acetic acid (sp. gr. 1.04), when the precipitate remaining will be quite red in color, then add about 1 c.c. of acetic acid, and dilute the solution with boiling water, so that the beaker may be about four-

Filtering and
washing
the pre-
cipitate.

fifths full. Heat to boiling, and when the solution has boiled one minute, lower the light, filter as rapidly as possible through a 5½-inch (140-mm.) filter, and wash once with hot water. The filtrate should run through clear, but in a few minutes it will appear cloudy by the precipitation of the ferric oxide, which has been formed by the exposure of the filtered solution to the

Precautions.

air. The points to be observed are the red color of the precipitate and the clearness of the solution when it first runs through. Ferric phosphate being white, the red color of the precipitate shows that enough ferric salt was present in the solution to form ferric phosphate with all the phosphoric acid, and enough more to color the ferric phosphate red with the excess of ferric oxide.

When the precipitate has drained quite dry, pour about 15 c.c. of HCl into the beaker in which the precipitation was made, warm it slightly so that the acid may condense on the sides and dissolve any adhering oxide, wash off the cover into the beaker, add about 10 c.c. of bromine-water, pour this on the filter containing the precipitate, allowing it to run around the edge of the filter, and let the solution run into a No. 1 Griffin's beaker. Wash out the beaker once or twice, and then wash the filter well with hot water. If the acid in the beaker is not sufficient to dissolve the precipitate completely, drop a little strong acid around the edge of the filter before washing it with hot water. The scaly film of difficultly soluble oxide which sometimes forms on boiling the acetate precipitate is caused by the presence of too much acetate of ammonium, but when the instructions given above are carefully carried out it never appears. Evaporate the solution in the small beaker nearly to dryness to get rid of the excess of HCl, add to it a filtered solution of 5 or 10 grammes of citric acid (according to the size of the precipitate of Fe_2O_3, etc.) dissolved in 10 to 20 c.c. of water, then 5 to 10 c.c. of magnesia-mixture and enough NH_4HO to make the solution faintly alkaline. Stand the beaker in cold water, and when the solution is perfectly cold, add to it one-half its volume of strong NH_4HO and stir it well. When the precipitate of $Mg_2(NH_4)_2P_2O_8$ has begun to form, stop stirring, and allow it to stand in cold water for ten or fifteen minutes, then stir vigorously several times at intervals of a few minutes, and allow it to stand overnight. Filter on a small ashless filter, and wash with a mixture of 2 parts of water and 1 part of NH_4HO containing 2.5 grammes of NH_4NO_3 to 100 c.c.

Dry the filter and precipitate, and ignite them at a very low temperature at first so as to carbonize the filter without decomposing the precipitate, which may then be readily broken up

Solution of the precipitate.

Cause of the difficultly soluble film.

Precipitation of the $Mg_2(NH_4)_2P_2O_8$.

Filtering and burning the precipitate.

with a platinum wire. Raise the heat gradually, and finally ignite at the highest temperature of the Bunsen burner. When the precipitate is perfectly white, cool and weigh. Then fill the crucible half full of hot water, add from 5 to 20 drops of HCl, and heat until the precipitate has dissolved. Filter off on another small, ashless filter any SiO_2 or Fe_2O_3 that may remain, ignite, and weigh. The difference between the two weights is the weight of $Mg_2P_2O_7$, which, multiplied by 0.27836, gives the weight of P.

When Titanium is Present.

When a solution of ferric chloride containing TiO_2 and P_2O_5 is evaporated to dryness, a compound of $TiO_2.P_2O_5$ and Fe_2O_3 is formed, completely insoluble in dilute HCl.*

Iron ores and pig-irons containing TiO_2 require, therefore, a somewhat different method of treatment from that given above.

Treatment of the insoluble residue.

Dry and ignite the residue of graphite, silica, etc., from the solution of the pig-iron, so as to burn off all the carbon. Moisten this residue with cold water, add 5 to 10 drops of H_2SO_4 and enough HFl to dissolve the silica, and evaporate until fumes of SO_3 are given off. While this is going on, proceed with the deoxidation of the filtrate as described above, but when the SO_2 has been driven off do not pass H_2S through the solution, but

Treatment of the precipitate of ferric phosphate.

cool it, and proceed with the acetate precipitation. Instead of dissolving the precipitate, after washing it as described above, dry the filter and precipitate in the funnel, being careful not to heat it so as to scorch the filter. Clean out any of the precipitate which may have adhered to the sides of the beaker in which the precipitation was made, by wiping it with filter-paper, and dry this paper with the filter and precipitate.

When the precipitate is quite dry, transfer it to a small porcelain mortar. The precipitate may be readily detached from

---

* Published in Report on Methods employed in the Analysis of the "Iron Ores," Tenth Census U.S., vol. xv. p. 512. I first noted this fact in 1878.

the filter by rubbing the sides of the latter together over a large
piece of white, glazed paper, so that any little particles that fall
out may be seen. Roll up the filter with the bits of paper which
were used to wipe out the beaker, wrap a piece of platinum
wire around it, burn it on the lid of the crucible in which the
graphitic residue was treated, and transfer the ash to the mortar.
Grind the precipitate and ash with 3 to 5 grammes of Na_2CO_3 *Fusion of the precipitate.*
and a little $NaNO_3$, and transfer it to the crucible containing
the residue which was treated by HFl and H_2SO_4. Clean the
mortar and pestle by grinding a little more Na_2CO_3, and add
this to the other portion in the crucible. Fuse the whole for
half an hour or more, cool, dissolve the fused mass in hot water,
filter from the insoluble Fe_2O_3, etc.,* acidulate the filtrate with
HCl, add a few drops of NH_4HSO_3, boil off all smell of SO_2,
and pass H_2S through the hot solution to precipitate any arsenic
that may be present. Pass a current of CO_2 through the solu- *Precipitation of the As.*
tion to expel the excess of H_2S, filter off the As_2S_3, and to the
filtrate add a sufficient amount of Fe_2Cl_6 solution to combine
with all the P_2O_5 as $Fe_2(PO_4)_2$ and leave a slight excess. Add
a slight excess of NH_4HO, which should throw down a red
precipitate, while the solution is alkaline to test-paper; then add
acetic acid to slightly acid reaction, boil, and filter off the
$Fe_2(PO_4)_2$ and Fe_2O_3, and wash with hot water. Dissolve the
precipitate in HCl, allow the solution to run into a small beaker, *Precipitation of the Mg_2 $(NH_4)_2$ P_2O_5.*
evaporate until the solution is syrupy, add citric acid and mag-
nesia-mixture, and precipitate the $Mg_2(NH_4)_2P_2O_5$ as described
above. Unless the amount of phosphorus is very small, a second
fusion of the insoluble residue of Fe_2O_3, etc., is necessary. The *Necessity for re-fusing the residue.*
two filtrates can then be added together, acidulated with HCl,
and the remainder of the process carried out as directed above.
To avoid the fusion of the acetate precipitate with Na_2CO_3, which

---

* This Fe_2O_3, etc., contains all the titanium that was in the pig-iron as titanate of
soda, and must be kept for the estimation of that element when it is to be determined.

is always troublesome, the method for the determination of phosphorus may be modified (in many cases with advantage, and generally when titanium is not to be estimated) as follows: After filtering off the insoluble matter, graphite, silica, etc., ignite it, burn off the graphite, and treat the residue with HFl and H_2SO_4, evaporate down until the excess of H_2SO_4 is driven off, and fuse with Na_2CO_3. Treat the fused mass with water, and filter. Acidulate the filtrate with HCl, and add it to the main

solution, which has been deoxidized in the mean time with bisul-phite of ammonium. Expel the last traces of SO_2 from the united filtrates by boiling and passing a current of CO_2 through the solution, as previously directed. If the solution remains clear, pass H_2S through it, and filter off the precipitated sulphides. Cool the solution, and make the acetate precipitation as directed

on page 84. The only danger to be apprehended now is the tendency of titanic acid to separate out and carry phosphoric acid with it when in the evaporation of the HCl solution of the acetate precipitate the liquid becomes concentrated. To avoid this, the evaporation must be watched very carefully, and citric acid added as soon as the titanic acid begins to separate. Then, if the separation has not proceeded too far, the phosphoric acid may be precipitated in the usual way. If, however, the separation of titanic acid is not checked in time, proceed with the evapo-ration as directed on page 85, add 5 c.c. strong HCl, and warm gently. The solution will nearly always clear, but if it does not, then add citric acid and a slight excess of ammonia, and filter. Stand the filtrate aside, burn off and fuse the precipitate with Na_2CO_3, dissolve in water, filter, acidulate the filtrate with HCl, add a little Fe_2Cl_6 solution, a slight excess of ammonia, and acidulate with acetic acid. Boil, filter off the precipitate of phosphate and oxide of iron, dissolve in a little HCl, allow the solution to run into a small beaker, evaporate down, and add it to the ammoniacal filtrate from the separated titanic acid obtained above. Add excess of magnesia-mixture, and precipitate the phosphoric acid in the usual way. When the solution Other sources of error. becomes cloudy after deoxidation with NH_4HSO_3, and remains so after acidulating with HCl, proceed as directed above, but dry, and ignite the filter containing the precipitate by H_2S and that on which the acetate precipitate was filtered, fuse with Na_2CO_3, treat with water, filter, acidulate with HCl, pass H_2S through the solution, filter, add a little Fe_2Cl_6 solution, and precipitate by ammonia and acetic acid. Add the solution of this precipitate, after filtering it off, to the solution of the main acetate precipitate, and proceed as before.

Instead of adding citric acid and magnesia-mixture to the Removing the Fe as FeS before precipitating the $Mg_2(NH_4)_2 P_2O_8$. solution of the acetate precipitate, Fresenius,* and afterwards Spiller,† advised the method of adding citric acid, excess of ammonia, and sulphide of ammonium, filtering off the precipitated sulphide of iron, and, after evaporating to small bulk, adding magnesia-mixture and ammonia. When the bulk of the iron precipitate is not too great, this is quite unnecessary, for Shown to be unnecessary. many determinations have shown that with an excess of magnesia-mixture, ammonium magnesium phosphate is absolutely insoluble in both citrate of iron and ammonium and citrate of aluminium and ammonium.

The precipitate is also insoluble in ammonia-water (1 part of NH_4HO to 2 parts of water).

The Molybdate Method.

Svanberg and Struve‡ first discovered the reaction on which this method is based, and Sonnenschein§ first used it quantitatively. Weigh 5 grammes of drillings into a No. 4 Griffin's beaker, and add, with the proper precautions (page 65), 40 c.c. strong HNO_3. Instead of using HCl to hurry the solution, it Solution. is better, when the action slackens, to add water very cautiously

---

* Jour. für Pr. Chem., xlv. 258.   † Jour. Chem. Soc. (2), iv. 148.
‡ Jour. für Pr. Chem. xliv. 291.   § Jour. für Pr. Chem., liii. 339.

from time to time until the metal is completely dissolved. Evaporate to dryness in the air-bath, replace the cover, and heat for one hour at a temperature of about 200° C. in order to decompose all the carbonaceous matter,* otherwise the precipitation of the phospho-molybdate will be incomplete. Allow the beaker to cool, dissolve the precipitate in 30 c.c. HCl, evaporate to dryness to render the silica insoluble, redissolve in 30 c.c. HCl, and evaporate carefully until the excess of HCl is driven off, shaking the beaker from time to time to prevent the formation of a crust of dry chloride of iron. Cool the beaker, and dilute the solution with twice its volume of cold water. Filter on a small, washed German filter, 3-inch (75-mm.), or on the Gooch crucible. In the latter case the precipitation of the phospho-molybdate may be made in the small flask into which the solution is filtered. The washing should be done with cold water after dropping a little dilute HCl around the edge of the filter. The filtrate and washing should not exceed 50 or 60 c.c. in volume. Add to the solution 50 to 100 c.c. molybdate solution,† heat it to 40° C. in a water-bath carefully kept at this temperature, and allow it to stand in the bath for about four hours. Filter on a small, washed filter, and wash thoroughly with dilute molybdate solution (1 part of solution to 1 part of water) until a drop of the filtrate gives no reaction for iron with ferrocyanide of potassium. Stand the filtrate aside in a warm place to see whether any further precipitation of phospho-molybdate of ammonium takes place; if it does, it must be filtered off and treated like the main precipitate. Pour 2 or 3 c.c. strong NH_4HO on the precipitate, stir it up with a fine jet of hot water, and allow the solution to run into the flask or beaker in which the precipitation of phospho-molybdate was

Margin notes:
Destroying the carbonaceous matter.

Removal of the SiO₂.

Volume of the solution.

Temperature of the solution.

Solution of the filtered phospho-molybdate.

---

* In 1877 I discovered the necessity for destroying the carbonaceous matter, and communicated the fact to Hunt and Peters, who mentioned it in the Metallurgical Review, vol. ii. p. 365.

† See page 59.

made. When it has all run through the filter, replace the flask
or beaker by a small beaker of a little over 100 c.c. capacity,
remove any phospho-molybdate that may have adhered to the
sides of the original flask or beaker, by means of the ammoniacal nitrate, and then pour this back on the filter and allow it
to run through into the small beaker. Wash out the beaker or
flask with hot water and pour it on the filter with the addition
of a little more NH₄HO. Unless the precipitate of phospho-
molybdate is very large, this amount of NH₄HO should dissolve it, and a very little more washing should be sufficient.
If the precipitate is very large, it may be necessary to use more
NH₄HO and more wash-water, but under all circumstances the
amount of NH₄HO and of wash-water should be as small as is
consistent with perfect solution of the precipitate and thorough
washing of the beaker and filter. When the precipitate is
small, the filtrate and washings should amount to about 25 c.c.
Neutralize the solution with strong HCl; if the yellow phospho-
molybdate begins to precipitate, add NH₄HO until it redissolves,
and if there should remain a flocculent white precipitate, probably silica, after the solution is quite alkaline, filter it off.
Then to the cold alkaline liquid add, very slowly, 10 c.c.
magnesia-mixture stirring constantly, and after the magnesia-
mixture is all in, add one-third the volume of the solution of
strong NH₄HO and stir vigorously. It is well to stand the
beaker in cold water and stir the solution several times after
the precipitate has begun to crystallize out. After standing
about four hours, it may be filtered off on a very small ashless
filter and washed with dilute ammonia-water (1 part NH₄HO to
2 parts water) containing 2.5 grammes nitrate of ammonium to
the 100 c.c. Dry, ignite very carefully to burn off the carbonaceous matter, and finally heat for ten minutes over the blast-
lamp to volatilize any molybdic acid that may have been
precipitated with the Mg₂NH₄P₂O₇ cool, and weigh. Fill the
crucible half full of hot water, add 5 to 10 drops HCl, and

heat for a few minutes to dissolve the $Mg_2P_2O_7$. Pour the contents of the crucible on a small ashless filter, wash, ignite, and weigh the small residue that may remain undissolved. The difference between the two weights is the weight of $Mg_2P_2O_7$, which contains 27.836 per cent. phosphorus.

Direct weighing of the phospho-molyb-date. Many chemists, following Eggertz,* prefer to weigh the yellow phospho-molybdate direct instead of dissolving it and precipitating as $Mg_2(NH_4)_2P_2O_8$. In this event take 1 gramme of the drillings and proceed exactly as directed above, but use only about one-third the amount of HNO_3 and HCl for the solution. Before adding the molybdate solution, the volume of the filtrate from the silica should amount to only about 25 c.c. Add 50 c.c. of the molybdate solution, allow it to stand four hours at a temperature of 40° C., and filter off the precipitated phospho-molybdate on a Gooch crucible; wash first with dilute molybdate solution, and finally with water containing 1 per cent. of HNO_3, dry in an air-bath heated to 120° C., and weigh as $(NH_4)_3 11MoO_3PO_4$ (approximate formula), containing 1.63 per cent. of phosphorus. In the absence of a Gooch crucible, use counterpoised filters † for weighing the phospho-molybdate. The points of special importance are:

Precautions necessary. First, the necessity for destroying all the carbonaceous matter by heating the nitric acid solution, after evaporation, to a sufficiently high temperature to effect this with certainty.

Second, the avoidance of an excess of HCl in the final solution before precipitating by molybdate solution.

Third, when the phospho-molybdate is weighed directly, the necessity for rendering the silica insoluble.

Fourth, the danger of heating the solution above 40° C. after adding the molybdate solution, as arsenic, when present, precipitates with the phosphorus if the solution is heated to a higher temperature.

---

* Jour. für Pr. Chem., lxxix. 496.   † See page 28.

Fifth, the danger of causing a precipitation of molybdic acid with the phospho-molybdate by heating the solution to a temperature approximating 100° C.

Variations in the details.

Some chemists prefer to drive off the HCl entirely by adding HNO_3 to the hydrochloric acid solution, and boiling down nearly to dryness once or twice before filtering off the silica.

Others, after filtering off the silica, add NH_4HO until a slight permanent precipitate appears, then the molybdate solution, which is sufficiently acid to redissolve the slight precipitate of ferric hydrate, and leave the solution quite clear, with the exception of the precipitate of phospho-molybdate. Others supersaturate the hydrochloric acid solution with NH_4HO, and redissolve with the least possible amount of HNO_3 before adding the molybdate solution. Many of these are matters of personal preference, but the safest plan for the beginner is to follow the instructions first given until he has sufficient knowledge and experience to judge of the value of these variations, or to invent some for himself.

The Combination Method.

Riley * was the first to suggest the precipitation of phosphorus as phospho-molybdate, preceded by a separation of the phosphoric acid from the mass of the ferric chloride by deoxidation and precipitation by the acetate method. This method was worked out afterwards by A. Wendel, of the Albany and Rensselaer Steel Company, S. Peters, of the Burden Iron Company, and J. L. Smith.†

Details of the method.

Proceed as directed for the determination of phosphorus by the *Acetate Method*, using 1 gramme of borings and proportional amounts of reagents until having dissolved the acetate precipitate in HCl, evaporate to dryness, redissolve in a very little HNO_3, dilute to 20 c.c. with water, add a slight excess of NH_4HO, redissolve the precipitated ferric oxide in HNO_3,

---

* Jour. Chem. Soc., 1878, vol. i. p. 104.   † Chem. News, xlv. 195.

and add 30 c.c. molybdate solution.   Heat to 40° C. for an
hour, filter, wash with water containing 1 per cent. of HNO_3,
dry, and weigh.

When Titanium is Present.

When phosphorus is determined in pig-irons containing titanium, burn off the residue of carbon, silica, etc., treat it with
HFl and H_2SO_4, evaporate, and heat until the greater part of the
H_2SO_4 is driven off.   Fuse with 2 or 3 grammes of carbonate
of sodium, dissolve in water, filter, acidulate the filtrate with
HNO_3, add 50 c.c. molybdate solution, and heat to 40° C. for
four hours.   Filter, wash, and add this precipitate to the one
obtained in the filtrate from the carbon, silica, etc.   If any slight
insoluble matter should remain on the filter upon dissolving in
NH_4HO the phospho-molybdate obtained in the filtrate from the
carbon, silica, etc., burn it, fuse it with carbonate of sodium, and
test it also for phosphorus.

Variable
composi-
tion of the
phospho-
molyb-
date.

As remarked above, page 92, the formula given for the dried
phospho-molybdate of ammonium is approximate only.   The
composition of the salt seems to vary very much, the percentage
of phosphorus in it being given by various authorities from
1.27 to 1.75.   It seems to depend upon various circumstances,
such as the presence or absence of HCl in the solution, the
degree of acidity, the temperature at which the precipitation is
effected, the length of time the solution stands before the precipitate is filtered off, the size of the precipitate, the state of
concentration of the solution, and even the amounts of the iron
and ammonium salts present.

The precau-
tions it ne-
cessitates.

This fact must be borne in mind when the phosphorus is
determined by direct weighing of the phospho-molybdate, and
every effort must be used to effect the precipitations always
under as nearly as possible the same conditions.

RAPID METHODS.

Volumetric Method.*

This method gives an indirect determination of P by means of the estimation of the MoO_3 in the phospho-molybdate of ammonium, in which form the P is precipitated. The MoO_3 is reduced to a lower state of oxidation by the reducing action of Zn and H_2SO_4, and the reduced oxide is titrated with a standardized permanganate solution, MoO_3 being again formed by the reaction.

Reduction of MoO_3 by Zn and H_2SO_4.

The ratio of P to MoO_3 in the yellow precipitate being known, the amount of P present may easily be calculated when the amount of MoO_3 is known.

The MoO_3 is not reduced by Zn and H_2SO_4 to Mo_2O_3, but to a mixture of oxides corresponding to the formula $Mo_{12}O_{19}$.

The action of permanganate on this oxide is as follows:

$$5Mo_{12}O_{19} + 17(K_2OMn_2O_7) = 60MoO_3 + 17K_2O + 34MnO.$$

17 molecules of permanganate being equivalent to 60 molecules of MoO_3, 1 molecule of permanganate, which can oxidize 560 parts of iron, oxidizes $Mo_{12}O_{19}$ to 508.23 parts MoO_3. Hence a solution of permanganate has a strength, in terms of MoO_3, 90.76 per cent. of its strength against iron. The phospho-molybdate contains $24MoO_3$ to $1P_2O_5$, the phosphorus being 1.794 per cent. of the MoO_3.

For convenience in reckoning, a permanganate solution is used of which 1 c.c. = .0001 P. Its strength against iron is 1 c.c. = .006141 Fe. Its strength against MoO_3 is 90.76 per cent. of this, or .005574 MoO_3. 1.794 per cent. of this, = .0001, is its strength against P.

Oxidation of $Mo_{12}O_{19}$ to MoO_3 by permanganate.

In the case of steel, dissolve 5 grammes, in a 6-inch dish, in 75 c.c. HNO_3 of 1.20 specific gravity. Support a 6-inch watch-glass over the dish, so that the edge of the glass is about half an

---

* Prepared by Mr. F. A. Emmerton for this volume.

inch above the rim of the dish. Boil down rapidly on an iron plate, and heat thirty minutes on the hot plate after the residue looks dry. At the end of this time the smell of acid should
have disappeared. Let the dish cool, add 40 c.c. strong HCl, put the cover down tight on the dish, and heat at a gentle temperature for a few minutes, till the oxide of iron spattered on the cover is softened, then boil down till all but 15 c.c. of the acid is gone. The latter part of the process requires close attention, as it is necessary that at its completion the solution should be very concentrated, and yet that there should be very little chloride dried upon the sides of the dish. Let the dish cool a little, lift up the large watch-glass, and rinse off the lower side of it with 40 c.c. strong HNO_3, which is allowed to flow into the dish. Then cover the solution with an inverted watch-glass 1 inch smaller in diameter than the dish, so that in the subsequent boiling down of the solution the liquid condensing on the inner side of the watch-glass will run back to the sides of the dish instead of to the middle, and will thus aid in preventing
the formation of a crust about the edge of the liquid. Place the dish thus covered on a hot plate, and boil the solution down to about 15 c.c. in bulk. Take the dish from the plate, and move it about so as to moisten with the solution what crust may have formed. In this way, with a little skill, a perfectly clear and highly concentrated solution may be obtained, from which, practically, all the HCl has been expelled.

Dilute this solution, when somewhat cooled, to about 40 c.c. with water, and wash it into a 400 c.c. flask, bringing the solution to about 75 c.c. Add strong ammonia, shaking after each addition to make a thorough mixture of the ammonia with the precipitated ferric hydrate. Continue adding ammonia, shaking after each addition, till the mass sets to a stiff jelly, then add a few c.c. more, shake well, and be satisfied that there is a strong smell of ammonia in excess. Then add strong HNO_3 gradually, shaking well after each addition, until the liquid begins to get thinner. After the precipitate has all dissolved and the solution shows a very dark color, add a little more HNO_3, enough to bring the solution to a clear amber color. At this stage the solution will be 150 to 300 c.c., generally about 250 c.c., in bulk. Put a thermometer into the liquid and observe its temperature: if below 85° C., heat carefully over a lamp-flame till it is raised to this temperature; if above 85° C., cool to that temperature by immersion of the flask in water. When at 85°, add at once 40 c.c. of molybdate solution.* Close the flask with a rubber stopper, wrap it in a thick cloth, and shake up and down violently for five minutes. At the end of this time the precipitate will all be down.

[margin: Precipitation of the phospho-molybdate of ammonium.]

Collect the precipitate on a filter, using the filter-pump, and wash thoroughly with HNO_3 diluted with fifty times its bulk of water. No difficulty is experienced in getting practically all of the precipitate from the flask to the filter. If a thin film of the precipitate should adhere to the walls of the flask, it may be removed by a portion of the ammonia used in dissolving the yellow precipitate previous to the reduction with zinc and sulphuric acid. Have ready a 500 c.c. flask in which have been put 10 grammes of granulated zinc, roughly weighed out. Put the moist filter with the precipitate on a funnel in the neck of this flask; punch a hole in the point of the filter, and wash the precipitate into the flask with ammonia, 1 in 4. This can be done thoroughly without using more than 30 c.c. ammonia. Then pour into the flask 80 c.c. hot dilute sulphuric acid, 1 in 4, and cover the neck with a small funnel. Heat quickly on an iron plate till rapid solution of the zinc begins, and then heat gently for ten minutes. At the end of this time the reduction is complete. To separate the liquid from the undissolved zinc, pour it through a large folded filter, rinse the flask

[margin: Reduction of MoO_3.]

---

* The molybdate solution used is made by dissolving 100 grammes molybdic acid in a mixture of 300 c.c. strong ammonia and 100 c.c. water, and pouring this solution into 1250 c.c. HNO_3 of 1.20 specific gravity.

with cold water, and, after these washings have run through, fill up the filter once with cold water. The filtration on a large folded filter exposes the liquid but a very short time to the air. The zinc is decanted into the filter with the liquid, on which it continues to act till the latter has drained through.

Titration by perman-ganate solution. The filtrate, amounting to 400–500 c.c., is then ready for titration with permanganate, which is run in until the liquid is colorless. During the reduction of the MoO_3 the liquid takes on successively the colors pink, plum, pale olive-green, and dark olive-green, the darkness of the final color depending on the amount of MoO_3 reduced. The moment the reduced liquid is exposed to the air on the filter it loses its green, and takes on a port-wine·color, but this change does not seem to be due to an appreciable amount of oxidation, the oxidation of the reduced liquid taking place slowly, as was shown by Werncke.

In titrating, the wine color becomes fainter, and finally disappears, leaving a perfectly clear liquid, in which one drop of permanganate produces a plain pink color.

Pig-iron. In the case of irons, dissolve 5 grammes, and get the HNO_3 solution as described above. Wash this into a graduated 100 c.c. flask, dilute to the mark, mix, pour through a dry filter into a dry bottle, using the filter-pump. From the filtrate draw off 80 c.c. with a pipette, and in this amount, holding 4 grammes of the iron taken for analysis, finish the determination. In this way what may be a tedious filtration and washing is avoided, and the bulk of the solution is kept constant.

Iron-ores. In the case of ores, dissolve 10 grammes in HCl, evaporate to dryness, take up with HCl, evaporate to small bulk, and expel the HCl by boiling down with 40 c.c. strong HNO_3. Then filter from the insoluble residue before going on with the determination.

Machine for shaking the flasks. A mechanical device may be used for shaking the flasks during precipitation, which is very convenient, especially when a great many determinations have to be made. It consists of a box, the inside of which is about three-fourths of an inch higher and one-half of an inch wider than the stoppered flask. It has a door in front, which closes tight; a leather strap, having a loop in the middle just large enough for the neck of the flask to pass through, is placed in the box so that one end is fastened permanently to the box on one side, and the other end passes out on the other side, and is fastened on the outside of the box by a screw-clamp. In putting the flask into the box the neck is passed up through the strap, and the free end of the strap on the outside is pulled down tight, till the flask is pressed firmly on the bottom of the box. The strap is then held securely in place by the compression of the screw-clamp. The box, which may have two or more such compartments in it, is mounted on an upright which slides between guides and is given an up-and-down stroke of about six inches by a simple arrangement of pulleys and a crank. When run at about 100 strokes per minute, it gives a very satisfactory shaking. It takes only a few seconds to fasten a flask into the box, and as many more to take it out. This appliance thus saves considerable time and exertion.

The box prevents any considerable loss of heat during the shaking, so that the liquid is kept, during the precipitation, between the limits of temperature which insure a precipitate of correct composition.

Jones's Reductor.*

To facilitate the reduction of the molybdic acid Mr. Jones makes use of the arrangement he calls a "reductor," which is practically a piece of apparatus designed for filtering the solution of metal through a column of powdered zinc under reduced pressure. The apparatus shown in Fig. 51 is the reductor, and is described by Mr. Jones as follows:

---

* Prepared by Mr. Clemens Jones for this volume.

The reductor apparatus consists of two cups or bulbs, A and B, of about 300 c.c. capacity, the outlets of which connect alternately by means of a two-way stop-cock, C, into the joint-tube D.

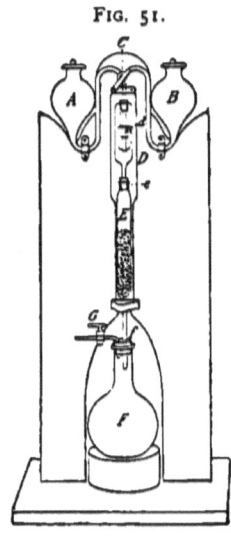

FIG. 51.

This tube D is provided with a pack-ing-space, d, which is filled with an as-bestos roll kept in place by a rim of cork. The tube moves up and down freely. At its lower end, e, it is ground to fit the detachable tube E. The tube E is for the pulverized zinc; its lower end is drawn out to a smaller tube, f, penetrating a rubber cork in which are two holes. The stopcock G connects with the vacuum-pump. The tube E is disconnected by pushing it up, grasping the neck of the flask F with one hand, removing with the other the wooden block which supports the flask, and then detaching the flask.

The tube E now rests on the little shelf shown in the cut. This is drawn out, and frees the tube at its ground-joint, e.

A wad of fine glass wool, sufficiently thick to make a good filter, is inserted into the detached tube E, which is then filled for four-fifths of its length with pulverized zinc. The tube holds about 300 grammes, which is enough for over sixty filtrations. The tube is then replaced by reversing the manner of removal. Connection is then made with the filter-pump, and the apparatus is ready for use.

Pulverized zinc which passes through a twenty-mesh sieve but fails to pass through a thirty-mesh sieve is of about the proper size.

Washing the Zinc.—It is first necessary to wash the column of zinc with dilute sulphuric acid. This acid is made of 1 part of acid of 1.84 sp. gr. and 2 parts of distilled water, and is used throughout in all work upon the determination of both

iron and phophorus. Of this about 30 c.c. is taken, diluted to
300 c.c., and transferred to the cup A. The stopcock G is opened
for suction, and then the two-way cock C is turned to empty
the cup A. A vacuum of from five to ten inches or more must
be used, since the large volume of disengaged hydrogen retards
the filtration.

The cup and the column of zinc are then washed free from
acid by five rinsings with water. To do this direct a stream of
water so that it encircles the cup from top to bottom two or
three times, during which time it is being rapidly sucked away
by the vacuum. This operation must be repeated four times,
and is then finished for this tube-full of zinc.

The correction for iron contained in the zinc may be taken
by filtering the fifth washing into a fresh flask. The flask is
then detached, and permanganate solution introduced, drop by
drop, until the reaction is obtained. The reading of the burette
is the deduction for the subsequent filtration. With the proper
conditions this reading will rarely amount to 0.1 c.c., and frequently will be as low as 0.03 c.c.

In determining phosphorus by reducing the molybdic acid,
proceed as follows:

Filter off and wash the yellow salt by means of the Bunsen
filtering-flask, and transfer the funnel and stopper to a fresh
clean flask. The stem of the funnel should be washed with
water. Dissolve the phospho-molybdate precipitate in ammonia,
0.96 sp. gr., without puncturing the filter-paper. Filter off the
solution, using the filter-pump. Wash with ammonia and once
or twice with water, using small quantities. Suck dry, and
remove the Bunsen filtering-flask and stopper to a suitable bell-
jar. Pour the ammonia solution into a small beaker, washing
out the flask with water. Place the flask under the bell-jar,
and again filter the ammonia solution through the original
filter-paper, the stopper with the funnel being placed in the top
tubulure, this time washing the paper thoroughly.

Washing the zinc.

Dissolving the phospho-molyb-date.

Wash the zinc in the reductor as described above. Then add 30 to 50 c.c. of sulphuric acid, 1.32 sp. gr. (1 part sulphuric acid, 1.84 sp. gr., to 2 parts distilled water), to the ammoniacal solution. Dilute the solution with water to about 300 c.c., transfer to the reductor, washing out the flask, and filter through the reductor, washing the zinc in the reductor as before. Titrate in the flask direct. The correction for zinc is as described above.

Reducing the molybdic acid.

It is of course possible to obtain a correction for zinc for each determination by filtering through the reductor an equal volume of dilute sulphuric acid, titrating, and deriving the correction in the usual way. It is desirable to use a separate reductor, especially for phosphorus determinations. This method of reduction effects a saving in time of from fifteen to twenty minutes.

Direct Weighing of the Phospho-Molybdate.

Instead of using the volumetric method, some chemists prefer to weigh the yellow precipitate. Mr. Wood's method * is as follows :

Wood's method.

Dissolve 1.63 grammes steel in a six-ounce Erlenmeyer flask in 30 c.c. warm nitric acid, 1.2 sp. gr., place the flask over a Bunsen flame and evaporate down to 10 or 15 c.c., hastening the evaporation by blowing a gentle current of air into the flask.

Heat 50 c.c. of molybdate solution to 50°–55° C., add it to the solution in the flask, and shake well. Complete precipitation should take place in from three to five minutes. Filter on the pump in a 7 c.m. Munktell's No. 1 filter which has been previously washed, dried at 100° C., and weighed. Wash with dilute nitric acid, suck dry, wash once with alcohol and thoroughly with ether, and place the filter containing the precipitate in a funnel in an air-bath heated to 110° C. The funnel in the bath

---

* Communicated to the author. Mr. Wood states that the details adapting this to a "rapid method" were worked out by Mr. J. A. Nichols, of the Homestead Works.

is connected with the exhaust so that the precipitate and filter are thoroughly dried in from one to three minutes, according to the size of the precipitate. Weigh, and 1 milligramme of precipitate will be equal to .001 per cent. of phosphorus in the steel.

In the case of pig-iron and spiegel, the metal after solution Pig-iron and spiegel. in nitric acid, 1.2 sp. gr., is diluted with 20 c.c. water, 5 drops of hydrofluoric acid are then added, the solution is boiled for two or three minutes, filtered through asbestos on the pump, and concentrated to 15 c.c.

15 c.c. of chromic acid is added, the solution is boiled down again and precipitated as above. The hydrofluoric acid prevents the separation of gelatinous silica, but does not interfere with the precipitation of the phosphorus.

This method will not work with ferro-manganese, as the combined carbon is not completely oxidized to prevent the precipitation of all the phosphorus.

The solutions referred to above are prepared as follows:

Molybdic acid solution: To 1200 c.c. water add 700 c.c. Reagents used. ammonia, sp. gr. 0.88, and 1 pound molybdic acid; when the molybdic acid is dissolved add 300 c.c. nitric acid, sp. gr. 1.42, and cool. Pour this solution into a mixture of 4800 c.c. water and 2000 c.c. concentrated nitric acid. Filter for use after standing twenty-four hours.

Chromic acid solution: 1.42 sp. gr. nitric acid saturated with chromic acid.

DETERMINATION OF MANGANESE.

The Acetate Method.

Dissolve 1 gramme of drillings in 15 c.c. HNO_3, 1.2 sp. gr., in a No. 2 Griffin's beaker. Evaporate to dryness in the airbath, and heat to decompose carbonaceous matter. Allow the beaker to cool, add 10 c.c. HCl, heat carefully until all the

Fe$_2$O$_3$ is dissolved, evaporate to dryness to get rid of all the
HNO$_3$, redissolve in 10 c.c. HCl, and evaporate carefully until
the solution is almost syrupy.   Dilute with cold water to about
100 c.c., and filter off the insoluble matter, allowing the filtrate

For steel and
puddled
iron filtra-
tion un-
necessary.

and washings to run into a No. 6 Griffin's beaker.   In the case
of steel or puddled iron the filtration may be omitted, the solution being poured into the large beaker, and the rinsings of
the small beaker added.   To the solution in the large beaker,
which should amount to about 200 c.c., add a solution of car-

Neutraliza-
tion with
Na$_2$CO$_3$.

bonate of sodium very slowly, stirring vigorously.   The solution
will finally become very dark red in color, and the precipitate
formed will redissolve very slowly.   Add the solution of carbonate of sodium 2 or 3 drops at a time, stir well, and allow the
solution to stand several minutes, to see whether the precipitate
will redissolve or not.   When, under these circumstances, a
decided precipitate remains, add 2 drops of HCl, stir well, and
allow the solution to stand for some minutes; if the solution
does not clear, add 2 drops more, and stir again.   If the first
part of the operation has been carefully conducted, this amount
of HCl will usually be sufficient, but if, for any reason, too
large a precipitate has been formed, it may require a few drops

Importance
of avoid-
ing excess
of HCl

more.   It is important, however, that no more HCl be added
than just enough to redissolve the precipitate formed by the
carbonate of sodium, and, to insure this, the solution should
be well stirred and allowed to stand a sufficient length of time
after each addition of HCl.   The solution may be so dark in
color that it is difficult to see when the precipitate does finally
disappear, but by standing the beaker on a piece of white
paper the light reflected through the bottom of the beaker will
greatly diminish the difficulty.   When, under this method of
procedure, the solution clears, add 2 grammes of acetate of
sodium dissolved in a few c.c. of water, stir well, and dilute
the solution to about 700 c.c. with boiling water.   Heat it to
boiling, and allow it to boil for about ten minutes, then remove

it from the tripod, and allow the precipitated hydrate and basic acetate of iron to settle. Decant the clear, supernatant fluid on a large washed German filter, throw the precipitate on, and wash it two or three times with boiling water, allowing the filtrate to run into a large beaker or flask, from which it can be transferred to a platinum or porcelain dish and evaporated rapidly. When the precipitate has drained quite dry, by means of a platinum spatula transfer it to the beaker in which the precipitation was first made; dissolve the precipitate which remains adhering to the filter, and that which remains on the blade of the spatula, by pouring around the edge of the filter and on the spatula held over it 10 c.c. HCl diluted with twice its volume of hot water, allowing it to run into the beaker containing the precipitate. Wash the filter free from chloride of iron with cold water, and heat the beaker containing the precipitate until the latter is dissolved. Cool the solution, and repeat the precipitation, filtration, and resolution of the precipitate precisely as in the first case, adding this filtrate to the first one. Precipitate, filter, and wash a third time in the same manner, evaporate all the filtrates down together until they are reduced to about 300 c.c. in volume, and transfer this solution to a No. 3 beaker.

Filtering off and redissolving the iron precipitate.

Evaporation of the filtrates.

If during the evaporation any manganese has become oxidized by exposure to the air, it forms a hard ring on the side of the capsule, and may be dissolved, after the solution is poured into the beaker, by two or three drops of HCl, and washed into the beaker. Should any oxide of iron separate out, pour the solution in the capsule through a small filter, allowing it to run into the beaker, wash the precipitate with hot water, dissolve it in a very few drops of dilute HCl, and let it run into a No. 1 beaker. Add just enough solution of carbonate of sodium to precipitate it, make it faintly acid with acetic acid, boil it, and filter into the main solution.

This solution now contains all the manganese, nickel, and

cobalt and the greater part of the copper which may have been
in the metal. Add to it 10 grammes of acetate of sodium and
a few drops of acetic acid, heat it to boiling, and pass a current
of H_2S through the boiling solution for fifteen minutes. This
will precipitate the copper, cobalt, and nickel. Filter off the
black sulphides, boil the filtrate to expel the excess of H_2S, let
the solution cool somewhat, and add bromine-water in excess.
If no precipitate forms at first, stand the solution, which should
be colored by the bromine-water, in a warm place for an hour
or two, to allow the precipitate of MnO_2 to separate out. If a
precipitate forms immediately, add bromine-water until, when
the precipitate settles, the solution is strongly colored by it, and
stand it aside for an hour or two. At the end of this time, the
precipitate having settled and the supernatant fluid being still
colored by the bromine, heat it carefully, finally to boiling, and
expel the excess of bromine; allow the precipitate to settle,
filter, wash very carefully, and avoid stirring up the precipitate
when it is on the filter, as it has a tendency to go through.
Dissolve the precipitate on the filter in sulphurous acid water
containing a little HCl; allow the solution to run into a platinum
dish, and wash the filter well. A little of the SO_2 water will
quickly dissolve any MnO_2 which may adhere to the beaker in
which it was precipitated, and this may be poured on the filter.
Boil the solution in the dish to expel the excess of SO_2, add
5 to 20 c.c. of a clear filtered solution of microcosmic salt, heat
to boiling, and add, with constant stirring, NH_4HO drop by
drop. When the precipitate of phosphate of ammonium and
manganese begins to form, stop adding NH_4HO, and stir until
the precipitate becomes crystalline. When this change occurs,
add one more drop of NH_4HO; the additional precipitate formed
will be curdy, but a few seconds' continued stirring at the boiling
temperature will change it to the silky crystalline condition.
Continue the addition of NH_4HO in exactly this manner until
the precipitate is all down and further additions of NH_4HO fail

Separation
of Cu, Ni,
and Co
from the
Mn.

Precipita-
tion of
MnO_2 by
Br.

Precipita-
tion of Mn_2
$(NH_4)_2$
P_2O_8—Aq.

to change the silky appearance. Add a dozen drops of NH_4HO in excess, remove the dish from the light, and stand it in ice-water until perfectly cold. Filter on an ashless filter, wash with cold water containing 10 grammes of nitrate of ammonium (dissolved in water made faintly alkaline with NH_4HO and filtered) in 100 c.c. until the filtrate gives no reaction for HCl, dry, ignite, and weigh as $Mn_2P_2O_7$, which contains 38.74 per cent. Mn. During the precipitation of the phosphate of ammonium and manganese the stirring must not be discontinued for an instant, as the solution has a great tendency to bump when the precipitate is allowed to settle. The crystalline condition of the precipitate, which is absolutely necessary for the success of the determination, can be most readily brought about by the means described above. It can, of course, be accomplished by adding an excess of NH_4HO at once, but it will require much more boiling and stirring than the method above described. The final precipitation as phosphate of ammonium and manganese, due to Dr. Gibbs, is much the most accurate method known. A common practice, however, is to wash the bromine precipitate of hydrated binoxide of manganese, dry, ignite, and weigh as Mn_3O_4, which contains 72.05 per cent. Mn. There are two objections to this method of procedure: first, the difficulty of washing the MnO_2 free from sodium salts; secondly, the uncertainty as to the exact state of oxidation of the ignited oxide of manganese. The first of these objections Eggertz claims to overcome by washing the precipitated MnO_2 with water containing 1 per cent. of HCl. It may also be overcome, or rather the danger may be avoided, by using no fixed alkalies. By this method, nearly neutralize the HCl solution of the iron or steel by NH_4HO, then add a solution of carbonate of ammonium exactly as directed above for carbonate of sodium, and finally, instead of acetate of sodium, add acetate of ammonium (5 c.c. of NH_4HO slightly acidulated by acetic acid). Evaporate the filtrates obtained in this way to about 500 c.c., transfer to a flask of about 1 litre capacity, and

Solution of NH_4NO_3 for washing the precipitate.

Weighing as Mn_3O_4.

Objections to this.

Avoiding use of fixed alkalies.

cool. When perfectly *cold*, add 3 or 4 c.c. bromine, shake well, and when the solution is strongly colored all through by bromine, add an excess of NH_4HO, and heat to boiling. Filter, wash with hot water, dry, ignite, and weigh as Mn_3O_4.

Variable composition of ignited oxide of manganese.

The second objection seems, according to Pickering,[*] to be well founded, the amount of manganese in the ignited oxides varying from 69.688 per cent. to 74.997 per cent., according to the temperature to which they were heated and other undetermined conditions. This cause of error may be avoided by weighing the precipitate as MnS, containing 63.18 per cent. Mn.

Weighing as MnS.

This method, due to H. Rose,[†] is carried out as follows : Ignite the oxide in a porcelain crucible, allow it to cool, mix it with 5 or 6 times its volume of flowers of sulphur, place the crucible on a triangle, and insert the bowl of a clay tobacco-pipe, which should be large enough to quite fill the top of the crucible and too large to reach to the precipitate. Pass through the stem a current of dry hydrogen until all air is expelled, heat the crucible gradually to as high a heat as a good Bunsen burner will produce, cool in the current of hydrogen, and weigh as MnS.

General Remarks on the Acetate Method.

Source of error in acetate method.

The chief source of error in the acetate method, as it is usually practised, is in the addition of too much acetate of sodium, whereby the manganous chloride is changed to manganous acetate, which, according to Kessler,[‡] is readily decomposed to manganous oxide and acetic acid. Under these circumstances, a larger amount of manganese is precipitated with the iron than would be the case if a less amount of acetate of sodium were added. When acetate of sodium is added to ferric chloride, the

Amount of $NaC_2H_3O_2$ necessary.

reaction may be written, $6NaC_2H_3O_2,3H_2O + Fe_2Cl_6 = 6NaCl + Fe_2(C_2H_3O_2)_6 + 3H_2O$; and to precipitate the iron as ferric acetate

---

[*] Chem. News, xliii. 226.　　　　[†] Rose, Quant. Anal. (French ed.), p. 104.

[‡] Chem. News, xxvii. 14.

in 1 gramme of metal would necessitate the use of 8 grammes of acetate of sodium. But, as Kessler in the same article remarks, when a solution of ferric chloride is treated with carbonate of sodium and HCl exactly as described above, a liquid is formed which contains 14 times its equivalent of *ferric hydrate* in solution. Consequently ½ gramme of acetate of sodium would be sufficient to precipitate 1 gramme of iron as ferric hydrate and basic acetate. In order, however, to precipitate the manganese as MnO_2 by bromine, it is necessary to convert all the manganous chloride into manganous acetate : consequently an excess of acetate of sodium is added before adding bromine. If, when making the acetate precipitation, the solution contains any ferrous chloride, a "brick-dust" precipitate is usually formed, which generally passes through the filter, and is very difficult to dissolve or manage in any way. It is usually the shortest and best plan, in this event, to start a fresh portion and throw away the other.

Brick-dust precipitate.

The Nitric Acid and Chlorate of Potassium Method.

(*Ford's Method.*)

The acetate method is at best very tedious, and when the amount of manganese is very small it is of course desirable to work on larger amounts than 1 gramme of the sample, but the iron precipitate in this event is so large that it becomes very difficult to manage it properly. With Ford's method, however, there is almost no limit to the amount which can be operated upon, and many experiments have shown that with proper precautions it is an extremely accurate process. The reaction on which the process is based was first noticed by Hannay[*] in 1878; but Ford[†] first worked out the method in its present practical form. Dissolve 5 grammes of borings in a No. 3 beaker in 60 c.c. HNO_3, 1.2 sp. gr., evaporate down until the solution is

Method for steel and puddled iron.

---

[*] Jour. Chem. Soc., xxxiii. 269.   [†] Trans. Inst. Min. Engineers, ix. 397.

almost syrupy, then add 100 c.c. strong HNO_3, 1.4 sp. gr., and 5 grammes $KClO_3$. Stand the beaker on a tripod with a thin piece of sheet asbestos, about 1 inch (25 mm.) in diameter, in the centre of the wire gauge or on the air-bath, and heat the solution to boiling. Boil the solution fifteen minutes, remove the light, add 50 c.c. strong HNO_3 and 5 grammes $KClO_3$, replace the light, and boil fifteen minutes longer, or until the yellowish fumes from the decomposition of the $KClO_3$ are no longer given off. Cool the solution as rapidly as possible by standing the beaker in cold water, filter on the pump, using the cone* or glass filtering-tube with asbestos filter,† and wash two or three times with strong HNO_3, which must be free from nitrous fumes.‡ Nitrous acid reduces MnO_2 to MnO, which then dissolves in HNO_3. Its presence may be recognized by the yellow color it imparts to HNO_3, and it may be removed by blowing air through the acid. It is always formed in HNO_3 which has been exposed to sunlight, and for that reason this acid should be kept in a dark place. Suck the precipitate dry, and transfer it, with the asbestos filter, to the beaker in which the precipitation was made. Pour into the beaker 10 to 40 c.c. strong sulphurous acid water, which will dissolve the precipitate almost instantly. By pouring it through the cone or filtering-tube, any adhering precipitate will be dissolved and carried into the beaker. As soon as the precipitate is dissolved, add 2 to 5 c.c. HCl, and filter from the asbestos into a No. 1 beaker, washing with hot water. Heat the filtrate until the excess of SO_2 is driven off, add bromine-water until the solution is strongly colored with it, and boil off the excess of bromine. Add NH_4HO until the solution smells quite strongly of it, boil for a few minutes, and filter into a No. 3 beaker. Wash several times with

Marginal notes:
Filtering the cold solution.

Effect of N_2O_3 in HNO_3.

Separation from small amounts of Fe_2O_3 by NH_4HO.

---

* See page 26.   † As described under Methods for Determination of Carbon.

‡ It is always well to transfer the filtrate and washings to a No. 4 beaker, add 2 grammes $KClO_3$, and boil again, to see whether any further precipitate of MnO_2 is formed.

hot water, remove the beaker, dissolve the ferric hydrate on the filter in dilute hot HCl (1 part of acid to 3 of water), allowing the solution to run back into the beaker in which the precipitation was made, and wash the filter with hot water. Boil this filtrate for a few minutes to drive off the chlorine which may be present from the solution of any little MnO_2 precipitated with the ferric hydrate, reprecipitate by NH_4HO as before, filter, and repeat the solution, precipitation, and filtration, allowing all the filtrates from the ferric hydrate to run into the No. 3 beaker. Acidulate this solution, which will be about 300 or 400 c.c. in volume, with acetic acid, heat to boiling, and pass H_2S through the boiling solution for ten or fifteen minutes. Filter into a platinum dish from any sulphide of cobalt, which is the only metal likely to be present with the manganese; boil off the H_2S after adding a little HCl, add microcosmic salt, and precipitate, filter, ignite, and weigh, as directed on pages 106 and 107, as $Mn_2P_2O_7$.

Separation from cobalt.

Steels containing much Silicon.

In steel high in silicon, 0.2 per cent. and over, the gelatinous silica formed is very apt to clog the filter when operating as described above, and it is better to dissolve the sample in HCl, evaporate to dryness, being careful not to heat it too hot, redissolve carefully in 50 c.c. strong HNO_3, boil down until nearly syrupy to destroy all the HCl, redissolve in 100 c.c. strong HNO_3, and precipitate as directed above.

Instead of dissolving in HCl, Mr. Wood suggests adding a few drops of hydrofluoric acid to the nitric acid solution before evaporating. This seems to work extremely well, and saves much time in the case of high silicon steels. It may also be used to advantage in the case of pig-iron instead of the method given below.

HFl to prevent precipitation of gelatinous SiO_2.

Pig-Iron.

Dissolve 5 grammes in 50 c.c. dilute HCl (1 part HCl to 1 part water), filter on a washed German filter into a No. 3 beaker, evaporate to dryness, redissolve in 50 c.c. strong HNO_3, and proceed as in the case of "steel high in silicon."

Spiegel and Ferro-manganese.

It is best to use only 1 gramme of spiegel or ferro-manganese of 20 to 40 per cent. manganese and .5 gramme of very high, 60 to 80 per cent., ferro-manganese. In the latter, indeed, it is better to use the acetate method with NH_4HO and $NH_4C_2H_3O_2$, and, omitting the precipitation by bromine, boil off the H_2S from the filtrate from the insoluble sulphides, after adding HCl, and then precipitate by microcosmic salt as directed above.

Variation in acetate method for ferro-manganese.

RAPID METHODS.

Volumetric Methods.

Volhard's Method.*

This method is based on the principle announced by Morawski and Stingl,† that when permanganate of potassium is added to a neutral manganous salt all the manganese is precipitated, in accordance with the reaction $4KMnO_4 + 6MnSO_4 + 4H_2O = 10MnO_2 + 4KHSO_4 + 2H_2SO_4$. When all the manganous salt is oxidized, the solution is colored by the permanganate, which thus indicates the end reaction. The permanganate used for titrating iron ores may be used for this determination, and, its value being determined, as directed, in terms of Fe, the calculation for Mn is as follows: The reaction, when permanganate is added to a solution of ferrous sulphate, is $10FeSO_4 + 2KMnO_4 + 8H_2SO_4 = 5Fe_2(SO_4)_3 + 2MnSO_4 + K_2SO_4 + 8H_2O$, or 2 molecules of permanganate oxidize 10 molecules of $FeSO_4$. Now, as 2 molecules of permanganate oxidize 3 molecules of manganous sulphate, while 2 molecules of permanganate oxidize 10 molecules of ferrous sulphate, the oxidizing power of the per-

Calculation of strength of permanganate.

---

* Liebig's Annalen, Band cxcviii. p. 318; Chem. News, xl. 207.

† Chem. News, xxxviii. 297.

manganate is only three-tenths as great in the former case as it is in the latter, and its value in Mn is to its value in Fe as 3 is to 10, or $\frac{55}{56} \times \frac{3}{10} = \frac{165}{560}$. Therefore the value of the permanganate in Fe multiplied by $\frac{165}{560}$ or 0.2946 $=$ its value in Mn. Dissolve 1.5 grammes of borings in a platinum or porcelain dish in 25 c.c. HNO_3, 1.2 sp. gr. When solution is complete, add 12 c.c. dilute H_2SO_4 (1 part concentrated H_2SO_4 and 1 part water), and evaporate to dryness, as directed on page 20, heating until fumes of H_2SO_4 are given off in order to destroy all the carbonaceous matter. Or dissolve in HNO_3 as above, evaporate to dryness, and heat on the tripod until the carbonaceous matter is destroyed; dissolve in 15 c.c. HCl, add 12 c.c. dilute H_2SO_4 as above, and evaporate until fumes of H_2SO_4 are given off. Allow the dish to cool, add 100 c.c. water, and heat until all the ferric sulphate is dissolved. Wash into a carefully graduated 300 c.c. flask, so that with the washings the solution may not exceed 200 c.c. in volume, and add solution of carbonate of sodium until the precipitate which is first formed dissolves only with difficulty. Then add slowly zinc oxide* suspended in water, shaking well after each addition until the iron is precipitated, which will be shown by the sudden coagulation of the solution. The precipitate will then settle, leaving a slightly milky supernatant liquid. Fill the flask exactly to the mark on the neck (300 c.c.), and mix thoroughly by pouring the entire contents of the flask into a large, clean, dry beaker, and back again into the flask, repeating this several times. Allow the precipitate to settle for a few minutes, and pour the solution through a large, *dry* filter. Fill a 200 c.c. pipette with this filtrate, which will, of course, represent exactly 1 gramme of the sample, run it into a flask of about 500 c.c. capacity, heat to boiling, and add 2 drops of HNO_3, sp. gr. 1.2. Now add permanganate solution slowly from a burette, shaking

Details of the method.

---

* See page 58.

after each addition to mix the solution and facilitate the collection of the precipitated hydrated peroxide of manganese. When the reaction is nearly finished, the solution will be slightly colored by the permanganate, but the color disappears after shaking the flask and allowing it to stand for a moment. Finally, however, a drop or two will give the solution a permanent pink color, which will not disappear for several minutes. The number of c.c. of the permanganate solution used multiplied by the factor found (the Fe factor of the permanganate multiplied by .2946) is the amount of manganese in the sample. If, during the addition of the permanganate, the solution should become cool and the precipitate fail to collect and settle quickly, heat the solution, but not quite to the boiling-point. This method is applicable for all samples except those containing very minute amounts of manganese. In working on spiegel, take .75 gramme, then, using two-thirds of the filtrate, the amount will be calculated on .5 gramme.

Applicable except for very minute amounts of Mn.

Williams's Method.

This method, which consists in precipitating the MnO_2 by Ford's method, filtering, washing, dissolving in H_2SO_4 with a measured volume of some reducing agent, such as oxalic acid or ferrous sulphate, and titrating the excess by permanganate, was first used by Williams.* Regarding the precipitate by $KClO_3$ in a nitric acid solution as MnO_2, the reaction in dissolving it might be expressed thus: $MnO_2 + 2FeSO_4 + 2H_2SO_4 = MnSO_4 + Fe_2(SO_4)_3 + 2H_2O.$ or $MnO_2 + H_2C_2O_4 + H_2SO_4 = MnSO_4 + 2CO_2 + 2H_2O.$ Therefore 1 molecule of MnO_2 oxidizes 2 molecules of ferrous sulphate or 1 molecule of oxalic acid, and, the excess of oxalic acid or ferrous sulphate unoxidized having been determined by a solution of permanganate, the difference between this excess and the amount originally added is the amount oxidized by the MnO_2.

Oxidizing power of MnO_2.

---

* Trans. Inst. Min. Engineers, x. 100.

We therefore require two standard solutions, one of perman- ganate and one of ferrous sulphate, ammonium ferrous sulphate, or oxalic acid. The permanganate solution used for iron deter- minations answers perfectly. A solution of ferrous sulphate is perhaps the most satisfactory, and is prepared by dissolving 10 grammes of the crystallized salt, $FeSO_4,7H_2O$,* in 900 c.c. water and 100 c.c. strong H_2SO_4. It will keep perfectly in a glass- stoppered bottle in the dark for a long time. One c.c. of this solution will be equal to about .002 gramme Fe, or nearly .001 gramme Mn, and if the permanganate is of the usual strength, say 1 c.c. $=$ .007 gramme Fe, 1 c.c. of the permanganate will equal about 3.5 c.c. of the ferrous sulphate. The permanganate solution having been carefully standardized, measure 50 c.c. of the ferrous sulphate solution by means of a pipette into the dish,† dilute to about 1 litre, and run in permanganate solution from a burette, stirring constantly until the first permanent pink tint appears. The reading of the burette will give the value of 50 c.c. ferrous sulphate in permanganate, and consequently by a simple calculation its value in Fe and Mn. Suppose, for instance, 1 c.c. permanganate solution $=$ .0068 gramme Fe, or (according to the proportion given above, $112:55::Fe:Mn$) $=$ .00334 gramme Mn. Then if 14.1 c.c. permanganate $=$ 50 c.c. ferrous sulphate, 100 c.c. ferrous sulphate will be equivalent to 28.2 c.c. permanganate. In using oxalic acid, dissolve 2.25 grammes of the crystallized acid, $H_2C_2O_4,2H_2O$, in 1 litre of water, and determine its strength by measuring 50 c.c. into the dish, diluting with *hot* water, adding 5 c.c. H_2SO_4, and titrating with permanganate.

The details of the method are as follows: Weigh out 5 grammes of the sample of puddled iron, pig-iron, or steel, and proceed as directed on p. 110 *et seq.;* but after filtering and washing the precipitated MnO_2 with strong HNO_3, suck the pre- cipitate as dry as possible, and then wash out the beaker in

---

* See page 55.   † See Determination of Iron in Iron Ores.

which the precipitation was made with cold water. Pour this water on the precipitate, and repeat the operation two or three times to get rid of all the HNO_3. Suck the precipitate as dry as possible, transfer it with the asbestos to the beaker in which the precipitation was made, measure into the beaker 100 c.c. of the standard ferrous sulphate solution (or 100 c.c. oxalic acid solution and 10 c.c. H_2SO_4), and stir until the MnO_2 is all dissolved. When using oxalic acid it is necessary to heat gently to about 60° C. Wash the solution and asbestos into the dish, dilute to about 1 litre (with oxalic acid use hot water), and titrate with permanganate. We will suppose, for example, that it requires 10.2 c.c. permanganate to give the permanent rose tint; then, as 100 c.c. ferrous sulphate = 28.2 c.c. permanganate, there would be the equivalent of 28.2 — 10.2 = 18 c.c. of permanganate in ferrous sulphate oxidized by the MnO_2 precipitate. One c.c. of permanganate being equivalent to .00334 gramme Mn, 18 c.c. = .06012 gramme Mn, and, 5 grammes of the sample having been taken, .06012 ÷ 5 = .01202 × 100 = 1.202 per cent. Mn.

Example.

FIG. 52.

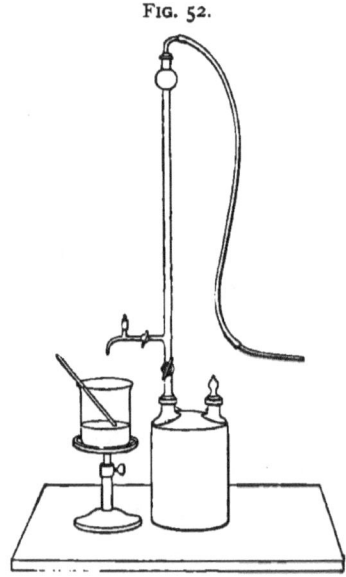

Fig. 52 shows a very convenient piece of apparatus designed by Mr. E. A. Uehling in 1884.*

Apparatus for ferrous sulphate solution.

It is especially useful when it is necessary to rapidly add a constant volume of a standard reagent, for instance, a measured

---

* Communicated to the author by Mr. A. L. Colby, of the Bethlehem Iron Company.

excess of ferrous sulphate in volumetric determination of manganese after precipitation with potassium chlorate.

The burette-tube extends to the bottom of the Wolff bottle, which holds 2 litres. Enough air is supplied, without danger of dust or evaporation of solution, by means of a pin-hole drilled in the neck of the bottle and through the hollow glass-stopper. The bottle may be blackened to preserve the solution from the action of light.

Spiegel and Ferro-manganese.

When working on spiegel or ferro-manganese, take .5 gramme of the sample and proceed in the same manner as directed for steel or iron; but it is better to use a standard solution of ferrous sulphate containing 30 grammes of $FeSO_4,7H_2O$ to the litre for very high ferro-manganese.

As there seems to be some uncertainty as to the exact composition of the oxide of manganese,* the permanganate solution may be standardized as follows: Determine the absolute amount of manganese in a finely-ground and well-mixed sample of spiegel or ferro-manganese by a gravimetric method, then treat .5 gramme of the same sample exactly as described above, and, having found the number of c.c. of permanganate that are equivalent to 100 c.c. of the ferrous sulphate solution, the amount of manganese in the sample divided by the number of c.c. of permanganate equivalent to the ferrous sulphate oxidized by the oxide of manganese in the sample, gives the value of the permanganate solution. Thus, if 100 c.c. ferrous sulphate solution require 28.2 c.c. permanganate to give the rose tint upon titration, the sample of spiegel contains 14.50 per cent. Mn, and the ferrous sulphate remaining after the solution of the oxide of manganese in 100 c.c. requires 6.5 c.c. permanganate to give the rose tint upon titration (using

Composition of the oxide of manganese.

Standardizing by spiegel of known value.

---

* Stone, Trans. Inst. Min. Engineers, xi. 323, xii. 295, 514; Mackintosh, Trans. Inst. Min. Engineers, xii. 79, xiii. 39.

Example. .5 gramme of the sample, of which 1 gramme contains .1450 gramme Mn), the calculation would be as follows: 28.2 c.c. — 6.5 c.c. = 21.7 c.c. = .0725 gramme Mn, or 1 c.c. permanganate is equivalent to $\frac{.0725}{21.7}$ = .00334 gramme Mn.

*Deshays's Method.**

This method is based on the fact that nitrate of manganese, when boiled with excess of nitric acid and peroxide of lead, is oxidized to permanganic acid, which is reduced again by a standard solution of arsenite of sodium.

Dissolve .5 gramme of steel or pig-iron in a No. 0 Griffin's beaker, or in a test-tube, in 30 c.c. nitric acid, 1.2 sp. gr., and boil until solution is complete and the evolution of nitrous fumes ceases. Remove from the burner, and add cautiously 1–3 grammes of dioxide of lead, or red lead, free from manganese,

Washing the lead precipitate. and dilute with hot water to about 60 c.c. Heat the solution to boiling, and as soon as it commences to boil stand the beaker or test-tube aside and allow the lead salt to settle. When tolerably clear, decant the solution and boil the residue with 50 c.c. nitric acid and water (1 part acid to 3 parts water). Decant as before, and repeat the operation until the supernatant fluid is colorless. Filter the decantations through asbestos and titrate with a standard solution of arsenite of sodium. The standard solution may be prepared of a convenient strength by dissolving 4.96 grammes of arsenious acid together with 25 grammes of carbonate of sodium in water and diluting to 2–2½ litres.

Standardizing the arsenite of sodium solution. To standardize this solution, treat a steel containing a known amount of manganese, as described above, and calculate the value of each c.c. of the standard solution by dividing the per cent. of manganese in the steel by the number of c.c. required to destroy the color of the permanganic acid. Or take a measured quantity of a standardized solution of permanganate of potas-

---

* Bull. Soc. Chim. de Paris, June 20, 1878.

sium and see how many c.c. of the arsenite of sodium are equal
to 1 c.c. of the permanganate solution. Then the value of the
permanganate solution in iron, multiplied by $11/56$ is equal
to its value in manganese, according to the equation,

$$10FeSO_4 + 2KMnO_4 + 8H_2SO_4 = 5Fe_2(SO_4)_3 + K_2SO_4 + 2MnSO_4$$
$$+ 8H_2O.$$

or 10 atoms of Fe correspond to 2 atoms of Mn, or 560 parts
by weight of Fe = 110 parts by weight of Mn. From this we
get the weight of Mn to which 1 c.c. of the arsenite of sodium
is equivalent, from which the percentage of manganese in the
steel is calculated.

The details of this method have been very carefully worked
out by Mr. H. C. Babbitt, of the Wellman Steel Company, who
has used it for many years. He finds that ordinary red lead is
quite as effective as the more expensive dioxide, and in an interesting series of experiments he shows that results obtained by
filtering off a portion of the first solution obtained by boiling
with red lead and titrating are not accordant, and that the only
method of getting thoroughly reliable results is by washing out
all the permanganic acid and decanting as described above.

Pattinson's Method (for Spiegel and Ferro-manganese).

This method is based on the precipitation of manganese as
MnO_2, from a solution of $MnCl_2$, by hypochlorite of calcium
and carbonate of calcium in the presence of ferric chloride (the
presence of the latter salt or of chloride of zinc being necessary
to prevent the precipitation of any manganese in a lower state
of oxidation than MnO_2).* Dissolve .5 gramme of spiegel or
ferro-manganese in a No. 5 beaker in 15 c.c. HNO_3, 1.2 sp. gr.,
evaporate to dryness, and heat to destroy carbonaceous matter.
Redissolve in HCl, and boil down to remove HNO_3, but not

---

* Jour. Chem. Soc., xxxv. 365.

to dryness, add a few drops of HCl, and dilute with 10 c.c.
water.   Add carbonate of calcium diffused in water, until the
solution becomes reddish by neutralization of the free acid, then
add 5 or 6 drops HCl and 100 c.c. of a solution of bleaching
powder (hypochlorite of calcium), made by treating 15 grammes
of the powder with 1 litre of water and filtering.   Now pour in
about 300 c.c. of boiling water, which will raise the temperature
of the solution to about 70° C., and add carbonate of calcium,
with constant stirring, until all the iron is precipitated.   If the
supernatant fluid has a pink color, due to the formation of a
little permanganate, add a few drops of alcohol, which will reduce
it.   Filter on a large filter, wash untill the filtrate is free from
chlorides, place the filter and its contents in the beaker in which
the precipitation was made, and add 100 c.c. of standard solution
of ferrous sulphate, made as directed on page 115.   When the
precipitate is dissolved, transfer the solution to the dish, dilute
to about 1 litre, titrate the excess of ferrous sulphate as directed
on page 115, and calculate the percentage of Mn as there
directed.

The Color Method (for Steel).

This method was first suggested by Pichard,* and was used
essentially in its present form by Peters.†   It is now in very general use in steel-works, and takes rank with the color carbon
method in its usefulness.   It requires one or more standard
steels in which the manganese has been most carefully determined by a gravimetric method.   When a number of samples
are to be tested at the same time, as is usually the case, a bath
like the one shown in Fig. 77 is necessary, but for the man-

Chloride of
calcium
bath.

ganese color method it should contain a solution of chloride of
calcium, which boils at 115° C.‡   It is, of course, very neces-

---

* Comptes-Rendus Hebd. des Séances de l'Acad. des Sciences, Dec. 30, 1872.

† Chem. News, xxxiii. 35.

‡ This latter modification is due to Mr. S. A. Ford.

sary in a method of this kind that the operations should always be conducted as nearly as possible under the same conditions, and that the standard should always be dissolved at the same time as the samples to be tested. Weigh out .2 gramme of Details of the method. each sample and of the standard, and place them in 8-inch test-tubes properly numbered. Pour into each test-tube 15 c.c. HNO_3, 1.2 sp. gr., cover each with a small glass bulb or very small funnel, and stand the test-tubes in the holes in the top of the bath, as shown in the sketch, Fig. 77. Heat in the bath at 100° C. until solution is complete. Pour the contents of a test-tube into a 100 c.c. tube, wash the test-tube out with cold water, adding it to the solution in the 100 c.c. tube, and finally dilute to the 100 c.c. mark. Mix thoroughly by placing the thumb over the top of the tube and turning it upside down several times. Draw out 10 c.c. of this solution with a pipette graduated to deliver 10 c.c., and let it run into the test-tube in which the solution was made. Treat each sample in this way, including the standard. The tube is merely washed out with water, but the pipette can be best cleaned by drawing it full from the 100 c.c. tube of the fresh sample, throwing the contents away, and filling it a second time to deliver into the test-tube. Stand the test-tubes in the rack again, add to each 3 c.c. HNO_3, 1.2 sp. gr., replace the bulbs or funnels, and stand the rack in the chloride of calcium bath, the solution in which should now be boiling. When the *solutions in the test-tubes* begin to boil, add to each .5 gramme fine peroxide of lead* and boil exactly five minutes. The PbO_2 can readily be measured by a small platinum spoon, made to hold about .5 gramme. It is necessary that the solutions in the test-tubes should boil, Necessity for boiling the solutions in the tubes. and it is easy to assure one's self of this fact by looking down into the test-tubes after the action caused by the addition of the PbO_2 has ceased. Remove the rack from the bath at the

---

* See page 57.

expiration of the five minutes, and stand it with the test-tubes in cold water, to cool the solutions and allow the insoluble lead salt to settle.   The insoluble matter settles to the bottom of the tube in a heavy compact mass, leaving the supernatant fluid perfectly clean.   When this occurs, which is usually within the space of half an hour, the solutions are ready to be decanted into the comparison-tubes.*   In working on a number of steels we will suppose that we use two standards, one containing 1.2 per cent. of manganese, the other .6 per cent.   As we weighed out .2 gramme, diluted the solution to 100 c.c., and took 10 c.c. in which to determine manganese, the amount taken corresponds to 0.02 gramme of the sample; and if we dilute the solutions of the standards after decanting into the comparison-tubes to 24 c.c., one c.c. will correspond to .05 per cent. in the high, and .025 per cent. in the low, standard.   Decant each solution in turn into a comparison-tube, and dilute it until it has the exact tint and depth of color of the standard to which it most nearly approximates when first decanted.   The percentage of manganese is found by multiplying the number of c.c. to which the sample has been diluted by .05 or .025, according to the standard with which it has been compared. If, however, the solution of a sample when first decanted and before dilution should be lighter in color than the lower standard, the latter may, after the other samples have all been finished, be diluted to 30 c.c., when each c.c. will correspond to .02 per cent. manganese, or, if this color is not sufficiently light, to 40 c.c., when each c.c. will correspond to .015 per cent. manganese.   When even this color is not sufficiently light, a lower standard must be used for comparison, or a larger amount of the sample taken for solution.   The comparison of the colors should be made in a camera or box, as shown in Fig. 79.

Comparing the colors.

---

* See Fig. 78.

The direct rays of the sun should not be allowed to shine on the solutions, and a northern light for the comparisons is preferable to any other.

DETERMINATION OF CARBON.

Carbon differs from all other elements in iron and steel in that it is supposed to exist in several conditions, and analytical chemistry supplies the means of distinguishing between at least two of these conditions. Until within a few years it was considered to exist in two forms, as graphite and as combined carbon. To Karsten is due the recognition of the fact that graphite is a form of pure carbon, and not a compound of carbon and hydrogen. It is always present as a mechanical mixture, and is thus distinguished from the other form, which was supposed to be combined chemically with the iron. Of late years the opinion has been growing that "combined carbon" exists in at least two conditions in steel, but as yet chemical methods for separating and distinguishing between these conditions have failed, so far as quantitative work is concerned. The analytical methods here given are:

The Determination of Total Carbon,
The Determination of Graphitic Carbon, and
The Determination of Combined Carbon.

The conditions in which carbon exists in iron and steel.

DETERMINATION OF TOTAL CARBON.

We may divide the methods for the determination of total carbon in iron and steel into the following classes:

A. The direct treatment of the borings or drillings without previous separation of the iron, including:

1. Direct combustion in a current of oxygen (Berzelius).

2. Combustion with chromate of lead and chlorate of potassium (Regnault).

3. Combustion with oxide of copper in a current of oxygen (Kudernatsch).

4. Solution and oxidation of the borings by CrO_3 and H_2SO_4 (Brunner modified by O. Gmelin).

B. Removal of the iron by volatilization, and subsequent combustion of the carbon, including:

1. Volatilization in a current of chlorine (Berzelius, Wöhler).

2. Volatilization in a current of hydrochloric acid gas (Deville).

C. Solution of the iron, and combustion or weighing of the residue, including:

1. Solution in double chloride of copper and ammonium, filtration, and weighing or combustion of the residue (Pearse and McCreath).

2. Solution in double chloride of copper and potassium, filtration, and combustion of the residue in oxygen (Richter).

3. Solution in chloride of copper, and combustion of the residue (Berzelius).

4. Solution in iodine or bromine, and combustion with chromate of lead, or weighing, of the residue (Eggertz).

5. Solution by fused chloride of silver, and combustion of the residue (Berzelius).

6. Solution of the iron in sulphate of copper, filtration, and combustion of the residue in a boat in a current of oxygen (Langley).

7. Solution of the iron in sulphate of copper, and oxidation of the residue by CrO_3 and H_2SO_4 (Ullgren).

8. Solution of the iron in sulphate of copper, filtration, and combustion of the residue, mixed with oxide of copper in vacuo under the Sprengel pump, the volume of CO_2 being measured (Parry).

9. Solution in dilute HCl by the aid of an electric current, and combustion of the residue (Binks, Weyl).

10. Oxidation of the iron by atmospheric air and moisture, solution of the ferric oxide by HCl, filtration, and combustion of the residue (Berthier).

A. 1. Direct Combustion in a Current of Oxygen.

This method requires the sample to be reduced to a very fine state of subdivision, otherwise some of the metal in the centre of the lumps becomes coated with oxide, and the carbon in it escapes combustion. Weigh out into a porcelain or platinum boat, about 3 inches (75 mm.) long,* 1 to 3 grammes of the sample, and spread it as evenly as possible over the bottom of the boat. Place the boat in the porcelain tube B, Fig. 58, by means of the rod C, replace the stopper P, and turn on a current of oxygen from the cylinder O, the stopcock R being open and Q closed. The apparatus will now appear as in the cut. The description of the apparatus is given on page 132 *et seq.*, the only difference being that for this determination the U-tube H and roll of silver in the tube B are omitted. The precautions necessary in weighing the absorption apparatus, consisting of the bulb I and tube J, are also described fully on page 135. When the tube is full of oxygen, the absorption apparatus being weighed and attached, light the burners in the furnace, beginning at the forward end, and, when they are all lighted, maintain the temperature of the tube at a good red heat for forty-five minutes. Should the solution in the bulb I begin to recede, owing to the rapid absorption of oxygen by the metal in the boat, increase the flow of oxygen, and regulate it so that the gas may never

---

* I obtained better results by using a platinum boat about 6 inches (150 mm.) long provided with a cover of platinum-foil, through which a semicircular cut was made about every ½ inch (12 mm.). On raising these pieces to an angle of 45° they formed a series of little wings, which directed the current of gas flowing along the upper part of the tube down into the boat. It is difficult to get a sufficiently high temperature in a porcelain tube, but the results obtained in a platinum tube were very satisfactory. (See Jour. of Anal. and App. Chem., 1891, p. 125.)

pass through the bulb I more rapidly than 3 or 4 bubbles in a second. At the expiration of the forty-five minutes, shut off the current of oxygen at O, close the stopcock R, open Q, and start the current of air by opening T gradually, so that the water may flow into the lower bottle F. Turn down the lights in the furnace slowly, to avoid cracking the tube, finally turn them out, and allow the current of air to run through the apparatus until the oxygen is expelled. This will usually be accomplished by running out half the water in the bottle F. Close the stopcock T, remove the absorption apparatus, and weigh it. The increase of weight will be CO_2, due to the carbon in the sample, and it contains 27.27 per cent. carbon.

2. Combustion with Chromate of Lead and Chlorate of Potassium.

Preparation of the combus-tion-tubes. This method, like the preceding one, requires the sample to be very finely powdered. Take a piece of combustion-tubing about 32 inches (800 mm.) long, ½ inch (12 mm.) internal diameter, and $\frac{1}{16}$ inch (1.5 mm.) thick in the walls; heat it in the middle by means of a blast-lamp until it softens, draw the ends apart slightly, and then, keeping the ends parallel, draw it out, as shown in Fig. 53. Allow it to cool, scratch it in the

FIG. 53.

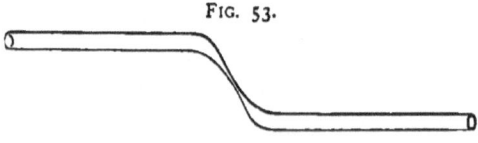

middle with a file, and break it. This gives two tubes each about 16 inches (400 mm.) long. Fuse the large ends slightly so as to round the sharp edges, but avoid contracting the tube. Wash the tubes thoroughly, using a rod with a piece of dark-colored silk or linen on the end; then if any lint remains on the inside of the tube it can be easily seen. Dry the tubes by heating them carefully and drawing air through them, then fuse the small ends and cork the large ends to keep out the dust. Weigh out 1 to 3 grammes (1 gramme of pig-iron, spiegel, or ferro-manganese, 3 grammes of steel) of the sample, and grind it thoroughly in a small mortar with 15 times its weight of fused and powdered chromate of lead and 1½ times its weight of fused and powdered chlorate of potassium or bichromate of potassium. Bichromate of potassium is to be preferred, as a little chlorine is sometimes given off by chlorate of potassium when used in this manner.   Place the combustion-tube in a stand, as shown in Fig. 54, and push down into the end, with a clean glass rod, a little ignited asbestos.   The asbestos should not be tightly packed, as it will prevent the air from passing in freely at the end of the operation. Place a small, dry, perfectly clean funnel in the end of the tube, and pour through it enough of the pure powdered chromate of lead to fill the tube for about one inch of its length. Hold the mortar under the funnel so that anything that falls from it may go into the mortar, and charge the mixture into the tube by means of a small platinum spatula.   Clean out the mortar by grinding in it two or three successive small portions of chromate of lead, charging each into the tube through the funnel.   Remove the funnel, cork the tube, and, holding it in a horizontal position with the tail up, tap it gently to get a clear space for the passage of the gas from one end of the tube to the other. Place the tube in the combustion-furnace, remove the cork, and insert in its place a smooth velvet cork, through the centre of which passes one end of a Marchand U-tube.   The half of this tube nearest the combustion-tube contains anhydrous sulphate of copper,* and the other half granulated dried chloride of

Details of the method.

FIG. 54.

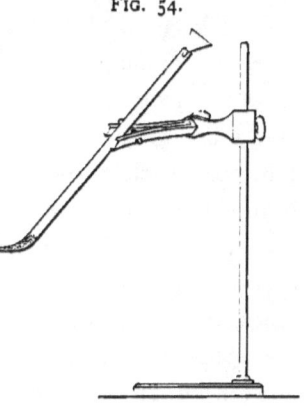

---

* See page 53.

calcium, the two reagents being separated by a small plug of fibrous asbestos loosely packed. Weigh, and attach the absorption apparatus and safety-tube.   Apply suction at the end of the rubber tube on the forward end of the safety-tube, and draw a few bubbles of air through the potash-bulb. Allow the liquid to recede gradually; if it maintains its level in the bulb for a few minutes, the joints of the apparatus may be considered tight, but if it gradually falls, it is proof that there is a Testing the tightness of the connections. leak, and the joints must all be tightened. If, after pushing the cork as far as possible into the end of the combustion-tube and binding all the rubber connections, another trial still shows a leak, a fresh cork must be substituted. When the joints are all tight, light the burner at the forward end of the tube, and each burner successively as the flow of gas slackens, bringing the tube over each burner to a red heat before lighting the next one.   Maintain the whole length of the tube up to the asbestos at a good red heat until the flow of gas entirely ceases. Then pass a piece of rubber tubing attached to a purifying apparatus well over the tail of the tube, which should be cool enough to be handled, break the point of the tail inside the tubing, lower the lights a little, and, by means of the aspirator-

FIG. 55.

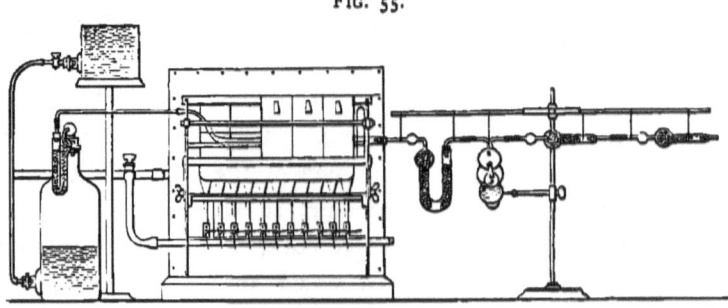

bottles, force about 1 litre of air through the apparatus. It will now appear as in Fig. 55. Turn out the lights, and detach and weigh the absorption apparatus, with the precautions mentioned on page 134. The increase of weight will be the CO_2 due to the carbon in the sample. This contains 27.27 per cent. carbon.

3. Combustion with Oxide of Copper in a Current of Oxygen.

Prepare the combustion-tube as directed in the last method, and pour on the asbestos in the end of the tube enough oxide of copper to fill the tube to the height of about an inch (25 mm.). Mix the weighed sample, 1 to 3 grammes in a fine state of division, with at least 20 times its weight of finely-powdered pure oxide of copper, charge it into the tube as directed on page 127, rinse out the mortar with a little more of the same material, and finally fill the tube to within an inch (25 mm.) of the end with granulated oxide of copper. Make the combustion exactly as directed in the last method, page 128. If the combustion is to be made in a current of oxygen, which is much the best plan, instead of drawing the combustion-tube out to a point and sealing it, it may be drawn out straight, as shown in Fig. 56. In this

Details of the method.

Using a current of oxygen.

FIG. 56.

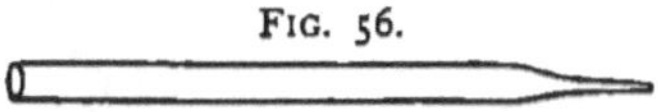

case, attach to the drawn-out end when the tube is in the furnace a purifying apparatus for oxygen and air, as shown in Fig. 58, and conduct the operation as directed on page 125.

4. Solution and Oxidation of the Borings by CrO_3 and H_2SO_4.

Fig. 57 shows the details of the apparatus for carrying out this method. M is the U-tube for purifying the air. It contains fused caustic potassa. A is the flask for oxidizing and dissolving the sample. The piece of glass tubing N bent at a right angle is drawn out slightly at the lower end, over which a piece of soft gum tubing is fitted, forming a stopper, which fits tightly in the top of the bulb-tube when air is forced through the apparatus. B is a bulb-tube for introducing the reagents. The lower

Description of the apparatus.

9

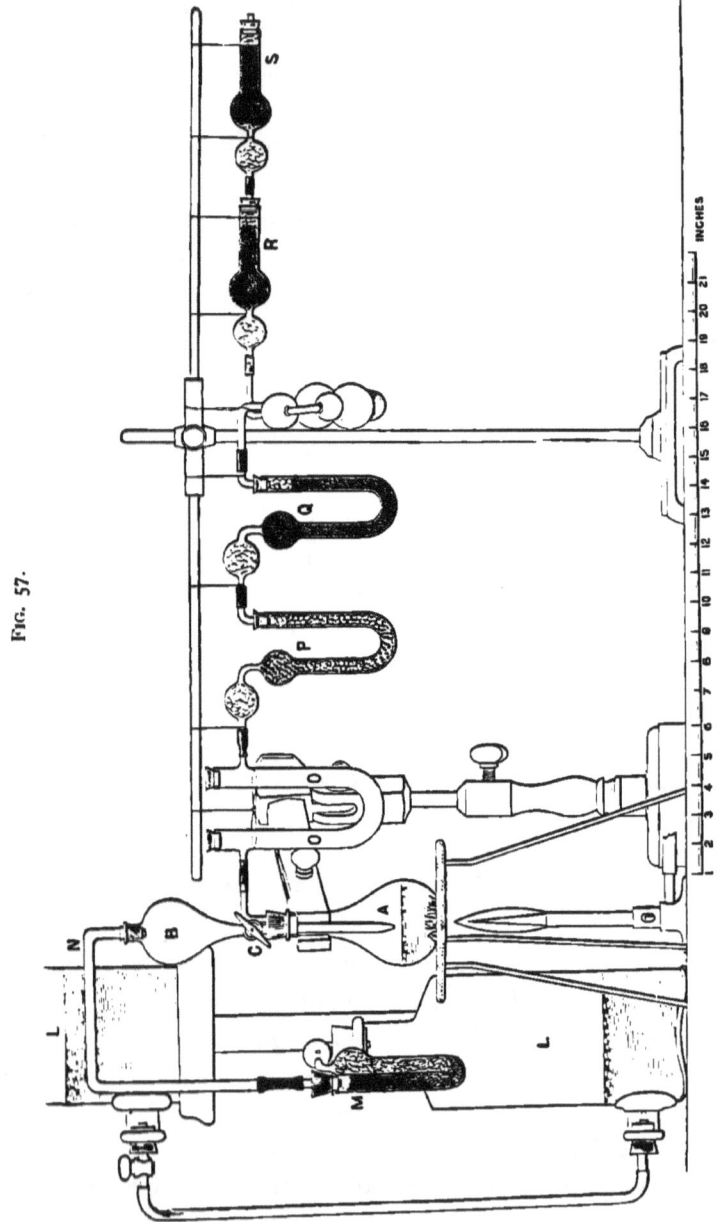

FIG. 57.

end is drawn out so that the orifice is quite small. O contains strong H_2SO_4. P contains dry pumice, Q granular chloride of calcium, and the small bulb of Q contains slightly moist cotton-wool. The object of the moist cotton-wool is to introduce the gas into the absorption apparatus with the same amount of moisture it has when it leaves it. The drying property of H_2SO_4 being greater than that of chloride of calcium, without the interposition of the slightly moist cotton-wool the gas would enter the absorption apparatus with less moisture than it would have on leaving it, and the increase of weight would be less than the amount due to the CO_2 absorbed. The Liebig bulb and the U-tube R form the absorption apparatus, and S the safety-tube. Weigh out into A 1 gramme of pig-iron, spiegel, or ferro-manganese, or 3 grammes of steel or iron ; fit in tightly the rubber stopper carrying the bulb-tube B, and attach the other tubes and the weighed absorption apparatus as described above. Close the glass stopcock C, and draw a few bubbles through the potash-bulb by applying suction at the end of the safety-tube. Allow the solution in the potash-bulb to recede, and see that it maintains its level for several minutes, to insure the tightness of all the joints. Introduce through the bulb-tube 10 or 15 c.c. of a saturated solution of chromic acid, and then 100 c.c. of strong H_2SO_4 which has been heated to boiling with a little chromic acid, cooled, and allowed to stand over crystals of chromic acid to become saturated. The H_2SO_4 should be run in very carefully, to cover the chromic acid already at the bottom of the flask. Now introduce in the same way 50 c.c. of H_2SO_4, 1.10 sp. gr., which will float on the top of the concentrated acid. Close the stopcock C, and heat the flask gradually almost to the boiling-point of the solution. When no more gas is given off, attach the purifying apparatus, open the stopcock C, and start a current of air through the apparatus by means of the bottles L, L. Lower the light under A gradually, finally extinguish it, and, after passing 2 litres of air through the apparatus,

Different drying properties of H_2SO_4 and $CaCl_2$.

Details of the method.

Testing the tightness of the apparatus.

detach, and weigh the absorption apparatus, with the precautions mentioned on page 136. The increase of weight is the weight of the CO_2, due to the carbon in the sample: it contains 27.27 per cent. carbon.

B. 1. Volatilization of the Iron in a Current of Chlorine, and Subsequent Combustion of the Carbon.

Weigh out 1 gramme of pig-iron or 3 grammes of steel into a porcelain boat about 3 inches (75 mm.) long, and treat it exactly as described on page 73 *et seq*. The boat when withdrawn from the tube contains the carbon, slag, and oxides, and nearly all of the non-volatile chlorides, such as $MnCl_2$. When the sample contains much manganese, it is necessary to treat the residue in the boat with cold water, filter it on a small plug of ignited asbestos, return it to the boat, and dry it before burning

This method not suitable for spiegel and ferro-manganese.

it off. As this adds very considerably to the time required for the determination, it is best to adopt some other method for the determination of carbon in such materials as spiegel and ferro-manganese. Introduce the boat into the tube B of the

Description of the combustion apparatus.

apparatus, Fig. 58. This apparatus consists of a ten-burner combustion-furnace A, through which runs the porcelain tube B. This tube is about 25 inches (625 mm.) long, and ¾ inch (18 mm.) internal diameter. It projects 6 inches (150 mm.) outside the furnace at each end, and the sheet-iron screens L prevent the heat from reaching the stoppers P and S. The

Preparation of the oxide of copper plugs.

tube is filled for a length of 6 inches (150 mm.), or from about the middle of the tube to the forward end of the furnace, with oxide of copper, which is best made by rolling up tightly a piece of coarse copper gauze 6 inches (150 mm.) long until it makes a roll *nearly* filling the bore of the tube, and heating it

Roll of silver.

for an hour in a current of oxygen. A piece of thin sheet-silver 4 inches long, and forming a roll completely filling the bore of the tube, is placed just in front of the oxide of copper: it serves to absorb any chlorine given off during the combus-

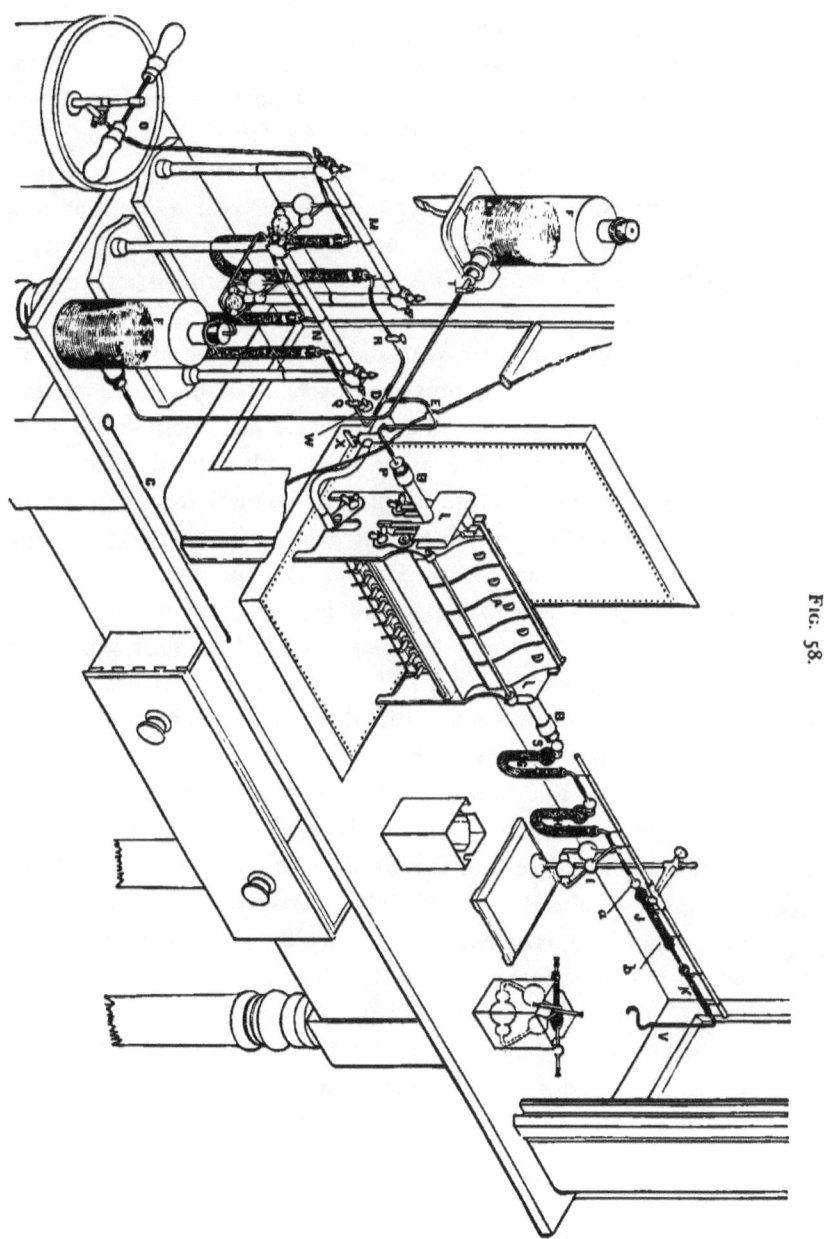

FIG. 58.

tion.* A roll of copper gauze 2 inches long, with a loop in one end, thoroughly oxidized, is pushed in after the boat con-

Oxygen.
taining the carbon. The cylinder O contains oxygen under

Air.
pressure. The bottles F, F serve to force air through the apparatus to replace the oxygen at the end of the operation. The stopcock T serves to regulate the flow of water, and consequently of air. When all the water has run from the upper into the lower bottle, it is siphoned out of the latter and returned to the former.

Purifying
apparatus
for oxygen
and air.
The purifying apparatus M and N, for oxygen and air respectively, consist of Liebig potash-bulbs filled with caustic potassa, 1.27 sp. gr., and U-tubes, the sides next the potash-bulbs filled with dry pumice, and the other sides with chloride of calcium. The glass stopcocks Q and R shut off the purifying apparatus on their respective sides when the oxygen or air is passing through the other set. The T-tube D connects the two sets of apparatus, the third limb passing through the glass in the side of the hood, and connecting by means of the bent-glass tubes with the rubber stopper P, which fits in the porcelain tube B. All

Danger of
using rub-
ber tubes.
the connections are made with glass tubes joined together by rubber tubing, the ends of the glass tubing being brought close together inside the rubber. This is to avoid carrying the oxygen or air through rubber tubing, which gives off volatile hydro-

Drying and
purifying
apparatus
for CO₂.
Asbestos
stopper.
carbons. The Marchand U-tube G contains anhydrous sulphate of copper to absorb any HCl which may be evolved during the combustion. It is joined to the tube B by a rubber stopper or by an asbestos stopper,† made by pressing wet fibrous asbestos into a mould of the proper shape. When sufficient pressure is applied in making the stopper it becomes very hard. When dry it can be bored easily, and makes an excellent stopper for this purpose. The U-tube H contains granulated dried chloride of

---

* This roll of silver must be occasionally removed and ignited in a current of hydrogen to remove the chlorine.

† J. F. White, Amer. Chem. Jour., iii. 151.

calcium.* The absorption apparatus consists of the Liebig bulb Absorption apparatus.
I and the drying-tube J. I contains caustic potash, 1.27 sp. gr.
It is filled by attaching a short piece of rubber tubing to one
end and applying suction to it, the other end being immersed
in the potassa solution, which has been poured into a capsule.
The end must be wiped dry with a little filter-paper, and the
inside of the tube dried in the same way. When filled, the bulb
should contain the solution as shown in Fig. 59. When attached

to the apparatus, the gas passes first into
the large bulb, and, the bulbs being inclined, the gas bubbles through the solution in the three bottom bulbs. It is
fitted with a loop of platinum wire, as
shown in Fig. 59. The drying-tube J
contains fused chloride of calcium. The
small bulb *a*, Fig. 58, contains a plug of
cotton-wool, and another plug of the same
material is inserted after the chloride of
calcium at *b*. K is a safety-guard tube,

FIG. 59.

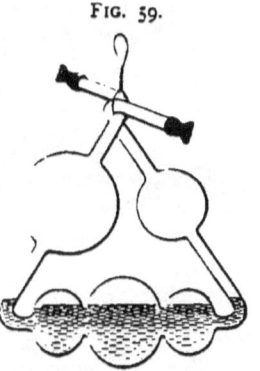

Safety-guard tube.

to prevent moisture from getting into the tube J during the combustion. The short rubber tube V is used to draw a little air
through to test the tightness of the joints. All the stoppers in
the various U-tubes and drying-tubes are of rubber. The copper
rod C is used to introduce the boats, etc., into the tube B, running the crooked end through the hole W in the glass side of the
hood. When not attached to the apparatus, the ends of the
potash-bulb I and drying-tube J are closed by little caps of rubber
tubing † (Fig. 59) made like the tips for "policemen." When on
the balance, however, they should be closed with short pieces
of rubber tubing containing bits of capillary glass tubing, as
shown in Fig. 60. The forward end of the drying-tube is closed
in the same way. These openings are too small to allow the

---

* See page 52.   † See page 31.

condition of the atmosphere to affect the weight of the bulbs by loss or gain of moisture, but they serve to equalize the pressure

FIG. 60.

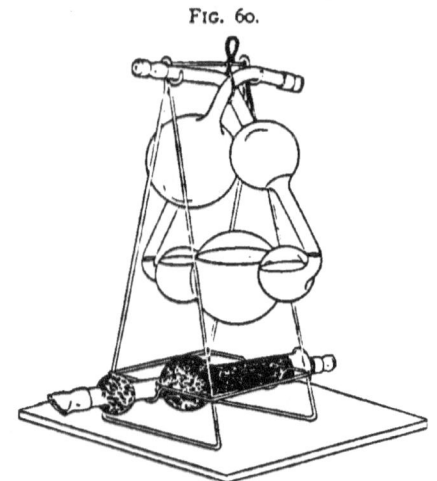

and make it unnecessary to reopen the balance-case until the bulbs are weighed.

It is very necessary in filling the potash-bulb to avoid getting any of the solution on the outside of the bulb, and it is well to see that both the bulb-tube and the drying-tube are perfectly clean. Wipe off the potash-bulb and drying-tube with a piece of linen, not silk (a clean linen handker-

Precautions
in weigh-
ing the
absorp-
tion ap-
paratus.

chief that does not leave lint on the glass is very good for this purpose), and place them on the balance.

The little wire stand shown in Fig. 60 is very convenient for holding the absorption apparatus in the balance, as it brings all the weight on the pan instead of putting the greater part on the beam alone, as is the case when the potash-bulbs are suspended from the hook on the end of the beam. The latter arrangement puts more weight on one pan than on the other, thus throwing the needle out of the vertical. Allow them to remain about thirty minutes to get the exact temperature of the balance, and

weigh. Attach the absorption apparatus as shown in the sketch, Fig. 58, insert the boat in the tube by means of the rod C, push-ing it up against the oxide of copper, insert the short roll of oxidized gauze as far as the inside of the screen L, and close the tube with the stopper P. Shut the stopcocks R and Q, and, by applying suction at V, draw a few bubbles through the potash-bulb I. When the liquid recedes in the potash-bulb, it should keep its level for a few minutes; if it does not, there is a leak in some of the connections, which must be discovered and stopped before proceeding with the combustion. When everything is tight, open R and start a slow current of oxygen through the apparatus. Light the two forward burners of the furnace, turning them low to heat the oxidized copper gauze, raise the heat gradually until·the tube appears red, and then light the last burner to heat the short roll of oxidized copper gauze. As soon as this end of the tube is hot, light the third burner from the forward end, and a few minutes afterwards the fourth burner, which is directly under the forward end of the boat. Light each burner in succession from this one until all are lighted and turned high enough to heat the tube red-hot. Allow them to burn for fifteen minutes, then shut off the oxygen, close R, open Q, and by means of the stopcock T start a current of air through the apparatus. By means of the gas-cock X lower all the lights of the furnace together very slowly, to avoid cracking the tube, and finally turn them out. About 1 litre of air should run through at the rate of about 3 bubbles a second; this will about half empty the upper bottle L. Close T and Q, detach the absorption apparatus, close the ends of I and J with the little rubber caps, and, after wiping the bulb and tube gently with the linen handkerchief to remove any moisture caused by the handling, place them on the balance. Weigh with the same precautions as before; the increase in weight is CO_2, which contains 27.27 per cent. carbon. When several com-

When making a number of combustions.

bustions are to be made in succession, as soon as the absorption apparatus is detached as directed above, remove the boat from the tube, replace it with another containing a second sample, attach a second absorption apparatus which has just been weighed, and proceed with the combustion. While the second combustion is in progress, the first absorption apparatus may be weighed, and the weight then obtained can be used for the first

Necessity for renewing KHO solution frequently.

weight of the absorption apparatus for a third combustion. Before the absorption apparatus shall have increased .5 gramme in weight from the original weighing, the potash-bulb must be

Condition
in which
apparatus
is kept
when not
in use.
emptied and refilled with a fresh solution. When the final combustion for the day is finished, place a piece of glass rod in the open end of the connection of H, remove the boat from the tube B, replace the short roll of oxidized copper gauze in the tube, insert the stopper P, but not tightly, open R and Q, and loosen the stopper in the bottle F. Place pieces of glass rod in the ends of the safety-tube K, to prevent access of moisture.

Whenever the apparatus has been out of use for a day, before making a combustion or set of combustions remove the piece of glass rod from the forward end of the U-tube H, insert in its place a piece of glass tubing drawn out at the forward end to a small orifice, start a current of oxygen through the apparatus, light the burners in the furnace, raising the heat very gradually, keep the tube at a red heat fifteen minutes, turn off the oxygen, start the air, lower the burners gradually, and pass a litre of air through

Good results
cannot be
obtained
in very
damp,
warm
weather.
the apparatus. It will then be ready for the combustion. In very damp weather it is almost impossible to get good results, the condensation of moisture on the absorption apparatus rendering the weighing extremely difficult even when the utmost care is used.

2. Volatilization of the Iron in a Current of Hydrochloric Acid Gas, and Subsequent Combustion of the Carbon.

The process is exactly the same in this method as in that just described, a current of hydrochloric acid gas being substituted

for one of chlorine. The apparatus for generating this gas is the same as the one used for chlorine, common rock-salt in pieces about as large as a filbert being substituted for binoxide of manganese, and sulphuric acid, diluted with two-thirds its bulk of water, for hydrochloric acid.

C. 1. Solution in Double Chloride of Copper and Ammonium, Filtration, and Weighing or Combustion of the Residue.

Weigh 1 gramme of pig-iron, spiegel, or ferro-manganese into a No. 2 Griffin's beaker, and add 100 c.c. of saturated solution of the double chloride of copper and ammonium* and 7.5 c.c. HCl. For steel or puddled iron, weigh 3 grammes† into a No. 3 beaker, and add 200 c.c. of the double chloride of copper and ammonium solution and 15 c.c. strong HCl. Stir the solution constantly with a glass rod for some minutes at the ordinary temperature. The more it is stirred the more rapid will be the solution of the iron Solution and of the precipitated copper. The beaker, carefully covered, of the
sample. may now be placed on the top of the air-bath or on a cool part of the sand-bath, but the solution should never be heated hotter than 60° or 70° C., and it should be stirred as often as practicable.

As the most tedious part of the determination of carbon in steel is frequently that which has to do with the decomposition of the steel and the solution of the precipitated copper, particularly with low steels, the samples being nearly always in lumps, and the analyst does not wish to separate these larger particles for fear that the fine stuff alone may not represent a true average, the

FIG. 61.

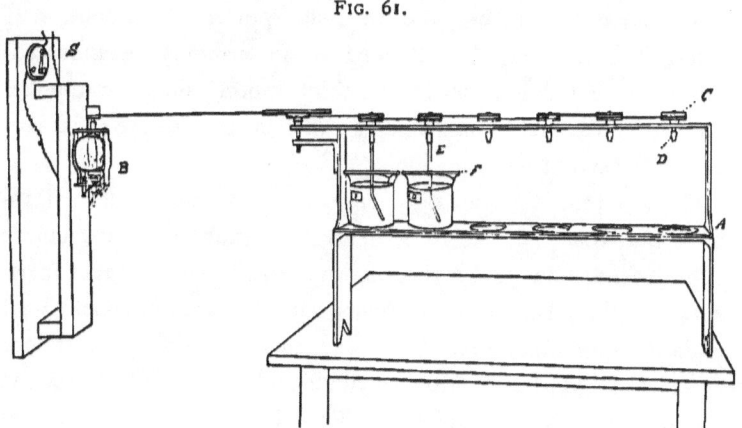

machine shown in Fig. 61 is very useful. It consists of a framework A of brass, cast in one piece for the sake of rigidity. It is fastened to the table by lugs and screws not shown in the cut.

---

* See page 54.   † See page 37, " Factor Weights."

The shelf, on which the beakers stand, has on it a piece of asbestos board with holes to fit exactly the bottoms of the beakers to prevent them from moving. To further increase the stability of the beakers (which should be of very heavy glass) their bottoms are ground on a glass plate with fine emery until they have a good bearing surface all around.

Description of stirring-machine.

The tops, which are covered when on the machine with a plate of glass, F, ground on one side and perforated to allow the passage of the stirring-rods E, are likewise ground, so that when slightly moistened the ground glass prevents almost entirely all movement of the covers on the beakers when the machine is in motion.

The small wooden pulleys C are fitted with brass spindles, which run through the upper cross-piece and have on their lower ends pieces of rubber tubing, which serve to hold the stirring-rods. The stirring-rods are bent as shown in the cut, to give the proper motion to the liquid. A small motor, B, adapted to the strength of the current, furnishes the requisite power. The motor, if properly wound, may be attached to an ordinary incandescent lighting current, but a sewing-machine motor run by a dipping battery of three bichromate cells is sufficient to give the necessary number of revolutions.

Necessity for acidulating the solution.

The fact that it is not only unnecessary to use a neutral solution, but that the use of a neutral solution gives inaccurate results, seems now to be thoroughly established by the experiments of the American members of the International Steel Standard Committee. The best practice is to add about 10 per cent. of HCl to the solution of double chloride. The reactions occurring may be considered as $Fe + CuCl_2 = FeCl_2 + Cu$ and $Cu + CuCl_2 = 2CuCl$. The part taken by the chloride of ammonium does not seem very clear, but the fact remains that the precipitated copper is much more soluble in the double chloride of copper and ammonium than in any other menstruum. When the precipitated copper is all, or very nearly all, dis-

solved, which is usually the case in half an hour after the solution of double chloride of copper and ammonium is added to
the drillings, run a little
of the acidulated double
chloride by means of the
rod around the sides of
the beaker, wash off the
rod into the beaker with
a jet of water, and let
the beaker stand for a
few minutes to allow the
carbonaceous matter to
settle. The best form
of filtering-apparatus is
shown in the annexed
sketches. It consists of
the perforated platinum

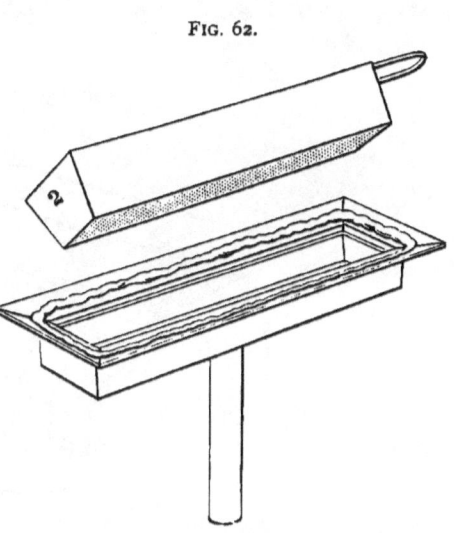

FIG. 62.

Filtering on
perforated
platinum
boat.

boat (Fig. 62), which fits in the platinum holder. To prepare
the boat for use, place it in the holder, as shown in Fig. 63,
attach the pump, but do not start it. Fill the boat with prepared asbestos* suspended in water, pour enough around the
outside of the boat to fill the space *a*, Fig. 63, and start the
filter-pump. Continue pouring the suspended asbestos into the
space *a*, Fig. 63, until enough is drawn into the joint to make
a good packing. By pressing it in all round with a spatula
the joint may be made very tight. Pour enough of the suspended asbestos into the boat to make a good, thick felt, and
press it down firmly all over the bottom of the boat with
something like the square end of a lead-pencil, to make it
compact. Detach the pump, remove the boat from the holder
carefully so as to leave the packing on the sides of the holder,
and move it up with the end of a spatula, so that it will re-

Method of
preparing
the boat.

---

* See page 26.

main as shown in Fig. 62. Place another boat in the holder, press the packing into the joint *a*, Fig. 63, with the end of a spatula, fill the boat with suspended asbestos, and start the

FIG. 63.

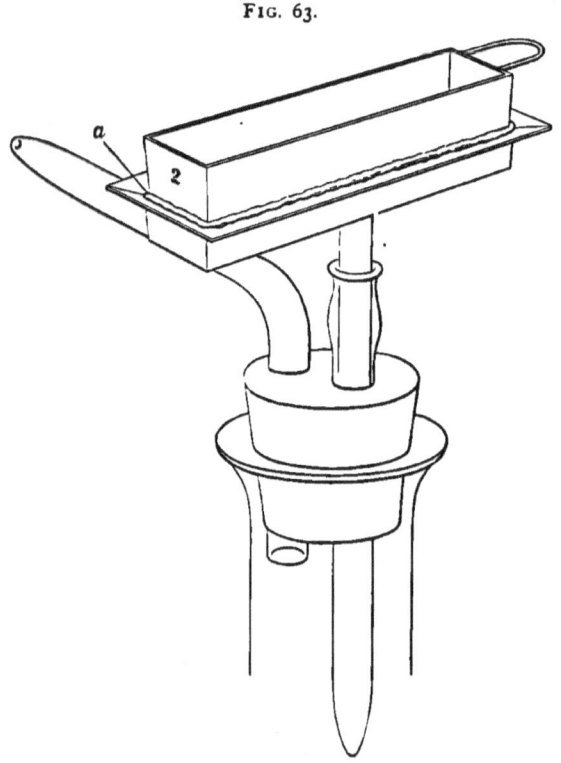

pump. If necessary, pour a little of the finer suspended asbestos fibre into the joint to make it perfectly tight, and prepare the felt in the boat as before. Dry the boats, and ignite them in the combustion-tube, two at a time, in a current of oxygen. Fit one of these prepared boats in the holder, press the packing into the joint as before, first moistening it slightly if it has become dry, start the pump, and pour into the boat enough suspended asbestos, which has been ignited in oxygen, to form a thin film on the top of the felt. This film will hold the silica, phosphate of iron, etc., from the carbonaceous residue, and, after the combustion, will usually turn up at the edges, so that it can be readily detached from the main felt, leaving the boat ready for another filtration.

The boat being thus prepared, pour into it the solution of the iron or steel, guiding the stream by a small glass rod held against the tip of the beaker. The solution, if the joint *a*, Fig. 63, is tight, and the pump works well, will usually run through the felt as rapidly as it can be poured into the boat. When the supernatant fluid has all run through, transfer the carbonaceous matter to the boat by a fine stream of cold water from a washing-flask. Pour into the beaker about 10 c.c. of dilute hydrochloric acid, run it all around the inside of the beaker by means of the rod to dissolve any adhering salt, wash off the glass rod and wash down the sides of the beaker with a jet of water, and decant the acid into the boat, filling the boat almost up to the edge. Wash the carbonaceous matter in the boat thoroughly with hot water by filling the boat from the beaker and allowing it to suck through dry, but do not attempt to throw a jet of water into the boat from the washing-flask, as it will be almost certain to throw some of the carbonaceous matter from the boat or cause it to crawl over the side. In decanting the water from the beaker, the lip must not be allowed to touch the surface of the liquid in the boat, as a film of carbonaceous matter will run up the inside of the beaker. Pour a little dilute acid into the joint between the boat and holder, allow it to suck through the packing, and wash it several times with hot water. The carbonaceous matter from pig-iron, puddled iron, spiegel, ferro-manganese, and ingot steel usually washes like sand, but that from steel which has been hardened, tempered, hammered, or rolled is apt to be more or less gummy, stopping the filter and rendering the filtration and washing prolonged and tedious. It is also apt to adhere more or less to the sides of the beaker, and must be wiped off by a little wad of ignited fibrous

Filtering on the prepared boat.

Differences in speed of filtration of different samples.

asbestos, held in a pair of platinum-pointed forceps like those shown in Fig. 64. This wad is then placed in the boat. When

the carbonaceous matter is thoroughly washed and sucked dry, detach the pump, remove the boat from the holder, wipe it off carefully with a piece of silk, place it in a dish covered with a watch-glass, and dry it in a water-bath or in an air-bath at 100° C. When dry, insert the boat in the tube (Fig. 58), and burn off the carbon as directed

Platinum combustion-tube.

on page 136. Instead of the porcelain tube, a platinum tube of the dimensions shown in Fig. 66 may be used to very great advantage. The rear end has a ground joint (Fig. 65), which may be

FIG. 65.

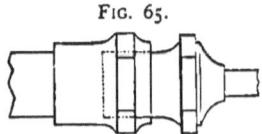

made perfectly air-tight. The tube has a strengthening band of German silver at B, Fig. 66, and the part P, which is of phosphor-bronze, is ground in. To prevent the tube from sagging when it is hot, the rear end is supported at P, Fig. 66, by a wire from the top of the hood. A piece of platinum gauze ½ inch long (12 mm), rolled up rather loosely, fills the forward end of the tube, then the tube is filled for a distance of about 6 inches (150 mm.) with granular oxide of copper, followed by another piece of platinum gauze of the same size as the first, and a similar roll 2 inches long, with a loop, is pushed in after the boat, the rear end coming just forward of the screen L. The limb of the U-tube G nearest the platinum tube contains anhydrous cuprous chloride* and the forward limb anhydrous cupric sulphate.† H contains dried, *not fused*, chloride of calcium, and in the bulb next to G is a small wad of cotton-wool, which should be moistened with a single drop

The purifying train.

of water before each set of combustions. G and H are called the purifying train, and when the apparatus is not in use they should be detached from the tube and the ends closed with pieces of

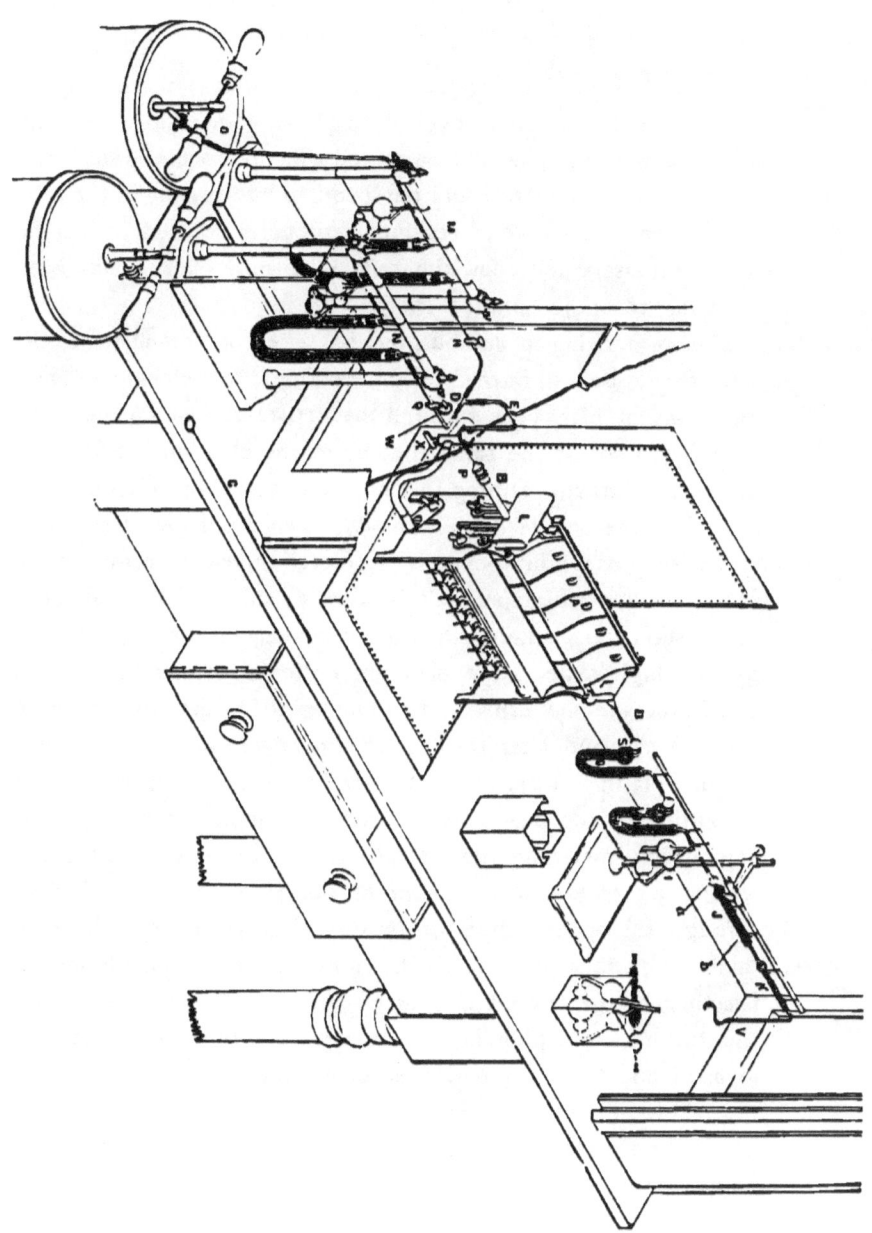

glass rod. The object of the cuprous chloride is to absorb any chlorine that may come over during the combustion. If any should come over it would be mixed with hydrochloric acid and moisture, and all then would be absorbed by the salts in the tube B. If the carbonaceous residue is properly washed it will be found necessary to renew the salts in G only after it has been used for 25 or 30 combustions.*

Necessity for burning out the tube before making a combustion. Before making a combustion, or series of combustions, the tube should be well burned out by heating it to redness and passing a current of oxygen through the apparatus, heating the small tube S red-hot at the same time by means of a small blast-lamp or Bunsen burner. During this operation fumes of sulphuric acid issue from the end of S, and usually, when the flame of the lamp is carried out to this point, it is colored green, showing that a small amount of copper salt is also volatilized. In making a combustion the platinum should not be heated above a low red, as at a high temperature platinum becomes permeable by CO_2. The burners in the furnace should be lighted in the order directed on page 137, and, after they are all lighted, ten minutes are ample to burn off the carbonaceous matter in the boat. From the time of putting in the boat, fifty minutes are ample for finishing the combustion, including the displacement of the oxygen by air.

Cylinder of compressed air. Instead of the arrangement of bottles F, F for forcing air through the apparatus shown in Fig. 58, a second cylinder containing air under pressure, as shown in Fig. 66, is much more satisfactory, as the current can be controlled with perfect accuracy, the trouble of siphoning the water from the lower bottle is avoided, and there is no danger of passing gases or fumes from the laboratory into the apparatus.

The time required when using a porcelain tube is somewhat longer, owing to the danger incurred of cracking the tube if the

---

* For a detailed account of the experiments on determination of carbon in steel see Prof. Langley's paper, Transactions of the Inst. of Mining Eng., Pittsburg International Meeting, October, 1890, and Jour. of Anal. and App. Chem., 1891, page 121.

heat is increased or diminished too rapidly. A platinum tube shorter than the one here figured is not to be recommended, as it cannot contain enough oxygen to burn the carbon to CO_2, and a consequent loss is often unavoidable. Duplicate results by this method should rarely vary more than .005 of a per cent. carbon. When using 3 grammes of the sample, the percentage of carbon is obtained by dividing the weight of CO_2 by 11 and multiplying by 100.

Instead of the perforated boat and holder described above, the carbonaceous residue may be filtered in a small platinum tube fitting inside the combustion-tube. It is made as represented in Fig. 67. The small perforated disk of platinum rests on a seat in the tube as shown in the sketch. The felt in the disk is prepared in the same way as directed for the boat, and, after drying the carbonaceous residue, the disk is moved upward in the filtering-tube before inserting the latter in the combustion-tube, to allow the gas to pass through the filtering-tube during the combustion. The boat has several advantages over the filtering-tube, the principal one being that the boat has a much larger filtering-surface, and, besides, there is no danger of the felt being disturbed during the filtering, while the disk in the tube may be loosened in its seat and allow some of the carbonaceous matter to pass around it. If the boats when not in use are kept carefully covered, the same felts may be used for a large number of filtrations; but occasionally they become clogged, and then it is better to renew them.

Filtering in a platinum filtering-tube.

Fig. 67.

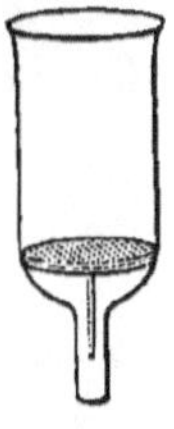

Instead of either of these forms of filtering-apparatus, a simple glass tube, as represented in Fig. 68, may be used. The closely-coiled spiral of platinum wire fits in the tube as shown in the sketch. On this is placed a rather thick layer of ignited long-fibre asbestos, and ignited asbestos suspended in water is poured over it to make a solid felt. The tube may be used in a stand, as represented in Fig. 69, or it may be used with the

Glass filtering-tube.

filter-pump under very gentle pressure.   Filter and wash the
carbonaceous matter, and while still moist transfer it to the boat

FIG. 68.

FIG. 69.

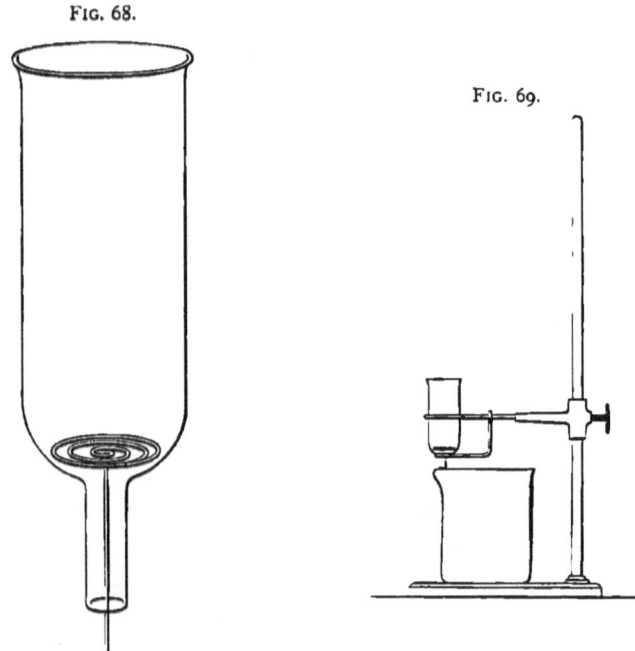

(Fig. 70) by opening out the sides of the boat, inverting the tube
over it, and allowing the felt and spiral to slide out of the tube.
Wipe off any carbonaceous matter that may remain on the sides

FIG. 70.

Boats of
platinum-
foil.

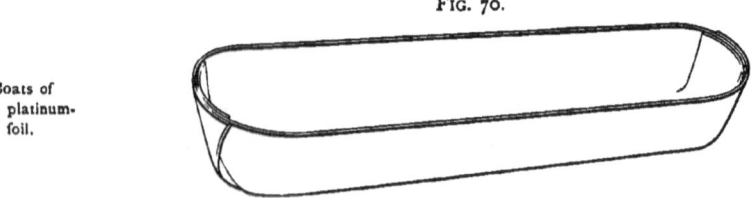

of the tube, or that may have adhered to the spiral in removing
it, with little wads of fibrous asbestos held in the forceps (Fig. 64).
Place these wads in the boat, bend the sides of the latter into

their proper shape, dry the boat and contents at 100° C., insert the boat in the porcelain or platinum tube, and burn off the carbonaceous matter as before directed. This boat is made by cutting a piece of platinum-foil in the shape shown in Fig. 71, and bending it up over a brass former into the shape shown in Fig. 70.

FIG. 71.

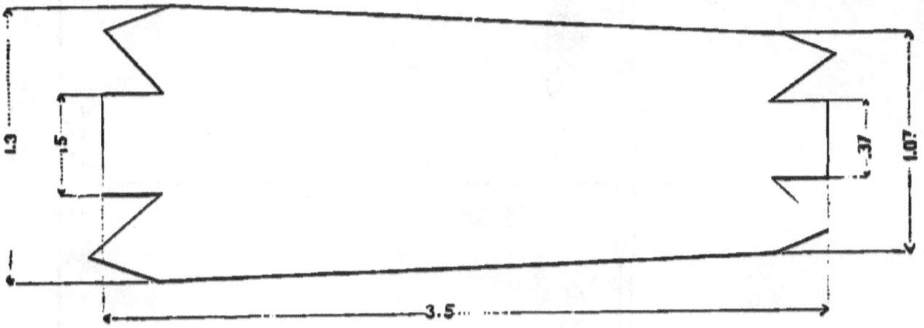

Instead of burning the carbonaceous matter in a current of oxygen, it may be burned by H_2SO_4 and CrO_3 in the arrangement shown in Fig. 72. P' is an empty U-tube, O is a tube containing sulphate of silver dissolved in strong H_2SO_4, P contains anhydrous sulphate of copper, Q granular dried chloride of calcium,* the Liebig bulb and drying-tube R constitute the absorption apparatus, S is the safety-guard tube, and L, L constitute the arrangement for passing air through the apparatus. The air is freed from CO_2 in passing through the U-tube M filled with lumps of fused caustic potassa. Transfer the carbonaceous matter and asbestos to the flask A, insert the stopper carrying the bulb-tube B, close the stopcock C, and connect the apparatus as shown in Fig. 72, including the weighed absorption apparatus. See that the joints are all tight, and then pour into B 10 c.c. of a saturated solution of chromic acid, admit it to the flask A by opening the stopcock C, and then pour

Combustion of the residue in CrO_3 and H_2SO_4.

---

* The bulb of Q contains a wad of slightly moistened cotton-wool, as described on page 131.

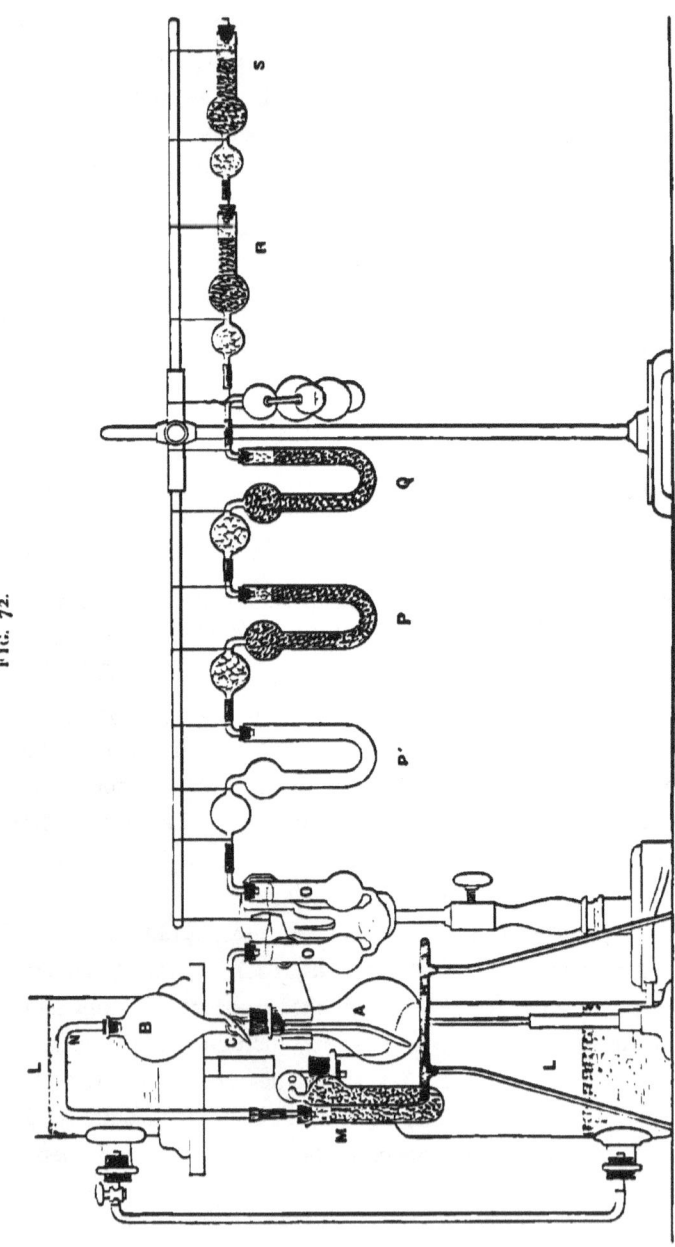

FIG. 72.

into B 100 c.c. strong H_2SO_4 which has been heated almost to boiling with a little CrO_3. Let this run into A slowly, connect the air-apparatus by the tube N, and start a slow current of air through. Light a very low light under A, and increase it gradually until the liquid is heated to the boiling-point. Gradually lower the light while the current of air continues to pass, and when about 1 litre of air has passed through the apparatus after the light is extinguished, detach and weigh the absorption apparatus, with the precautions mentioned on page 136.

The carbonaceous residue may also be weighed directly instead of being burned off. In this method, filter on a Gooch crucible or on counterpoised filters,* dry at 100° C., and weigh. Burn off the carbonaceous matter and weigh the residue: the difference between the two weights is carbonaceous matter, which contains about 70 per cent. of carbon † in steel or iron free from graphite. Of course this method of direct weighing is applicable only to samples when all the carbon is in the so-called combined condition.

Weighing the dried residue.

2. Solution in Chloride of Copper and Chloride of Potassium, Filtration, and Combustion of the Residue in Oxygen.

As a solvent this salt has no advantage over the ammonium salt, but the presence of carbonaceous matter in the latter, which can only be removed by repeated crystallizations, has brought the potassium salt into use. Solution is almost, if not quite, as rapid with the potassium salt as with the ammonium salt, and the price is decidedly in favor of the former. The absence of volatile constituents is another advantage, for it is quite possible that chloride of ammonium if left in the carbonaceous residue may be decomposed in the red-hot oxide of copper and form some compound capable of being absorbed by the caustic potassa in the Liebig bulb of the absorption apparatus. The only satisfactory

Advantages of the potassium salt.

---

* See page 27.　　　† Amer. Chem. Jour., iii. 245.

way to test a solution of double chloride is to make several determinations on a standard steel with each fresh lot of the solvent.

3. Solution in Chloride of Copper, and Combustion of the Residue.

The only disadvantage in the use of this reagent is the
length of time required to dissolve a sample of steel in it. Even
with a strongly acid solution and constant stirring, unless the
sample is very finely divided, it may require several days for its
complete solution.

4. Solution in Iodine or Bromine, and Combustion with Chromate of Lead, or Weighing, of the Residue.

The determination by this method, when iodine is used, is
carried out exactly as directed for the estimation of "Slag and
Oxides," page 79, the residue being filtered on asbestos, dried,
and burned with chromate of lead or oxide of copper, as directed
in A. 2, page 126 *et seq*. The residue may also be filtered on
a counterpoised filter * or Gooch crucible, washed, dried at 100°
C., weighed, the carbonaceous matter burned off, and the residue weighed. The difference between the weights is the amount
of carbonaceous matter, which contains, according to Eggertz,†
59 per cent. of carbon. It also contains about 16 per cent. of
iodine, so that the residue cannot be burned in a current of
oxygen, nor with CrO_3 and H_2SO_4. If bromine is used instead
of iodine, great care must be taken in adding the bromine, 10
c.c. bromine for 5 grammes of iron or steel, as the action is
very violent, and unless the bromine is added very slowly and
the solution kept as near 0° C. as possible, there will be oxidation, and, consequently, loss of carbon. The details of the
method when bromine is used are otherwise the same as when
iodine is the solvent.

Margin note: Weighing the resi-due.

---

* See page 27.
† Percy, Iron and Steel, page 891.

5. Solution by Fused Chloride of Silver, and Combustion of the Residue.

Fuse in a porcelain crucible 20 grammes of chloride of silver, and see that the button when cold has a smooth, flat surface on top. Place the button in a porcelain dish about 6 inches (15 cm.) in diameter, and pour on the button 3 grammes of drillings. Add 300 c.c. cold distilled water containing 2 drops of HCl, place the dish on a ground-glass plate, and cover it with a bell-glass to exclude the air during the time occupied in dissolving the sample. It is not necessary that the sample should be in drillings, as a single piece will be dissolved in this way. The chloride of silver should weigh at least 6 times as much as the sample of iron or steel. The reaction is a simple substitution, $Fe + 2AgCl = FeCl_2 + 2Ag$, by galvanic action, but secondary reactions occur, including the decomposition of water, both hydrogen and oxygen being taken up by the carbon at the moment of its liberation. A slight excess of oxygen over the amount necessary to form water with the hydrogen is taken up and a little hydrogen is liberated. There is a tendency, of course, for the ferrous chloride when formed to oxidize, consequently the air must be excluded. The decomposition requires several days, as many as ten if the sample of steel or iron is in a single piece and not very thin. The metallic silver is quite cohesive, and is readily separated from the carbonaceous residue. When the action is finished, remove the mass of silver, washing off any of the carbonaceous matter adhering to it, add a little HCl to dissolve any ferric oxide which may have formed, filter off, and burn the carbonaceous matter by one of the methods previously described.

Details of the method

6. Solution of the Iron in Sulphate of Copper, Filtration, and Combustion of the Residue in a Boat in a Current of Oxygen.

Weigh 3 grammes of steel into a No. 3 beaker, and add 150 c.c. of solution of sulphate of copper, made by dissolving 200

Prepara-
tion of
sulphate
of copper
solution.
grammes of the copper salt in water, adding a dilute solution of
caustic soda until a slight permanent precipitate appears, allowing
it to settle, filtering through asbestos, and diluting to 1 litre. For
pig-iron, spiegel, and ferro-manganese, use 1 gramme, and 50 c.c.
of sulphate of copper solution. Heat the solution gently, and stir
well until decomposition is complete. Filter in a glass filtering-
tube on asbestos, as described on page 147. Wash well with
water, transfer to a boat, as directed on page 148, dry, and burn
in a porcelain tube, as directed for A. 1, page 125. The results
are apt to be a little low, owing to the difficulty of thoroughly
oxidizing the mass of copper mixed with the carbonaceous
matter.*

Instead of filtering off the mass of copper, carbonaceous matter,
etc., decant the clear supernatant fluid through the filtering-tube,
wash several times by decantation, and then dissolve the copper
in double chloride of copper and ammonium, chloride of copper,
or ferric chloride. Filter, wash the residue with a little dilute
HCl, and then with cold water, transfer to a boat, and burn as
directed on page 132 et seq.

7. Solution of the Iron in Sulphate of Copper, and Oxidation of the Residue by $CrO_3 + H_2SO_4$.

Treat the sample with solution of sulphate of copper, as in
the method just described. Allow the precipitated copper and
carbonaceous matter to settle, pour off the clear supernatant
liquid, and transfer the residue to the flask A (Fig. 72, page 150)
by means of a platinum spatula and a fine jet of water. The
water used should not exceed 20 or 25 c.c.† The apparatus is
that sketched in Fig. 72, the only difference being that the tube

---

* See report of the U. S. Board appointed to test iron, steel, and other metals,
vol. i. p. 284.

† The borings may be treated with the sulphate of copper solution in the flask
A, and the clear liquid drawn off with a pipette. This will avoid the necessity for
transferring the residue.

O contains merely a little strong H_2SO_4. Effect the combustion exactly as described on page 149.

8. Solution of the Iron in Sulphate of Copper, Filtration, and Combustion of the Residue, mixed with Oxide of Copper in Vacuo under the Sprengel Pump, the Volume of CO_2 being measured.

Treat 1–3 grammes of drillings exactly as described under C. 6, page 153, filter on ignited asbestos in a glass tube, dry the residue, consisting of copper, carbonaceous matter, and asbestos, mix it with about 50 grammes of pure oxide of copper, and charge it into a glass combustion-tube, as directed under A. 2, page 127. The end of the combustion-tube should not be drawn out at an angle, however, but rounded and thickened in the flame, as shown in Fig. 73. When the residue has been transferred to the tube, soften the forward end in the flame, draw it out, bend it at right angles, and, after cutting off the large end, fuse the edges of the small tube. The combustion-tube should originally be about 18 inches (450 mm.) long, the drawn-out part 4 inches (100 mm.) long, and $\frac{1}{4}$ inch (6 mm.) in diameter. Place the tube in the combustion-furnace, and attach the Sprengel pump, as shown in the sketch, Fig. 74. The combustion-tube is connected with the Sprengel pump by the tube b, and the joints at a and c are made by connecting the ends of the tubes together with short lengths of rather heavy pure gum tubing well wired. Before the ends of the tubes are connected, a rubber stopper is forced over the end of b at a, and another over the end of b at c. These stoppers support short pieces of glass tubing of about $\frac{5}{8}$ inch (16 mm.) inside diameter. After the ends of the tubes are connected, the stoppers are pushed up so that the joints are entirely within the large tubes, which are then filled, the one at a with water, and that at c with glycerine. To the end of the pump is attached a tube, d, the end of which

FIG. 73.

Preparation of the combustion-tube.

Making the joints.

bends upward; it rests in the mercury-trough as shown in the
sketch. When the apparatus is properly connected, light a
burner under the forward part of the combustion-tube, which

FIG. 74.

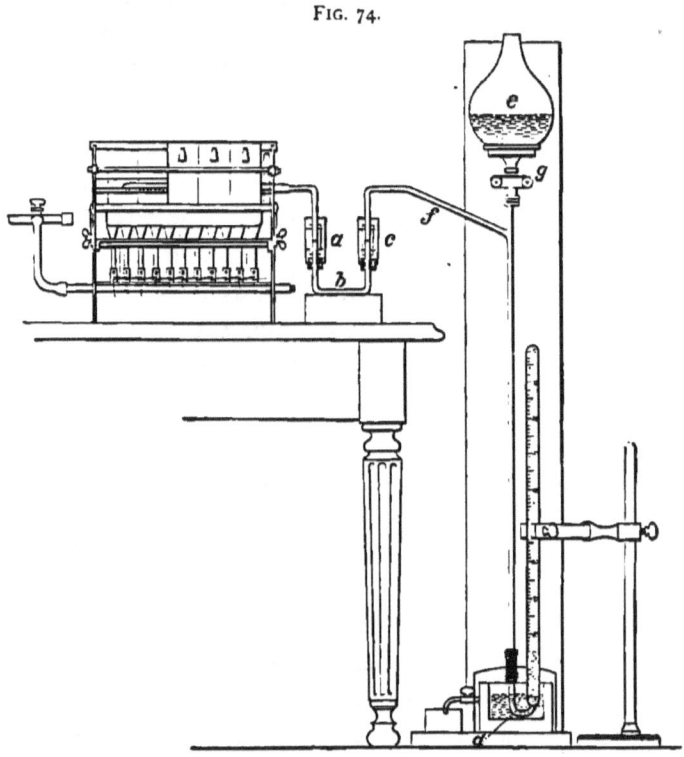

contains only oxide of copper, and start the pump by opening
carefully the screw-clamp *g*, the funnel *e* being full of mercury.
Regulate the flow of mercury so that it does not rise into the
connecting-tube *f*.

When the vacuum is complete, the mercury will fall with a
clicking sound; then close the screw-clamp *g*, place over *d* a
carefully calibrated glass tube of 100 c.c. capacity graduated in
$\frac{1}{10}$ c.c., filled with mercury, and heat the combustion-tube gradually to redness for its entire length. When no more gas is given

off, lower all the burners a little, start the pump slowly, and transfer all the gas to the graduated tube. Stop the pump, transfer the graduated tube to a mercury cistern by means of a capsule containing mercury, and adjust the tube so that the mercury will be at the same height inside and outside the tube. Read the volume of the gas, which is pure CO_2, and also take the temperature by means of a thermometer hanging near the tube, and the height of the barometer. As the carbonaceous matter contains hydrogen, which by the combustion is oxidized to H_2O, we must correct the volume of gas obtained from temperature, barometric pressure, and tension of aqueous vapor to reduce it to the volume it would occupy in the dry state at 0° C. and 760 mm. pressure, the condition in which the weight of a litre of CO_2 has been determined. The coefficient of expansion of gases from 0° C. to 100° C. has been determined to be .3665 ; they expand, therefore, for 1° C. $\frac{.3665}{100} = .003665$. To reduce the volume of a gas at any given temperature to the volume it would occupy at 0° C., we have the equation $\frac{a}{1 + (b \times .003665)} = x$, in which a is the volume it occupies at the observed temperature b, and x is its volume at 0° C. The tension of aqueous vapor, or the volume it occupies at a given temperature, measured in mm., is given in the table. Take from this table the tension of aqueous vapor at the observed temperature and subtract it from the height of barometer observed at the same time; this gives the *actual pressure* under which the gas was at the moment the volume was read. Now, as the volume of a gas is inversely as the pressure to which it is exposed, we have: As 760 : the *actual pressure* :: the corrected volume at 0° C.: the actual volume at 760 mm. and 0° C. As 1 litre of CO_2 at 760 mm. bar. and 0° C. weighs 1.9663 grammes, 1 c.c. of CO_2 under the same conditions weighs .0019663 gramme. Multiply the actual volume of CO_2 obtained above in c.c. by .0019663, and the result is the weight of the CO_2 in grammes.

Correction of the volume for pressure, temperature, and tension of aqueous vapor.

9. Solution in Dilute HCl by the Aid of an Electric Current, and Combustion of the Residue.

Description of the apparatus. The arrangement shown in Fig. 75 may be used in carrying out the details of this method. It consists of a No. 3 Griffin's beaker, in which is a piece of platinum-foil, the wire from which connects with the negative pole of the battery; a small basket of very fine platinum gauze is supported from a

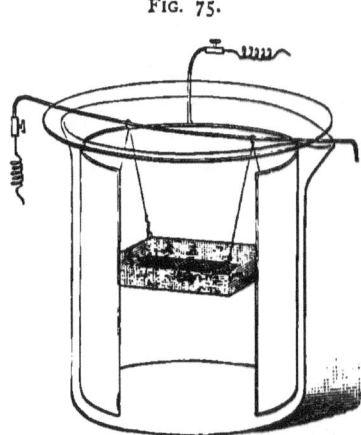

FIG. 75.

platinum wire, on one end of which is a clamp connecting with the positive pole of the battery. The battery is usually a single Bunsen or Grove element, and the intensity of the current should be regulated by varying the distance between the foil and the basket, or by introducing resistance-coils in the connections, so that no gas is given off from the iron. Hydrogen, of course, is given off abundantly from the surface of the foil, and the iron dissolves in the acid as ferrous chloride. Weigh into the basket from 1 to 5 grammes of the sample, which should be in pieces and not in powder. Suspend the basket from the wire, having previously connected the rest of the apparatus and poured into the beaker a mixture of 200 c.c. water and 50 c.c. HCl, and regulate the intensity of the current as directed above. By looking through the solution, a stream of colorless ferrous chloride will be seen falling to the bottom of the beaker, but when the current is too strong the iron becomes passive, and chlorine is given off at the positive pole, which oxidizes the iron and colors the descending current yellow with ferric chloride. When the sample is in a

Details of the method.

single piece, the solution requires eight to ten hours. The carbonaceous matter usually retains the form of the sample. When solution is complete, disconnect the battery, remove the foil from the liquid, wash the carbonaceous matter from the basket with a jet of cold water, filter it off, and determine the amount of carbon by one of the methods previously given.

10. Oxidation of the Iron by Atmospheric Air and Moisture, Solution of the Ferric Oxide in HCl, Filtration, and Combustion of the Residue.

This is the only method for the determination of carbon in iron or steel in which the carbon is not liberated in the presence of an acid or of a metallic salt, and the details are given here because the method may be useful in a study of the composition of the liberated carbonaceous matter. Weigh the sample, in as finely divided a condition as possible, into a flat-bottomed porcelain dish, moisten it with water, cover the dish carefully, and allow it to stand twenty-four hours. Add 20 or 30 c.c. of water, stir it well, and decant the water and the iron-rust which has formed into a beaker. Scatter the sample evenly over the bottom of the dish to expose the iron as much as possible to the action of the moist air, and cover the dish and beaker carefully. Repeat this operation once or twice a day until the iron is completely oxidized. Siphon off as much of the clear liquid in the beaker as possible, dissolve the oxide of iron in dilute HCl, filter, and determine the carbon by one of the previously described methods.

DETERMINATION OF GRAPHITIC CARBON.

Karston gave the first information in regard to the existence of graphite in pig-iron, and he suggested dissolving the sample in HNO_3 with the addition of a few drops of HCl, in HCl alone, or in dilute H_2SO_4, boiling the residue with caustic potassa, filtering, washing again with HCl, and finally with water, and weighing the residue as graphite.   A very interesting comparison of the results obtained by the use of different solvents is given by Drown,* and many experiments seem to show that the amount of graphite found varies with the different acids used to dissolve the sample, and also with the variations of treatment when the same acid is used.   The usual method is as follows: Treat 1 gramme of pig-iron or 10 grammes of steel with an excess of HCl, 1.1 sp. gr.   When all the iron is dissolved, boil for a few minutes, allow the graphite to settle, and decant the supernatant fluid on an asbestos filter, using either the perforated boat, Fig. 63, or the filtering-tube, Figs. 67 and 68.   Wash several times with hot water by decantation, then pour on the residue in the beaker 30 c.c. of a solution of caustic potassa, sp. gr. 1.1, and, when the effervescence ceases, heat the solution to boiling.   Filter on the same filter, transfer the graphite, etc., to the filter, wash with hot water again, and finally with alcohol and ether.   Burn the graphite by one of the methods given under "Determination of Total Carbon," and from the weight of CO_2 obtained calculate the percentage of carbon existing as *graphite*.   It frequently happens, when the sample is a high steel, that the residue which remains after treating it as above is black, and contains carbon, but it is not crystalline in appearance, and bears no resemblance to graphite.   The same steel will dissolve completely in HNO_3, and when filtered will not leave a trace of carbon on the felt.   Steels containing graphite give appreciably less carbon when dissolved in HNO_3 than when dissolved in HCl.   It is, of course, possible that a small amount of very finely divided graphite may be oxidized by the HNO_3, but, taking everything into consideration, it would seem that the method giving probably the most accurate and certainly the most uniform results is as follows: Dissolve the weighed sample in HNO_3, sp. gr. 1.2, using 15 c.c. of acid to each gramme taken for analysis.   Filter on the perforated boat or on an ignited

Solution in HCl.

Comparison of results obtained by dissolving in HCl and HNO_3.

Solution in HNO_3.

* Trans. Inst. Min. Engineers, vol. iii. p. 42.

asbestos filter, in a glass tube, transfer the residue to the filter, and wash thoroughly with hot water. Treat the residue on the filter with hot caustic potassa solution, 1.1 sp. gr. (as the Si is all oxidized to SiO_2 there will be no effervescence), wash thoroughly with hot water, then with a little dilute HCl, and finally with hot water. Burn the carbon by one of the methods previously mentioned and calculate the CO_2 obtained to carbon, and call the result *graphite*.

DETERMINATION OF COMBINED CARBON.

Indirect Method.

Having determined the total carbon and the graphite, by subtracting the latter from the former we obtain the amount of carbon existing in the *combined condition*.

Direct Method.

This method was first introduced by Eggertz,[*] in 1862, and is now used in every steel-works of any importance in the world. It is based on the fact that when steel containing carbon is dissolved in HNO_3, 1.2 sp. gr., the carbon, which sometimes at first separates out in flocks of a brownish color, is eventually dissolved, giving to the solution a depth of color directly proportionate to the amount of combined carbon in the steel. To use this in practice it is only necessary to determine very accurately the amount of combined carbon contained in a steel, by a combustion method, and to compare the depth of color in a solution of this standard with that of any unknown steel, in order to ascertain the amount of carbon in the latter. There is, however, a limitation in the application of this method, which was at first entirely overlooked, and even now is not generally understood. Reference was made on page 123 to the fact that combined carbon

Limitation in the use of this method.

---

[*] Jern-Kontorets Annaler, 1862, p. 54: 1874, p. 176; 1881, p. 301 ; Chem. News, vii. p. 254; xliv. p. 173.

is now believed to exist in two conditions in steel, or rather that under certain circumstances a portion of the combined carbon changes its condition, and, from a chemical point of view, while it is still combined carbon, in that it is soluble in HNO_3, it fails to impart so dark a color to its nitric acid solution as it did in its original state. The circumstances under which a change of this kind occurs are quite well known, and are merely those occasioned by the mechanical treatment to which steel is submitted, such as hammering, rolling, hardening, tempering, etc.* It may be stated, then, as a general proposition, that *the standard steel for the color-test should be of the same kind and in the same physical condition as the samples to be tested.*

To obtain the best results samples should be taken from the original ingots that have not been reheated, rolled, or hammered ; Bessemer steel should be compared with Bessemer, crucible with crucible, open hearth with open hearth ; the standard should contain approximately the same amount of carbon as the samples to be tested, and should have as nearly as possible the same chemical composition. The only elements that seem to have any decided effect on the color of the nitric acid solution are copper, cobalt, and chromium.

Details of the method.

Weigh out carefully .2 gramme of each sample, including the standard, into test-tubes 6 inches (150 mm.) long and ⅝ inch (16 mm.) in diameter. The test-tubes should be perfectly clean and dry, and each one marked with the number of the sample on a small gummed label near the top. A little wooden rack (Fig. 76) is convenient for holding the test-tubes in the weighing-room, and to avoid all chance of error the tube is not placed in the rack until the sample has been weighed and is ready to be transferred.

---

* Two very interesting papers on this subject will be found in the Chem. News, J. S. Parker, "On the Varying Condition of Carbon in Steel," xlii. p. 88; T. W. Hogg, "On the Condition of Carbon in Steel," xlii. p. 130. In my own practice I have seen one-third of the total carbon changed from the combined form to the *graphitic* in a high carbon steel by heating and hammering the ingot.

A little platinum or aluminium dish about 1½ inches (40 mm.) in diameter, with a spout, and furnished with a counterpoise (Fig. 44, page 36), is very convenient for holding the drillings, which are brushed from it into the test-tube with a camel's-hair brush. A very excellent form of water-bath is shown in Fig. 77. It may be provided with a constant level arrangement, consisting of

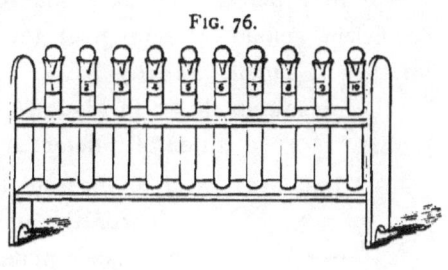

FIG. 76.

a tubulated bottle, the height of the end *b* of the vertical tube *a* fixing the level of the water in the bath. A is the bath, and B the rack. The top of the rack is of sheet-copper, perforated to receive the test-tubes, the bottoms of which rest on the coarse

Description of water-bath.

FIG 77.

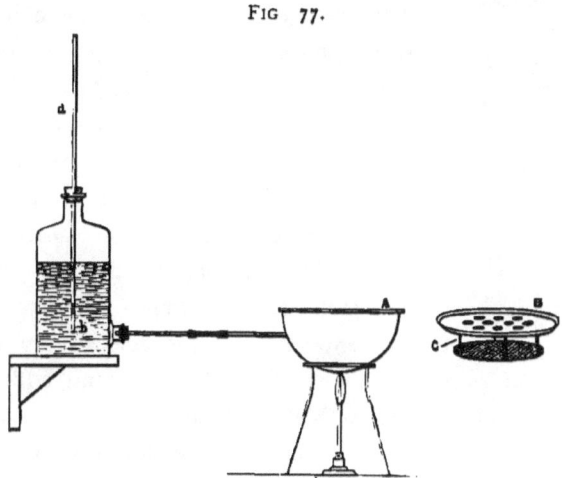

copper gauze, which is joined to the top by the uprights C. The top of the rack rests on a flange around the top of the bath.

Place the test-tubes in the rack B, and stand the rack in the bath which contains cold water. Drop into each test-tube, from a pipette, the proper amount of HNO₃, sp. gr. 1.2. For steels containing less than .3 per cent. carbon use 3 c.c. HNO₃; from .3 to .5 per cent. carbon, 4 c.c.; from .5 to .8 per cent., 5 c.c.; from .8 to 1 per cent., 6 c.c.; and over 1 per cent., 7 c.c. An insufficient amount of acid gives the solution a slightly darker tint than it should properly have.

The apparatus shown in Fig. 78 * is useful for the rapid addition of different measured quantities of nitric acid to the samples.

FIG. 78.

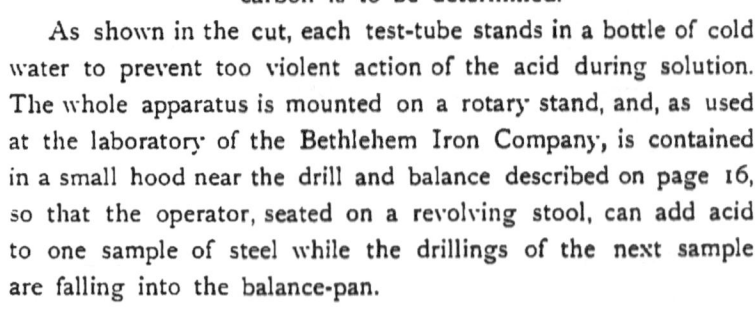

It consists of a glass reservoir holding 750 c.c., communicating below with four burettes graduated to *deliver* various quantities of acid up to 10 c.c. Each burette is furnished with a loose-fitting glass cap. The burettes are fitted with three-way glass stopcocks, so that a quarter of a revolution connects them with the reservoir, and when the proper amount of acid has run in, the stopcock is turned another quarter, which shuts off the reservoir and completely empties the burette, thus delivering the exact amount of acid measured, into the test-tube containing the weighed sample of steel in which carbon is to be determined.

As shown in the cut, each test-tube stands in a bottle of cold water to prevent too violent action of the acid during solution. The whole apparatus is mounted on a rotary stand, and, as used at the laboratory of the Bethlehem Iron Company, is contained in a small hood near the drill and balance described on page 16, so that the operator, seated on a revolving stool, can add acid to one sample of steel while the drillings of the next sample are falling into the balance-pan.

---

* Communicated to the author.

The apparatus, as here shown, is a modification by Mr. Albert L. Colby, chemist of the Bethlehem Iron Company, of an apparatus first designed by Mr. E. A. Uehling in 1884.

The HNO_3 is made by adding its own volume of water to acid of the usual strength, 1.4 sp. gr. It should be absolutely free from chlorine or hydrochloric acid, as, according to Eggertz, .0001 gramme Cl in a nitric acid solution of .1 gramme iron in 2.5 c.c. HNO_3 gives a decided yellow color. The HNO_3 should be added slowly, to prevent violent action, and the drillings should not be too fine, for the same reason. Place in the top of each test-tube a small glass bulb * or a very small funnel, and heat the water in the bath to boiling, and boil until all the carbonaceous matter is dissolved, shaking the tubes from time to time to prevent the formation of any little film of oxide. The time required for solution is for low steels about twenty minutes, and for high steels (over 1 per cent. carbon) forty-five minutes. After entire solution of the carbonaceous matter, prolonged heating tends to make the color lighter; therefore, as soon as the absence of small bubbles and the disappearance of any brownish flocculent matter show complete solution, remove the rack from the bath and stand it in a dish of cold water. The dish should be about the same size as the bath, so that the top will be covered by the top of the rack, thus excluding the light from the solutions, in which case the color will not fade for a long time. Under all circumstances the solutions should be kept out of the light, and especially out of direct sunlight, as much as possible. If there should be necessarily, in the steels operated on at one time, a wide range in carbon, the test-tubes should be removed from the bath as fast as their respective contents are dissolved and placed in cold water in a dark place. The appearance of the drillings will often give an idea of the approxi-

Proper strength of HNO_3.

Time required for the solution.

---

* These bulbs are easily made by sealing one end of a glass tube in the blowpipe flame, heating it, blowing a bulb of the proper size, allowing it to cool, heating it above the neck, and drawing it out as shown in Fig. 76.

mate carbon contents of a sample, but when there is no clue whatever, it is best to begin by adding 3 c.c. HNO_3 to the weighed portion in the test-tube, and increase the amount 1 c.c. at a time as the depth of color of the solution or the amount of flocculent carbonaceous matter indicates

FIG. 79.

Comparing the colors.
a higher carbon percentage. To compare the colors of the solutions, pour the standard into one of the carbon tubes (Fig. 79), wash out the test-tube with a little cold water, add it to the solution in the carbon tube, and dilute to a convenient amount.

This dilution should be sufficient to make the volume of the diluted standard at least twice as great as the volume of acid originally used to dissolve the sample, as this amount of water is necessary to destroy the color due to the nitrate of iron. It should not, however, greatly exceed this amount, and should be in some convenient multiple of the carbon contents of the standard in tenths of a per cent. Thus, if a standard contains .45 per cent. carbon, dilute the solution in the carbon tube to 9 c.c.,

Comparison-tubes.
then each c.c. will equal .05 per cent. The carbon tubes should be about ½ inch (12 mm.) in diameter, holding at least 30 c.c., and graduated to $\frac{1}{10}$ c.c. The tubes should have exactly the same diameter, and the glass should be perfectly colorless and have walls of the same thickness. They should, of course, be most accurately graduated.

Wood's modifications for low steels.
Mr. E. F. Wood,* of the Homestead Works, leaves the lower ends of the tubes free from graduations to give a clear space for comparing the colors. He considers this especially necessary in low steels, for which he uses 1 gramme of the sample, dissolves in 25 c.c. of nitric acid, boils for five to seven minutes in a glycerine bath at 140° C., and compares in tubes ¾ inch (18 mm.) in diameter.

---

* Communicated to the author.

The standard having been prepared, pour the solution of the sample to be tested into another carbon tube, rinse the test-tube into it with a little cold water, and compare the colors. If the solution of the sample is darker than that of the stand-ard, add water little by little, shaking the tube well to mix the solution until the shades are exactly the same. Allow a minute or two for the solution to run down the walls of the tube, and read the volume. If the standard was diluted as above, then, of course, each c.c. will equal .05 per cent. carbon, and if the volume of the sample is 10.5 c.c. it will contain .525 per cent. carbon. If the solution of the sample when first transferred to the tube should be lighter in color than the standard, a lower standard must be used, or this one may be diluted to, say, 13.5 c.c., in which case the number of c.c. divided by 3 will give the percentage of carbon in tenths. The color may be com-pared by holding the two tubes in front of a piece of white paper held towards the light, but a camera made of light wood and blackened inside is most convenient, and at night is quite invaluable. It is shown in Fig. 80, and consists of a box 3½ inches (90 mm.) high inside, 1½ inches (38 mm.) wide at one end, and 5 inches (127 mm.) at the other. It is 24 inches (610 mm.) long, and is supported on a rod, which can be raised and lowered to suit the convenience of the ob-server. The small end is closed by a piece of ground-glass, which slides in through a slot on top 1 inch (25 mm.) from the end. Immediately beyond this is an-other slot to receive a thin piece of faintly blue glass, which is inserted when the tests are made at night, using an oil-lamp

FIG. 80.

Description of camera.

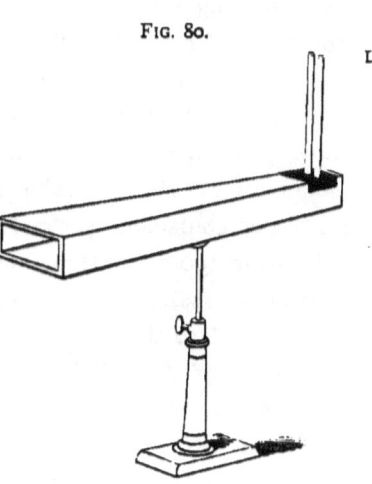

placed on a stand just beyond the camera. In fact, in many steel-works, to avoid the differences between the colors as seen by daylight and lamplight, *all* comparisons are made in a dark room, using a box or camera and an oil-lamp. Two holes in the top of the camera just inside the ground-glass screen receive the carbon tubes, the ends of which rest on a piece of black cloth on the bottom of the camera inside. Another piece of black cloth fastened across the top of the camera, covering the top of the ground-glass slide, and having holes just large enough to admit the tubes, excludes all light except that at the back of the tubes. A north light is much the best for comparing the colors, and, as to most observers the left-hand tube appears a little the darker, the color will be exactly matched when, the tubes being reversed, the left-hand tube still appears a little the darker of the two.

Use of permanent standards. Instead of diluting the solutions to agree with a standard, as above described, some chemists use a rack of permanent standards, as suggested by Britton.* The principal difficulty heretofore attending the use of permanent standards has been the impossibility of preventing their fading; but, according to Eggertz,† this is now entirely overcome by the method of preparing them suggested by Prof. F. L. Ekman. The details are as follows: Dissolve 3 grammes of neutral ferric chloride in 100 c.c. water containing 1.5 c.c. HCl; dissolve 2.1 grammes cupric chloride in 100 c.c. water containing .5 c.c. HCl; dissolve 2.1 grammes cobaltic chloride in 100 c.c. water containing 5 c.c. HCl, using the neutral salts in all cases. These solutions will contain about .01 gramme *Preparation of the solution.* of the metal to the c.c., and by adding to 8 c.c. of the iron solution 6 c.c. of the cobalt solution, 3 c.c. of the copper solution, and 5 c.c. water containing .5 per cent. HCl, a liquid is obtained which has a color approximating to that obtained by dissolving .2 gramme of steel, containing 1 per cent. of carbon, in HNO_3, and

---

* Chem. News, xxii. 101.   † Chem. News, xliv. 173.

diluting to 10 c.c., or .1 per cent. carbon to the c.c. Prepare a number of test-tubes of the size described on page 162, but in this case it is essential that they should be of exactly the same diameter, and that the glass should be as nearly colorless as possible. By successive dilutions with water containing .5 per cent. HCl, of the normal solution prepared as above, make solutions of about the proper strength for the series required.

The variations should be about .02 per cent. between the different tubes of the series, corresponding to, say, the even hundredths. There should be about 10 c.c. of solution in each tube, and then the color of each should be compared with a standard steel, diluted to the exact strength required in the permanent standard. For example, if the standard steel contains .4 per cent. carbon, and you wish to get the exact color for the .32 per cent. carbon tube in the permanent series, then dissolve .2 gramme of the standard exactly as directed on page 164, pour the solution into a carbon tube, and dilute it in accordance with the formula, carbon required : carbon of standard : : 10 c.c. : the number of c.c. required, or, in this case, 32 : 40 : : 10 c.c. : 12.5 c.c. Therefore dilute the solution in the carbon tube to 12.5 c.c., pour 10 c.c. into a test-tube exactly like those used for the permanent standards, and compare it with the .32 per cent. carbon tube. If the color of the permanent solution is not exactly the same, correct it by adding portions of the solutions of the iron, cobalt, or copper salts, or water containing .5 per cent. HCl. The iron salt or HCl alone gives a yellowish, the cobalt salt a brownish, and the copper salt a green-

FIG. 81.

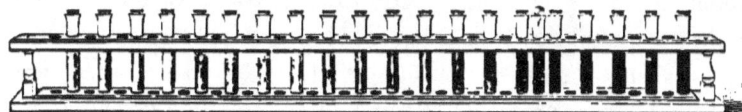

ish, tone to the solution. The standards may now be arranged in a rack, as shown in Fig. 81. The colors of the permanent standards once fixed, the samples to be analyzed are treated exactly

Details of
method
when
using per-
manent
standards
as described on page 164, the test-tubes used being precisely like those containing the permanent standards, and each one carefully graduated to contain 10 c.c. When the samples (.2 gramme each) are dissolved and cooled, dilute each solution in turn with cold water to 10 c.c., mix thoroughly, and compare it with the standards in the rack, by which means the carbon may be estimated to the nearest hundredth of a per cent.

In testing white cast iron, use only .05 gramme, dissolve in 7 c.c. HNO_3, dilute the standard to some convenient amount approximating 20 c.c., and compare as quickly as possible to avoid the precipitation of carbonaceous matter, which is apt to occur under these circumstances. The graphite in ordinary gray pig-iron, and sometimes even in steels, renders filtration necessary. In this case

add to the cold acid solution one-half of its volume of water, filter through a small, dry, ashless filter into the carbon tube, wash with as little water as possible, and compare as usual.

For steels very low in carbon, the color test, as above described, becomes uncertain, but Stead* has suggested and elaborated a
method which gives excellent results. It is based on the fact that the carbonaceous matter liberated from iron and steel is soluble in the caustic alkalies as well as in HNO_3, while the color which it imparts to the alkaline solution is about $2\frac{1}{2}$ times as great as that which it gives to the acid solution. For this method is required, besides the HNO_3, 1.2 sp. gr., a solution of caustic soda 1.27 sp. gr. Weigh 1 gramme of each sample, including the standard, into a No. 1 beaker, add 12 c.c. HNO_3, and heat on the bath until solution is complete, which, in the case of puddled iron or low steel, is in about five or ten minutes. Add to each 30 c.c. of boiling water and 13 c.c. of the soda solution, stirring well. Pour each solution in turn into a glass measuring-jar, dilute to 60 c.c., mix thoroughly, allow the solution to settle, filter through a dry filter, and receive 15 c.c. of each sample in a carbon tube. Those samples

---

* Jour. Iron and Steel Institute, 1883, No. 1, p. 213.

whose solutions are darker than that of the standard contain, of course, more carbon than the standard. Dilute the solutions in turn until the colors agree with that of the standard. The percentage of carbon is deduced from the equation $\frac{a}{15} \times b = x$, in which a is the percentage of carbon in the standard, 15, of course, the number of c.c. taken of each solution, b is the number of c.c. in the diluted sample, and x is the percentage of carbon in the sample. Take those samples whose solutions are lighter than that of the standard, and dilute the standard until its color is the same as that of the darkest of

FIG. 82.

Stead's chromometer.

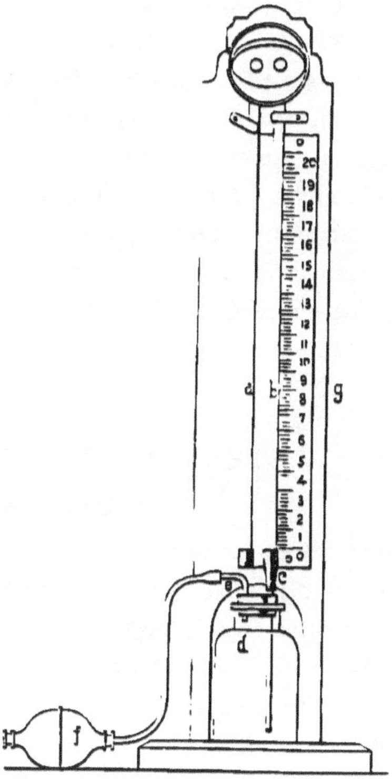

the samples, read the volume, and dilute it for the next darkest, and so on through the series. The percentage of carbon in each sample is then deduced from the equation $\frac{a}{b} \times 15 = x$, the letters having the meaning given above. They may also be compared by pouring into measuring-tubes until the colors appear equal when looked at from above. The carbon in this case is inversely as the length of the column. To facilitate the comparison, Stead (*loc. cit.*) has devised a very simple instrument based on this last principle. It consists (Fig. 82) of two parallel tubes of any convenient diameter fastened to a frame. The tube b is open at both ends, but is contracted at the point c. The contracted end passes through the stopper of the bottle *d*, and reaches almost to the bottom of the bottle. A small tube, *e*, which ends just below the stopper, is connected with a bulb syringe, *f*. The tube *a* is closed at the lower end, and contains a small, solid, glazed china cylinder, which rests on the bottom. A similar cylinder rests just above the contraction in the tube *b*, and the tubes are so arranged that the upper flat surfaces of the cylinders are on the same level, and exactly the same distance from the open tops of the tubes. The scale *g* is graduated in .02 up to .20 from the level of the upper surfaces of the cylinders to a point marked on the tube *a*, 10 inches (254 mm.) above. A solution of a standard steel containing .2 per cent. carbon, prepared as above, is placed in the bottle *d*, and a similar solution of a sample to be tested is poured into the tube *a* up to the mark. By squeezing the bulb *f* a column of the standard solution is forced up the tube *b*, and when, by looking into the mirror, placed at an angle of 45°, the color in the two columns appears equal in intensity, the percentage of carbon is read off on the scale opposite the top of the column in *b*. The alkaline solution is said to keep its color unaltered for a month when not exposed to direct sunlight.

DETERMINATION OF TITANIUM.

By Precipitation.

Only traces or very minute amounts of titanium are found in steel, but notable quantities exist in some kinds of pig-iron. As pointed out by Riley,* when pig-iron containing titanium is dissolved in HCl a portion of the titanium goes into solution, while the remainder is found with the insoluble matter. The insoluble portion, as noticed on page 86 *et seq.*, contains P_2O_5. It is a curious fact that while TiO_2 interferes with the deter-

---

* Jour. Chem. Soc., xvi. 387.

mination of P_2O_5 by its tendency to form upon evaporation to dryness an insoluble phospho-titanate, so P_2O_5 interferes with the determination of TiO_2 by partially preventing the precipitation of TiO_2 from its boiling sulphuric acid solution. The best method, therefore, for the determination of titanium is to proceed exactly as for the determination of phosphorus when titanium is present, as directed on page 86 *et seq.*, until the residue from the aqueous solution of the carbonate of sodium fusion is obtained. Dry this residue, transfer it to a large platinum crucible, preferably the one in which the carbonate of sodium fusion was made, burn the filter, add its ash to the residue, and fuse the whole with 15 or 20 times its weight of bisulphate of potassium. In fusing with bisulphate of potassium it is necessary to begin with a very low heat, and to raise the temperature very slowly and carefully to a low red heat, as the mixture has a strong tendency to boil over the top of the crucible whenever the temperature is increased too rapidly. When the lid of the crucible is raised, fumes of SO_3 should come off, and the fusion should be kept at this point for several hours, or until it is quite clear and the whole of the ferric oxide has been dissolved. Incline the crucible as far as possible on one side while the fused mass is still liquid, and allow it to cool in this position. The mass will harden in a cake on the side of the crucible, and can be readily detached without bending the sides of the crucible. Place the crucible and lid in a No. 4 beaker, and suspend in the beaker a little platinum wire-gauze basket containing the fused mass, as shown in Fig. 75, page 158. Pour into the beaker 50 c.c. of strong sulphurous acid water, and fill the beaker to the top of the fused mass in the basket with cold water. Under these circumstances the fused mass dissolves quite rapidly, as the concentrated solution falls to the bottom, and the iron is at the same time deoxidized. Without the basket, it is necessary to stir the liquid constantly, and the time occupied in dissolving the fused mass is much prolonged. When solution is

Insoluble phospho-titanate.

Separation from P_2O_5 by fusion with Na_2CO_3.

Fusion with $KHSO_4$.

Solution of the bisulphate in water.

complete, remove the basket, the crucible, and the lid from the beaker, wash them with a jet of cold water, and filter the solution into a No. 5 beaker. Add a filtered solution of 20 grammes acetate of sodium and one-sixth the volume of the solution of acetic acid, 1.04 sp. gr., to the filtered solution, and heat to boiling. The titanic acid is precipitated almost immediately in a flocculent condition, and quite free from iron. Boil for a few minutes, allow the titanic acid to settle, filter, wash with hot water containing a little acetic acid, dry, ignite, and weigh as TiO_2, which contains 60.00 per cent. Ti. Instead of fusing the residue from the aqueous solution of the carbonate of sodium fusion with bisulphate of potassium, the operation may be hastened as follows:

Treatment of Na_2CO_3 fusion with H_2SO_4.

Transfer the residue to the large crucible, as before directed, and fuse with 5 grammes of dry carbonate of sodium. Allow the crucible to cool, and then pour into it very gradually strong H_2SO_4. When the effervescence slackens, warm the crucible slightly, and continue the addition of H_2SO_4 and the careful application of heat until the fusion becomes liquid and the ferric oxide is all dissolved. Heat carefully until copious fumes of SO_3 are given off, allow the crucible to cool, and pour the contents, which should be just fluid when cold, into a beaker containing about 250 c.c. of cold water. Add to it 50 c.c. of a strong aqueous solution of sulphurous acid, or 2 or 3 c.c. of bisulphite of ammonium, filter if necessary, nearly neutralize by NH_4HO, allow it to stand until it is entirely decolorized, add 20 grammes acetate of sodium and one-sixth its volume of acetic acid, 1.04 sp. gr., and precipitate the TiO_2 as before.

By Volatilization.

Drown* suggested the method of determining titanium by volatilizing it in a current of chlorine gas. The details, with

---

* Trans. Inst. Min. Engineers, viii. 508.

some modifications, are as follows. Treat the sample exactly as directed for the determination of silicon, *by volatilization in a current of chlorine gas*, page 73 *et seq.*

To the filtrate from the silica, page 76, add a slight excess of NH_4HO. acidulate with acetic acid, boil, filter, wash, and ignite the precipitate. As this precipitate may contain a little ferric oxide (carried over mechanically as Fe_2Cl_6), phosphoric acid, tungstic acid, etc., fuse it with a little carbonate of sodium, dissolve the fused mass in hot water, filter, wash, dry, and ignite the residue, which will contain all the titanic acid as titanate of sodium, and any iron that may have been present as Fe_2O_3. The filtrate will contain the P_2O_5, etc. Fuse the ignited residue with a little carbonate of sodium, treat it in the crucible with strong H_2SO_4, as directed on page 174, and determine the TiO_2 in the manner there described.

DETERMINATION OF COPPER.

For the determination of copper the precipitate by H_2S, obtained in the determination of phosphorus, page 84, may be used, but in this case the precipitate must be filtered off before getting rid of the excess of H_2S, after which, if any additional precipitate of As_2S_3 is thrown down in the filtrate, it must be filtered off before proceeding with the determination of phosphorus. Dry and ignite the filter with the precipitate of CuS, etc., in a porcelain crucible, burn off all the carbon from the paper, allow the crucible to cool, and digest the precipitate at a gentle heat with HNO_3 and a few drops of H_2SO_4, keeping the crucible covered with a small watch-glass. When the CuS is entirely dissolved, remove the watch-glass and evaporate the solution until all the HNO_3 is expelled and fumes of SO_3 are given off. Allow it to cool, add enough water to dissolve all the $CuSO_4$, heating gently, if necessary, and wash the solution into a platinum crucible. Place the crucible in the little brass holder (Fig. 83), and attach the weighed platinum cylinder and connect the battery. The battery should consist of three Daniell's 2-quart cells, arranged as shown in Fig. 84. The connectors a, b pass through the sides of the box (which should be kept covered), and, the jars being

FIG. 83.

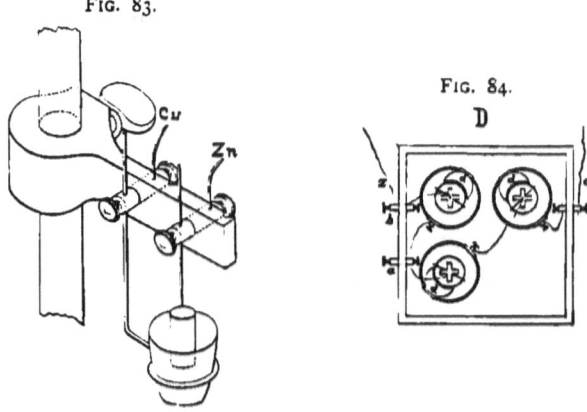

FIG. 84.

connected as shown in the sketch, by simply changing the wire from a to b, three cells are brought into action instead of two. For depositing the small amount of copper found in iron or steel, two cells furnish a sufficiently strong current. The platinum cylinder should weigh about 3 or 4 grammes; it is lowered into the liquid until it is just clear of the bottom of the crucible, and the crucible is covered with two small pieces of glass to prevent liquid being carried off by the escaping gas. It is much neater to deposit the copper on the cylinder than in the crucible, as it weighs less, is quite as easy to wash and dry, and there is no danger of any silica or dirt from the solution being covered by the deposited copper. When the copper is all deposited, usually in two or three hours, remove the cylinder, wash it with cold water, then with alcohol, dry at 100° C., cool, and weigh. The increase of weight is Cu.

In pig-irons containing titanium it is necessary to use a separate portion for the determination of copper. In steels, the solution in the flask from the determination of sulphur (page 61) may be used for the determination of copper. In this case, wash the contents of the flask into a No. 5 beaker, nearly neutralize with NH_4HO, add 5 c.c. HCl, heat the solution to boiling, and pass H_2S through the boiling solution for fifteen or twenty minutes, filter, wash with hot water, and treat the precipitate as directed above. In the case of pig-irons, however, it is best to dissolve in aqua regia, evaporate to dryness, redissolve in HCl, filter, reduce the iron in the filtrate with NH_4HSO_3, boil off the excess of SO_2, and precipitate by H_2S. Instead of using H_2S, the copper may be precipitated in a sulphuric acid solution by hyposulphite of sodium. Dissolve 5 grammes of the sample in a mixture of 150 c.c. H_2O and 12 c.c. strong H_2SO_4. Dilute to about 500 c.c. with hot water, heat to boiling, and add 3 grammes of hyposulphite of sodium dissolved in 10 c.c. hot water. Boil for a few minutes, allow the precipitate to settle, and filter and wash with hot water. Dry the precipitate, which besides the CuS will consist of the graphite, silica, etc.; transfer it to a small beaker, burn the filter, and add the ash to the main portion. Digest the whole with aqua regia, dilute with hot water, filter, wash, add a few drops of H_2SO_4, and evaporate until fumes of SO_3 are given off, cool, dissolve in water, transfer to the platinum crucible, and determine the copper by the battery as directed above.

Instead of determining the copper by electrolysis, it may be determined as subsulphide, Cu_2S, or as oxide, CuO. To determine it as Cu_2S, dilute the sulphate obtained by any of the methods mentioned above with water to about 50 c.c., add an excess of NH_4HO, filter from Fe_2O_3, etc., wash with ammoniacal water, and pass H_2S through the cold solution. Filter, wash with H_2S water, dry the filter and precipitate, transfer the latter to a small porcelain crucible, burn the filter, and add its ash to the precipitate. Add to the precipitate in the crucible about twice its volume of flowers of sulphur and ignite it in a current of hydrogen, as directed for the determination of manganese as MnS, page 108. Weigh as Cu_2S, which contains 79.82 per cent. Cu.

Determina-
tion as
CuO.   Instead of igniting the precipitate obtained above as Cu_2S, the copper may be determined as CuO, as follows : Dissolve the sulphide in aqua regia in a small porcelain dish, evaporate nearly dry, dilute with hot water, heat to boiling, and add a slight excess of a dilute solution of caustic soda or potassa. Filter on a small ashless filter, wash with hot water, dry, transfer the precipitate to a platinum crucible, burn the filter and add its ash to the precipitate, moisten the whole with HNO_3, and heat very gently at first, but increase the heat slowly to redness. Cool, and weigh as CuO, which contains 79.85 per cent. Cu.

DETERMINATION OF NICKEL AND COBALT.

Treat 3 grammes of the drillings exactly as directed for the determination of manganese by the acetate method, page 103 *et seq.* The precipitate by H_2S, page 106, will contain all the nickel and cobalt and a portion of the copper contained in the sample. Filter this precipitate on a small washed filter, wash with H_2S water containing a little free acetic acid, dry and ignite the filter and precipitate, and transfer them to a No. 1 beaker. Dissolve in HCl with a few drops of HNO_3, evaporate to dryness, redissolve in 10–20 drops of HCl, dilute with hot water to about 50 Separation
from Cu. c.c., heat the solution to boiling, and pass a stream of H_2S through the boiling solution to precipitate any copper that may be present. Filter, wash with hot water, evaporate the filtrate to dryness, moisten the dry mass with 4 or 5 drops of HCl, add 20 or 30 drops of cold water, and then 2 or 3 grammes of nitrite

of potassium (KNO_2)* dissolved in the least possible amount of water, and acidulated with acetic acid. The presence of cobalt is shown by the formation of a bright yellow precipitate of the double nitrite of cobalt and potassium, ($KNO_2)_6 Co_2(NO_2)_6 + Aq.$ Stir the solution, and allow it to stand twenty-four hours, with occasional stirring. Filter on a small ashless filter, wash with water containing acetate of potassium and a little free acetic acid, remove the filtrate which contains the nickel, and wash the precipitate and filter free from acetate of potassium with alcohol. Ignite the filter and precipitate carefully in a porcelain crucible, being careful not to raise the temperature high enough to fuse the precipitate; transfer to a very small beaker, and digest in HCl and a little $KClO_3$. Evaporate to dryness, redissolve in 3–5 drops of HCl, dilute with cold water, add about 1 gramme of acetate of sodium, and boil for an hour to precipitate the small amount of Fe_2O_3 and Al_2O_3 that is always present. Filter, to the filtrate add excess of NH_4HO and NH_4HS, and heat to boiling. As soon as the precipitate of CoS has settled, filter, wash with water containing a little NH_4HS, dry and ignite the precipitate and filter, in a platinum crucible. When all the carbon is burned, allow the crucible to cool, pour in a little HNO_3, heat carefully, and finally evaporate to dryness. Add a few drops of H_2SO_4, digest until the sulphide and oxide are changed to sulphate of cobalt, drive off the excess of H_2SO_4, heat finally to dull redness for a few moments, cool, and weigh as $CoSO_4$, which contains 38.05 per cent. of cobalt. Heat the filtrate from the double nitrate of cobalt and potassium to boiling, add a slight excess of caustic potassa, boil for a few minutes, filter, and wash the precipitate of oxide of nickel with hot water. Dissolve the precipitate on the filter with HCl, allow the solution to run back into the beaker in which the oxide of nickel was precipitated, and wash the filter with hot water. Evaporate

Margin notes: Separation of Ni and Co. Determination of Co. As $CoSO_4$. Determination of Ni.

---

* See page 47.

the solution to dryness, redissolve in 3–5 drops of HCl, dilute
with cold water to about 50 c.c., add about 1 gramme of acetate of sodium, boil for about an hour, filter off any Fe_2O_3 and
Al_2O_3, and wash with hot water. To the filtrate add an excess
of NH_4HS (a brown color shows the presence of nickel), acidulate with acetic acid, heat to boiling, and pass a current of
H_2S through the boiling solution until the precipitated sulphur
and sulphide of nickel agglomerate. Filter, wash with H_2S water,

As Ni_2S or
NiO. dry and ignite the filter, and precipitate. Allow the crucible
to cool, add a little carbonate of ammonium to the precipitate,
heat to dull redness, and volatilize any sulphuric acid that may
have been formed as sulphate of ammonium, cool, and weigh as
Ni_2S or NiO, which contains 78.55 per cent. of nickel. The
nickel and cobalt may also be weighed in the metallic condition by precipitating them by the battery from the ammoniacal

Determina-
tion by
electroly-
sis as Ni
+ Co. solutions of the sulphates. If it is not desired to separate them,
evaporate the filtrate from the precipitated sulphide of copper
with an excess of H_2SO_4 until the HCl is driven off and fumes
of SO_3 appear, allow the beaker to cool, add about 5 c.c. water,
then an excess of NH_4HO, filter if necessary, transfer to a platinum crucible, and precipitate on the small cylinder (Fig. 83,
page 176) in a strongly ammoniacal solution, using three cells of
the battery. Wash the cylinder with water, then with alcohol,
dry at 100° C., and weigh as Ni + Co. To determine the nickel
and cobalt separately, precipitate the cobalt as double nitrite of

Determina-
of Co. cobalt and potassium, treat the ignited cobalt precipitate with
an excess of H_2SO_4, heat until fumes of SO_3 are given off, dilute a little, make the solution strongly ammoniacal, and precipitate the cobalt as above directed. Precipitate the NiO, in

Determina-
of Ni. the filtrate from the cobalt, by KHO solution, filter, wash, dissolve on the filter in HCl, evaporate the solution with H_2SO_4,
add excess of NH_4HO, and precipitate the Ni by the battery
as above.

For the analysis of nickel steel, which contains from 2 to 3 per cent. of nickel, use 1 gramme of the sample, and, after obtaining the precipitate of NiS as described above, burn it with the filter in a porcelain crucible, allow it to cool, add a little pure powdered sulphur, and ignite in a stream of hydrogen gas as described on page 108. Weigh as Ni_2S.

DETERMINATION OF CHROMIUM AND ALU-
MINIUM.

Weigh 5 grammes of drillings into a flask of about 500 c.c. capacity, and pour in 20 c.c. strong HCl diluted with 3 or 4 times its bulk of water. Close the flask with a rubber stopper carrying a valve which is made as follows. Bore a hole through the centre of a rubber stopper, and insert a piece of glass tubing long enough to extend from the small end of the stopper to a distance of 1 inch (25 mm.) beyond the large end. Take a piece of heavy soft rubber tubing 2 inches (50 mm.) long, and cut a longitudinal slit in the middle about ½ inch (12 mm.) long. Close one end of the tube with a piece of glass rod ½ inch (12 mm.) long, and fit the other end over the glass tube in the stopper for a distance of ½ inch (12 mm.). This valve allows the gas to escape from the flask, but prevents air from entering it, so that the iron is not oxidized, but remains dissolved as ferrous chloride. Heat the dilute acid in the flask if necessary, and when the iron or steel is entirely dissolved remove the stopper, drop a small piece of Na_2CO_3 into the flask, and close it with a solid rubber stopper. Cool the flask with its contents as quickly as possible, and dilute the solution with cold water until the flask is three-fourths full. Add $BaCO_3$,* shaking constantly until the solution appears milky with the excess of $BaCO_3$. Loosen the stopper to allow the CO_2 to escape, shake

---

* See page 50.

the flask at intervals for several hours, and allow it to stand over-night, the stopper being pushed well into the neck. The precipitate will consist of all the Al_2O_3, Cr_2O_3, Fe_2O_3 from the solution, as well as P_2O_5, etc., and the graphite and silica that were insoluble in the dilute acid; it should be quite white from the excess of $BaCO_3$ added. Filter as rapidly as possible, wash with cold water, dissolve on the filter in dilute HCl, allow the solution to run into a small beaker, clean out the flask with the same acid, and wash it and the filter well with hot water. The insoluble matter left on

Cr and Al insoluble in HCl

the filter may contain some chromium and aluminium insoluble in dilute HCl, and usually in the form of slag, or in puddled iron as oxides. This may be ignited, treated with HFl and H_2SO_4, evaporated to dryness, fused with Na_2CO_3 and KNO_3, and the Cr_2O_3 and Al_2O_3 determined, or the solution of the fused mass in dilute HCl added to the filtrate from the insoluble matter. Boil this filtrate, add a slight excess of H_2SO_4 to precipitate all the barium, allow the precipitate of $BaSO_4$ to settle, filter, and wash with hot water.

Separation of Cr and Al from Fe by NH_4HS.

Evaporate the filtrate to get rid of the excess of acid, dilute with cold water, add sufficient tartaric or citric acid to hold the iron in solution, add an excess of NH_4HO, and to the solution, which should be perfectly clear, an excess of NH_4HS. Allow the precipitated FeS to settle, filter, wash with water containing NH_4HS, evaporate the filtrate to dryness in a large platinum crucible, heat to redness to volatilize the ammonium salts, and burn the carbon

Separation of Cr and Al by Dexter's method.

formed from the decomposition of the tartaric acid. Fuse the residue with 6 parts Na_2CO_3 and 1 part KNO_3, dissolve out in water,* transfer to a beaker, add 2 or 3 grammes $KClO_3$, rinse out the crucible with HCl, add it to the solution, and then add a slight excess of HCl. Evaporate to syrupy consistency on the water-bath, adding a little $KClO_3$ from time to time to decompose the excess of HCl.† Redissolve in water, add an excess of carbonate

---

* If the fusion or its concentrated aqueous solution is not yellowish in color there is no chromium present.

† Dexter, Pogg. Annal., 89, 142.

of ammonium to precipitate the Al_2O_3, and boil off all smell of ammonia. The alumina will be precipitated as phosphate, wholly or in part, if the sample contains phosphorus, while the chromium is in solution as chromate of potassium or sodium. Filter, wash with hot water, reserve the filtrate and washings, redissolve the precipitate on the filter in HCl, allowing the solution to run into a small beaker, evaporate to dryness to render any silica insoluble, redissolve in HCl, filter, to the filtrate add excess of NH_4HO and NH_4HS, boil, filter on a small ashless filter, wash with hot water, ignite, and weigh as Al_2O_3, which contains 53.01 per cent. Al. Acidulate the solution containing the chromium with HCl, heat to decompose the excess of $KClO_3$, add a little alcohol, and evaporate to dryness to render silica insoluble. The chromium is now in the condition of Cr_2O_3; redissolve in HCl, dilute, filter off any silica that may be present, to the filtrate add an excess of NH_4HO, boil, filter on a small ashless filter, wash well with hot water, ignite, and weigh as Cr_2O_3, which contains 68.48 per cent. of chromium. As the precipitates of Al_2O_3 and Cr_2O_3 may both contain P_2O_5, it is necessary to fuse each of them, after weighing, with a little Na_2CO_3, dissolve in water, filter, acidulate with HNO_3, and determine the P_2O_5 by the molybdate method, or acidulate with HCl, add a little citric acid and magnesium mixture, and determine the P_2O_5 as $Mg_2P_2O_7$. Calculate the amount of P_2O_5, subtract its weight from that of the Al_2O_3 and Cr_2O_3 respectively, and calculate the remainder to Al and Cr, as directed above.

Determination of Al.

Determination of Cr.

Separation of Al_2O_3 or Cr_2O_3 from any P_2O_5

Instead of separating the aluminium and chromium by HCl and $KClO_3$, as directed above, the better method suggested by Genth * may be used, which is as follows: Dissolve in water the fusion of the residue from the volatilization of the ammonium salts and the decomposition of the tartaric acid, transfer it to a platinum dish, add a few grammes of nitrate of ammonium, and evaporate down on a water-bath until the solution is syrupy,

Separation of Al_2O_3 and Cr_2O_3 by Genth's method.

---

* *Chem. News, vi. 32.*

adding NH_4NO_3 from time to time until the addition fails to produce any further evolution of NH_4HO from the solution. Add a little carbonate of ammonium towards the end of the operation, and when the solution is syrupy and smells very faintly of ammonia, dilute and filter from the Al_2O_3, which treat as directed above. To the filtrate add a strong aqueous solution of sulphurous acid, boil off the excess of SO_2, and add NH_4HO to alkaline reaction. Boil, filter, wash, ignite, and weigh the Cr_2O_3, which must be tested for P_2O_5 as above directed. To

Determination of Cr alone. determine chromium alone in iron or steel, treat 5 grammes with HCl, precipitate by $BaCO_3$, filter, and wash the insoluble matter and precipitate, as directed above. Place a clean beaker under the funnel, pierce the filter, and wash the contents into the beaker. Clean the flask and filter with hot dilute HCl, and wash them thoroughly with hot water, allowing all the acid and washings to run into the beaker. Add enough HCl to dissolve the soluble part of the precipitate (Fe_2O_3, Cr_2O_3, Al_2O_3, $BaCO_3$), dilute, boil, and precipitate the Cr_2O_3, etc., with NH_4HO. Boil off all smell of ammonia, allow the precipitate to settle, and wash well with hot water. Dry, and transfer the precipitate to a platinum crucible, carefully separating it from the filter, ignite the filter, and add its ashes to the precipitate in the crucible. Before heating the precipitate, add to it in the crucible 3–6 grammes Na_2CO_3 and ½ gramme KNO_3 (with pig-irons it is necessary to add 2–3 grammes KNO_3 to oxidize the graphite), and mix thoroughly. Heat gradually to fusion, and finally raise the heat until all the KNO_3 is decomposed. Cool, treat the fused mass with hot water, filter from Fe_2O_3, wash well with hot water, acidulate the filtrate with HCl, and evaporate to dryness with a little alcohol. Redissolve in HCl, dilute, filter from SiO_2, and in the filtrate precipitate the Cr_2O_3 by NH_4HO. Filter, wash thoroughly, dry, ignite, and weigh as Cr_2O_3. This precipitate may contain also some Al_2O_3 and P_2O_5, which must be separated in very accurate determinations, and the amounts subtracted from the first weight of Cr_2O_3.

Stead's Method.*

Weigh off 6–12 or 24 grammes steel, place in 600 c.c. beaker, cover with watch-glass, dissolve it in HCl (strong), evaporate to dryness, redissolve in HCl, filter into 1000 c.c. beaker through an ashless filter, wash filter containing silica, nearly neutralize the filtrate with dilute ammonia, and boil filtrate, which should measure about 500 to 600 c.c. Add to the solution 1 or 2 c.c. of saturated solution of ammonium phosphate, and then a large excess of sodium hyposulphite, boil till all SO_2 has passed off (half an hour's boiling should be sufficient); just before filtering add 20 c.c. of a saturated solution of ammonium acetate, stir to mix, and filter through an ashless filter, wash precipitate and filter 5 or 6 times, add to the beaker from which the solution and precipitate had been formed 10 c.c. HCl, heat to boiling, re-move the vessel containing the filtrate, and place instead of it under the funnel a platinum dish, and pour over the filter the boiling acid. Rinse out the beaker and wash all soluble mat-ter on the filter with a fine jet, evaporate the solution to dry-ness in the platinum dish, and heat, to drive off excess of acid, on the sand-bath to a temperature of 300° or 400° F.

Add from 2 to 5 grammes pure sodium hydrate made from sodium free from alumina and about 2 c.c. water. Heat gently over a rose-burner for ten minutes, maintaining the mass in a fluid state all the time. Cool and add water, and boil till solu-tion is complete. Make the bulk of the solution to 300 c.c. and note the temperature exactly. Shake well and filter through an ashless filter. Measure off 250 c.c. at the original temperature, equal to 5–10 or 20 grammes steel. If any yellow tint is ob- Indication servable chromium may be present. In such a case the phos- of chro-phate of alumina must be neutralized with HCl and precipitated mium. by ammonium carbonate, taking care to boil the solution well to free from excess of ammonia before filtering. Filter off

---

* Prepared by Mr. J. E. Stead, of Middlesboro', England, for this volume.

through an ashless filter, dry, burn off, and weigh, dissolve precipitate in HCl and determine P_2O_5 in it, and deduct the weight found from the weight of the original precipitate. If chromium is absent, neutralize the solution with HCl as before described, boil and add excess of sodium hyposulphite, and boil for half an hour, filter off precipitate, burn, and weigh as pure aluminium phosphate, which contains 22.18 per cent. of aluminium.

Carnot's Method.*

M. Carnot states that the method is very similar to that published by Mr. J. E. Stead in the Journal of the Society of Chemical Industry, 1889, page 965, but that he has used and taught it at the École des Mines for eight years. It is founded on the reaction that he pointed out in 1881, that aluminium is precipitated as the neutral phosphate from a boiling solution faintly acid with acetic acid. The precipitation succeeds equally well when the solution contains iron, if the ferric salt has been previously reduced to ferrous by hyposulphite of soda.

Treat 10 grammes of the iron or steel in a platinum dish covered with a piece of platinum-foil with hydrochloric acid, and when solution is complete, dilute and filter into a flask, washing the carbon, silica, etc., on the filter thoroughly with distilled water. Neutralize the solution with ammonia and carbonate of soda, but see that no permanent precipitate is formed, then add a little hyposulphite of soda, and, when the liquid at first violet becomes colorless, 2 or 3 c.c. of a saturated solution of phosphate of soda and 5 or 6 grammes of acetate of soda dissolved in a little water. Boil the solution about three-quarters of an hour, or until it no longer smells of sulphurous acid. Filter, and wash the precipitate of phosphate of alumina, mixed with a little silica and ferric phosphate, with boiling water. Treat the precipitate on the filter with hot dilute hydrochloric acid, allow the solution to run into a platinum dish, evaporate to dryness,

---

* A. Carnot, Moniteur Scientifique, 1891, p. 14.

and heat at $100°$ for an hour to render the silica insoluble. Dissolve in hot dilute hydrochloric acid, filter from the silica, dilute to about 100 c.c. with cold water, neutralize as before, add a little hyposulphite in the cold, then a mixture of 2 grammes of hyposulphite and 2 grammes of acetate of soda, wash, and weigh as $AlPO_4$, which contains 22.18 per cent. of aluminium.

Volumetric Method for Chromium.

Galbraith [*] has suggested a rapid method for the determination of chromium when it is present in appreciable amounts, as in chrome steel or chrome pig-iron. Dissolve 1–3 grammes of the sample in dilute H_2SO_4 (1 part H_2SO_4 and 6 parts water), add permanganate of potassium in crystals until the iron is all oxidized and the liquid is quite red in color, then add as much more to oxidize the chromium to CrO_3. Heat the solution to boiling, and boil until the permanganate is all decomposed and there remains a precipitate of oxide of manganese. Filter, wash with hot water, to the filtrate add a measured volume of standardized ferrous sulphate, and determine the excess of ferrous sulphate by a standard solution of permanganate. From the amount of ferrous sulphate oxidized by the CrO_3 calculate the amount of Cr. The reaction is $6FeSO_4 + 2CrO_3 + 6H_2SO_4 = 3Fe_2(SO_4)_3 + Cr_2(SO_4)_3 + 6H_2O$, or 1 equivalent of chromic acid will oxidize 3 equivalents of ferrous sulphate to ferric sulphate. Therefore, if the value of the permanganate is known in metallic iron, and consequently the value of the ferrous sulphate (it being standardized by the permanganate) in metallic iron, the amount of chromium is calculated as follows: 3 equiv. $Fe = 168$: 1 equiv. $Cr = 52.14$ :: the value of the ferrous sulphate oxidized by the CrO_3 in Fe : its value in Cr; or multiply the value of the ferrous sulphate oxidized, in Fe, by $\frac{52.14}{168} = .3103$. The titration is effected in the manner directed for the determination of iron in iron ores.

---

[*] Chem. News, xxxv. 151.

DETERMINATION OF ARSENIC.

By Precipitation with H₂S.

When iron or steel is dissolved in dilute HCl, the arsenic which may be present, according to Wöhler, is not evolved as AsH_3, but is dissolved as $AsCl_5$, and, unless the solution is very acid, upon heating it a white flocculent precipitate of ferric arseniate is formed. It is, therefore, possible to use the solution in the flask from the determination of sulphur in steel by evolution (page 59 *et seq.*) for the estimation of arsenic. If this is not available in the case of steel, or in the case of pig-iron when the residue must be treated for S, dissolve 10 grammes of drillings in a flask in 40 c.c. HCl and 100 c.c. water, dilute with hot water to 750 c.c. and pass a current of H_2S for thirty minutes, fill the flask to the neck with water, cover it with a watch-glass, and stand it in a warm place overnight. When the precipitate has settled and the solution smells but faintly of H_2S, filter, preferably on a Gooch crucible, and wash with cold water. Transfer the filter or asbestos felt, with the precipitate, to a small beaker, pour about 10–20 c.c. KHS solution into the flask, to dissolve any precipitate that may have adhered to the sides, and add it to the precipitate in the beaker. Digest for some time at a gentle heat, filter, wash with water containing a little KHS, acidulate the filtrate slightly with HCl, and stand it in a warm place until the smell of H_2S has nearly disappeared. Filter on a Gooch crucible, wash with water, dry the precipitate and felt (or wash with alcohol), extract with disulphide of carbon, transfer the felt and precipitate to a small beaker, and digest with HCl and $KClO_3$. Filter, wash with as little water as possible, add a small crystal of tartaric acid and a slight excess of NH_4HO, and cool the solution. If the solution remains clear, as it will in the absence of tin, add 5 c.c. of magnesium mixture and ½ the volume of the solution of NH_4HO. Stir the solution vigorously from time to time, keeping it cool by immersing the beaker in ice-water, and allow it to stand twelve hours. Filter on a Gooch crucible, wash the precipitate of $Mg_2(NH_4)_2As_2O_8 + Aq$ with the ammonia-water containing nitrate of ammonium, used for washing the $Mg_2(NH_4)_2P_2O_8$ (page 85), dry at 103° C. for half an hour, then increase the heat very gradually to redness, and ignite strongly for a few minutes. Weigh as $Mg_2As_2O_7$, which contains 48.30 per cent. of As. If the sample contains tin, the solution obtained above will become cloudy upon the addition of NH_4HO. In this case pass a current of H_2S through the ammoniacal solution until the precipitated oxide of tin is dissolved, then add magnesium mixture and ammonia, and precipitate the arsenic as directed above.

When tin is present.

By Distillation.

Lundin * has suggested the following method of determining arsenic, which gives very good results : Dissolve 10 grammes of drillings in a large beaker in HNO_3, 1.2 sp. gr., transfer the solution to a platinum or porcelain dish, add 50 c.c. H_2SO_4, and evaporate down until copious fumes of sulphuric acid are given off. Cool the dish, add 50 c.c. of water, and evaporate again until the excess of H_2SO_4 is driven off, and the ferric sulphate is so dry that it can be readily transferred to a flask of about 500 c.c. capacity. Add to the mass in the flask 15 grammes finely-powdered ferrous sulphate, pour in 150 c.c. strong HCl, and close the flask with a stopper carrying a tube bent twice at right angles and connected by a rubber tube with a 50 c.c. pipette, the point of which dips about ½ inch (12 mm.) into 300 c.c. of water in a beaker, as shown in Fig. 85. Heat the liquid in the flask gradually until it boils, and continue the distillation until the wide part of the burette becomes heated. The arsenic acid in the solution is reduced by the ferrous sulphate, and, in the strong hydrochloric acid solution, is distilled over

Reduction to AsCl₃.

---

* Jern-Kontorets Annaler, 1883, p. 360; Chem. News, li. 115.

as AsCl$_3$. About half an hour is required to effect this, and when the wide part of the pipette is heated remove the light,

FIG. 85.

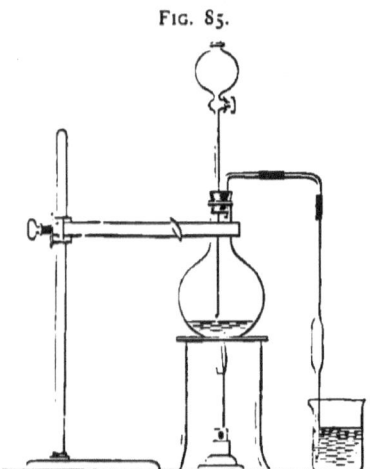

disconnect the pipette, heat the solution in the beaker to about 70° C., and pass a rapid current of H$_2$S through it until it is completely saturated. Remove the excess of H$_2$S by a current of CO$_2$, and when the solution smells very faintly of H$_2$S, filter off the yellow precipitate of As$_2$S$_3$ in a Gooch crucible, or on a counterpoised filter,* wash with water, then with alcohol, then with pure disulphide of carbon, dry at 100° C., and weigh as As$_2$S$_3$, which contains 60.93 per cent. of As.

DETERMINATION OF ANTIMONY.

Antimony is a very rare constituent of iron or steel, but very minute amounts have been found in spiegel. To determine antimony, treat 10 grammes of the drillings as directed for the determination of arsenic by precipitation with H$_2$S, page 188. Evaporate off the excess of NH$_4$HO from the filtrate from the Mg$_2$(NH$_4$)$_2$As$_2$O$_8$ + Aq, add a slight excess of HCl, dilute to about 300 c.c. with water, and pass a current of H$_2$S through the solution. Expel the excess of H$_2$S by a current of CO$_2$, filter on a very small ashless filter, or on a disk of paper on the bottom of a Gooch crucible, wash with water, and dry the precipitate and filter. Separate the precipitate, and treat the filter in a small weighed porcelain crucible with *fuming* HNO$_3$.

---

* See page 27.

When it is dissolved, evaporate down, add more HNO_3 if necessary, evaporate to dryness, and heat to destroy the organic matter. When the residue in the crucible is quite white, allow it to cool, add the precipitate, and treat it with *fuming* HNO_3, evaporate to dryness, and finally ignite to drive off the sulphuric acid formed, cool, and weigh as Sb_2O_4, which contains 78.95 per cent. Sb. When tin is present, and the arsenic has been precipitated from a sulphide of ammonium solution,* acidulate the filtrate from the precipitate of $Mg_2(NH_4)_2As_2O_8 - Aq$ with HCl, and when the solution smells but faintly of H_2S, filter on a small ashless filter, wash with water, alcohol, and finally with disulphide of carbon, dry the precipitate and filter, and treat them with fuming HNO_3, evaporate down, but not to dryness, add an excess of dry Na_2CO_3, transfer the mass to a silver crucible, add some pure fused NaHO, and fuse the whole for some minutes. Allow the crucible to cool, dissolve the fused mass in water, transfer it to a beaker, and add $\frac{1}{3}$ the volume of alcohol, .83 sp. gr. Stir several times, and allow the precipitate of metantimonate of sodium to settle, filter, and wash with a solution consisting of equal volumes of alcohol and water containing a little Na_2CO_3 solution. The filtrate contains the tin, or tin and arsenic. Dissolve the precipitate of metantimonate of sodium on the filter in HCl containing tartaric acid, allow the solution and washings to run into a small beaker, dilute to about 300 c.c., and precipitate the sulphide of antimony by H_2S. Filter off, and determine the antimony as Sb_2O_4 as above directed.

Separation from tin.

DETERMINATION OF TIN.

Tin is a most unusual constituent of steel or iron, but has been found in the former in cases where scrap from tinned iron,

---

* The precipitated sulphides from acidulated KHS solution may be treated directly in this way without precipitating the arsenic as $Mg_2(NH_4)_2As_2O_8 + Aq$.

from which the tin has been removed by a chemical process, has been melted in the open-hearth furnace as a portion of the charge. Proceed as in the determination of antimony, until the sulphides from the acidulation of the KHS solution have been filtered on a small ashless filter and washed thoroughly with a solution of acetate of ammonium made slightly acid with acetic acid. It is not possible to wash the precipitate with water, as the sulphide of tin has a strong tendency, under these circumstances, to pass through the filter. Dry the precipitate and filter, transfer the precipitate to a weighed porcelain crucible, burn the filter, and add its ash to the precipitate, add a little sulphur, and ignite in a current of H_2S, as directed for the determination of manganese as MnS, page 108. Any arsenic present will be volatilized, but it is not possible to weigh the tin as sulphide, as its composition is not constant. Heat the crucible carefully, and roast the precipitate with access of air, heat it strongly two or three times with carbonate of ammonium to volatilize any sulphuric acid that may have been formed, cool, and weigh as SnO_2, which contains 78.81 per cent. Sn.

Ignition in H_2S volatilizes As.

DETERMINATION OF TUNGSTEN.

Dissolve 1 to 10 grammes of the drillings in HNO_3, 1.2 sp. gr., evaporate to dryness in the air-bath, redissolve in HCl, dilute slightly, and boil for some time. The tungstic acid is deposited as a yellowish powder. Dilute, filter, wash with hot water containing a little HCl, and finally with alcohol and water. The precipitate consists of WO_3 mixed with more or less SiO_2, graphite, and perhaps a little Fe_2O_3, TiO_2, etc. Dry and ignite the filter and precipitate, and burn off the carbon. Allow the crucible to cool, moisten the precipitate with water, add a little H_2SO_4 and an excess of HFl. Evaporate to dryness under a hood, and ignite to drive off the H_2SO_4. Fuse the residue with 5 times its weight of Na_2CO_3, allow it to cool, dissolve in water, filter from any insoluble matter, and wash with water containing a little Na_2CO_3. The filtrate contains all the tungsten, as tungstate of sodium. Nearly neutralize with HNO_3, and boil off the CO_2, allow the solution to cool slightly, and add a faint but distinct excess of HNO_3. Add an excess of mercurous nitrate,* and then mercuric oxide diffused in water,* until the free acid is all neutralized. The tungsten is all precipitated as mercurous tungstate, and can be washed perfectly free from all sodium salts with hot water. The method of neutralizing the solution with mercuric oxide is due to Dr. Gibbs,† and makes of a very uncertain method an extremely accurate one. Allow the precipitate to settle, filter on an ashless filter, wash with hot water, and dry the filter and precipitate. Separate the precipitate from the filter, burn the filter in a platinum crucible, add the precipitate, and heat it under a hood with a good draft, increasing the heat gradually to a bright red. The mercury volatilizes, and there remains only WO_3. Cool, and weigh as WO_3, which contains 79.31 per cent. of W.

Precipitation as mercurous tungstate

Schöffer ‡ has suggested the method of dissolving the steel or iron in the double chloride of copper and ammonium. The tungsten remains in the insoluble matter, which he filters off, ignites, fuses with Na_2CO_3, and finally precipitates as WO_3 with mercurous nitrate. This method has no advantage over the one first given, and has the disadvantage of contaminating the WO_3 with P_2O_5, and also with any chromium and arsenic which may be in the sample.

DETERMINATION OF VANADIUM.

Vanadium is occasionally found in pig-iron, and may be determined with great accuracy by the following method: Treat 5

---

* See page 56.   † Amer. Chem. Jour., v. 373.   ‡ Chem. News, xli. 31

grammes of the drillings with 50 c.c. HNO_3, 1.2 sp. gr., in a No. 4 beaker. When all action has ceased, transfer the liquid to a porcelain dish, evaporate to dryness, and heat at a gradually increasing temperature over a Bunsen burner until the nitrates are nearly all decomposed and the mass separates easily from the bottom and sides of the dish. Transfer the cooled mass to a porcelain or agate mortar, and grind it thoroughly with 30 grammes of dry Na_2CO_3 and 3 grammes of $NaNO_3$. Transfer to a large platinum crucible, and fuse well for about an hour at a high temperature. Run the fused mass well up on the sides of the crucible, allow it to cool, dissolve in hot water, and filter. Dilute the filtrate to about 600 c.c., and add nitric acid carefully to get rid of the carbonic acid. Boil off the latter, but be careful to keep the solution always slightly alkaline. Add nitric acid drop by drop until the solution is just acid, then add a few drops of carbonate of sodium solution to render the solution faintly but decidedly alkaline, boil for a few minutes, and filter. To the filtrate add a few drops of nitric acid to make it faintly acid, when the appearance of a yellowish coloration is an indication of the presence of vanadic acid. Add to the solution a few c.c. of mercurous nitrate,* and then an excess of mercuric oxide in water,* to render the solution neutral† and insure the complete precipitation of all the mercurous vanadate. With the mercurous vanadate are precipitated also all the phosphoric, chromic, tungstic, and molybdic acids as mercurous salts. Heat to boiling, filter, and wash the precipitate. Dry it, separate the paper, burn it in a platinum crucible, add the precipitate, heat carefully to expel the mercury, and finally heat to full redness. Fuse the brownish-red mass remaining in the crucible with a small amount of Na_2CO_3 and a pinch of $NaNO_3$, dissolve the cooled mass in a small amount of water, and filter into a small beaker. Add to the solution pure chloride of ammonium in excess (about 3.5 grammes to each 10 c.c. of solution),

Marginal notes:

Indication of V_2O_5.

Precipitation as mercurous vanadate.

---

* See page 56.   † Am. Chem. Jour., v. 373.

and allow it to stand for some time, stirring occasionally. Vana-
date of ammonium, insoluble in a saturated solution of chloride
of ammonium, separates out as a white powder. It is necessary
to keep the solution decidedly alkaline, and a drop or two of am-
monia must be added from time to time. The appearance of the
faintest yellowish tint to the solution is evidence that the solution
has become slightly acid, and this must be corrected or the result
will be too low. Filter on a small ashless filter, wash first with a
saturated solution of chloride of ammonium containing a drop or
two of ammonia, and then with alcohol. Dry, ignite, moisten with
a drop or two of nitric acid, ignite, and weigh as V_2O_5, which
contains 56.22 per cent. of vanadium.

Precipitation as vanadate of ammonium.

Precautions.

DETERMINATION OF NITROGEN.

This method is based on the reaction by which the nitrogen
in iron or steel is converted into ammonia by HCl during the
solution of the steel in this reagent.

It was first published by A. H. Allen,[*] with many interest-
ing details and results. The modifications of the method as
described by Mr. Allen are by Prof. J. W. Langley,[†] of Pitts-
burg, and consist essentially in the use of caustic soda freed from
nitrates and nitrites by the copper-zinc couple and subsequent
distillation of all ammonia formed, and in a few details of
manipulation.

The reagents required are:

Hydrochloric Acid of 1.1 sp. gr., free from Ammonia, which
may be prepared by distilling pure hydrochloric acid gas into
distilled water free from ammonia. To do this, take a large flask
fitted with a rubber stopper carrying a separatory funnel-tube
and an evolution-tube, fill it half-full of strong hydrochloric

Pure HCl.

---

[*] Chem. News, xli. 231.   [†] Communicated to the author.

acid, connect the evolution-tube with a wash-bottle connected with a bottle containing the distilled water. Admit strong sulphuric acid free from nitrous acid to the flask through the funnel-tube, apply heat as required, and distil the gas into the prepared water.

Test the acid by admitting some of it into the distilling apparatus, described farther on, and distilling it from an excess of pure caustic soda, or determine the amount of ammonia in a portion of hydrochloric acid of 1.1 sp. gr., and use the amount found as a correction.

Caustic soda.   *Solution of Caustic Soda,* made by dissolving 300 grammes of fused caustic soda in 500 c.c. of water, and digesting it for twenty-four hours at 50° C. on a copper-zinc couple, made, as described by Gladstone & Tribe, as follows: Place 25–30 grammes of thin sheet zinc in a flask and cover with a moderately-concentrated, slightly warm solution of sulphate of copper. A thick spongy coating of copper will be deposited on the zinc. Pour off the solution in about ten minutes and wash thoroughly with cold distilled water.

Nessler reagent.   *Nessler Reagent.* Dissolve 35 grammes of iodide of potassium in a small quantity of distilled water, and add a strong solution of bichloride of mercury little by little, shaking after each addition, until the red precipitate formed dissolves. Finally the precipitate formed will fail to dissolve, then stop the addition of the mercury salt and filter. Add to the filtrate 120 grammes of caustic soda dissolved in a small amount of water, and dilute until the entire solution measures 1 litre. Add to this 5 c.c. of saturated aqueous solution of bichloride of mercury, mix thoroughly, allow the precipitate formed to settle, and decant or siphon off the clear liquid into a glass-stoppered bottle.

Standard NH_4Cl solution.   *Standard Ammonia Solution.* Dissolve 0.0382 gramme of chloride of ammonium in 1 litre of water. One c.c. of this solution will equal 0.01 milligramme of nitrogen.

Distilled Water free from Ammonia. If the ordinary distilled water contains ammonia, redistil it, reject the first portions coming over, and use the subsequent portions, which will be found free from ammonia. Several glass cylinders of colorless glass of about 160 c.c. capacity are also required. Ammonia-free distilled water.

The best form of distilling apparatus consists of an Erlenmeyer flask of about 1500 c.c. capacity, with a rubber stopper, carrying a separatory funnel-tube and an evolution-tube, the latter connected with a condensing-tube through which a constant stream of cold water runs. The inside tube, where it issues from the condenser, should be sufficiently high to dip into one of the glass cylinders placed on the working-table. Distilling apparatus.

The determination of nitrogen is made as follows: Place 30 c.c. of the caustic soda, which has been treated with the copper-zinc couple, in the Erlenmeyer flask, add 500 c.c. of water, and distil until the distillate gives no reaction with the Nessler reagent. While this part of the operation is in progress, dissolve 3 grammes of the carefully-washed drillings in 30 c.c. of the prepared hydrochloric acid, using heat if necessary. Transfer the solution to the bulb of the separatory funnel-tube, and when the soda solution is free from ammonia drop the ferrous chloride solution into the boiling solution in the flask, very slowly. The ferrous hydrate formed is apt to stick to the bottom and sides of the flask and cause it to break. When about 50 c.c. of water has been collected in the cylinder, remove it and substitute another cylinder. Dilute the distillate in the cylinder to 100 c.c. with the special distilled water, and add 1½ c.c. of Nessler reagent. Take another cylinder, pour into it 100 c.c. of the special distilled water, add 1 c.c. of the chloride of ammonium solution and 1½ c.c. of the Nessler reagent. Compare the colors in the two cylinders, and add ammonia solution to the contents of the latter cylinder until the colors of the solutions in the two cylinders correspond after standing about ten minutes. When about 100 c.c. has distilled into the second cylinder, replace it and test it as before. Continue the distillation until Details of the method.

the water comes over free from ammonia, then add together the number of c.c. of ammonia solution used, divide the sum by three, and each 0.01 milligramme will be 0.001 per cent. of nitrogen in the steel.

DETERMINATION OF IRON.

The combined carbon in steel and iron interferes with a direct determination of the amount of metallic iron by solution of the drillings in hydrochloric or sulphuric acid and direct titration. It is always necessary to oxidize the iron and carbonaceous matter in the solution, and the process may be carried out as follows:

By solution.   Dissolve .5 gramme of the drillings in a small flask, as described for the determination of iron in iron ores, in HCl, add $KClO_3$ in small crystals until the iron is all oxidized and an excess of $KClO_3$ is present, boil until all the yellow fumes have disappeared, and then proceed as in the determination of iron in iron ores, page 201. Instead of chlorate of potassium, permanganate of potassium or chromic acid may be used to oxidize the iron and destroy the carbonaceous matter. In pig-irons the most satisfactory
By fusion.   method is to fuse .5 gramme of the borings in a large platinum crucible with 10 grammes Na_2CO_3 and 2 grammes KNO_3, dissolve in hot water, transfer to a small beaker, allow the ferric oxide to settle, decant on a small filter, and wash several times by decantation. After the last decantation, remove the beaker containing the filtrate and place the beaker containing the ferric oxide under the funnel. Dissolve any adhering oxide in the crucible with HCl, dilute slightly, and pour it on the filter to dissolve the small amount of oxide, allowing the solution to run into the beaker. Wash the filter if necessary, add more HCl to the solution in the beaker, evaporate down, transfer to a small flask, deoxidize, and titrate as before. In the case of puddled iron, it is necessary to subtract the iron in the "slag and oxides" from the total iron obtained as above to get the amount of *metallic iron* in the sample.

METHODS FOR THE ANALYSIS

OF

IRON ORES.

A FEW words in regard to the proper method of taking samples of iron ores may not be amiss, for unless the sample truly represents the lot from which it is taken, the subsequent work of the analyst is useless, if not misleading. Method of sampling iron ores.

In drawing a sample, note carefully the relative amounts of fine ore and lumps in the lot to be sampled, and see that this proportion be observed in the whole amount taken. A small trowel may be used for taking the fine ore, and only about a teaspoonful should be picked up at one time. In taking pieces from the lumps, it will never do to merely chip the outside, but each lump as selected should be broken and chippings taken from both the inside and the outside, and no piece taken should be larger than a cherry. In sampling from cars or wagons these points should be observed in each car or wagon, for it is rarely the case that the ore even from one mine is so uniform as to render this precaution unnecessary. In some cases the lumps are covered with dirt or gangue, making the outside of the lump poorer in iron than the inside, and on the other hand the lumps are merely masses of dirt coated with ore. Then the fine stuff may be much richer than the lumps, or it may be merely dirt or gangue, while it almost always contains more hygroscopic water than the lumps. The sample should be taken in tin cans with close-fitting lids, and the amount should be proportioned to the size of the lot sampled. Two pounds to ten tons is a good rule for large lots. Preserving samples.

DETERMINATION OF HYGROSCOPIC WATER.

Break the sample down quickly to about pea size, mix thoroughly in a large glazed earthenware or metal dish, and weigh out from ½ to 1 kilo. into a copper box about 4½ inches (114 mm.) long, 3¾ inches (95 mm.) wide, and 1½ inches (38 mm.) deep, and dry in a water- or air-bath at 100° C. for at least twelve hours, or until it ceases to lose weight. Fig. 86 shows a convenient form

Fig. 86.

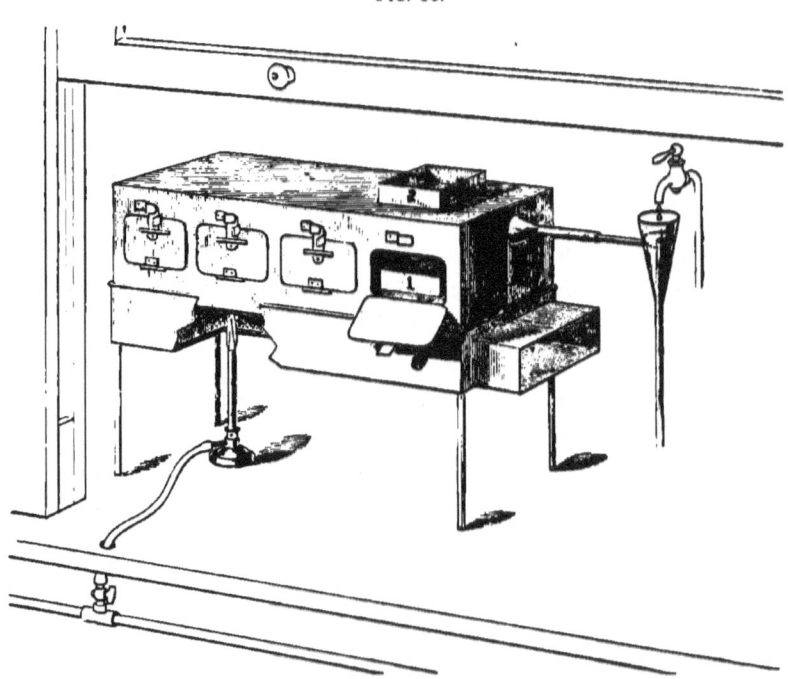

of water-bath. The boxes are numbered, and each one is provided with a counterpoise stamped with the same number as the box, to facilitate the weighing. When a supply of water is not available to run the constant level shown in Fig. 86, the device, on the principle of Marriott's flask, as shown in Fig. 77, page 163,

Device for constant level.

may be used. The position of the end *b* of the tube *a* fixes the level of the water in the bath.

A balance sensitive to .1 gramme is sufficiently accurate for weighing these samples. The loss of weight in grammes divided by 5, when ½ kilo. of ore was originally used, gives the percentage of hygroscopic water in the sample. Grind the dried sample very fine, mix it well, heat as much of it as may be required for the analysis, in the water-bath, and put it while still hot into a perfectly dry, glass-stoppered bottle.

Balance for weighing samples.

DETERMINATION OF TOTAL IRON.

Very few iron ores are completely decomposed by hydrochloric acid, the insoluble residue usually containing more or less iron, as silicate, titaniferous iron, etc. The disregard of this fact may occasion grave errors in the determination of iron, and, unless a previous examination has shown the absence of iron in the insoluble residue, it is best to proceed as follows: Weigh 1 gramme of the finely-ground sample into a No. 1 beaker, add 10 c.c. HCl, and digest it on the sand-bath until the residue appears quite white and flotant, or until the acid appears to have no further action. When the ore contains carbonaceous matter, add a little $KClO_3$. Wash off the watch-glass with a fine jet of water, remove it, and evaporate to dryness in the air-bath. Redissolve in about 5 c.c. HCl, dilute with 10 c.c. water, allow to settle, and decant the clear liquid into a flask (B, Fig. 88) of about 50 to 75 c.c. capacity. Transfer the residue to a small filter, fitted in a funnel placed in the neck of the flask, with as little water as possible, and wash with cold water from a fine jet. Transfer the filter to a small platinum crucible, burn it off, allow the crucible to cool, and pour on the residue 20 or 30 drops of H_2SO_4 and about twice

Residue insoluble in HCl.

Treatment of the ore.

Treatment of the insoluble residue by H_2SO_4 and HFl.

as much HFl. Heat carefully, and, if the residue is dissolved, evaporate off the HFl, allow the liquid to cool, and dilute slightly, when it will be ready to add to the solution in the flask, which shall have been deoxidized in the mean time by one of the methods explained farther on.

Occasionally this treatment fails to decompose the insoluble residue, in which case it is necessary to heat the crucible until the greater part of the H_2SO_4 shall have been driven off; then **Treatment with $KHSO_4$.** add about .5 gramme $KHSO_4$, and heat gradually until the $KHSO_4$ is quite liquid and fumes of SO_3 are given off whenever the lid of the crucible is raised. When all the black specks have disappeared, allow the crucible to cool, and dissolve the salt in the crucible with hot water and a few drops of HCl.

Several methods are used for the deoxidation of the solution of ferric chloride, but the one in general use is by adding metallic zinc to the solution. The iron is deoxidized according to the reaction $Fe_2Cl_6 + Zn = 2FeCl_2 + ZnCl_2$, while the excess of HCl is decomposed and hydrogen liberated, $2HCl + Zn = ZnCl_2 + 2H$. As all zinc contains a small amount of iron, the amount added to **Deoxidation by metallic zinc.** the solution should be roughly weighed. Add then to the solution in the flask 3 grammes of granulated zinc,* and, when the evolution of hydrogen has somewhat slackened, heat the flask slightly. The neck of the flask is closed by a small funnel, which allows the hydrogen to escape while the liquid is caught on the funnel and falls back into the flask. It sometimes happens as the solution becomes neutralized that a basic salt of peroxide of iron is thrown down, giving the solution a reddish color; in this case add a few drops of HCl, and when the solution finally becomes **End of the reaction.** colorless add a few drops more of HCl. If this fails to produce a yellowish coloration, the solution may be considered deoxidized. **Final addition of H_2SO_4.** Pour in through the funnel the solution of the residue insoluble in HCl, and add gradually a mixture of 10 c.c. H_2SO_4 and 20 c.c.

---

* See page 57.

H₂O. This addition of H_2SO_4 is a very necessary part of the operation, for it not only serves to dissolve the remainder of the zinc which is unacted on when the deoxidation is complete, but it supplies the proper amount of sulphate of zinc and iron, which makes the end reaction with permanganate of potassium as sharp as if no HCl were present in the solution. As soon as all the zinc is dissolved, wash down the funnel inside and out and the neck of the flask with a fine jet of water, filling the flask almost full, cool the flask in water, and when the solution is quite cold transfer it to a large white dish of about 1500 c.c. capacity (see A, Fig. 88, page 208). Wash the flask and funnel well with cold water, pour the rinsing into the dish, and make the solution up to about 1000 c.c. Run in from a burette a standard solution of permanganate of potassium (Marguerite's method), the value of which has been carefully determined by one of the methods described farther on. At first the color of the permanganate is destroyed almost as soon as it touches the liquid in the dish, which should be stirred carefully with a glass rod. The permanganate should be added more and more slowly until towards the end of the operation it is added only drop by drop. The liquid in the dish gradually assumes a yellowish tint, which is deeper the larger the amount of iron in the ore. Finally a drop of the permanganate seems to destroy the yellow color, and the next drop gives the liquid a very faint pink tinge. This is the end of the reaction. Take the reading of the burette, and then add another drop, which will cause the solution to become decidedly pink in color. The number of c.c. of the standard solution used when the reading was taken, less a small correction for the zinc, etc., noted farther on, multiplied by the value of 1 c.c., gives the amount of metallic iron in the ore.

Titration by permanganate solution.

The reductor, Fig. 87, is also useful for reducing ferric salts to ferrous; the only disadvantage is that it seems necessary to have the iron present as sulphate, which necessitates evaporating off the hydrochloric acid used in dissolving ores. The description of the

Jones's reductor.

reductor is on page 100, and the method of using it in iron determinations is as follows:*

The conditions essential to the accurate determination of iron by this method are: That the iron must be in the state of ferric sulphate; that the solution of ferric sulphate must be dilute; that the least traces of hydrochloric and nitric acids must be absent. There should not be over 50 c.c. sulphuric acid, 1.32 sp. gr., in 300 c.c. of the ferric solution ready for reduction.

For iron ores, and in almost all cases, this ordinarily presents no difficulties. If the solution is in strong sulphuric acid, it must be reduced in bulk, or diluted to such an extent as to avoid violent action in contact with zinc. The volume of the solution should not exceed 350 c.c.

Preparing the reductor. The reductor should now be filled with zinc and washed as required. If there is still enough zinc remaining in the tube from previous reductions, a single washing will usually suffice. The ferric solution is now brought to the reductor and transferred to one or both of the cups A and B, washing out the beaker or flask three or four times with water.

Details of manipulation. The stopcock G of the reductor is opened, and the two-way stopcock C is set to discharge the solution, which is then filtered through the zinc. The cup is then rinsed out five times with water as described. The stopcock G is then closed to relieve the pressure, and the flask F is detached. The solution has now a volume of about 400 to 500 c.c. In this manner a solution of ferric sulphate is instantaneously and completely reduced in two minutes. The burette is now filled to the zero mark as described, and the solution is titrated in the flask direct.

A little practice will enable the operator to give a continuous circular motion to the flask held in the right hand, with the left hand in control of the flow of the permanganate from the burette.

---

* Prepared by Mr. Clemens Jones for this volume.

The average time by this means for the reduction and accurate titration of a ferric solution is four minutes. The burette B (50 c.c. to $\frac{1}{10}$ c.c.), shown in Fig. 87, consists of the gradu-

Fig. 87.

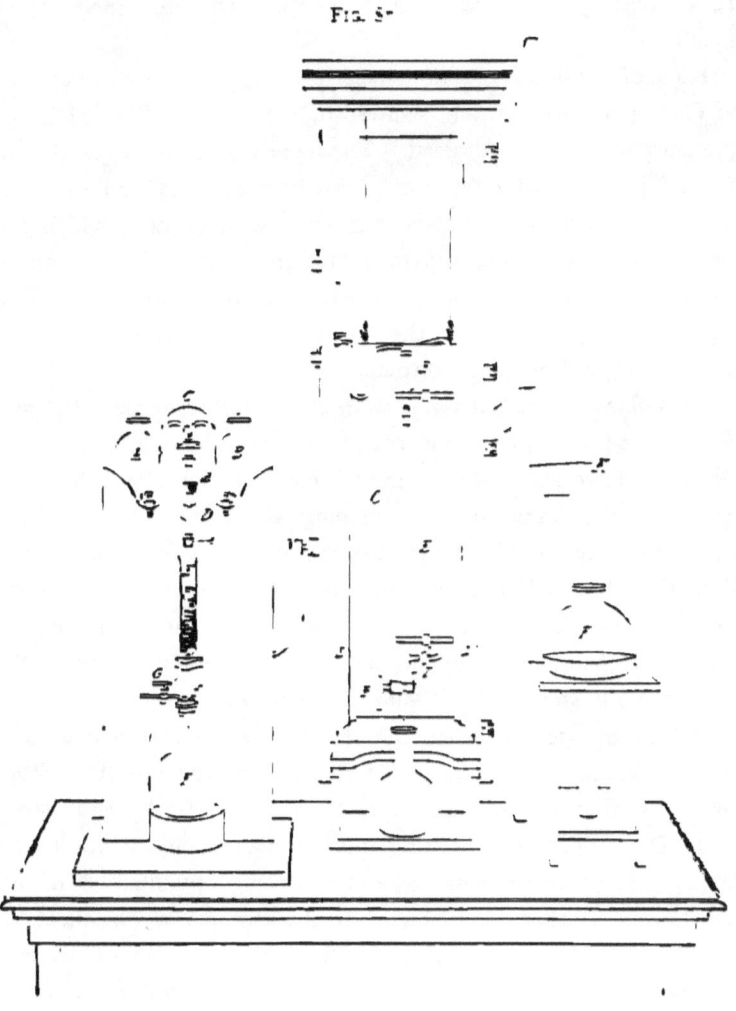

ated glass tube proper, and an arm, E, fused to it below the 50 c.c. mark. At its top are rubber connections with the blast-aspirator, shown in the cut. By means of the stopcock D connection through E is established with the glass reservoir F. The burette is clamped securely to a slide, C, which is counterpoised, and moves freely on guides between two parallel sides, L, L, suitably mounted in a frame, and through their whole length.

Back of the burette a porcelain scale may be fixed, graduated to correspond with it, and secured to the slide, in front of which the burette may be adjusted. The reservoir F is suspended in a shelf placed within the frame, and is introduced into the side-door K, shown open, and is then encased in a box, which has an annular hole in the top to admit the prong of the tube E, the slide C being previously raised. The reservoir is so placed that when the slide is at the lowest point the inlet-prong has a safe margin from the bottom.

If a float is used, it remains in the burette permanently, and is caught on a stage of fine platinum wire supported by a spiral, when it descends within one-half inch of the inlet-tube. In operation, the reservoir F, containing about two litres, is filled with the solution of permanganate and placed in position; the slide C is lowered until the zero marks are brought in the direct line of vision; blast is admitted to the aspirator by the brass valve V, and the suction produced is communicated to the burette, both stopcocks, H and D, being closed.

When the float is used, the stopcock H is first opened, the suction lifting the float to the zero mark in the burette. Stopcock H is then closed, and, while the float slowly descends, stopcock D is opened, admitting the permanganate solution and allowing the float to sink without enclosing any bubbles of air. The burette is then filled exactly to the zero mark. In titration, the blast must, of course, be shut off, and the column of solution connected with the outside atmosphere by turning a suitably-arranged stopcock of the aspirator. If the float is not employed, stopcock H remains closed, and by opening stopcock D the burette is filled in the manner described above.

Reservoir for permanganate solution.

To cleanse the burette, allow the solution partially filling it to run out. Stopcock H is then closed, suction is again produced by starting the aspirator as described, and a beaker of water is held so that the burette tip is in the water. On opening the stopcock H, the water rises in the burette. This is then run out by again stopping the aspirator, and the operation is repeated until the burette is perfectly clean. Should the burette require further cleansing, hydrochloric acid may be used in the same manner. This is then washed out with water as before, and the burette may then be dried in a few minutes by turning on the blast gently, and reversing the aspirator by simply closing its main outlet with a rubber cap, allowing the current of air to pass down through the burette and out through the open stopcock H. By closing the outside doors the apparatus is protected from light. The apparatus is always ready for use. Twenty accurate titrations can be easily made in an hour's time.

Another form of burette which is extremely convenient and has the great advantage of dispensing with the glass stopcock, which is liable to stick at a critical moment, or break without warning, is shown in Fig. 88.

The burette is attached to the wooden stand by bands of German silver or of nickel. The top of the burette is closed by a rubber stopper carrying a glass tube of small bore connected by rubber tubing with a small glass tube attached to the back of the burette-stand. To the end of this tube, near the base of the burette-stand, is attached a short piece of heavy-walled gum tubing, *a*, passing under a compressor fixed to the base of the stand. Fig. 89 shows the form and construction of the clamp or compressor. By applying suction at the end of the tube *b* the standard solution may be drawn up into the burette a little above the zero mark, and the compressor closed down on the tube *a*, holding the liquid in the burette until the admission of air through the tube *a* allows the liquid to flow out of the burette. The entire practical value of this

FIG. 88.

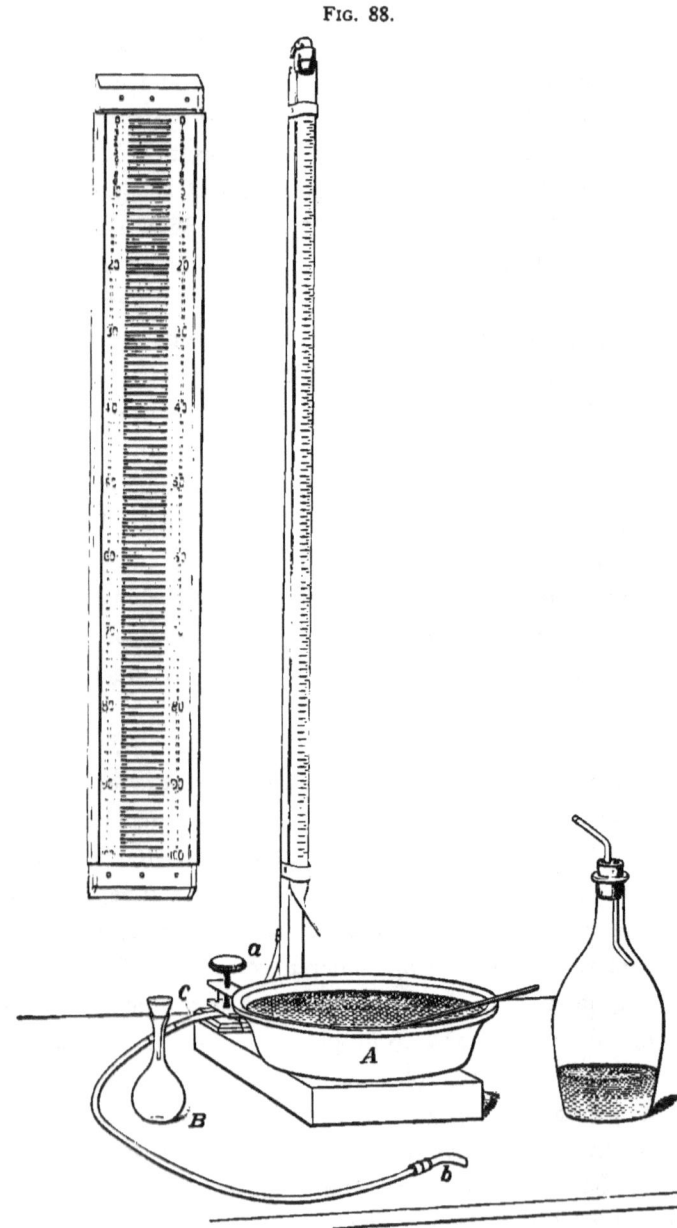

burette* depends on placing a drop or two of water in the tube *a,* which, flowing to the point of compression, not only closes the tube hermetically when the clamp is screwed down, but makes

it possible, by a slight movement of the clamp, to admit the smallest quantity of air to the burette, and thus to permit the liquid to flow from the burette at any desired rate. The flow is thus controlled by the left hand while the solution in the dish is stirred with the right. Towards the end of the operation a single drop may be made to flow from the burette,

FIG. 89.

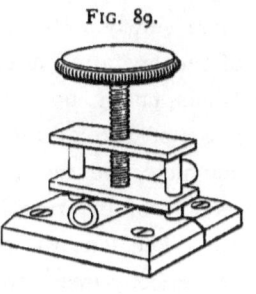

when the clamp is closed (not too tightly), by compressing the tube *a* at the point *c* with the thumb, and forcing a little air into the burette. Even a fraction of a drop may be obtained by touching the point of the burette with the stirring-rod. The scale shown in the sketch is fixed on the wall, so that the eye may always be kept at the proper level in taking the readings of the burette.

When using a standard solution of bichromate of potassium (Penny's method), the end reaction is not rendered apparent by a change in the color of the solution, but the presence or absence of ferrous salt in the solution is determined by taking a drop from the dish on the end of the stirring-rod and allowing it to run into a drop of a dilute, freshly-made solution of ferricyanide of potassium placed on a white tile or capsule. Dissolve a very small crystal of ferricyanide of potassium in a few c.c. of water, and place a number of drops of the solution on a white tile or on a flat-bottomed capsule. Run the carefully standardized solution of bichromate of potassium from the burette into the deoxidized iron solution previously placed in a white dish. The solution, at first colorless, changes gradually to a decided chrome-green from

---

* The suggestion of Mr. Thos. H. Garrett, of Philadelphia.

14

the reduction of the chromic acid. Test the progress of the oxidation of the iron solution by transferring a drop of it on the end of the stirring-rod to one of the drops of ferricyanide. As the blue color produced becomes less intense, add the bichromate more slowly and make the test more frequently, towards the end of the operation after the addition of each drop of bichromate.

End of the reaction.

When, finally, no color appears in the test-drops, even after the lapse of several moments, the oxidation of the ferrous salt is complete, and the amount of bichromate used, less a small correction for the zinc, is the measure of the amount of iron in the

Purity of ferricyanide.

ore. The ferricyanide of potassium employed must, of course, be perfectly free from ferrocyanide: it may be tested by adding a drop of ferric chloride solution to one of the drops of ferricyanide solution, the absence of any resulting blue color in the test-drops being proof of the purity of the ferricyanide. As towards the end of the operation the frequent tests become rather

Duplicate determinations.

tedious, some analysts prefer to make the determinations in duplicate, using the first to get an approximate result rather quickly, and the second to get the exact result after running in at once a little less than the amount of bichromate shown to be necessary by the first test.

Treatment of ores completely decomposed by HCl.

When the ore is completely decomposed by HCl, a separate treatment of the residue is unnecessary, and the ore may be weighed at once into the flask and treated with 10 c.c. HCl and a little $KClO_3$ when organic matter is present. When the ore is completely decomposed, and any Cl from the $KClO_3$ driven off, add 30 c.c. of water, and proceed with the deoxidation as previously described.

Deoxidation by NH_4HSO_3.

Necessary in the presence of TiO_2.

Instead of deoxidizing the solution of ferric chloride by zinc, it may be deoxidized by a solution of bisulphite of ammonium. In fact, the deoxidation by zinc is not practicable in ores containing much TiO_2, for the TiO_2 is reduced by metallic zinc to Ti_2O_3, imparting a purple or blue color to the solution, and acting like a solution of ferrous salt on the standard solution of permanganate.

In deoxidizing a solution of ferric chloride by this method it should be placed in a flask of 120 c.c. capacity, and two or three small spirals of platinum wire added to facilitate the subsequent boiling. Add cautiously to the solution (which should not exceed 40 c.c. in volume) enough ammonia to produce a slight permanent precipitate of ferric hydrate, which remains even after vigorous shaking. Add now 5 c.c. of a strong solution of NH_4HSO_3,* shake vigorously, and warm the flask gently. As the color of the solution—at first a deep red—fades, increase the heat, and finally heat to boiling. When the solution is quite colorless, add to it the solution of the residue and 100 c.c. H_2SO_4 mixed with 20 c.c. H_2O. Boil the solution until all the sulphurous acid is driven off. The pieces of platinum wire will cause the gas to be given off freely at the bottom of the flask, and the funnel in the neck will prevent the access of air and the loss of any portion of the solution. When the escaping steam no longer smells of SO_2, place the flask in cold water, wash down the funnel and the neck of the flask, filling the latter quite full of water, and when the solution is quite cold transfer it to a dish and titrate with a standard solution.

Details of the method.

A third method of deoxidizing the solution of ferric chloride is sometimes used, in which the reducing agent is a solution of stannous chloride. The details of the method are as follows:† Dissolve 1 gramme of the ore in 30 c.c. strong HCl (if necessary, filter off, ignite, and fuse the residue with a little Na_2CO_3, dissolve in water and HCl, and add to the main solution), transfer to a flask, dilute to 500 c.c., and heat to boiling. Add to the boiling solution, very cautiously, a clear acid solution of $SnCl_2$ containing about 10 grammes Sn to the litre. When the yellow color of the ferric chloride solution becomes very faint, add the $SnCl_2$ solution drop by drop, and test the former for ferric salt by transferring a drop of it on the end of a rod to a drop of a

Deoxidation by $SnCl_2$.

---

* See page 44.   † Stock and Jack, Chem. News, xxxi. 63.

dilute fresh solution of sulphocyanate of potassium on a white tile or capsule. A number of drops of the sulphocyanate should be placed on the surface of the tile or capsule, so that the tests may be made frequently, and without any delay, during the

Test for the
end of the
reduction. reduction. After each addition of the $SnCl_2$ solution the liquid in the flask should be allowed to boil for a few moments, then a drop taken from it on a rod should be transferred quickly to one of the drops of sulphocyanate. When the color produced in the sulphocyanate is only a faint pink the deoxidation may be considered perfect. It is, however, possible that an excess of $SnCl_2$ may have been added, and it is therefore necessary to test the effect of the addition of the first two or three drops of the standard solution of bichromate of potassium (perman-

Test for
excess
of $SnCl_2$
solution. ganate cannot be used) to the liquid. The reading of the burette having been observed, transfer two or three drops of the bichromate solution to the liquid in the flask, and test it again with the sulphocyanate. If the result is a decided increase in the intensity of the coloration, transfer the solution to the dish and finish the titration with the bichromate solution. The reduction of the ferric chloride solution is expressed by the formula $Fe_2Cl_6 + SnCl_2 = 2FeCl_2 + SnCl_4$.

Methods for Standardizing the Solutions.

Conditions
affecting
the accu-
racy of
the valu-
ation of
the stand-
ard. It is of the utmost importance that the value of the standard solution employed should be determined with the greatest accuracy if the results obtained by its use are to be anything but mere approximations to the truth. To do this, not only should the reagents employed be pure, but the conditions under which the standard is fixed should be, as nearly as practicable, those under which it is employed in actual use. The conditions referred to are not only those of temperature, dilution, etc., but of the actual chemical composition of the liquid acted on by the standard solution by which its value is determined.

The best reagent to employ is a solution of ferric chloride

Preparation
of ferric
chloride
solution.

of known strength. To prepare this, dissolve 100 grammes of
wrought iron (free from manganese and arsenic, and in which the
phosphorus has been accurately determined) in nitric acid, evaporate to dryness in a capsule, and heat until the nitrate of iron is
largely decomposed and the mass separates easily from the bottom
and sides of the capsule. Transfer to a piece of platinum-foil
with the edges turned up, and heat for some time in a muffle
at a very high temperature, or heat it, a portion at a time, in a
crucible at the highest temperature obtainable by a blast-lamp.
Grind the entire mass very fine in an agate mortar, dissolve in
HCl, evaporate to dryness, redissolve in dilute HCl, filter to get
rid of SiO_2, and dilute the solution to about 4 litres. Twenty c.c.
of this solution will contain about .5 gramme Fe, and it may be
kept indefinitely in a glass-stoppered bottle sealed with paraffine,
or after being thoroughly mixed it may be preserved in a number
of smaller bottles properly secured.

Preserva-
tion of
the solu-
tion.

Wash out and dry thoroughly three of the small flasks used
for deoxidizing the solutions of the ores, weigh them to within
1 mg., and measure into each a portion of the ferric chloride
solution ranging from 15 to 25 c.c. in volume. Weigh the flasks
and their contents; the differences between the first and second
weights are the weights of the ferric chloride solution taken.
Transfer the solution carefully from each flask to a platinum dish,
dilute, boil, precipitate by NH_4HO, filter, wash, dry, ignite, and
weigh the precipitate with the precautions mentioned farther
on. The precipitate is $Fe_2O_3 + P_2O_5$. Subtract from this weight
the amount of P_2O_5 in this weight of the material, and the remainder will be the weight of Fe_2O_3 in the amount of solution used.
Suppose, for example, that the original iron contained .1 per cent.
P, this would be equivalent to 0.229 per cent. P_2O_5, but, as the iron
has been oxidized to Fe_2O_3, the percentage of P_2O_5 in the iron as
oxide would be only $\frac{7}{10}$ as great as in the iron itself, the weight as
oxide being $\frac{10}{7}$ as great as it was as Fe. Therefore multiply .229
per cent. by .7 for the percentage of P_2O_5 in the Fe_2O_3, which

Determina-
tion of the
strength
of the
ferric
chloride
solution.

Example
to illus-
trate the
method.

gives .16 per cent. P_2O_5. If we further suppose that the weight of $Fe_2O_3 + P_2O_5$ obtained was .8131 gramme, .16 per cent. of this would be .0013 gramme, the weight of P_2O_5 in the precipitate, and .8131 — .0013 = .8118 gramme, the weight of Fe_2O_3 in the amount of solution taken. Divide this weight by the weight of the solution, and the result is the weight of Fe_2O_3 in 1 gramme of the solution of ferric chloride. Take the mean of the three results obtained in this way, and call this result the value of the ferric chloride solution in Fe_2O_3, or multiply by .7 for its value in Fe.

To standardize the permanganate or bichromate solution, weigh out three portions of the ferric chloride solution into the flasks, reduce them by the method selected, and titrate the reduced solutions exactly as directed above. Before calculating the strength of the standard solution a small correction must be applied to the burette reading, due to the fact that a definite amount of oxidizing solution is required to produce the end reaction in all cases where permanganate is used, and, when bichromate is used, in those cases where zinc has been the deoxidizing agent.

Determination of the correction for zinc, etc.

Treat 3 grammes of zinc in a small flask with 5 c.c. HCl and 20 c.c. H_2O, add gradually 10 c.c. H_2SO_4 and 20 c.c. H_2O. When the zinc has all dissolved, place the flask in cold water until the solution is cold. Wash it out into the dish, dilute to 1 litre, add 20 c.c. ferric chloride solution (free from ferrous salt), and drop in the standard solution until the end reaction is obtained. Subtract the correction thus obtained from every burette reading. To calculate the strength of the standard solution, therefore, subtract the correction from the burette reading, and the result is the absolute volume of the standard solution required to oxidize the ferrous salt in the solution operated on. Knowing then the weight of the ferric chloride solution used, the amount of Fe in each gramme of the solution, and the volume of the standard required to oxidize this amount, the value of each c.c. of the standard solution is found by multiplying the weight of ferric chloride solution used by the value of each gramme in Fe, and dividing the amount by the number of c.c. of the standard used in titrating. The mean of the results obtained in the three portions used should be taken as the value of the standard solution. An example will illustrate the method of computation, and, as logarithms very much facilitate these calculations, they will be given in the example as well.

Weight of empty flask	22.8817
Weight of flask + ferric chloride solution	40.0640
Weight of ferric chloride solution used	17.1823 = log. 1.2350813
Value of ferric chloride solution, determined as on	
p. 213 . . . . 1 gramme = .03227 gramme Fe = log. 8.5087990—10	
Fe in ferric chloride solution used . . . . . .55448 gramme = log. 9.7438803—10	
Burette reading after titration . . . . = 82.0 c.c.	
Less correction 0.25	
Corrected reading . . . . 81.75 c.c. = log. 1.9124878	
1 c.c. standard solution—.0067826 gramme Fe = log. 7.8313925—10	

Of course in calculating the amount of Fe in an ore it is only necessary to get the logarithm of the corrected reading (page 214) and add it to the logarithm of the standard solution as found above, the number corresponding to the resulting logarithm being the weight of Fe in grammes in the ore. This multiplied by 100 will give the percentage.

Very fine iron wire may be used to standardize the solutions, instead of a standard solution of ferric chloride. Weigh into the reducing flasks from .4 to .6 gramme of fine iron wire (page 55) which has been carefully rubbed with fine sand-paper and wiped clean with a linen rag. Dissolve in 10 c.c. HCl and 20 c.c. H_2O, with the addition of a few small crystals of $KClO_3$. Deoxidize carefully, and titrate as before directed. Multiply the weight of iron wire by .998 to get the absolute amount of Fe used, apply the proper correction to the burette reading, and calculate the value of the standard.

Ferrous sulphate, $FeSO_4.7H_2O$,* containing 20.1439 per cent. Fe, or the double sulphate of iron and ammonium $FeSO_4,(NH_4)_2SO_4,6H_2O$,† containing 14.2857 per cent., or almost exactly ¼ of its weight of Fe, may be used instead of ferric chloride solution or iron wire to determine the value of the standard solutions. The pure salts are generally weighed off, dissolved in water with 10 c.c. H_2SO_4, added and titrated direct, but they are not so satisfactory in use as the first and second methods described. It is important to have the standard solutions of the proper strength; that is, neither too dilute nor too concentrated for convenience in working. As iron ores rarely contain more than 60 per cent. metallic iron, a standard solution 100 c.c. of which are equal to .66 gramme Fe will be found sufficiently concentrated to avoid the necessity of refilling the burette for a determination; and where ores much poorer than this are habitually used the solutions may be correspondingly more dilute.

When permanganate of potassium is added to a solution of ferrous sulphate the reaction is $10FeSO_4 + 2KMnO_4 + 8H_2SO_4 = 5Fe_2(SO_4)_3 + K_2SO_4 + 2MnSO_4 + 8H_2O$, or 316.2 parts by weight of $KMnO_4$ will oxidize 560 parts by weight of Fe, or 3.727 grammes $KMnO_4$ to the litre will give a solution of about the strength required.

In the case of bichromate of potassium the reaction is $6FeSO_4 + K_2Cr_2O_7 + 7H_2SO_4 = 3Fe_2(SO_4)_3 + K_2SO_4 + Cr_2(SO_4)_3 + 7H_2O$, or 294.5 parts by weight of $K_2Cr_2O_7$ will oxidize 336 parts of Fe, or 5.785 grammes of bichromate of potassium dissolved in 1 litre of water will give a solution 100 c.c. of which will be equivalent to about .66 gramme Fe.

To prepare the solutions, therefore, dissolve the above weights, or multiples of them, in pure distilled water, allow the solution to stand for some little time, filter through asbestos, and dilute to the proper volume. Mix thoroughly by shaking in the bottle, and standardize as above directed. The solutions should be kept in glass-stoppered bottles in a dark closet, and the bottles should be well shaken whenever the solution is used.

DETERMINATION OF IRON EXISTING AS FeO.

Many iron ores contain iron in the state of FeO, and this FeO may be either soluble or insoluble in HCl. To determine the FeO soluble in HCl, weigh 1 gramme of the finely-ground ore into the flask A, Fig. 90, of about 100 c.c. capacity. Close the flask with a rubber stopper fitted with the two glass tubes B and C, and place it in the position shown in the sketch. Connect the tube C by means of a piece of rubber tubing with the bent tube D dipping below the surface of the water in the beaker E. Pass a current of CO_2 through the tube B until all the air is expelled, then remove for a moment the rubber tube connecting B with the source of CO_2, and by means of a small funnel and rubber connector introduce into the flask A, through B, 10–12 c.c. strong HCl, and establish the current of CO_2 as before. Heat the flask carefully, and when the ore is entirely decomposed, or the HCl ceases to exert any further action on it, remove the source of heat, stop the current of CO_2 for a moment, cool the flask with the hand, and allow the partial vacuum thus formed to draw the water from E back into A. Turn on the current of CO_2 again, place a dish of cold water under the flask A, and allow the solution to cool. Dissolve in a small flask 3 grammes of metallic zinc in 10 or 15 c.c. H_2SO_4, diluted with the proper quantity of water, cool it, and have it ready to pour into the titrating-dish by the time the solution in the flask A is cool. Wash out the solution of the ore from the flask A into the dish, add the zinc solution, dilute to 1 litre, and titrate with a standard solution. Subtract from the burette reading the proper correction, calculate the percentage of Fe, divide by 7, and multiply by 9. The result is

FeO soluble in HCl.

the percentage of FeO in the ore soluble in HCl. Allow the solution in the dish to stand for a few minutes, when all the undecomposed particles of ore will settle. Draw off the greater part of

FIG. 90.

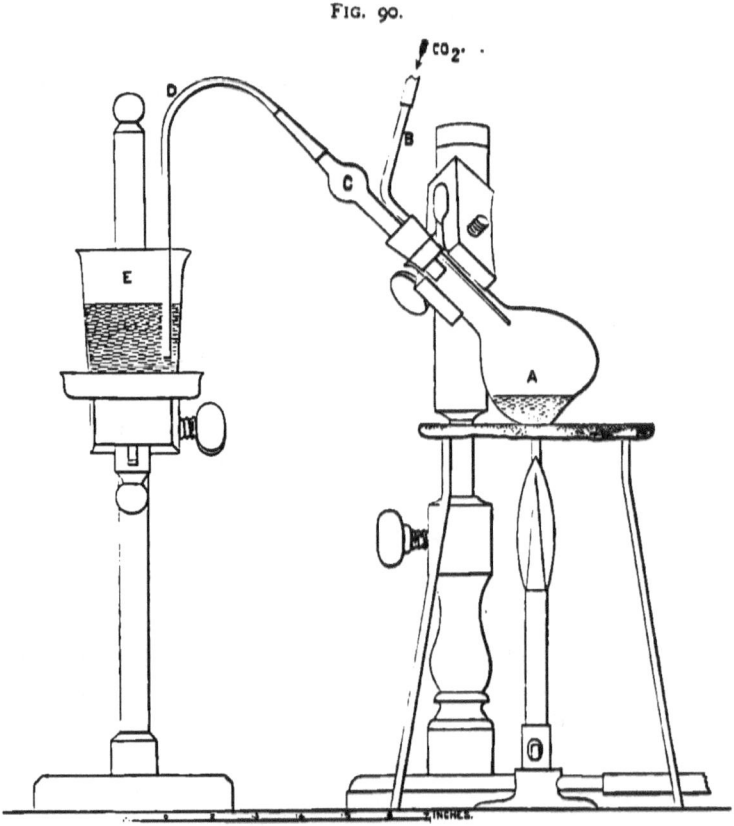

the clear supernatant fluid with a siphon, wash the sediment into a beaker with a jet of cold water, filter on a thin felt* in a Gooch crucible, and wash the sediment on the felt with cold water. Transfer the felt and sediment to a platinum crucible, pour into the crucible 5–10 c.c. HCl and about half the quantity of HFl,

---

* The asbestos of which the felt is made must be free from FeO.

cover the crucible, and place it in the water-bath shown in Fig. 91. The crucible rests on a platinum triangle fixed over the hole in the centre of the tip of the bath. Around this hole is a groove

FIG. 91.

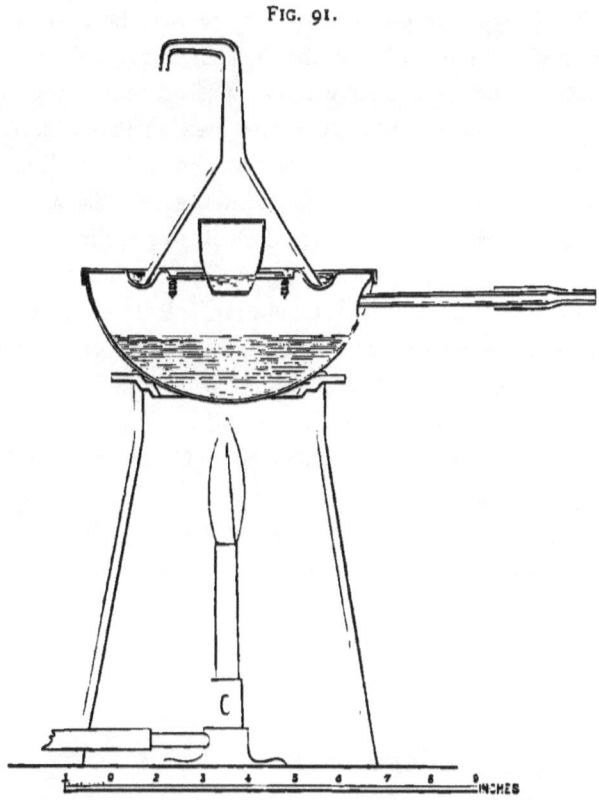

in which a funnel stands as shown in the cut, while the water in the groove forms a tight joint.* Pass a current of CO_2 or coal-gas through the tube in the side of the bath, as figured in the cut, to exclude the air, and heat the bath until the residue and felt are completely dissolved. Wash the crucible out into the titrating-

---

* Avery, Chem. News, xix. 270; Wilbur and Whittlesay, Crook's Select Methods, page 133.

dish, into which have been poured just previously 3 grammes of zinc dissolved in H_2SO_4 and enough cold water to make the solution up to nearly 1 litre. Titrate, and calculate the amount of FeO as before.

Separate portions for FeO soluble and insoluble in HCl.

Of course separate portions of the ore may be used to determine the FeO soluble and insoluble in HCl, but it is more troublesome, and experience has shown that it is no more accurate, and in some cases less accurate, than the method just described.

Total FeO in one operation.

The total FeO may also be determined in one operation by treating 1 gramme of the ore direct in the crucible with 20 c.c. HCl and 20 c.c. HFl, but it is often difficult to get the ore perfectly dissolved even by prolonged heating in the bath, and the ore must be ground very fine in the agate mortar. It is necessary to remove the funnel from time to time, raise the lid of the crucible, and stir the contents with a platinum wire.

When the ore is completely decomposed by HCl, or when the portion undecomposed contains no FeO, the treatment of the residue is unnecessary.

When an ore contains much organic matter, an accurate determination of FeO is often impossible, as the solution of the ore in HCl reduces some of the ferric salt.

DETERMINATION OF SULPHUR.

Sulphur exists in two conditions in iron ores, as sulphur in the form of sulphides and as sulphuric acid in the form of sulphates.

Total sulphur by fusion.

To determine the total sulphur, weigh 1 gramme of the finely-ground ore into a large platinum crucible, add to it 10 grammes of Na_2CO_3 and a little KNO_3 (less than 1 gramme).* Mix

---

* See pages 46 and 48. It is well to make a blank determination, using the same amounts of Na_2CO_3, KNO_3, and HCl, applying the amount of $BaSO_4$ found as a correction.

thoroughly with a platinum wire, and heat carefully over a large Bunsen burner or blast-lamp until the mass appears perfectly liquid and in a tranquil state of fusion. Run the fusion well up on the sides of the crucible, allow it to cool, and treat it in the crucible with boiling water. Pour the liquid into a tall, narrow beaker, treat the crucible again with boiling water, and repeat the operation until all the sodium salts are dissolved and nothing remains in the crucible except the unavoidable stains. Stir the liquid in the beaker well, and allow the oxide of iron to settle. If the solution is colored red or green, it is proof of the presence of manganese in the ore; add a few drops of alcohol, which will precipitate the manganese as oxide, leaving the solution colorless unless the ore contains chromium, in which case the solution will be yellowish. Decant the supernatant liquid on a small filter, allowing the filtrate to run into a No. 4 beaker, fill the small beaker nearly full of hot water, stir well, and allow to settle. Decant again on the filter, and repeat the operation once more. Acidulate the collected filtrates with HCl (about 20 c.c. will be required), evaporate to dryness in the air-bath, redissolve in water with a few drops of HCl, filter into a No. 3 beaker, heat the filtrate to boiling, and add 10 c.c. of a solution of chloride of barium.* Allow to stand for some hours, filter on the Gooch crucible or on a small ashless filter, ignite, and weigh as $BaSO_4$, which multiplied by .1376 gives the weight of S. The insoluble portion from the aqueous solution of the fusion may be used to determine the total iron in the ore, and is very convenient for this purpose in ores difficult to dissolve. Pour into the crucible in which the fusion was made about 10 c.c. HCl, place the lid on the crucible, and warm the crucible slightly to dissolve the adhering oxides, dilute with about an equal bulk of water, and pour it on the small filter through which the aqueous solution was decanted, allowing it to run into the beaker which contains the residue of oxide of iron,

Evidence of manganese and chromium.

Determination of iron in the residue from the fusion.

---

* See page 51.

etc. Wash out the crucible, pouring the washings on the filter, and wash the filter free from iron with a jet of cold water. Evaporate the solution in the beaker to dryness, redissolve in 10 c.c. HCl, and transfer the solution of ferric chloride, the silica, etc., to one of the small flasks, deoxidize, and titrate as directed.

The sulphur which exists as sulphuric acid in an iron ore is usually combined with either calcium or barium: as sulphate of calcium or of any of the other alkaline earths except barium, of the alkalies, or of the metals, it is soluble in HCl; as sulphate of barium it is practically insoluble. We may, therefore, deter-

Determination of soluble sulphates. mine the soluble sulphates as follows: Boil 10 grammes of the ore with 30 c.c. HCl and 60 c.c. water, filter from the mass of the undissolved ore, evaporate the filtrate to dryness, redissolve in HCl and water (1–2), filter into a No. 2 beaker, nearly neutralize by NH_4HO, heat to boiling, and precipitate by $BaCl_2$ solution. Filter and wash the precipitate, ignite, and weigh as $BaSO_4$, which contains 34.352 per cent. SO_3.

Determination of sulphate of barium. To determine the sulphuric acid which exists as sulphate of barium, treat 10 grammes of the ore with 50 c.c. HCl until the ore appears to be decomposed. Evaporate to dryness, redissolve in dilute HCl (1–3), dilute, filter, and wash the insoluble matter thoroughly. Ignite and fuse the insoluble matter with Na_2CO_3, treat the fused mass with hot water, and filter. In the filtrate is the sulphuric acid as sulphate of sodium, while the barium remains on the filter as carbonate of barium. It is safer to calculate the sulphate of barium from the amount of barium rather than from the amount of sulphuric acid, as the ore may contain sulphides (pyrites, etc.), which are not decomposed by HCl, but are decomposed and partly oxidized by fusion with Na_2CO_3. The other forms of barium besides the sulphate (silicate and carbonate) are readily decomposed by HCl, and are not likely to be found with the barium in the insoluble residue. It is, of course, possible to suppose the coexistence of silicate or carbonate of barium and of sulphate of calcium in an ore, and the consequent formation of sulphate of barium when the ore is decomposed by HCl; but, as the soluble sulphuric acid is determined in one operation and the insoluble in another,* the total amount of sulphuric acid existing as such is determined, and the object of the analysis attained. To determine the barium, then, treat the insoluble matter obtained by the filtration of the aqueous solution of the fusion by dilute HCl, evaporate to dryness to render SiO_2 insoluble, redissolve in water with a few drops of HCl, filter into a No. 2 beaker, heat the filtrate to boiling, and add a few drops of H_2SO_4 diluted with a little water. Allow the precipitate to settle, filter, wash, ignite, and weigh as $BaSO_4$, from which weight calculate the amount of SO_3 in the ore insoluble in HCl. To find the amount of sulphur existing as sulphides, subtract from the total S the amount of S in the SO_3 found as sulphates.

S as sulphides.

DETERMINATION OF PHOSPHORIC ACID.

Treat 5 or 10 grammes of the finely-ground ore in 30 or 60 c.c. HCl. (With low phosphorus ores use 10 grammes; with others, 5 grammes.) When the ore is decomposed, evaporate to dryness, redissolve in 20 or 40 c.c. HCl, dilute, filter, and proceed exactly as directed in the determination of phosphorus in iron and steel, page 81 *et seq.* The weight of the $Mg_2P_2O_7$ multiplied by .63788 gives the weight of the P_2O_5. The weight of the phospho-molybdate of ammonium multiplied by .03735 gives the weight of the P_2O_5.

Solution of the ore.

Titanic acid is very generally found associated with iron ores, and may be regarded as one of the usual constituents.

Precautions when TiO_2 is present.

---

* The insoluble matter from the treatment of 10 grammes of the ore with HCl for the determination of soluble sulphates, page 222, may be used to determine the sulphate of barium.

As mentioned on page 86 its presence, if overlooked, may lead to serious errors in the determination of phosphoric acid. When an ore contains much titanic acid it may readily be recognized by the peculiar milky appearance of the solution when it is diluted preparatory to filtering off the insoluble matter, and by the strong tendency it shows to run through the filter as soon as the attempt is made to wash the insoluble matter with water. Smaller quantities of titanic acid may be recognized by the clouding of the solution when it is deoxidized by bisulphite of ammonium, as noted on page 89. In the latter case, however, this clouding may be caused by the formation of sulphate of barium when the ore contains the latter element in the form of carbonate or silicate. Silica in the solution may also cause a cloud under those circumstances which closely resembles that caused by titanic acid, while sulphate of barium may readily be distinguished from either by its granular appearance and its tendency to settle to the bottom of the beaker.

Means of recognizing titaniferous ores.

Ores containing barium.

The insoluble residue from the solution of the ore in HCl should, therefore, be treated to recover any P_2O_5 which may have remained insoluble in combination with TiO_2.* An additional test for the presence of titanic acid, and one that rarely fails even with very small amounts, is to dissolve the insoluble matter from the aqueous solution of the fusion of the residue from the HFl and H_2SO_4 treatment of the insoluble residue from the ore, in dilute HCl, allowing it to run into a test-tube and adding metallic zinc. When titanic acid is present the solution becomes first colorless, and then pink or purple, and finally blue from the formation of Ti_2O_3. The simplest way is to pro-

Additional test for titanic acid.

* When HFl is not available, fuse the residue with Na_2CO_3, treat the fused mass with hot water, filter, acidulate the filtrate with HCl, evaporate to dryness to render SiO_2 insoluble. Redissolve in water with a little HCl, filter, and add the filtrate to the main solution, or add a little Fe_2Cl_6, and make a separate acetate precipitation in this portion, adding the solution to the solution of the main acetate precipitation.

ceed as directed an pages 88 and 89 when using the acetate method, or on page 94 when using the molybdate method. These methods are not practicable, however, when the ore contains a very large amount of TiO_2, and recourse must be had to the method described on page 86 *et seq.*, involving the fusion of the acetate precipitate and the residue from the treatment of the insoluble matter with HFl and H_2SO_4, with Na_2CO_3 and a little $NaNO_3$. It is best to pursue this method at any rate whenever TiO_2 is also to be determined, as the same portion can be used for the estimation of both TiO_2 and P_2O_5, and the aggregate labor involved is much lessened.

Fusion of the acetate precipitate with Na_2CO_3, etc.

DETERMINATION OF TITANIC ACID.

The determination of titanic acid has always presented many difficulties, and its separation from a large amount of oxide of iron and alumina has been far from satisfactory, besides being most tedious. The principal sources of error in the estimation of titanic acid in iron ores are the tendency of P_2O_5 to prevent the precipitation of TiO_2 by boiling, when its sulphuric acid solution contains P_2O_5 and ferrous sulphate, and the liability of Al_2O_3 to separate out with the TiO_2 when the latter is precipitated under the circumstances above mentioned. There is also a mechanical difficulty, caused by the adhesion of the precipitated TiO_2 to the bottom and sides of the beaker, from which it can sometimes be removed only by boiling with a strong solution of caustic potassa. The admirable series of experiments carried out by Dr. Gooch [*] on the separation of aluminium and titanium suggests a method which renders the determination of TiO_2 in iron ores much less troublesome, while adding greatly to the accuracy of the results.

Difficulties in the precipitation of TiO_2.

---

[*] Proceedings Am. Acad. Arts and Sciences, New Series, vol. xii. p. 435.

Details of the method.

In carrying out the details of the method, dissolve 5 or 10 grammes of the ore in HCl, and proceed exactly as in the determination of P_2O_5, by fusing the residue from the treatment of the insoluble matter by HFl and H_2SO_4 and the acetate precipitate with Na_2CO_3 and a little $NaNO_3$,* and then complete the operation exactly as described in the determination of Ti in pig-iron.†

Principles involved.

The essential points in this method are—1. Separation of the TiO_2 from the mass of Fe_2O_3 by acetate of ammonium in the deoxidized solution. 2. Separation from all the P_2O_5 and the greater part of the Al_2O_3 by fusion with Na_2CO_3, by which means a titanate of sodium insoluble in water is formed, and at the same time phosphate and aluminate of sodium soluble in that menstruum. 3. Separation from the last traces of Al_2O_3 from the iron, calcium, etc., by precipitating the TiO_2 in the thoroughly deoxidized solution in the presence of a large excess of acetic acid and some SO_2, the sulphuric acid being all in the form of sulphate of sodium. The addition of a large excess of acetate of sodium, by which this latter condition is effected, converts all the sulphates of iron, calcium, etc., into acetates, and precipitates the TiO_2 almost instantaneously as a hydrate, which is flocculent, settles quickly, shows no tendency to run through the filter, and is washed with the greatest ease. It sometimes happens that a little FeO is precipitated with the TiO_2, and the latter, after ignition, appears discolored; in this case fuse with a little Na_2CO_3, add H_2SO_4 to the cold fused mass, dissolve, and repeat the precipitation with acetate of sodium in the presence of sulphurous and acetic acids exactly as in the first instance.

A number of experiments covering all the points involved in this method show it to be extremely accurate and entirely trustworthy.

---

* See page 86 *et seq.* † See page 172 *et seq.*

DETERMINATION OF MANGANESE.

When manganese alone is to be determined in an ore, any one of the methods described under the determination of manganese in iron and steel, page 103 *et seq.*, may be used. The most convenient, however, is Ford's method with the modifications necessary in the analysis of pig-iron, page 111. The only change requisite is to evaporate the solution in HCl to dryness to render silica insoluble before filtering off the insoluble matter. Ford's method.

In using the acetate method it is, of course, necessary that all the iron should be in the form of Fe_2Cl_6, and also that there should be no oxidizing agent in the solution. Even a very small amount of $FeCl_2$ will cause the formation of a " brick-dust" precipitate, which cannot be kept from passing the filter while some of the iron remains dissolved in the acetate solution. When, therefore, the ore contains FeO, it should be oxidized by HNO_3 or $KClO_3$, and the excess of the oxidizing agent removed by evaporation with HCl. The acetate method.

When the ore contains much organic matter it should be filtered off before attempting to oxidize the ferrous salt, as it is quite impossible in some cases to destroy the organic matter, and resolution of the evaporated mass in HCl causes a reduction of some of the ferric salt. FeO and organic matter in the ores.

Many manganiferous iron ores contain manganese in a higher state of oxidation than the protoxide, and the determination of the excess of oxygen is often necessary. All ores of this character when treated with HCl evolve chlorine gas, which is easily recognized by its yellowish-green color and peculiarly irritating odor. The reaction by which chlorine is liberated is $MnO_2 + 4HCl = MnCl_2 + 2H_2O + 2Cl$, or each molecule of $MnO_2 = 87$ corresponds to 2 molecules of $Cl = 70.90$. This reaction is the basis of Bunsen's method for the estimation of the amount of the MnO_2 in manganese ores, which consists in driving the liberated Cl into a solution of iodide of potassium, and determining the amount of Ores containing MnO_2.

iodine set free, by starch and hyposulphite solution. When the method given on page 68 *et seq.* for determining sulphur in steel is in use, the solutions employed in carrying out that method (with the exception of the iodine in iodide of potassium) can be used in this, or they may be prepared by the directions there given, for use in this method.

Weigh from .5 gramme to 1 gramme of the finely-ground ore into the flask *a*, Fig. 92, pour in 10 c.c. strong HCl, connect the

FIG. 92.

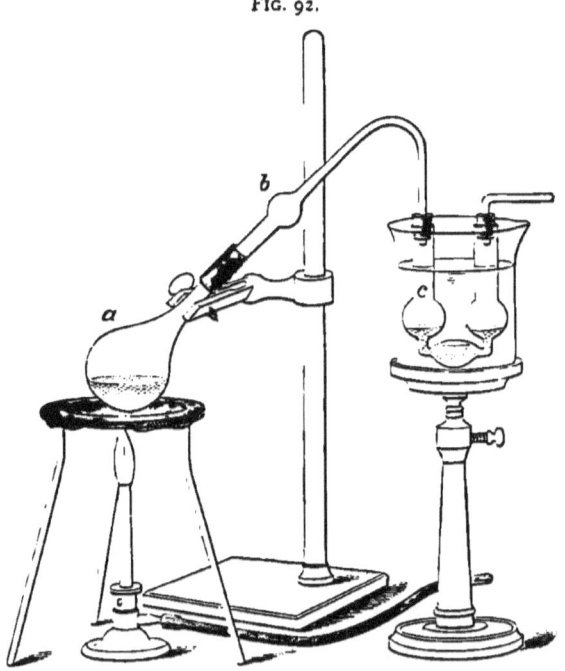

bent tube *b* quickly by means of a piece of gum tubing, and heat the flask gently at first and finally to boiling to drive all the Cl over into the tube *c*, which contains a strong solution of pure iodide of potassium free from iodate. This tube is placed in ice-water. When all the Cl has been expelled from the flask *a* and absorbed in *c*, detach the latter, wash its contents into a large dish, add a little starch solution, and run in the hyposulphite until the blue color just vanishes. If, as in the example given on page 70, Example. 1 c.c. of the hyposulphite solution is equal to .01267 gramme of iodine, and 1 equivalent of chlorine $= 35.45$ replaces 1 equiva· lent of iodine $= 126.85$ in the iodide of potassium, 1 c.c. of the hyposulphite solution would be equal to ($126.85 : 35.45 :: .01267 :$ .003541) .003541 gramme of chlorine; and, as 1 equivalent of $MnO_2 = 87$ is equal to 2 equivalents of chlorine $= 70.90$, 1 c.c. of the hyposulphite would be equal to ($70.90 : 87 :: .003541 : .004345$) .004345 grammes MnO_2.

In most laboratories, however, it is generally more convenient to determine the amount of MnO_2 in an ore by determining its oxidizing power on a solution of ferrous salt. The reaction is $2FeSO_4 + MnO_2 + 2H_2SO_4 = Fe_2(SO_4)_3 + MnSO_4 + 2H_2O$, or 2 equivalents of $Fe = 112$ are equal to 1 equivalent of $MnO_2 = 87$. Grind in an Determina-
tion by
means of
ferrous
sulphate. agate or Wedgwood mortar about 10 or 15 grammes of ferrous sulphate or ammonio-ferrous sulphate, and weigh out two portions, one of 2 grammes and one of 3 to 8 grammes, according to the quality of the manganese ore. One gramme of pure MnO_2 would oxidize 1.2874 grammes of Fe, equal to nearly 6.5 grammes of ferrous sulphate, or more than 9 grammes of ammonio-ferrous sulphate. Transfer the 2-gramme portion to the dish, add a large amount of water and about 5 c.c. HCl, and pour in 3 grammes of zinc dissolved in 10 c.c. H_2SO_4 diluted with enough water to dissolve the sulphate of zinc readily. Titrate with the standard solution of permanganate or bichromate of potassium in the usual way, and calculate the amount of iron in 1 gramme of the ferrous salt used. Weigh into the flask A, Fig. 90, page 218, 1 gramme of the finely-ground ore, and add to it the larger portion of the ferrous salt previously weighed out. Connect the flask as in Fig. 90, and pass in a current of CO_2 until the air has been driven out. Now pour into the flask A, by means of a small funnel attached to B, 10 c.c. HCl and 30 c.c. water, reconnect the CO_2 apparatus, and while the current of CO_2 is passing dissolve the ore, heating the flask, and shaking it from time to time as necessary. When the ore is all decomposed, stop the current of CO_2 for a moment, remove the light, and allow the water in E to flow back into the flask A. Transfer the solution to the dish, add 3 grammes zinc dissolved in H_2SO_4, and titrate it with the standard solution. From the titration of the ferrous salt calculate the amount of Fe in the amount used in the solution of the ore, and subtract from this the amount found by this last titration; the difference is the weight of Fe oxidized by the chlorine liberated from the MnO_2 in the ore. Then, as 112 parts of Fe correspond to 87 parts of MnO_2, multiply the above weight of iron by 87 and divide by 112, and the result is the weight of MnO_2 in the ore.

Calculation
of MnO
and
MnO₂.

The total Mn having been determined by one of the methods previously given, subtract from it the amount of Mn as MnO_2 (found by multiplying the weight of MnO_2 by .63218), and calculate the difference to MnO by multiplying by 1.2909.

DETERMINATION OF SILICA, ALUMINA, LIME, MAGNESIA, OXIDE OF MANGANESE, AND BARYTA.

Composi-
tion of
residue
insoluble
in HCl.

Treatment of iron ores with HCl leaves a residue which only in very rare instances consists of silica alone, being usually silicates of aluminium, calcium, and magnesium, mixed with an excess of silica. These silicates are often much more complicated, and contain, besides the substances enumerated above, protoxide of iron, soda, potassa, and oxide of manganese. With these silicates are occasionally found titanic acid, titaniferous iron, chrome iron ore, sulphate of barium, and ferrous sulphide, besides organic matter, and sometimes graphite. As this residue must be fused with Na_2CO_3 in order to decompose it, and the introduction of sodium salts into the main solution is not desirable, the two portions of the ore (the soluble and the insoluble in HCl) should be analyzed separately.

Weigh 1 gramme of ore into a No. 1 beaker, add 15 c.c. HCl, cover with a watch-glass, and digest at a gentle heat until the ore appears to be quite decomposed, add a few drops of HNO_3, heat until the action has ceased, and then wash off the cover with a fine jet of water, and evaporate to dryness. Redissolve in HCl, and evaporate to dryness a second time to render all the silica insoluble. Redissolve in 10 c.c. HCl and 30 c.c. water, filter, *Solution of* transfer all the residue to the filter (a small ashless filter) with a *the ore* fine jet of cold water, using a "policeman" to detach any adhering particles from the beaker, and wash the filter with a little HCl and plenty of cold water. Allow the filtrate and washings to run into a No. 3 beaker, and ignite and weigh the residue as "*Insoluble Silicious Matter.*"

Add to the insoluble matter in the crucible about ten times its *Analysis* weight of pure dry Na_2CO_3 and fuse it. Run the fusion well up *of the* on the sides of the crucible and treat it with hot water. Wash it *insoluble* out into a platinum dish, dissolve any particles adhering to the *matter* crucible in HCl, and add this to the solution in the dish. Acidulate with HCl, evaporate to dryness, moisten with HCl and water, evaporate to dryness a second time to render silica insoluble, then pour into the dish 5 c.c. HCl and 15 c.c. water, and stand it in a warm place for some time. Dilute with about 20 c.c. water, filter on a small ashless filter, wash well with hot water, receiving the filtrate and washings in a small beaker, dry, ignite, and weigh. Treat the ignited precipitate with HFl and a drop or two of H_2SO_4, evaporate to dryness, ignite, and weigh again. The differ- *SiO₂.* ence between the two weights is SiO_2. If the difference between the last weight and the weight of the empty crucible is more than a milligramme or two, the residue must be examined and its nature *Nature of* determined. This residue may consist of titanic acid, sulphate of *residue* barium, alumina, or sulphate of sodium (from imperfect washing *from HFl and H₂SO₄ treatment* of the silica). If it is titanic acid or alumina, the weight must be added to the weights of the Al_2O_3, etc.

Return the filtrate from the SiO_2 to the dish in which it was previously contained, heat to boiling, add a few drops of bromine-water and an excess of NH_4HO, boil until it smells but faintly of NH_3, filter on a small ashless filter, wash well with hot water, dry, ignite, and weigh as Al_2O_3, etc. Besides alumina this precipitate may contain titanic acid, sesquioxide of chromium, sesquioxide of iron, oxide of manganese, and phosphoric acid.

Return the filtrate from this precipitate to the dish, evaporate down to about 100 c.c., add oxalate of ammonium and ammonia, boil for a few minutes, allow the precipitate to settle, filter on a small ashless filter, ignite finally for five minutes over a blast-lamp, and weigh as CaO. To the filtrate from the oxalate of calcium add microcosmic salt and about one-third the volume of the solution of ammonia, cool in ice-water, stir vigorously several times, and allow to stand overnight so that the precipitated $Mg_2(NH_4)_2P_2O_8$ may settle properly, filter, wash with water containing one-third its volume of ammonia and about 100 grammes of nitrate of ammonium to the litre, ignite carefully, and weigh. Dissolve the precipitate in the crucible in a little water containing from 5 to 10 drops HCl, filter through a small ashless filter, which dry, ignite, and weigh. The difference between the two weights is $Mg_2P_2O_7$, which, multiplied by .36212, gives the weight of MgO.

When barium has been shown to exist in the ore, as noted on page 222, heat the filtrate from the Insoluble Silicious Matter to boiling, add a few drops of H_2SO_4, boil for a few minutes to allow the precipitate to settle, filter on a small ashless filter, allowing the filtrate and washings to run into a No. 5 beaker, dry, ignite, and weigh as $BaSO_4$, which, multiplied by .65648, gives the weight of BaO.

To the cold filtrate from the $BaSO_4$ add NH_4HO until the solu-

---

Marginal notes:

Al_2O_3, etc.

Possible constituents of this precipitate.

CaO.

MgO.

Analysis of the filtrate from the Insoluble Silicious Matter.

BaO.

tion is nearly neutralized, then add a solution of carbonate of am- Precipitation by acetate of ammonium. monium until a slight permanent precipitate is formed which fails to dissolve after vigorous stirring, and redissolve this by the careful addition of HCl, drop by drop, stirring well, and allowing the solution to stand for a short time after each addition of HCl. As soon as the solution clears, add a solution of acetate of ammonium, made by slightly acidulating 5 c.c. of NH_4HO by acetic acid, dilute to about 600 c.c. with boiling water, and boil for a few minutes. Allow the precipitate to settle, decant the clear liquid through a large washed German filter, pour the precipitate on the filter, and wash it two or three times with boiling water. With the aid of a platinum spatula return the precipitate to the beaker in which the precipitation was made, dissolving any portion remaining on the filter or adhering to the spatula in dilute HCl, allowing the acid to run into the beaker containing the precipitate. Wash the filter thoroughly with cold water, and evaporate the solution and washings to dryness. Redissolve in dilute HCl, filter into a large platinum dish, dilute with hot water,* heat to boiling, and add a slight excess of ammonia. Boil for a few minutes to make the precipitate granular and expel the excess of ammonia, and filter on an ashless filter (using the filter-pump and cone, page 26, with very slight pressure, if practicable. Dissolve any of the adhering particles of the precipitate in the dish in a very few drops of HCl, heating the bottom of the dish slightly, wash off the rod and cover, and wash down the sides of the dish with hot water, add a *slight* excess of ammonia, heat gently until the precipitate of ferric hydrate separates, wash this

---

* The distilled water used in the complete analysis of iron ores should never be heated in glass vessels for any length of time, as glass is sensibly attacked by it. An experiment in which distilled water free from residue was heated for twelve hours in a Bohemian flask showed that the water dissolved 52 milligrammes of solid matter to the litre, of which 26 milligrammes were SiO_2. The water should always be heated in platinum or porcelain dishes, or in tin-lined copper flasks. For convenience, the water may be poured into the washing-flasks for immediate use.

on the filter, and wash the precipitate thoroughly with hot water.
Dry the filter and precipitate carefully, transfer the latter to a
weighed crucible, burn the filter in a wire, add the ash to the
precipitate, and heat the crucible, keeping it carefully covered,
and raising the heat very gradually and slowly to expel the last
traces of moisture from the precipitate of ferric hydrate. Finally
heat the crucible to bright redness, and then to the highest temperature of the blast-lamp for about five to ten minutes. Cool,
ignite, and weigh as $Fe_2O_3 + Al_2O_3 + P_2O_5 (+ TiO_2 + Cr_2O_3 + As_2O_5)$.

$Fe_2O_3 +$
$Al_2O_3 +$
$P_2O_5.$

Add the filtrate and washings from the acetate precipitation to
those from the precipitation by ammonia, evaporate down to about
200 c.c. in a platinum dish, filter off any slight precipitate of Fe_2O_3
(which must be ignited, weighed, and the weight added to that of
the Fe_2O_3, etc.), add 20 to 30 drops of acetic acid, heat to boiling, and pass a current of H_2S through the solution for fifteen
or twenty minutes, keeping the solution hot during the passage
of the gas. Filter off the precipitated sulphides of copper, zinc,
nickel, and cobalt, wash with H_2S water containing a little free
acetic acid, and to the filtrate add excess of ammonia and sulphide of ammonium. Allow the precipitated sulphide of manganese to settle, decant the clear, supernatant liquid through a
filter, but before pouring the precipitate on the filter remove the
beaker containing the filtrate and substitute a clean beaker, for
the precipitate is almost certain at first to run through the filter.
Wash the precipitate and filter with water containing a little sulphide of ammonium, add the clear filtrate and washings together,
and stand them aside. Dissolve the precipitate of sulphide of
manganese on the filter in dilute HCl, and wash the filter thoroughly with hot water, receiving the solution and washings in a
small beaker. Heat to boiling to expel H_2S, and, when the excess
is driven off, destroy the last traces with a little bromine-water,
transfer the solution to a platinum dish, and precipitate by microcosmic salt and ammonia as directed on page 106. Filter, wash,

ignite, and weigh as $Mn_2P_2O_7$, which, multiplied by .50011, gives the weight of MnO.

Acidulate the filtrate from the sulphide of manganese with HCl, boil off all the H_2S, filter from the sulphur deposited by this operation into a platinum dish, add an excess of ammonia and oxalate of ammonium, filter off, ignite, and heat at the highest temperature of the blast-lamp for fifteen minutes, cool, and weigh as CaO.

Precipitate the magnesia in the filtrate as directed on page 232, and determine the weight of $Mg_2P_2O_7$, which, multiplied by .36212, gives the weight of MgO.

By adding the elements determined in the insoluble portion to the similar ones in the soluble portion, we get the total amounts of each in the ore. Thus, we have from the above analysis $SiO_2, Fe_2O_3 + Al_2O_3 + P_2O_5 + Cr_2O_3 + TiO_2 + As_2O_5$, MnO, CaO, and MgO, and it becomes, of course, necessary to calculate properly the iron in its different states of oxidation and to determine the amount of Al_2O_3 in the ore. It is much more accurate to determine in separate portions of the ore the amounts of P_2O_5, As_2O_5, Cr_2O_3, Fe_2O_3, and TiO_2 than to attempt to make the separation in the precipitate obtained in this portion. Therefore, knowing the amounts of these substances, the Fe_2O_3 from the volumetric determination of iron, as previously described, and the amount of each of the others as found by one of the methods given, add together the weights of the Fe_2O_3, the P_2O_5, the Cr_2O_3, the TiO_2, and the As_2O_5 in one gramme of the ore, and subtract the sum from the weight of the precipitate obtained in the above analysis, the result is the weight of Al_2O_3 in one gramme of the

ore.

Iron may exist in an ore in several conditions, as Fe_2O_3, as FeO, as FeS_2, as $FeAs_2$, etc. While it may not always be possible to determine the exact conditions in which it exists, the rule usually followed is, after subtracting from the sulphur existing as sulphides (page 223) the amount necessary to form sulphide of copper, sulphide of nickel, etc., to calculate the remainder as FeS_2 by multiplying the weight of S by 1.87336. The weight of S subtracted from this gives the weight of iron in the FeS_2. Now from the weight of $FeAs_2$ subtract the weight of arsenic, and the result is the weight of iron existing as Fe in the $FeAs_2$.* Add the Fe in the FeS_2 to the Fe in the $FeAs_2$, and subtract this weight from the Fe found as FeO, the remainder calculated to FeO is the amount of FeO in the ore. Subtract the total amount of Fe found originally by titration to exist as FeO from the total Fe found in the ore, and calculate the remainder to Fe_2O_3.

[margin: FeS_2. $FeAs_2$. FeO. Fe_2O_3.]

[margin: Method for ores containing little manganese.] When an iron ore contains only a very small amount of manganese, the acetate separation may be omitted in the method as given above, which simplifies and shortens the operation very materially. In this event transfer the filtrate from the insoluble silicious matter at once to a large platinum dish, heat to boiling, add a few c.c. of bromine-water and then excess of ammonia, boil, and filter the Fe_2O_3, etc., on an ashless filter, dry, ignite, and weigh, as described above. The manganese will be in the precipitate after ignition as Mn_3O_4, and the amount calculated from the determination of manganese made in a separate portion of the ore must be subtracted from the weight of the above precipitate in calculating the amount of Al_2O_3.

The lime and magnesia are determined in the filtrate from the Fe_2O_3, etc., providing, of course, that the ore contains only minute amounts of nickel, copper, etc.

[margin: Titaniferous ores.] The same general method described above is applicable when the ore contains quite a large amount of titanic acid, so much, in fact, as to cause the cloudiness in the filtrate from the insoluble silicious matter, as noted on page 224. Whenever an acetate separation is necessary in an ore of this character, the precipitate must be filtered on an ashless filter, and this filter, as well as the

---

* All the weights, of course, are calculated to 1 gramme of ore.

filter containing any insoluble matter from the resolution of the acetate precipitate, must be ignited and examined for TiO_2 by treating the residue with HFl and H_2SO_4, heating to redness, fusing with Na_2CO_3, dissolving in HCl and water, and precipitating by ammonia. The precipitate so obtained is to be filtered, ignited, and the weight added to that of the Fe_2O_3, etc. Ilmenite even, when very finely ground in an agate mortar, is frequently capable of being almost entirely decomposed by HCl, and when this is the case it is of advantage to use this method of analysis. It may be necessary, however, under certain circumstances to decompose the ore at the start by fusing with bisulphate of potassium. To carry out this method, weigh 1 gramme of the ore, which has been ground as fine as possible in an agate mortar, into a large platinum crucible, add 10 grammes of pure bisulphate of potassium,* and heat the crucible, carefully covered, over a very low light until the bisulphate is melted. It is necessary to watch this operation most carefully, for the bisulphate has a strong tendency to boil over, and only unremitting attention on the part of the analyst will prevent the loss of the analysis. It is well at the start to stand by the crucible and raise the lid slightly at very short intervals to watch the condition and progress of the fusion. The lid should be held just over the crucible and in a horizontal position, otherwise the particles which have spirted on it from the mass in the crucible may run to the edge of the lid and, when the latter is replaced, down the outside of the crucible. Raise the heat very gradually, keeping the mass just liquid and the temperature at the point at which slight fumes of SO_3 are given off when the lid is raised, until the bottom of the crucible is dull red. When the ore is completely decomposed, remove the light, take off the lid of the crucible, and incline the latter at such an angle that the fused mass may run together on one side of the crucible and as near the top as possible. Allow it to cool in this position;

Fusion with bisulphate of potassium.

Precautions necessary.

---

* See page 49.

when cold it is easily detached from the crucible. Place the crucible and lid in a No. 4 beaker half full of cold water, and the fused mass in the little basket, as shown in Fig. 75, page 158.

Solution of the fused mass. Pour into the beaker enough strong aqueous solution of sulphurous acid to raise the liquid to the top of the basket, and allow the fusion to dissolve, which may require twelve hours. Wash off with a jet of cold water, and remove the basket, the crucible, and lid, stir the liquid, which should smell strongly of SO_2, and allow the insoluble matter to settle. Filter on an ashless filter, wash well with cold water, dry, ignite, and weigh. Treat with HFl and 2 or 3 drops of H_2SO_4, evaporate to dryness, ignite, and weigh.

SiO_2. The difference between the weights is SiO_2. If any appreciable residue remains in the crucible, fuse with a little Na_2CO_3, treat with H_2SO_4, and add to the main filtrate. To the main filtrate, which should be quite colorless and which should smell strongly of SO_2, add a clear filtered solution of 20 grammes of acetate of sodium and one-sixth of its volume of acetic acid, 1.04 sp. gr., heat to boiling, and boil for a few minutes. Allow to settle, filter on an ashless filter, wash thoroughly with hot water containing one-sixth its volume of acetic acid, and finally with hot water, dry,

Treatment of impure precipitate of TiO_2. ignite, and weigh as TiO_2. This precipitate, however, may not be quite pure, as small amounts of ferric oxide and alumina may be carried down with it. The best plan to pursue is to fuse with Na_2CO_3, dissolve in water, filter, wash, dry, and fuse the insoluble titanate of sodium, etc., with Na_2CO_3, treat the cooled mass in the

TiO_2. crucible with H_2SO_4, and precipitate and determine the TiO_2 as directed above. The two filtrates from the treatment of the first precipitate of TiO_2 may contain a little oxide of iron and alumina. To recover this, boil down the last filtrate until the greater part of the sulphurous acid has been driven off, add bromine-water to oxi-

Fe_2O_3 and Al_2O_3 carried down with first precipitate of TiO_2. dize the iron, acidulate the aqueous filtrate from the carbonate of sodium fusion with H_2SO_4, add it to this solution, boil the united solutions down in a platinum dish to a convenient volume, and add a slight excess of ammonia. Boil the solution until it smells faintly but decidedly of ammonia. filter off, and wash slightly. Redissolve the precipitate in HCl and reprecipitate by ammonia. filter, wash, ignite, and weigh as $Fe_2O_3 - Al_2O_3$, to be added to the main precipitate. Boil the main filtrate and washings down in a large platinum dish after adding enough bromine-water to oxidize all the iron, add HCl from time to time when necessary to keep the iron in solution, and, when reduced to a convenient bulk, nearly neutralize by ammonia, and boil. Filter off and wash the precipitate two or three times, redissolve and reprecipitate by ammonia, filter, wash, dry ignite, and weigh as $Fe_2O_3 - Al_2O_3 - P_2O_5$. Fuse this precipitate for a long time and at a high temperature with Na_2CO_3, dissolve in water, wash by decantation, redissolve the residue of Fe_2O_3, etc. in HCl, and determine the iron by titration. Determine the alumina by difference, the P_2O_5 being determined in a separate portion. In the filtrate from the $Fe_2O_3 - Al_2O_3 + P_2O_5$, determine manganese, lime and magnesia in the usual way.

$P_2O_5 -$
$Al_2O_3 -$
P_2O_5

Fe_2O_3

Al_2O_3

Mn. CaO
MgO

DETERMINATION OF SILICA.

When silica alone is wanted in an ore a more rapid method is sometimes desirable. In this case dissolve 1 gramme of the ore in HCl, evaporate to dryness, redissolve in dilute HCl, filter on an ashless filter, wash, dry, ignite, and weigh the insoluble siliceous matter. Treat this in the crucible with HF, and a few drops of H_2SO_4, evaporate to dryness, ignite and weigh. It is evident now that if the insoluble siliceous matter contains calcium, magnesium, potassium, or sodium, the loss of weight, which in the absence of these elements would represent the SiO_2 volatilized as fluoride of silicon, will be decreased by the amount of sulphuric acid which, uniting with these elements, remains as a part of the residue in the crucible. It is a simple operation, however, to fuse this residue

Loss in weight
with HF
and
H_2SO_4

with Na_2CO_3, dissolve in water, acidulate with HCl, heat to boiling, add solution of $BaCl_2$ and filter off, and weigh the precipitated $BaSO_4$. This being accomplished, calculate the amount of SO_3, and add its weight to the loss by volatilization. The result is the weight of SiO_2. When the ore contains appreciable amounts of sulphate of barium this method is not admissible.

SiO₂. in margin

Separation of Alumina from Ferric Oxide.

Besides the indirect method for determining alumina, it is sometimes necessary or convenient to make a direct separation. The method usually taken, the iron and alumina being in solution in HCl, is as follows : Add to the solution about five times the weight of the oxides, of citric acid (tartaric acid may be used, but, as it is liable to contain alumina, citric acid is preferable) and excess of ammonia. If the solution remains clear, heat to boiling, and add a fresh solution of sulphide of ammonium until all the iron is precipitated. If the solution does not remain clear on the addition of ammonia, acidulate with HCl, add more citric acid, and then excess of ammonia. Allow the sulphide of iron to settle, decant the clear liquid through a washed filter, throw the precipitate on the filter, and wash it well with water containing sulphide of ammonium, changing the beaker into which the washings run before each addition of wash-water, and keeping the funnel well covered with a watch-glass. Unite the filtrate and washings, acidulate with HCl, boil until the precipitated sulphur agglomerates, filter into a platinum dish, and evaporate to dryness. Heat carefully until the chloride of ammonium is volatilized and there remains in the dish a mass of carbonaceous matter from the decomposition of the citric acid. The expulsion of the last traces of water from the chloride of ammonium nearly always causes loss by spirting, but the difficulty may be entirely avoided by placing the dish in one of the holes of the air-bath overnight, after having lightly coated the upper edge of the dish with paraffine or grease to prevent the chloride of ammonium from creeping over the top.

Margin notes: *Separation by citric acid, ammonia, and sulphide of ammonium.* ... *Danger of loss by spirting.*

This long heating expels the last traces of water without the least
disturbance, and the dish may be at once placed over a Bunsen
burner, and the mass in it decomposed without fear of loss.
Transfer the carbonaceous matter to a crucible, wiping out the
dish carefully with filter-paper, and placing these in the crucible
also. Burn off the carbon in the crucible, fuse the residue with
Na_2CO_3 and a little $NaNO_3$, treat with water, transfer to a platinum
dish, dissolve any adhering particles in the crucible in HCl, add
this to the solution in the dish, with enough HCl to acidulate
it, heat to boiling after diluting, add a slight excess of ammonia,
boil until the solution smells but faintly of NH_3, filter, wash
thoroughly, ignite, and weigh as Al_2O_3. This precipitate will Al_2O_3.
contain any P_2O_5, Cr_2O_3, and TiO_2 that may have been in the
original solution. They may be separated by the methods given Impurities.
on page 183 *et seq.* It is liable to contain also a little iron,
which is almost invariably held in solution by the sulphide of
ammonium.

Dissolve the precipitate of ferrous sulphide on the filter in
dilute hot HCl, allow the solution and washings to run into the
beaker in which the precipitation was made, add a little HNO_3,
evaporate to dryness, redissolve in as little dilute HCl as possible,
filter into a platinum dish, dilute, precipitate by ammonia, filter,
wash, dry, ignite, and weigh as Fe_2O_3. Fe_2O_3.

Rose * suggested the method based on the solubility of alu- Separation
mina in caustic potassa or soda. When the iron and alumina are by caustic
in solution, evaporate until syrupy in a platinum dish, add a strong soda.
solution of caustic soda or potassa until the solution is strongly
alkaline, and then add a large excess of the precipitant, and boil
for ten or fifteen minutes; or, pour the nearly neutral solution of
the chlorides into a boiling solution of caustic soda or potassa in
a platinum or silver dish, in a thin stream, stirring continually.
Filter, wash with hot water, carefully acidulate the filtrate with

---

* Chimie Anal. Quant. (French ed.), page 148.

HCl, and precipitate the alumina by ammonia, filter, wash, dissolve in HCl, evaporate to dryness to get rid of SiO_2, redissolve, filter, and determine as usual. As the Fe_2O_3 precipitated by caustic soda or potassa always contains alkali, it must be dissolved in HCl, precipitated by ammonia, filtered, and weighed in the usual manner.

Rose also suggested fusing the finely-ground ignited oxides in a silver crucible with potassium or sodium hydrate; but this method, as well as the other, is open to the objection that it is almost impossible to get caustic soda or potassa that does not contain alumina, and generally there would be more in the reagent than in the ore.

Objection
to the
method.

Volatiliza-
tion in a
current of
HCl gas
after re-
duction of
the Fe by
H.

Rivot suggested the following method: After weighing the ignited oxides of iron and aluminium, grind them very fine, and weigh them into a porcelain or platinum boat. Place the boat in a porcelain or platinum tube, and heat to redness in a current of hydrogen gas until no more H_2O appears to come off. Replace the hydrogen by a stream of HCl gas, reheat the tube, and continue the current as long as ferric chloride is given off. Remove the boat, and, if the residue is not white, repeat the operation. Weigh the remaining Al_2O_3, and calculate from the amount of the oxides used the total amount in the ore.

Rose's mod-
ification.

Rose modified this method by substituting a crucible and tube for the boat, etc. The apparatus as he used it is the same as that described for the determination of manganese as sulphide, page 108.

Separation
by hypo-
sulphite of
sodium.

Wöhler suggested the method of separating iron and alumina by boiling the nearly neutral solution with an excess of hyposulphite of sodium. The following modification of this method[*] appears to give excellent results, and has the advantage of doing away with a subsequent separation of P_2O_5 in those cases in which it has not been determined in another portion. The Fe_2O_3 and

---

[*] Communicated to me by Mr. S. Peters in 1879.

Al$_2$O$_3$ from 1 gramme of ore being in solution in HCl, dilute to 400 or 500 c.c. with cold water, and add ammonia until the solution becomes dark red in color, but contains no precipitate. Now add 3.3 c.c. HCl, 1.2 sp. gr., and 2 grammes phosphate of sodium, dissolved in water and filtered; stir until the precipitate formed is dissolved and the solution becomes perfectly clear again. Add now 10 grammes of hyposulphite of sodium, dissolved in water and filtered if necessary, and 15 c.c. of acetic acid, 1.04 sp. gr., heat to boiling, boil fifteen minutes, filter as rapidly as possible on an ashless filter, wash thoroughly with hot water, dry, ignite in a porcelain crucible, and weigh as AlPO$_4$, which, multiplied by .41847, gives the weight of Al$_2$O$_3$. It is necessary in burning off the precipitate to raise the heat very carefully until all the carbon has been burned off, as the AlPO$_4$ may fuse and make it almost impossible to burn off the carbon.

Peters's modification.

DETERMINATION OF NICKEL, COBALT, ZINC, AND MANGANESE.

For the determination of these elements use 3 grammes of ore, dissolve in HCl, add a little HNO$_3$ or KClO$_3$ to oxidize any FeO in the ore, evaporate to dryness, redissolve in HCl, and evaporate a second time if necessary to get rid of all HNO. As noted on page 227, when the ore contains much organic matter, dissolve in HCl (if there is much gelatinous silica, evaporate to dryness or the filtration will be much retarded), filter, add HNO$_3$ or KClO$_3$, evaporate to dryness, redissolve in HCl, and evaporate a second time if necessary, redissolve in 10 c.c. HCl and 20 c.c. water, dilute, filter into a No. 6 beaker, and proceed exactly as directed for the determination of manganese in iron and steel, page 104 *et seq.*, until the precipitate by H$_2$S is obtained and filtered off. Deter-

Solution of the ore.

MnO.

mine the manganese, if desired, in the filtrate, as directed on page 106, and calculate to MnO.

Dry and ignite the precipitated sulphides of nickel, cobalt, zinc, copper, lead, etc., in a porcelain crucible, transfer to a small beaker, and dissolve in HCl, with the addition of a drop or two of HNO_3. Evaporate to dryness, redissolve in 10 to 20 drops HCl, dilute to 50 or 60 c.c., heat to boiling, and pass a current of H_2S

Sulphides of copper, lead, etc.

through the boiling solution. Filter off the precipitated sulphides of copper, lead, etc., and wash with water containing H_2S. Evaporate to dryness the filtrate, which contains only nickel, cobalt, and zinc. To the dry salts in the bottom of the beaker add 2 drops of strong HCl, dilute to 150 c.c. with cold water, and pass H_2S through the solution until it is thoroughly saturated with the gas. If a white precipitate forms, it is sulphide of zinc. Allow to stand several hours, filter, wash with H_2S water (the sulphide of zinc has a tendency to pass through the filter, and consequently the beaker into which the filtrate is received must be changed before the precipitate is poured on the filter), dry, and ignite the precipitate. Heat it several times with carbonate of ammonium to drive off any sulphuric acid that may have been formed by the

ZnO.

ignition, cool, and weigh as ZnO. The precipitate is greenish white while hot and yellowish white when cold. If it should carry down a little cobalt from the solution, the ignited precipitate of ZnO is green when cold. Pass H_2S through the filtrate from the ZnS again, and, if no further precipitate appears, add a few drops of a solution of .5 gramme of acetate of sodium in 10 c.c. water. If this occasions a white precipitate, filter it off, after standing, as in the first instance; but if the precipitate is black (as it is almost certain to be if the instructions given above are strictly followed), add the rest of the acetate of sodium solution, heat the solution to boiling, while the passage of the H_2S is continued, allow the precipitate to settle, filter it off, ignite it, and treat it as directed for the separation and determination of nickel

Ni and Co.

and cobalt, page 178 *et seq.*

DETERMINATION OF COPPER, LEAD, ARSENIC, AND ANTIMONY.

Treat 10 grammes of the very finely ground ore with 50 c.c. HCl, add a little $KClO_3$ from time to time, and increase the heat gradually until the ore is perfectly decomposed. Dilute, filter into a No. 5 beaker, deoxidize with bisulphite of ammonium, as directed on page 82, drive off the excess of SO_2, and pass H_2S through the solution for fifteen or twenty minutes. Allow the solution to stand for some hours until the precipitate has settled completely and the solution smells but faintly of H_2S. Filter on a thin felt on the Gooch crucible or small cone, wash with cold water, and suck dry. Transfer the felt and precipitate to a small beaker, using a little asbestos wad in the forceps to wipe off any adhering precipitate from the large beaker and the crucible or cone, and digest it with a few c.c. of a colorless solution of sulphide of potassium. Dilute to about 100 c.c., filter on another felt, and wash with water containing a little sulphide of potassium. The solution contains the sulphides of arsenic and antimony dissolved in sulphide of potassium, while the sulphides of copper and lead remain in the felt. Return the felt with the precipitate to the beaker from which they were filtered, and digest with HCl, with the addition of HNO_3, until all the black sulphides are dissolved, dilute with a little hot water, and filter. Evaporate the filtrate, after adding a few drops of H_2SO_4, until fumes of SO_3 are evolved, allow to cool, dilute with 25 c.c. cold water, add one-half its bulk of alcohol, allow to settle, filter the precipitated $PbSO_4$ on the Gooch crucible, wash with alcohol and water, heat carefully over a low light, and weigh. Treat the precipitate in the felt under a slight pressure with a strongly ammoniacal solution of citrate of ammonium, to dissolve the $PbSO_4$, wash with hot water, and weigh. The difference between the two weights is $PbSO_4$, which multiplied by .68298 gives the weight of Pb, or multiplied by .78879 gives the weight of PbS.

Evaporate the filtrate from the $PbSO_4$ until the alcohol is

[margin note:] Separation of As and Sb from Cu and Pb by K_2S.

[margin note:] Pb and PbS.

driven off and the solution reduced to a convenient bulk, transfer
to a platinum crucible, and precipitate the copper on the small

**Cu and
Cu₂S.**

platinum cylinder by the battery, page 176. The weight of Cu
multiplied by 1.25284 gives the weight of Cu_2S.

Acidulate the filtrate of sulphide of pótassium containing arsenic and antimony in solution with HCl, and allow to stand in a
warm place until all the H_2S has been driven off and the sulphides
of arsenic and antimony mixed with the excess of sulphur have
settled completely. Filter on a thin felt, wash with warm water,
then with alcohol, and finally with bisulphide of carbon, to dissolve the excess of S. Transfer the felt and precipitate to a small

**Solution of
sulphides
of arsenic
and anti-
mony by
HCl and
KClO₃.**

beaker, add 5 c.c. HCl and a few crystals of $KClO_3$. Digest at
a low temperature for some time, adding occasionally a small crystal of $KClO_3$, finally heat a little, but not to a sufficiently high
degree to fuse any little particles of separated sulphur, keeping the
liquid always full of the products of decomposition of the $KClO_3$.
When all the sulphides of arsenic and antimony are dissolved,
dilute with about 20 c.c. of warm water, and add a few small
crystals of tartaric acid to keep the antimony in solution. Filter
from the asbestos, using as little wash-water as possible in order
to keep down the volume of the solution, add a slight excess of
ammonia to the filtrate, and if it remains clear 5 c.c. of magnesia
mixture and one-third the volume of the solution of NH_4HO.

**Mg₂(NH₄)₂
As₂O₈ ÷
Aq.**

Cool in ice-water, and stir vigorously from time to time to precipitate the $Mg_2(NH_4)_2As_2O_8 + Aq$.

Allow to stand overnight, filter, and determine the arsenic
as directed on page 189. If the acid solution above mentioned
becomes cloudy upon the addition of NH_4HO, acidulate carefully with HCl, and add a little more tartaric acid. Then proceed

**Mg₂As₂O₇
and
FeAs₂.**

as above directed. The weight of As calculated from the amount
of $Mg_2As_2O_7$, multiplied by 1.373, gives the weight of $FeAs_2$.

Acidulate the filtrate from the $Mg_2(NH_4)_2As_2O_8 + Aq$, which
contains none of the washings, with HCl so that the solution is
just acid to test-paper, dilute with hot water to about 250 c.c.,

and pass H_2S into the solution, heating it gradually to boiling. Drive off the excess of H_2S with a current of CO_2, filter on a felt in the Gooch crucible, wash with water, alcohol, and finally with bisulphide of carbon to dissolve any free sulphur, dry carefully, heat to a temperature slightly above 100° C., and weigh as Sb_2S_3. For the very small amounts of antimony that are found in iron ores this method is sufficiently exact. The weight of Sb_2S_3 multiplied by .71390 gives the weight of Sb.

Sb_2S_3 and Sb.

DETERMINATION OF THE ALKALIES.

As a rule, the alkalies in iron ores are found exclusively in the insoluble silicious matter, and when the sum of the weights of the SiO_2, Al_2O_3 etc., CaO, and MgO in the insoluble silicious matter falls much below the weight of the latter, it is always well to look for alkalies.

Dissolve 3 grammes of the ore in HCl, evaporate to dryness, redissolve in 10 c.c. HCl + 20 c.c. water, dilute, and filter into a platinum dish. Ignite the insoluble residue, treat it in the crucible with HFl and 10 to 30 drops H_2SO_4, evaporate down until copious fumes of SO_3 are given off, dissolve in water with a little HCl if necessary, transfer to a small platinum dish, dilute to 100 c.c., heat to boiling, and add excess of ammonia. Boil for a few minutes, and filter from the Al_2O_3 etc. into another platinum dish. Evaporate the filtrate to dryness, and heat until the chloride and sulphate of ammonium are volatilized. Treat the residue with a little water, heat to boiling, and add enough oxalate of ammonium to precipitate all the calcium, filter into another platinum dish, evaporate to dryness, and heat to dull redness. Treat the residue with a little water, heat the filtrate to boiling, add enough acetate of barium to precipitate all the H_2SO_4, boil, and filter. Evaporate the filtrate to dryness and heat to redness to decompose the acetates. Treat the

Treatment of insoluble silicious matter.

residue with water, filter from the insoluble carbonate of barium, add a few drops of barium hydrate, and evaporate again to dryness. Dissolve in a few c.c. of water, and filter into a weighed crucible.

Evaporate very low, and, if nothing separates out, add a few drops of HCl, evaporate to dryness, heat to very dull redness, cool, and weigh as KCl + NaCl. To the residue in the crucible add a little water, in which the residue should dissolve perfectly, and a solution of platinic chloride. Evaporate down in the water-bath until the mass in the crucible solidifies upon cooling, add a little water to dissolve the excess of platinic chloride, and then an equal volume of alcohol. Filter on a Gooch crucible, wash with alcohol until the filtrate runs through perfectly colorless, dry at 120° C., and weigh as K_2PtCl_6. This weight multiplied by .19395 gives the weight of K_2O. Then multiply the weight of K_2PtCl_6 by .30696, which gives the weight of KCl. Subtract this from the weight of KCl + NaCl previously obtained, and the difference is the weight of NaCl, which multiplied by .53077 gives the weight of Na_2O.

[margin: KCl + NaCl.]

[margin: K_2PtCl_6. K_2O. KCl. NaCl. Na_2O.]

To the filtrate from the insoluble silicious matter add an excess of ammonia, rub a little grease or paraffine on the edge of the dish, and evaporate the mass to dryness. This will render the Fe_2O_3 very compact and granular. Dilute with hot water, add a few drops of ammonia, filter into another platinum dish, add a few drops of H_2SO_4, evaporate to dryness, and ignite to drive off all the ammonia salts. Then proceed exactly as directed for the determination of the alkalies in the insoluble silicious matter. The alkalies in the insoluble silicious matter may also be determined by J. Lawrence Smith's method of fusion with carbonate of calcium and chloride of ammonium, as directed farther on.

[margin: Treatment of the portion of the ore soluble in HCl.]

[margin: Decomposition of insoluble matter by $CaCO_3$ and HN_4Cl.]

The chloride of ammonium, which is so troublesome in alkali determinations, may be decomposed * very easily by evaporating

---

* J. L. Smith, Am. Jour. Sci. and Art, 1871, 3d Ser., vol. i. (whole No. ci.) p. 269.

the solution down very low, transferring to a tall beaker or flask, and heating with a large excess of HNO_3,—3 or 4 c.c. HNO_3 to every gramme of NH_4Cl supposed to be present. The decomposition takes place at a temperature below the boiling-point of water, and when the action seems to be over, transfer to a porcelain dish, and evaporate to dryness after adding a few drops of H_2SO_4. Dissolve in water, filter into a platinum dish, and proceed with the analysis in the usual way.

DETERMINATION OF CARBONIC ACID.

Weigh 3 grammes of finely-ground ore into the flask A, Fig. 93, and connect the apparatus in the manner shown in the sketch. L, L are triculated bottles for forcing a current of air through the apparatus. The air is deprived of any CO_2 which it may contain by passing through the tube M, which is filled with lumps of caustic potassa. M is connected with the bulb-tube B by the tube N, a piece of gum tubing over the slightly tapering and making an air-tight connection with B. The tube O is empty, and serves merely to condense the mass of the steam from the flask A. P contains anhydrous $CaSO_4$, and Q contains chloride of calcium. The potash-bulb and the drying-tube R form the absorption apparatus, and S is a safety-tube filled with $CaCl_2$ to prevent R from absorbing moisture from the atmosphere. Weigh the absorption apparatus with the precautions mentioned on page 136, and connect the apparatus. Close the stopcock C, and draw a little air through the apparatus by means of a piece of gum tubing attached to the end of S. Allow the suction of the air to draw the solution up into the rear limb of the potash-bulb, and if it remains there for a reasonable length of time the connections may be considered tight. Pour into the bulb B 10 c.c. H_2SO_4 diluted with about 60 c.c. water, connect the tube

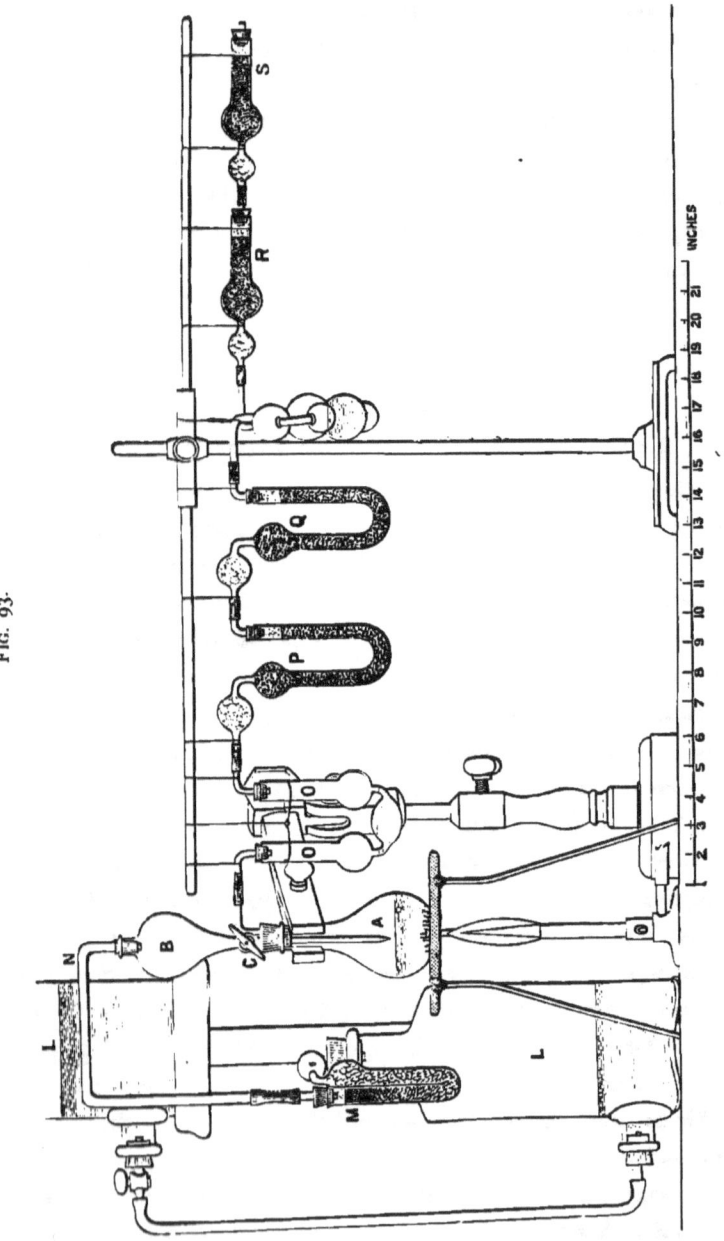

FIG. 93.

N, and by means of the stopcock C allow the acid to flow slowly into the flask A. When the acid has all run in, by opening slightly the stopcock in L, start a slow current of air through the apparatus. Warm the flask A, gradually increasing the heat until the solution boils, and continue the application of heat until a considerable amount of water has condensed in O. Allow it to cool while the current of air is continued, detach, and weigh the absorption apparatus. The increase of weight is the weight of CO_2.

CO_2.

DETERMINATION OF COMBINED WATER AND CARBON IN CARBONACEOUS MATTER.

The ores are very rare indeed in which the combined water can be accurately determined by simply heating them in a crucible and calling the loss by ignition "Water of Composition." Nor is the method of absorbing the moisture, driven off by heat, in a drying-tube much more reliable. The presence of pyrites, of organic matter, of graphite, and of binoxide of manganese serves to complicate the problem. The water of composition may indeed be determined with great accuracy by heating the ore in a tube with chromate of lead and bichromate of potassium, exactly as described for the determination of carbon in iron and steel by direct combustion, page 126 *et seq.* The increase of weight of the U tube which is attached to the end of the combustion-tube (and which should be filled in this case with granulated dried $CaCl_2$) is the weight of "Combined Water" in the amount of ore used. By attaching the absorption apparatus we likewise obtain the total CO_2 in the ore, or that existing as CO_2 in the carbonates, and that due to the oxidation of any carbon existing as carbonaceous or organic matter or as graphite. By subtracting from the weight of CO_2 thus obtained the amount of CO_2 existing as carbonate and determined by the method last given, and multiplying the

Loss by ignition.

Combustion with chromate of lead and bichromate of potassium.

Combined water.

difference by .27273, we get the weight of "Carbon in carbonaceous matter." When it is necessary to make a large number of
these determinations, the matter is very much simplified by using
the apparatus shown in Figs. 94 and 95.* Fig. 94 shows the

details of a form of tubulated platinum crucible suggested by Dr.
Gooch, which consists of the crucible with a flange at d into which
fits the cap. This cap consists of a conical cover, H, drawn up

FIG. 94.

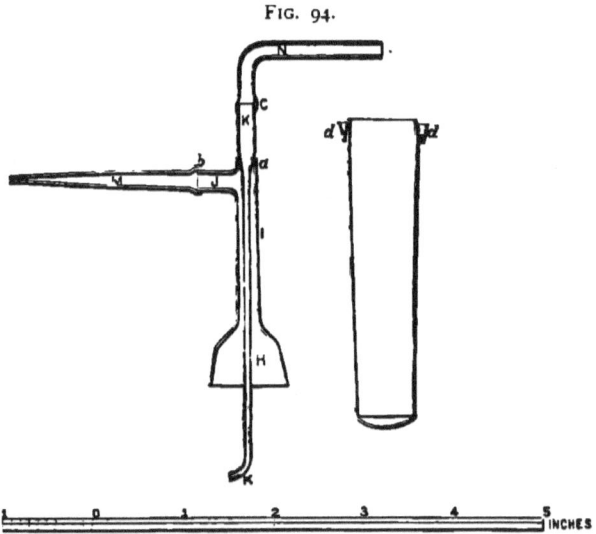

vertically into the tube I. The horizontal tube J is burned into I,
and through the centre of I passes the small tube K, which,
expanding at a, is burned into I at this point, sealing it securely.
The tubes N and M of glass are fused to K and J at C and b
respectively. In analyzing ores containing much water or carbonic acid, use 1 gramme; for others, use 3 grammes. Weigh the
finely-ground ore into a small agate mortar, and mix it thoroughly
with 7 to 10 grammes of previously fused bichromate of potassium, transfer it to the crucible A, Fig. 95, and place it in an air-bath

---

* Tenth Census of the U. S., Mining Industries, vol. xv. p. 519.

heated to 100° C. to drive off any hygroscopic moisture. When
perfectly dry, attach the cap B to the crucible, and stand the latter
in the triangle C.   Close the end N with a piece of rubber tubing
in the other end of which is fitted a piece of glass rod.   Attach
the weighed drying-tube D, filled with $CaCl_2$, to the horizontal
tube from B, by means of a thoroughly dried velvet cork.   Attach
the absorption apparatus E and F and the safety-tube G.   Fill the
outside of the flange *d* with small pieces of fused tungstate of

FIG. 95.

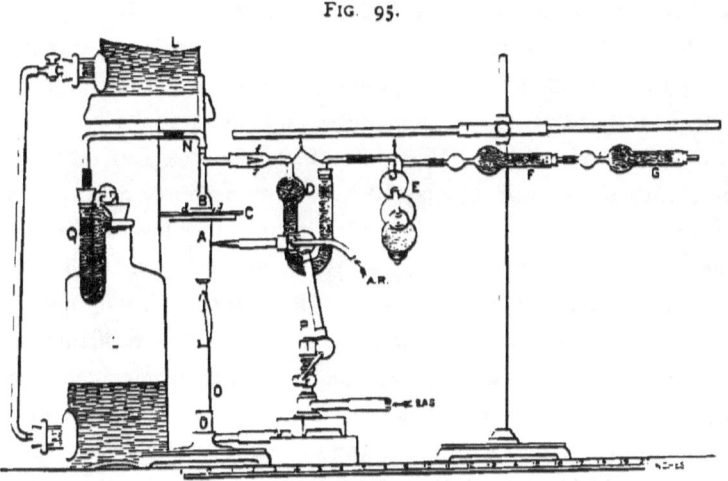

sodium, and, with a blow-pipe flame, melt them, having previously
immersed the lower end of A in a small beaker of ice-water.   The
expansion of the air in the crucible by the heat applied to melt the
tungstate of sodium will force some bubbles through the potash-
bulb E, and the subsequent cooling of the air in A will cause the
liquid in E to flow back into the rear bulb.   If the difference of
level thus produced be maintained for some minutes, the connections may be considered tight.   Connect N with the bottles L, as
shown in the sketch, and start a current of air through the apparatus.   The air is purified from CO_2 and moisture by passing through
Q, which is filled with fused caustic potassa.   Now, by means of the

blast-lamp P, heat the crucible just above the top of the mixture, and gradually carry the heat downward, increasing it at the same time. This will keep the mixture from frothing and choking the tube. Finally, heat the bottom of the crucible by the burner O, and continue the application of the heat for ten minutes. During the whole of the operation the air passes through N and K into the crucible and out through J and M (Fig. 94) into D (Fig. 95), and so through the apparatus. The moisture from the ore should not be allowed to condense in the wide part of D at *f,* but should be driven forward into the $CaCl_2$ by warming the tube at *f* with the flame from an alcohol lamp. Allow the apparatus to cool while the current of air is continued, then detach, and weigh the tube D and the absorption apparatus, and calculate the results, as directed on page 251. When detached from the apparatus, the wide end of the tube D may be closed by a short cork, covered with tin-foil to prevent the absorption of moisture from the atmos-

Cleaning the crucible. phere. To clean the crucible, remove it from the stand, and, holding it in a piece of asbestos board in an inclined position, melt the tungstate of sodium in the flange *d* with a blow-pipe flame and detach the cap. Dissolve out the bichromate by placing the crucible in a dish of hot water, clean out the ore, dissolve any adhering oxide in HCl, wash the crucible and cap with hot water, dry them, and they will be ready for another determination.

DETERMINATION OF CHROMIUM.

The small amount of chromium which is found in some iron ores is generally converted into chromate of sodium very readily by fusion with Na_2CO_3 and KNO_3. Fuse 1 or 2 grammes of the finely-ground ore with 10 times its weight of Na_2CO_3 and a little KNO_3. Treat the fused mass with water and wash it out into a small beaker. If the solution is colored by manganese, add a

little alcohol, which will precipitate the manganese, leaving the $\quad$ Indication
of the
presence
of chro-
mium
solution, if chromium is present, slightly yellow. If the solution
is colorless it may be considered proof of the absence of chromium. Otherwise filter, wash the insoluble matter on the filter,
dry it, grind it with ten times its weight of Na_2CO_3 and a little
KNO_3, fuse it, treat with water as before, filter, and add this filtrate
to the other. Acidulate the combined filtrates with HCl, evaporate
to dryness to render the silica insoluble, and reduce the chromic
acid to Cr_2O_3. Treat the mass with HCl, dilute, filter, and precipitate the $Cr_2O_3 - Al_2O_3$ by ammonia. Boil for some minutes, filter,
wash well with hot water, dry, and ignite the precipitate. Fuse
with as little Na_2CO_3 and KNO_3 as possible, treat with water, and
wash the solution into a platinum dish. Evaporate the solution $\quad$ Separation
from
Al_2O_3
until it is very concentrated, adding from time to time crystals of
nitrate of ammonium to change all the carbonated and caustic
alkali to nitrate. At each addition of the nitrate of ammonium
the solution effervesces, and carbonate of ammonium is given off.
When the solution is nearly syrupy, the addition of nitrate of ammonium no longer causes an effervescence, and the solution smells
faintly of ammonia, add a few drops of NH_4HO, and filter. By
this operation all the alumina, phosphate of aluminium, oxide of
manganese, etc., are precipitated, and there remain in solution
only the alkalies and the chromate of the alkalies. To the filtrate add an excess of sulphurous acid in water, which instantly
changes the color of the solution from yellow to green. Boil well,
add an excess of ammonia, boil for a few minutes, filter on an
ashless filter, wash well with hot water, dry, ignite, and weigh
as Cr_2O_3. $\quad$ Cr_2O_3

Chrome iron ore is best decomposed by Genth's [*] method of $\quad$ Chrome
iron ore.
fusing .5 gramme of very finely ground ore with bisulphate of
potassium, raising the heat very gradually until finally the highest
temperature of the lamp is attained, allowing it to cool, adding

---

[*] Chem. News, vol. vi. p. 31.

5 grammes Na_2CO_3 and 1 gramme KNO_3, and heating gradually to complete fusion, allowing it to remain so for fifteen or twenty minutes, treating with water, and proceeding as directed above.

DETERMINATION OF TUNGSTEN.

Digest from 1 to 10 grammes of the ore in HCl, adding HNO_3 from time to time. When the ore appears to be perfectly decomposed, evaporate to dryness on the water-bath (a higher temperature is not admissible, as it may render the WO_3 insoluble in NH_4HO), redissolve in HCl, and evaporate down again. Redissolve in HCl, dilute, filter, wash with acidulated water, and finally with alcohol. Treat on the filter with ammonia, allowing the filtrate to run into a platinum dish, evaporate to small bulk, add excess of ammonia, filter, if necessary, into a platinum crucible, evaporate carefully to dryness, heat gently to drive off the ammonia, and ignite. Weigh as WO_3.

DETERMINATION OF VANADIUM.

Fuse 5 grammes of the very finely ground ore with 30 grammes of Na_2CO_3 and from 1 to 5 grammes of $NaNO_3$, and proceed exactly as in the determination of vanadium in pig-iron, page 193. A second fusion of the residue from the aqueous solution of the first fusion is hardly ever necessary.

DETERMINATION OF SPECIFIC GRAVITY.

The specific gravity of iron ores is determined with much greater accuracy by using the powdered material than by using lumps of the ore. The little flask shown in Fig. 96 was designed for this purpose by the late Mr. James Hogarth,* and its use avoids two difficulties experienced in the use of the ordinary specific gravity bottle,—the expansion and overflow consequent upon transferring the flask at 60° F. to the higher temperature of the balance-case, and the necessity for waiting until the finely-divided particles of the ore shall have settled before inserting the stopper. These difficulties were overcome by melting a capillary tubulus to the lower part of the neck of the flask, and by grinding in

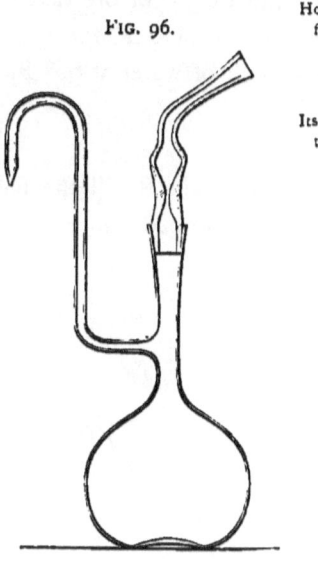

Fig. 96.

Hogarth's flask.

Its advantages.

a stopper having a small bulb above the capillary, to allow for expansion. The operation is conducted as follows: Transfer a weighed amount of the ore to the flask, add enough water to cover it, and heat it almost to the boiling-point by placing it in the water-bath. Place the flask under a bell-jar connected with an aspirator or air-pump, and expel all the air by allowing it to boil for some time at a reduced pressure. Remove it from the bell-jar, fill it up to the tubulus with cold water, insert the stopper, and cool the flask and its contents to about 60° F. By suction on the stopper draw water through the tubulus until it is slightly above the capillary of the stopper, at which point a mark is scratched. When the flask and its contents are exactly at 60° F.,

---

* Tenth Census of the U. S., vol. xv. p. 522.

adjust the volume exactly to the mark on the capillary by touch-ing a piece of blotting-paper to the end of the tubulus or by draw-ing a little water in through it.   Dry the flask, allow it to acquire the temperature of the balance-case, and weigh it.   Now, if W is the weight of ore taken, W' the weight of the ore and water at 60° F., and K the weight of the flask and its contents to the mark of water at 60° F., then

$$\text{sp. gr.} = \frac{W}{W + K - W'}.$$

To obtain K, fill the flask with boiled water, and treat it exactly as described above.

METHODS FOR THE ANALYSIS

OF

LIMESTONE.

DETERMINATION OF INSOLUBLE SILICIOUS MATTER, ALUMINA AND OXIDE OF IRON, CARBONATE OF CALCIUM, AND CARBONATE OF MAGNESIUM.

WEIGH 1 gramme of the powdered limestone, previously dried at 100° C., into a No. 1 beaker, cover with a watch-glass, and pour in 5 c.c. of HCl diluted with 25 c.c. of water and a little bromine-water. Digest on the sand-bath until all the action ceases, wash the watch-glass with a fine jet of water, and evaporate to dryness. Redissolve in 10 c.c. HCl diluted with 50 c.c. water, filter on a small ashless filter, wash well with hot water, dry, ignite, and weigh as *Insoluble Silicious Matter.* Heat the filtrate to boiling, add a slight excess of ammonia, boil for a few minutes, filter, wash once or twice. Dissolve the precipitate on the filter in a little dilute HCl, allowing the solution to run into the beaker in which the precipitation was made, wash well with water, dilute, boil, and reprecipitate by ammonia. Filter on a small ashless filter, allow this filtrate to run into the beaker containing the first one, wash well with hot water, dry, ignite, and weigh as Al_2O_3 and Fe_2O_3. Heat the united filtrates to boiling, add enough oxalate of ammonium to convert all the calcium and magnesium into oxalates.* Allow the precipitate of oxalate of

---

* 25 c.c. of the saturated solution is about the proper quantity.

calcium to settle for fifteen or twenty minutes, filter on an ash-less filter, wash with hot water, dry, ignite for some time over a Bunsen burner, and finally for fifteen minutes at the highest temperature of a blast-lamp. Cool in a desiccator, weigh quickly, ignite again over the blast-lamp for five minutes, cool, and weigh again. If this weight is the same, or nearly the same, as the

CaO.   previous one, call the amount CaO. If the second weight is much less than the first, ignite, and weigh again until the weight is constant. The weight of CaO multiplied by 1.78459 gives the

$CaCO_3$ weight of $CaCO_3$. Add to the filtrate from the oxalate of cal-

Quantity of microcosmic salt required.   cium 30 c.c. of a saturated solution of microcosmic salt (phosphate of sodium and ammonium), acidulate with HCl, and evaporate the solution to about 300 c.c. If during the evaporation any precipitate should separate out, redissolve it in HCl. Cool the evaporated solution in ice-water, and add ammonia drop by drop, stirring the solution, but being careful to avoid rubbing the sides of the beaker with the rod, as the precipitate of $Mg_2(NH_4)_2P_2O_8 + 12H_2O$ is liable to adhere with great tenacity to those points or lines where the rod has touched the sides or bottom of the beaker. Continue the addition of ammonia until the solution is decidedly alkaline, and then add an amount equal to one-fourth of the neutralized solution. After the precipitate has begun to form, stir vigorously several times, allow to stand over-night, filter on an ashless filter, rub off with a "policeman" any of the precipitate that may adhere to the beaker, wash with a mixture of 1 part ammonia and 2 parts water, containing 100 grammes of nitrate of ammonium to the litre, dry, ignite with great care, as directed on page 85, cool, and weigh as $Mg_2P_2O_7$,

MgO and $MgCO_3$.   which multiplied by .36212 gives the weight of MgO, and multiplied by .75760 gives the weight of $MgCO_3$.

Other substances found in limestones.   Limestones, besides the ordinary constituents mentioned above, may contain small amounts of phosphoric acid, sulphur as sulphate or as pyrites, titanic acid, organic matter, combined water, alkalies, manganese, fluorine, and in rare instances nearly all the metals found in iron ores. For most of these the methods described in the analysis of iron ores may be employed. Very often the amounts of silica and alumina are required in calculating mixtures for the blast-furnace, and, as the matter insoluble in HCl consists usually of silicates of alumina, lime, and magnesia, it would be necessary in accurate work to decompose the *Insoluble Silicious Matter* by fusion with carbonate of sodium and to make a separate analysis of it, as described on page 231. It is, indeed, much better to make the analysis in this way than to add the filtrate from the silica to the main solution, for the oxalate of calcium is sure to carry down some of the sodium salts with it and thus very materially complicate the analysis.

Determination of SiO₂.

After weighing the Al_2O_3 and Fe_2O_3 from the *Insoluble Silicious Matter* and that from the portion soluble in dilute HCl to determine the Fe_2O_3, fuse the two precipitates with a little carbonate of sodium, dissolve in water, acidulate with HCl in a beaker, add a few small crystals of citric acid to the clear solution, then excess of ammonia and sulphide of ammonium. Allow the precipitate of sulphide of iron to settle, filter, wash slightly, dissolve in HCl, add a little bromine-water, boil the solution, precipitate by ammonia, filter, wash, ignite, and weight as Fe_2O_3. The weight of Fe_2O_3 subtracted from the weight of the total $Al_2O_3 + Fe_2O_3$ gives, of course, the weight of Al_2O_3.

Fe_2O_3.
Al_2O_3.

The CaO and MgO in the *Insoluble Silicious Matter* should not be calculated as carbonates, but should be considered as existing as CaO and MgO.

CaO and MgO in Insoluble Silicious Matter.

To determine phosphoric acid in limestones, treat 20 grammes with dilute HCl, filter from the *Insoluble Silicious Matter*, to the filtrate add a few drops of ferric chloride solution, then ammonia until the solution is alkaline to litmus-paper,* and acetic acid to decided acid reaction. Boil for a few minutes, filter, wash once

Determination of P_2O_5.

---

* If the precipitate is not decidedly red in color, acidulate with HCl and add more ferric chloride solution.

with hot water, dissolve in HCl on the filter, allowing the solution to run into the beaker in which the precipitation was made, add the solution from the treatment of the *Insoluble Silicious Matter* mentioned below, dilute, and reprecipitate exactly as before with ammonia and acetic acid. Dissolve this precipitate on the filter in dilute HCl, allowing the solution to run into a No. 1 beaker, wash the filter with hot water, evaporate the solution down almost to dryness, and precipitate the P_2O_5 as directed on page 85.

Treatment of In-soluble Silicious Matter.

Ignite the *Insoluble Silicious Matter*, treat it with HFl and a few drops of H_2SO_4, evaporate until fumes of SO_3 are given off, fuse with Na_2CO_3, digest in water, filter, acidulate the solution with HCl, and add it to the solution of the first precipitate in the soluble portion as mentioned above.

Treatment of In-soluble Silicious Matter by direct fusion.

Instead of treating the *Insoluble Silicious Matter* with HFl and H_2SO_4, it may be fused at once with Na_2CO_3, the fused mass treated with water, filtered, the filtrate acidulated, evaporated to dryness, redissolved in water slightly acidulated with HCl, filtered, and the filtrate added to the solution of the first precipitate by ammonia and acetic acid as above.

Sulphur in limestone.

To determine sulphur in limestone, fuse 1 gramme with Na_2CO_3 and KNO_3 exactly as in the determination of sulphur in iron ores, page 220 *et seq.*

To determine sulphates, proceed as in the analysis of iron ores for these substances, page 222 *et seq.*

METHODS FOR THE ANALYSIS

OF

CLAY.

CLAY is essentially silica, mixed with silicates of aluminium, Composi- calcium, magnesium, potassium, and sodium. These silicates are tion of clay. hydrated, so that clay usually contains from 6 to 12 per cent. of water of composition. Besides these usual constituents, clay may contain oxide of iron, titanic acid, pyrites, organic matter, phosphoric acid, and occasionally some of the rarer elements, such as vanadium.

Clay being practically unacted on by HCl, it is necessary to Method of analysis. proceed as follows: Fuse 1 gramme of the finely-ground clay dried at 100° C. with 10 grammes of Na_2CO_3 and a very little $NaNO_3$. Run the fused mass well up on the sides of the crucible, allow it to cool, and treat it with hot water until thoroughly disintegrated, transferring the liquid from time to time to a platinum dish. Treat the crucible with HCl, add this to the liquid in the dish, acidulate with HCl, and evaporate to dryness in the air-bath. Treat the mass with water and a little HCl, evaporate again to dryness, and treat with 15 c.c. HCl and 45 c.c. water. Allow it to stand in a warm place for fifteen or twenty minutes, add 50 c.c. water, and filter on an ashless filter. Wash thoroughly with hot water acidulated with a few drops of HCl, dry, ignite, heat for three or four minutes over the blast-lamp, and weigh. Treat the precipitate with HFl and a few drops of H_2SO_4, evaporate to dryness, ignite, and weigh. The difference between the two weights is

SiO₂.

SiO$_2$. If any appreciable residue remains in the crucible, treat it with a little HCl, and wash it out into the filtrate from the silica. Transfer the filtrate from the silica to a large platinum dish, heat it to boiling, add an excess of ammonia, boil until the smell of NH$_3$ is quite faint, filter on an ashless filter, and wash several times with hot water. Stand the filtrate and washings aside, and treat the precipitate on the filter with a mixture of 15 c.c. HCl and 15 c.c. water, cold. Allow the solution to run into a small clean beaker, replace this by the platinum dish in which the precipitation was made, pour the solution on the filter again, and repeat this operation until the precipitate has completely dissolved. Wash out the beaker into the filter, wash the latter thoroughly with cold water, dry, and preserve it. Reprecipitate by ammonia, as above directed, filter on an ashless filter, wipe out the dish with small pieces of filter-paper, add these to the precipitate, and wash thoroughly with hot water. Dry, ignite the precipitate and filter, and the filter from the first precipitation, heat for a few minutes

Al₂O₃ – Fe₂O₃.

over the blast-lamp, cool, and weigh as Al$_2$O$_3$ and Fe$_2$O$_3$. Fuse the ignited precipitate with Na$_2$CO$_3$, treat the fused mass with water, wash it out into a small beaker, allow the residue to settle, decant off the clear, supernatant fluid, treat the residue with HCl, and determine the iron volumetrically, or add citric acid and ammonia, and precipitate the iron as sulphide. Filter, wash, dissolve in HCl, oxidize with bromine-water, and precipitate the Fe$_2$O$_3$ by ammonia. Filter, wash, dry, ignite, and weigh as Fe$_2$O$_3$. Subtract the weight of Fe$_2$O$_3$ from the Al$_2$O$_3$ + Fe$_2$O$_3$ found above,

Al₂O₃.

and the difference is Al$_2$O$_3$.

As the amounts of calcium and magnesium in clay are very small, the filtrate and washings from the second precipitation of

CaO and MgO.

Al$_2$O$_3$ + Fe$_2$O$_3$ may be rejected and the CaO and MgO determined in the first filtrate as directed on page 232.

Determination of alkalies.

To determine the alkalies in clay, treat 2 grammes of the finely-ground material in a platinum dish with 4 c.c. of strong H$_2$SO$_4$ and 40 or 50 c.c. of redistilled HFl. Stir it from time to time with a platinum wire or rod, heating carefully, until the clay is entirely decomposed and no more gritty substance can be felt under the rod. Evaporate to dryness, and heat until fumes of SO_3 are given off. The entire operation should be carried on under a hood with a good draft, as HFl is very poisonous, and the evaporation may be safely conducted on the little arrangement shown in Fig. 10, page 20. Allow the dish to cool, add about 50 c.c. water and a little HCl, and heat until the mass is all dissolved. If any of the clay has escaped decomposition, filter into another platinum dish, wash the insoluble matter on the filter, dry, ignite, and decompose it in the crucible with HFl and H_2SO_4. Dissolve the mass in the crucible after evaporating off the HFl, and add the solution to the main solution in the dish. Dilute this solution to 300 or 400 c.c. with hot water, heat to boiling, add an excess of ammonia, boil for a few minutes, and filter. Allow the precipitate to drain well on the filter, remove the filtrate, which should be in a platinum dish, to a light, and evaporate it down. Pierce the filter with a wire or rod, and wash the precipitate into the dish in which the precipitation was made with a jet of hot water. Dilute to 300 or 400 c.c., add a little ammonia, heat to boiling, filter, and wash several times with hot water. Add this filtrate to the first one, and evaporate to dryness. Heat until all the ammonium salts are volatilized, and proceed exactly as directed for the determination of alkalies in the *Insoluble Silicious Matter* from iron ores, page 247.

Instead of decomposing the clay by HFl and H_2SO_4, the method given by J. Lawrence Smith may be used for determining alkalies. Weigh 1 gramme of the finely-ground clay into a porcelain or agate mortar, add an equal weight of granular chloride of ammonium,* and grind the two together to mix them. Add 8 grammes of carbonate of calcium,† and grind the entire mass so as to obtain an intimate mixture of the whole. Transfer to a

---

* See page 45. † See page 52.

capacious platinum crucible, cover with a close-fitting lid, and heat carefully to decompose the chloride of ammonium, which is accomplished in a few minutes. Heat gradually to redness, and keep the bottom of the crucible at a bright red for about an hour. Allow the crucible to cool, and if the mass is easily detached from the crucible, transfer it to a platinum dish and add about 80 c.c. of water. Wash off the lid into the crucible with water, heat this to boiling, and wash the crucible out into the dish. Heat the water in the dish to boiling, and, when the mass has completely slaked, filter into another platinum dish and wash the mass on the filter with hot water. If the semi-fused mass in the crucible is not easily detached, place the crucible on its side in the dish, wash off the lid into the dish, add about 100 c.c. water, and heat until the mass disintegrates. Remove the crucible, wash it off into the dish, and filter as above directed. To the filtrate add about 1½ grammes of pure carbonate of ammonium, evaporate on the water-bath, or very carefully over a light, until the volume of the solution is reduced to about 40 c.c., add a little more carbonate of ammonium and a few drops of ammonia, and filter on a small filter. Evaporate the filtrate carefully after adding a few drops more of carbonate of ammonium to make certain that all the calcium has been precipitated. If any further precipitate appears, filter into a platinum crucible and evaporate to dryness. Heat carefully to dull redness to drive off any ammonium salts, and weigh the residue as $KCl + NaCl$. Separate the potassium and sodium as directed on page 248.

Water of composition.

Determine the water of composition by igniting 1 gramme of the clay for twenty minutes at a bright red heat, when the loss of weight will represent the water. In the presence of much organic matter or pyrites the method given for the determination of water of composition in iron ores, page 251, may be used.

Determination of TiO_2.

To determine titanic acid, treat 2 grammes of the finely-ground clay in a large platinum crucible with HFl and 5 c.c. H_2SO_4. Evaporate off the HFl, and heat carefully until the greater part of the H_2SO_4 is volatilized. Allow the crucible to cool, add 10 grammes of Na_2CO_3, and fuse for thirty minutes at the highest temperature obtainable by a Bunsen burner. Run the fused mass well up on the sides of the crucible, and allow it to cool. Treat the fused mass with water, transfer it to a beaker, and filter. Wash the insoluble matter slightly on the filter, dry, ignite, and fuse it again with Na_2CO_3. Dissolve in water as before, and filter. By this method of treatment nearly all the alumina will be dissolved and separated from the titanic acid. Fuse the insoluble matter left on the filter with Na_2CO_3, and determine the TiO_2 as directed on page 173.

When alkalies are determined, the precipitated alumina may be used for the determination of TiO_2. In this case dry the precipitate of Al_2O_3, etc., separate it from the filter, ignite the two filters, add the ash to the dried, not ignited, precipitate of Al_2O_3, etc., and fuse with Na_2CO_3 as above.

Determination of TiO_2 in the portion taken for the determination of alkalies.

METHODS FOR THE ANALYSIS

OF

SLAGS.

Composition of blast-furnace slags.

BLAST-FURNACE slags contain silica, alumina, lime, magnesia, and alkalies always, generally also ferrous oxide, manganous oxide, and sulphur, and occasionally titanic acid, small amounts of phosphoric acid, and such metallic oxides as may exist in the ores, fluxes, or fuel used in the furnace. Sulphur, which is occasionally present in considerable amounts, is considered to exist in the slag as sulphide of calcium.

The method used for the determination of the principal ingredients depends upon whether the slag is capable of being entirely or but partially decomposed by HCl.

In the first case weigh 1 gramme of the finely-ground slag into a platinum or porcelain dish, add 20 c.c. of water, and shake the dish until the material is thoroughly disseminated through the

Slags decomposed by HCl.

water. Add gradually 30 c.c. HCl, with constant stirring, and finally heat the dish carefully. The slag will dissolve completely to a clear liquid, but, after heating for a short time, will suddenly form a solid jelly. Evaporate carefully to dryness, treat with a few c.c. of dilute HCl and a little bromine-water, evaporate again to dryness, and add 15 c.c. HCl and 45 c.c. water. Allow to stand fifteen or twenty minutes in a warm place, add 50 c.c. water, filter on an ashless filter, wash thoroughly with hot water, dry, ignite, and weigh. Treat the material in the crucible with a little water, add 2 or 3 drops H_2SO_4 and enough HFl to dissolve it.

268

Evaporate to dryness, ignite, and weigh. The loss of weight is SiO_2. SiO_2.

Any residue in the crucible after the volatilization of the SiO_2 is to be added to the $Al_2O_3 - Fe_2O_3$. Heat the filtrate obtained above, diluted to 500 c.c., to boiling, add a slight excess of ammonia, boil for a few minutes, filter on an ashless filter, and wash two or three times with boiling water. Stand the filtrate aside, and pour on the precipitate in the filter a mixture of 15 c.c. HCl and 30 c.c. cold H_2O, allowing the solution to run into the dish in which the precipitation was made. Alumina precipitated in this way seems generally to dissolve more readily in cold than in hot dilute HCl, but it is often necessary to break up the precipitate on the filter with a rod, to pour the acid solution back on the filter several times after it has run through, and sometimes to pierce the filter with a rod or wire and wash the precipitate still undissolved into the dish. Wash the filter well with water, dry it, and keep it to ignite with the Al_2O_3, etc. Heat the filtrate and washings to boiling, reprecipitate by ammonia, filter on an ashless filter, clean off any adhering precipitate from the dish with filter-paper, add it to the precipitate on the filter, wash well with hot water, dry, ignite, after adding the filter on which the first precipitation was filtered, and weigh as Al_2O_3, etc. Add to this the weight of the residue from the treatment of the SiO_2 by H_2SO_4 and HFl.* and the sum is the total $Al_2O_3 - Fe_2O_3 - P_2O_5 + TiO_2$. Al_2O_3, etc.

Evaporate down to about 300 c.c. the two filtrates obtained above, transfer to a No. 3 beaker, add a few drops of ammonia and enough sulphide of ammonium to precipitate the manganese. Filter off, and determine the manganese as directed on page 234, in the "Analysis of Iron Ores." To the filtrate from the sulphide of manganese add a slight excess of HCl, boil until all the H_2S is driven off, filter from any precipitated sulphur, and determine the CaO and MgO as directed on page 259 *et seq.*, in the "Analysis of Limestone." CaO and
MgO.

---

* This residue should be examined for CaO.

Determi-
nation of
FeO.
To determine the FeO, fuse the ignited precipitate of Al_2O_3, etc., obtained above, with 5 grammes of carbonate of sodium, at a very high temperature, for at least thirty minutes. Allow the crucible to cool, treat the fused mass with water, transfer to a beaker, allow the insoluble matter to settle, decant the clear, supernatant liquid through a filter, and treat the residue with HCl. Pour the solution through the filter to take up any iron that may have been suspended in the liquid decanted through it, and determine the iron volumetrically or by precipitation as sulphide in the solution to which citric acid and an excess of ammonia have been

Slags con-
taining no
manga-
nese.
added, as on page 240. When the slag contains no appreciable amount of manganese, the precipitation by sulphide of ammonium, page 269, may be omitted and the CaO precipitated at once from the concentrated solution.

Slags that
are not
entirely
decom-
posed
by HCl.
For the analysis of slags that are not entirely decomposed by HCl, recourse must be had to fusion with Na_2CO_3 and a little $NaNO_3$, exactly as described for the analysis of clay, page 263 et seq. After filtering off the SiO_2 as directed, page 263, proceed with the analysis as described for slags decomposed by HCl, page

Reprecipi-
tation of
the CaO.
269 et seq. As, however, the oxalate of calcium is very liable to carry down sodium salts with it, it is always well, after igniting the oxalate of calcium, to dissolve it in dilute HCl, transfer the solution to a platinum dish, dilute to 300 c.c. with hot water, add an excess of ammonia, and precipitate boiling by 30 c.c. of a saturated solution of oxalate of ammonium. Filter, wash, ignite, and weigh in the usual manner.

Determi-
nation of
sulphur
in slags.
For the determination of sulphur in slags, fuse 1 gramme with Na_2CO_3 and a little KNO_3, and proceed exactly as directed for the determination of sulphur in iron ores, page 220 et seq. Calculate the total sulphur as CaS and the remainder of the calcium as CaO.

Alkalies,
TiO_2, etc.
For the determination of alkalies, titanic acid, etc., proceed as directed for the determination of these substances in clay.

Converter
slags, etc.
Converter slags, open-hearth slags, refinery slag, tap cinder, mill cinder, etc., are analyzed by the methods described for the

analysis of iron ores.   In the case of slags obtained from the Analysis of basic slag. manufacture of steel by the basic process, which usually contain very large amounts of phosphoric acid, proceed as follows: Treat 1 gramme of the finely-ground slag in a small beaker with 15 c.c. HCl and a little HNO_3 until it is decomposed.   Evaporate to dryness, redissolve in 10 c.c. HCl and 20 c.c. H_2O, dilute, filter off, and weigh the SiO_2.   To the filtrate diluted to 500 c.c. add a solu- SiO_2. tion of ferric chloride and a slight excess of ammonia, if the precipitate is not decidedly red in color, acidulate carefully with HCl, add more ferric chloride solution, and then a slight excess of ammonia.   Add acetic acid to slight acid reaction, heat to boiling, filter and wash slightly with boiling water, stand the filtrate aside, and dissolve the precipitate on the filter in HCl, allow the solution to run into the beaker in which the precipitation was made, wash the filter thoroughly with cold water, dilute the filtrate to about 400 c.c., add a slight excess of ammonia, and then acetic acid, boil, and filter as before.   Add this filtrate to the first, evaporate down, and determine the manganese, calcium, and magnesium, as directed in the case of blast-furnace slags, page 269.   Dissolve the MnO, CaO, and MgO. precipitate on the filter in HCl, dissolving any iron that may adhere to the beaker in a few drops of the same acid, pour it on the filter, and wash the beaker and filter well with water.   Allow the solution and washings to run into a No. 3 beaker, add about 10 grammes of citric acid and an excess of ammonia.   To this solution, which should be cold, and should measure about 300 c.c. add, drop by drop, 50 c.c. of magnesia mixture, stirring carefully, without touching the sides of the beaker with the rod.   Add about one-third the volume of the solution of ammonia, allow the beaker to stand in ice-water for some time, stir vigorously several times, and after a few hours filter (preferably on a Gooch crucible), wash with ammonia-water of the usual strength, ignite carefully, and P_2O_5. weigh as $Mg_2P_2O_7$.   Any alumina in the slag will be in the filtrate from the phosphate of ammonium and magnesium, and may Al_2O_3. be determined by the method on page 240.   Determine the iron

FeO.   volumetrically in a separate portion, and calculate to FeO. Determine any other elements present by the methods under " Analysis of Iron Ores."

Phosphoric acid cannot well be determined in basic slags by fusion with Na_2CO_3, as phosphate of calcium is not readily decomposed by this method, and its employment may lead to error.

METHOD FOR THE ANALYSIS

OF

FIRE-SANDS.

As sand contains comparatively very small amounts of alumina, lime, and magnesia, and a very large amount of silica, it is best to proceed as follows in the analysis: Weigh 2 grammes of the finely-ground sand into a large platinum crucible, moisten it with cold water, add 6 or 8 drops of H_2SO_4, and then gradually enough HFl to dissolve it. Evaporate to dryness (under a hood, of course), and heat to redness to drive off the H_2SO_4. Allow the crucible to cool, add a little Na_2CO_3, and fuse. Dissolve the cold fusion in water, add an excess of HCl, evaporate to dryness, redissolve in HCl and water, filter from SiO_2, and determine the Al_2O_3, CaO, and MgO as usual. Ignite 1 gramme of the sand and determine the loss, which will be water and organic matter (if present). _{removed}

It is well to note that in the presence of Al_2O_3 it is almost impossible to drive off all the SiO_2 by treatment with HFl and H_2SO_4, and the small amount of SiO_2 remaining after this treatment must be separated as directed above.

Add together the percentages of water, Al_2O_3, CaO, and MgO, subtract the sum from 100, and call the remainder SiO_2.

(marginal notes:) Treatment with HFl and H_2SO_4. — Al_2O_3, CaO, and MgO — Water. — SiO_2.

18

METHODS FOR THE ANALYSIS

OF

COAL AND COKE.

PROXIMATE ANALYSIS.

A PROXIMATE analysis affords a very rapid and comparatively simple way of classifying and valuing coal. From the nature of the material, the determinations cannot be absolute, but inferences may be drawn from the relative proportions of *Moisture, Volatile Combustible Matter,* and *Ash.* Therefore it is essential that the analysis should be performed in such a way as to obtain the most concordant results. The series of experiments carried out by Prof. Heinrichs,* of the Iowa State Geological Survey, show very clearly that by following a definite course of procedure and taking a few simple precautions the method may be made sufficiently accurate to accomplish satisfactorily the desired object. The details, which should in all cases be closely adhered to, are as follows: Weigh from 1 to 2 grammes of powdered coal into a crucible, heat for exactly one hour in an air-bath from 105° to 110° C., allow the crucible to cool, and weigh it. The loss of weight divided by the weight of coal taken and the result multiplied by

Moisture.   100 gives the percentage of *Moisture* in the coal. Weigh from 1

Volatile
Com-
bustible
Matter.
to 2 grammes of the powdered coal into a small platinum crucible, heat the crucible with the cover on by means of a Bunsen burner for three and a half minutes, then, without allowing the crucible

* Chem. News, xviii. 53.

to cool, heat it for three and a half minutes more at the highest temperature obtainable by means of a gas blast-lamp. Cool and weigh. Divide the loss of weight by the amount of material used, multiply by 100, subtract the percentage of *Moisture*, and the remainder is the percentage of *Volatile Combustible Matter*. This determination should always be made on a fresh portion of coal, *Fresh portion to be used.* and never on the portion used for the determination of *Moisture*.

After weighing the crucible for the determination of *Volatile Combustible Matter* as above, place it over a light in the position shown in Fig. 12 or Fig. 13, page 22, and burn off the carbon. This operation, which is liable to be tedious, may be hastened by breaking up and stirring the mass from time to time with a platinum rod or a piece of stiff wire. It is necessary to avoid producing too strong a draft in the crucible, as by this means par- *Precautions in burning off carbon.* ticles of the ash may be carried out and a fictitious value given to the coal or coke by the apparent increase of *Fixed Carbon* and corresponding decrease of *Ash*. When no particles of carbon are apparent in the ash, allow the crucible to cool, and weigh it. The difference between this weight and the last, divided by the weight of coal taken, and multipled by 100, gives the percentage of *Fixed Carbon*. *Fixed Carbon.*

The difference between the sum of the percentages of *Water*, *Volatile Combustible Matter*, and *Fixed Carbon* and 100 is the percentage of *Ash*. The sum of the percentages of *Fixed Carbon* and *Ash.* *Ash* is the percentage of *Coke* which the coal will yield. The *Coke.* appearance of the coke before burning off the *Fixed Carbon*, its hardness, etc., are often valuable indications of the coking qualities of the coal, and should be noted. The appearance, color, etc., of the *Ash* should likewise be noted.

ANALYSIS OF THE ASH.

The ash may be analyzed by the method given for the analysis of the *Insoluble Silicious Matter* in Iron Ores, page 231.

DETERMINATION OF SULPHUR.

Fusion with
Na₂CO₃
and
KNO₃.
Weigh out 1 gramme of the finely-ground coal or coke, and
mix it thoroughly, by grinding in a large agate or porcelain mortar, with 10 grammes of dry Na_2CO_3 and· 6 grammes of KNO_3.
During the mixing it is well to have the mortar on a large sheet
of white glazed paper, to catch any particles that may be thrown
from it. Transfer the mixture to a large platinum crucible, clean
the mortar by grinding a little Na_2CO_3 in it, transfer this and any
particles that may be on the paper to the crucible, cover the
latter with a lid, and place it on a triangle over a Bunsen burner.
Heat the crucible very carefully, and raise the heat very slowly,
cautiously removing the lid of the crucible from time to time to
see that the fusion does not boil over. It is very necessary that
none of the fused sodium or potassium salts be allowed to get on
the outside of the crucible, for they will certainly absorb sulphuric
or sulphurous acid from the burned gas, and thus vitiate the analysis. When the mass in the crucible is in a tranquil state of fusion,
run it up on the sides of the crucible, allow it to cool, treat it with
hot water, and wash it out into a small clean beaker. Filter from
the insoluble matter, acidulate the filtrate with HCl, and evaporate
to dryness. Redissolve in water with a few drops of HCl, filter,
dilute the filtrate to about 500 c.c., heat to boiling, and add 10–20
c.c. solution of chloride of barium.* Allow the precipitated sulphate
Washing the
sulphate
of barium.
of barium to settle, decant the clear, supernatant fluid through a
filter or through a felt on a Gooch crucible, heat the precipitate
with a solution of acetate of ammonium,† transfer it to the filter,
wash well with hot water, dry, ignite, and weigh as $BaSO_4$, which,
Method of
shorten-
ing the
operation.
multiplied by .13756, gives the weight of S. The time of the
operation may often be very much shortened by adding an excess
of ammonia to the acidulated filtrate of the aqueous solution of
the fusion, and boiling the solution while passing through it a
rapid current of carbonic acid gas. This precipitates the silica,

---

* See page 51.   † See page 45.

alumina, etc., and, after filtering this off, acidulate by HCl, and precipitate the sulphate of barium as above directed.

A blank determination, using the same amount of Na₂CO₃, KNO₃, and HCl, should always be made with every new lot of reagents, and the amount of BaSO₄ found, subtracted from the amount of BaSO₄ in every analysis before calculating the amount of S in the coal or coke.

Correction for S in reagents.

Besides the method given above, Eschka's* method is very often used. It is essentially as follows: Weigh out 1 gramme of the finely-ground sample, and mix it thoroughly in a mortar with 1 gramme of calcined magnesia and .5 gramme of dry carbonate of sodium, transfer the mixture to a crucible, and heat it over a Bunsen burner, having the crucible inclined in such a way that the flame may be applied to the bottom of the crucible, so that the heat, a dull red, shall extend only about one-third up from the bottom. Stir the mixture every few minutes with a platinum wire until the carbon is burned off and the ash is a dull yellow. This will generally require about one hour. Allow the crucible to cool, add to the mixture about 1 gramme of nitrate of ammonium, mix it in thoroughly with a glass rod, place the lid on the crucible, and heat it cautiously until the nitrate of ammonium is decomposed and the crucible is raised to a bright red heat. Allow it to cool, treat it with hot water, and transfer the contents to a beaker. Filter from the insoluble matter, acidulate the filtrate with HCl, and determine the S by precipitation as BaSO₄ in the usual way.

Eschka's method.

In reporting the results of a coal analysis the S should always be reported as a separate matter, and no attempt should be made to distribute it between the *Volatile Combustible Matter*, *Fixed Carbon*, and *Ash*. The reason for this is obvious when we consider the conditions in which S exists in coal, and the difficulty which attends any attempt to determine the amount existing in any one condition.

Method of reporting the amount of S in a coal.

---

* Chem. News, xxi. 261.

Sulphur is known to exist in coal in three conditions,—as a metallic sulphide, such as pyrites; as sulphate of calcium or barium; and as a sulphuretted hydrocarbon. In a proximate analysis of coal about one-half the sulphur in any pyrites present and all the sulphur existing as a sulphuretted hydrocarbon are probably driven off with the *Volatile Combustible Matter.* The rest of the sulphur from the pyrites is oxidized and driven off during the burning of the *Fixed Carbon* (sulphate of iron being easily decomposed at a bright red heat) unless the sulphuric acid formed is taken up by an alkali or alkaline earth.

The nearest approach we can make to a determination of the conditions in which the sulphur exists in any coal is to make a determination of the total sulphur by fusion, and a determination of the sulphuric acid in the ash. By subtracting the S found by the latter determination from the total S the difference may be taken to represent the amount existing as S (in the form of sulphide), and the amount found in the ash as that existing as SO_3 (in the form of sulphate). These results will be correct if the coal contains no carbonates of the alkalies or alkaline earths.

DETERMINATION OF PHOSPHORIC ACID.

Burn off 10 grammes of the coal or coke in a crucible, or, as in anthracite coal or coke this is a very tedious operation, burn it off in a large platinum boat in a tube in a current of oxygen. A boat 4 inches (102 mm.) long, and wide enough to fit in a tube $\frac{3}{4}$ of an inch (19 mm.) in diameter, will hold 10 grammes very easily, and by its use this amount of coke or anthracite coal may be burned off in a current of oxygen in about one and a half hours. Treat the ash with HCl to dissolve any phosphate of calcium, filter, and wash well with water. Stand the filtrate aside, dry, ignite, and fuse the insoluble matter with Na_2CO_3. Dissolve in water, filter from the insoluble matter, acidulate the filtrate with HCl, and evaporate to dryness. Redissolve in water and a little HCl, filter, add this filtrate to the HCl filtrate from the first treatment of the ash, add a little ferric chloride solution and a slight excess of ammonia. Acidulate with acetic acid, heat to boiling, boil for a few minutes, filter, and wash the precipitate once or twice with boiling water. Dissolve the precipitate in HCl, evaporate nearly to dryness, add citric acid, magnesia mixture, and ammonium, and precipitate as directed on page 85. Filter off, ignite, and weigh the $Mg_2P_2O_7$ as there directed. Or, after dissolving the acetate precipitate, as above, in HCl, evaporate down, and precipitate the P_2O_5 by molybdate solution, as directed on page 89 *et seq.*

METHODS FOR THE ANALYSIS

OF

GASES.

THE technical analysis of gases is of growing importance, and a knowledge of the methods of analysis and of the manipulation involved is now generally necessary to the iron chemist. For ease of manipulation, and for the accuracy of the results obtained by its use, Hempel's form of apparatus is generally to be preferred. It consists essentially of a burette for holding and measuring the gas B, Fig. 100 (the modified Winkler's gas-burette), and a pipette, G, Fig. 100, which holds the reagent. By means of the level-tube A, filled with water, the gas is forced into the pipette, where it is brought in contact with the reagent and afterwards returned to the burette and measured. By the use of a series of these pipettes, each filled with a separate reagent, the various constituents of the gas under examination are absorbed and their volumes estimated.

Hempel's apparatus.

COLLECTING SAMPLES.

Fig. 97 shows a very simple method for taking a sample of gas for analysis. The porcelain tube A passes through the brick-work into the flue through which the gas is carried. In the sketch a portion of the porcelain tube is cut away, to show the loose filaments of asbestos with which the tube is filled to keep dust or tarry matter from entering the burette. This asbestos must be put in very loosely, or else it will pack and interfere with the free passage of the gas. Where the gas, as from a producer, etc., is constantly examined, it is very convenient to have a valve fitted permanently to an iron pipe screwed or cemented into the flue, into which the porcelain tube may be fastened by means of a rubber or asbestos * stopper. A glass tube of about ¼ inch (6 mm.) diameter is fitted into the outer end of the porcelain tube

FIG. 97.

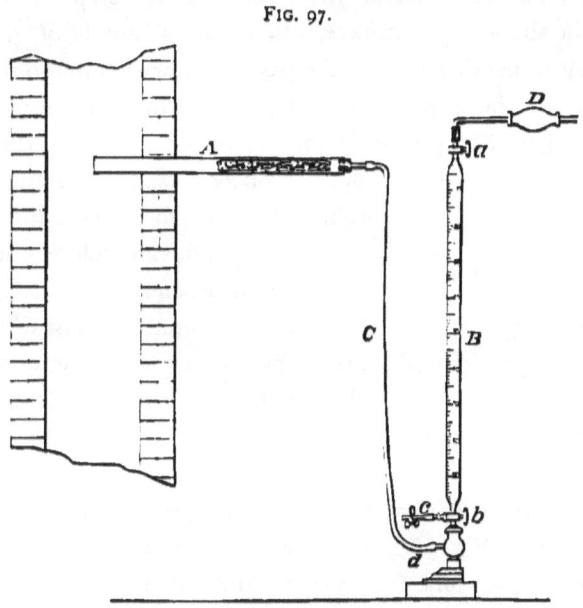

A, Fig. 97, by means of a rubber or asbestos stopper, and this glass tube is connected by means of the rubber tube C with the opening at the lower end of the burette *d*. If the gas is under pressure (as is rarely the case), it is only necessary to open the stopcocks and allow it to pass through the burette until the air is entirely displaced. Usually, however, it is necessary to draw the gas through; and the little india-rubber pump D attached to

Taking the sample in the burette.

----

* See page 134.

Aspirator
for draw-
ing gas
through
the bu-
rette.
the capillary tube at the upper end of the burette is very useful
for this purpose. It is fitted with a simple valve at each end, so
that by compressing the bulb in the hand its contents are dis-
charged through the outer end while the pressure closes the valve
at the burette end. When the bulb is released it resumes its shape,
the tension closing the outer valve and opening the one towards
the burette, through which the contents of the latter are drawn
into the bulb. A bulb of the usual size will empty a 100 c.c.
burette in about three strokes. In taking a sample of gas, turn
the 3-way stopcock *b* so that the passage is open through into the
burette, open the stopcock *a* at the upper end of the burette, and

pump the gas through slowly for five or six minutes. Close the

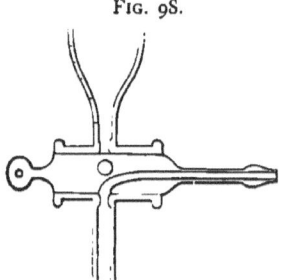

FIG. 98.

upper stopcock *a*, compress the rubber
tube C between the thumb and fingers
of the left hand, and, holding the tube
with the other hand, slide the left hand
towards the burette. This will compress the gas in the burette, and by
closing the stopcock *b* while the tube
C is thus held the gas in the burette
will be under pressure. In closing *b*,
it must be turned so that the passage is open from *d* out through
c, as shown in Fig. 98. Remove the burette to the laboratory,
attach the rubber tube C of the level-tube A, Fig. 100, to the end
of the burette, loosen the pinchcock E, and allow the water to
run through until it comes out through the rubber tube on the
end of the stopcock. Close E, and allow the burette and gas to

attain the temperature of the laboratory. Samples of gas for
analysis may also be taken in glass tubes drawn out at the ends
and closed by rubber tubes and pinchcocks or pieces of glass rod.
When the sample is to be taken to a distance, it may often be collected in a metal vessel with conical ends and tubes with well-
ground stopcocks. Glass vessels of the proper shape, holding
from half a litre to one litre, and fitted with glass stopcocks and

capillary tubes made for this purpose, may be purchased from dealers in chemical glass-ware. From these vessels or tubes the gas may be transferred to the burette by attaching to one outlet a *Transfer-ring to the burette.* tube filled with water and joined to the burette, likewise filled with water, placing the other end of the vessel in water, lowering the level-tube, and drawing the gas into the burette.

REAGENTS FOR THE PIPETTES.

Blast-furnace gas, producer gas, and, in general, gases made *Composition of gas.* by drawing or forcing atmospheric air through coal or coke, contain varying amounts of carbon dioxide (CO_2), oxygen (O), carbon monoxide (CO), hydrogen (H), methane, or marsh gas (CH_4), and nitrogen (N). The best absorbents are caustic potassa for CO_2, *Absorbents.* pyrogallol for O, and cuprous chloride in HCl for CO. Hydrogen is determined by ignition with excess of oxygen over palladium sponge, and marsh gas by ignition in a tube filled with cupric oxide. The pipettes required, therefore, are a simple pipette (G, Fig. 100) filled with caustic potassa, 1.27 sp. gr., for absorbing CO_2, which is readily filled by placing in the large tube of the *Method of filling a simple pipette.* pipette a small glass tube, which extends down to the bottom of the bulb and is connected outside with a small glass funnel by means of a piece of gum tubing. Pour the caustic potassa in *Caustic potassa pipette.* through the funnel until the large bulb of the pipette and the tube connecting the two bulbs are filled with the liquid. Draw the liquid into the capillary tube until it reaches to within a very short distance of the rubber tube on the end of the capillary, and close the rubber tube with a piece of glass tubing or a pinchcock, as shown in the sketch of the composite pipette, Fig. 99.

A composite pipette (Fig. 99) containing pyrogallol for absorb- *Method of filling a composite pipette.* ing oxygen is filled as follows : Dissolve 30 grammes of, pyrogallic acid in 75 c.c. of water, attach a funnel to the capillary tube

of the pipette by a piece of rubber tubing, and fill it with the solution. Attach a piece of rubber tubing to the other tube of the

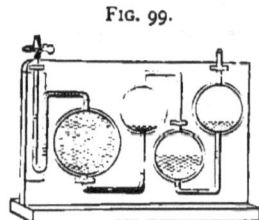

Fig. 99.

pipette, and by gentle suction exhaust the
air; this will cause the liquid to run rapidly through the capillary tube into the
pipette. Keep the funnel full until the
liquid which is drawn through the large
bulb into the second bulb fills the latter
to an inconvenient extent, then stop the
suction, and very carefully blow the liquid back into the large
bulb.   Fill the funnel again, and exhaust the air gently as
before. Repeat this until all the solution of pyrogallic acid has
been drawn in, and then with the same precautions draw in a
solution of caustic potassa, 1.27 sp. gr., until the large bulb and
the tube connecting the large bulb and the second bulb are filled
with the liquid, which is now an alkaline solution of pyrogallate

*Pyrogallol
pipette.*

of potassium.   Close the capillary tube as directed for the caustic
potassa pipette, page 283.   Insert the small tube and funnel in the
large tube of the composite pipette, as directed on page 283 for
filling the simple pipette, and pour a little water into the last bulb
of the composite pipette.   The amount of water poured in should
not be sufficient to fill the third bulb, for the pyrogallol rapidly
absorbs the oxygen of the air in the second bulb, and this contraction causes the water poured into the last bulb to rise in the third
bulb.   Therefore the amount of water should be small enough to
permit small bubbles of air to pass through to supply the contraction in the second bulb, and large enough to avoid emptying the
third bulb when the gas during an analysis is forced through the
capillary into the large bulb of the pipette.   The amount of pyrogallate of potassium from 30 grammes of pyrogallic acid is suffi-

*Absorbing
capacity
of pyro-
gallol.*

cient to absorb nearly 1500 c.c. of pure oxygen, so that a composite pipette filled in this way, and securely sealed by the water
in the third and fourth bulbs, will last for almost an indefinite
number of analyses.

Another composite pipette for absorbing carbon monoxide is Cuprous chloride pipette. filled, as above described, with a saturated solution of cuprous chloride in HCl, 1.1 sp. gr., and sealed with water. Each pipette Marking pipettes. should be distinctly labelled with the name of the reagent, so that no mistake can be made in using them.

It is worthy of note that the absorption of CO by cuprous Absorption of CO by cuprous chloride never perfect. chloride is purely mechanical, and is never absolutely perfect, so that a small amount of CO *invariably* remains in the gas after treatment in the cuprous chloride pipette. Moreover, whenever a gas absolutely free from CO is treated in a cuprous chloride pipette (which has been previously used to absorb CO) and returned to the burette, it will be found to have *increased* in volume, and subsequent combustion in a palladium tube will yield an amount of CO_2 corresponding to this increase counted as CO. If this fact is overlooked, the CO left in the gas will be counted as methane if a determination of this gas is made in the usual course of the analysis.

A composite pipette filled with bromine-water to absorb Bromine pipette for C_2H_4. ethylene (C_2H_4) is sometimes used, as this gas has been found in the gases from blast-furnace and producers using bituminous coal. But the amount of ethylene is very small, and a separate determination is rarely made, any small amount being absorbed and determined as CO.

ANALYSIS OF THE SAMPLE.

The burette containing the gas, with the level-tube filled with water attached, as mentioned on page 282, having attained the temperature of the laboratory, raise the level-tube and open the 3-way stopcock so that the passage is open for the water to enter the burette. If the gas is shown to be under a slight pressure, by raising or lowering the burette bring the water just to the stopcock (if the burette is graduated to read 100 c.c. from stopcock to stopcock, otherwise bring the water to the 0 mark), and close the stopcock. Then open the upper stopcock for an instant to allow the gas to assume the pressure of the atmosphere. Now open the 3-way stopcock to allow the water to enter the burette, hold the

level-tube so that the water in the tube and that in the burette are at the same level, and observe the reading of the burette. It is a very simple matter in this way to get exactly 100 c.c. of gas, which very materially simplifies the calculations. Connect the burette with the pipette containing caustic potassa by means of the capillary connecting-tube, as shown in Fig. 100. Some little skill is necessary in making this connection; the best way to arrange it is as follows: Attach one end of the capillary connecting-tube to the top of the burette by a piece of gum tubing, wiring it if necessary, then compress between the thumb and forefinger of one hand the rubber tube on the capillary of the pipette for its entire length above the pinch-cock (as shown in Fig. 99), then carefully introduce the end of the capillary connecting-tube into the end of the rubber tube, and release the rubber tube. If this is carefully done, the walls of the rubber tube between the pinchcock and the end of the capillary will remain in contact, showing that no air has been

FIG. 100.

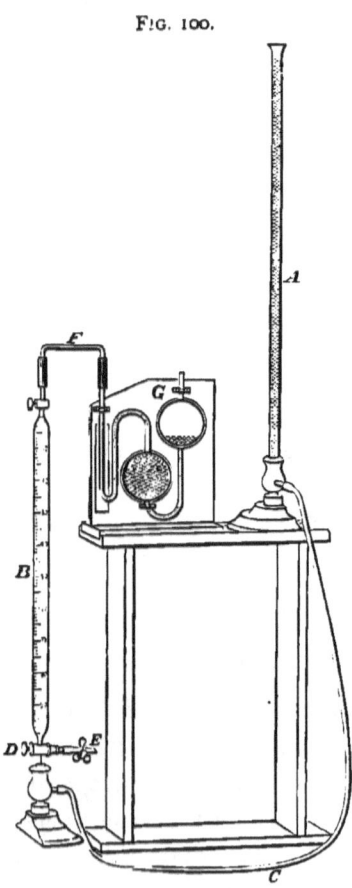

admitted. Force the end of the capillary tube down to the pinch-cock, and open the latter, allowing it to remain over the capillary, as shown in Fig. 101. The apparatus will now be in the position shown in Fig. 100. Open the upper stopcock of the burette, and then turn the 3-way stopcock D carefully to admit the water from the level-tube into the burette. As the water enters the burette the gas is forced over into the pipette G. Allow the water to fill completely the burette B and to enter the capillary tube F and fill it as far as the rubber connection between it and the capillary tube of the pipette G. Close the upper stopcock of the burette, place the pinchcock on the rubber tube between the capillary connecting-tube and the pipette, and remove the capillary connecting-tube F from the rubber tube of the pipette, leaving it attached to the burette. Take the pipette from the stand and shake it, to promote the absorption of the CO_2, which will require only a minute or two. Replace the pipette, attach the capillary connecting-tube F as before, remove the pinchcock, place the level-tube A on the floor, open the upper stopcock of the burette, and allow the water to run from the burette B into the level-tube A, drawing the gas from the pipette G into the burette B. When the caustic potassa solution has run back so as to fill the large bulb and the capillary of the pipette almost to the rubber connection, close the upper stopcock of the burette B quickly, replace the pinchcock on the rubber tube of the pipette G, detach the capillary connecting-tube F from the pipette, hold the level-tube A and the burette B together to get the water on an exact level, and take the reading of the burette. The difference between this reading and the original reading will be the number of c.c. of CO_2 absorbed; and if the original reading was 100 c.c., each c.c. absorbed will be one per cent. of CO_2 in the gas. If any other volume of gas was originally used, divide the number of c.c. absorbed by the number originally used, multiply this by 100, and the result is the percentage of CO_2 in the gas.

If ethylene is to be determined, pass the gas into the bromine-water pipette, back into the burette, then into the caustic potassa

Determination of CO_2.

Determination of C_2H_4.

pipette to absorb any bromine fumes, finally back into the burette, and take the reading as before. The contraction is ethylene.

Determination of O.

Now pass the gas into the pyrogallol pipette, shake the latter gently for four or five minutes to promote the absorption of the oxygen, return the gas to the burette, and note the reading. The contraction from the last reading is O.

Determination of CO.

Pass the gas in the same manner into the cuprous chloride pipette, detach and shake the latter gently at short intervals for five or six minutes to promote the absorption of the CO, return the gas to the burette, and take the reading. The contraction from the last reading is the CO absorbed by cuprous chloride.

Determination of H.

To determine the remaining CO and the H, the gas is mixed with oxygen and burned over spongy palladium. Fig. 101 shows the

Description of the apparatus.

arrangement of the apparatus. A is the palladium tube, B the burette, C a pipette filled with water, D a small gas-burner for heating the palladium tube, and E the gas-pipe attached to the wood-work of the pipette and connected by a rubber tube with a supply of gas. Instead of a gas-burner for heating the palladium tube a small brass spirit-lamp may be used, which is fastened to the pipette-stand by a clamp in such a position as to bring the flame under the palladium tube. With any ordinary furnace or producer gas which contains 50 per cent. and upwards of nitrogen, the best plan is to attach an oxygen-cylinder to the top of the burette, using a capillary tube and rubber connections, and fill the latter with oxygen

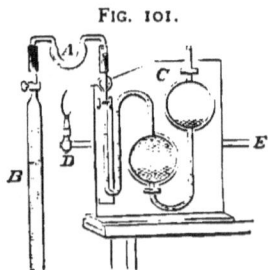

FIG. 101.

Transferring a portion of the unabsorbed gas.

gas. With water-gas, or when a supply of oxygen is not available, it is necessary to transfer a portion of the unabsorbed gas in the burette to another burette, and then to admit air to the first burette until it is nearly filled. Of course it makes the calculation a little more complicated to change the volume of the gas in this way during the progress of an analysis, but in the case of nearly pure water-gas the use of oxygen alone would probably lead to an explosion, while with other gases, in the absence of a supply of oxygen, simply filling the burette with air without letting out any of the gas might not admit enough oxygen to burn the hydrogen. After transferring a portion of the unabsorbed gas, read the burette carefully to get the volume of gas taken for combustion, and then *Divide the volume of gas taken for combustion by the total volume unabsorbed, and multiply by the amount originally taken for analysis;* the result is the number of c.c. of *the original gas*, to which the amount taken for combustion corresponds.

Calculating the volume of gas used.

After admitting air to the burette, which is done by standing the level-tube on the floor while the burette is on the table, opening the 3-way stopcock so that the water may run into the level-tube, and opening the upper stopcock of the burette until the proper amount of air has been drawn in, take the reading of the burette with care. Connect the apparatus as shown in Fig. 101, light the gas-jet D, open the upper stopcock of the burette B, and by opening very carefully the 3-way stopcock of the burette cause the gas to pass *very slowly* into the pipette C. The palladium tube should not be heated to redness, but to a temperature just below a dark-red heat. It is very necessary to avoid carrying over any water into the hot palladium tube, as it would be certain to crack it, and for this reason it is well to see that the capillary tube above the stopcock of the burette and both capillary ends of the palladium tube are dry before making the connections. Any little moisture may be removed by means of a very fine wire wrapped with thread. As the water from the combustion of the H in the palladium is liable to condense in the end of the tube near the pipette, it is always well to warm this gently with the flame of a small spirit-lamp or a piece of glowing charcoal, so as to drive all the moisture into the pipette, and thus prevent its being carried into the hot part of the palladium tube when the gas is returned into the burette. When the water has risen in the burette just above the upper stopcock, lower the level-tube and draw the gas

Precautions necessary to avoid breaking the palladium tube.

back very slowly into the burette. When the water in the pipette has risen to the usual position in the capillary, replace the pinch-cock on the rubber connection between the palladium tube and the capillary tube of the pipette, extinguish the light under the palladium tube, and, when the latter is cold, close the upper stop-cock of the burette, detach the apparatus, open the 3-way stop-cock fully, and take the reading of the burette.

Now, if there were no CO present in the gas before the com-bustion, the contraction would be due to the condensation of the H_2O formed by the combustion of the H, and, as 2 volumes of H unite with 1 volume of O to form H_2O, $\frac{2}{3}$ of the contraction would be H. In the presence of CO, however, there is an additional con-traction beyond that caused by the formation of H_2O, due to the fact that 2 volumes of CO uniting with 1 volume of O form 2 volumes of CO_2. By absorbing the CO_2 in the caustic potassa pipette, and then reading the burette, the second contraction is the

Calculating H and CO. volume of the CO_2, which is the volume of the CO. The first con-traction, then, is $\frac{2}{3}$ of the $H + \frac{1}{2}$ the CO, and the second contrac-tion being the volume of the CO, it may be stated thus:

first contraction $= \frac{2}{3}H + \frac{1}{2}$ second contraction,

or $\frac{2}{3}H =$ first contraction $- \frac{1}{2}$ second contraction ;

multiplying by $\frac{2}{3}$,

$H = \frac{2}{3}$ first contraction $- \frac{1}{3}$ second contraction.

Divide the number of c.c. of H and CO respectively as found above by the number of c.c. of the original gas to which the amount taken for combustion is equivalent, multiply by 100, and the result is the percentage of H and CO. This percentage of CO is to be added to the percentage found by absorption in cuprous

Total CO. chloride, and the result is the total CO.

Determina-tion of CH_4. There remain now in the burette only nitrogen and methane. The latter can be properly burned only at a red heat in contact with oxide of copper, forming H_2O and CO_2. By absorbing the CO_2 in a solution of caustic baryta, standardized by a normal solu-tion of oxalic acid, and then titrating the caustic baryta, the volume of CH₄ is at once indicated. As the normal solution of oxalic acid indicates the volume of CH₄ at 760 mm. of barometric pressure and 0° C. of temperature, the thermometer and barometer must be noted, and the correction made according to the table (Table V.).

Dissolve 5.6314 grammes of crystallized oxalic acid in 1 litre of water. 1 c.c. of this solution indicates 1 c.c. CO_2, or 1 c.c. CH₄, at 760 mm. barometric pressure and 0° C. Dissolve 14.0835 grammes of crystallized hydrate of barium in 1 litre of water. 1 c.c. of this solution is equal to about 1 c.c. of the oxalic acid solution.

The apparatus for the determination is shown in Fig. 102. It consists of a porcelain tube, EE, in the combustion-furnace F: the

FIG. 102.

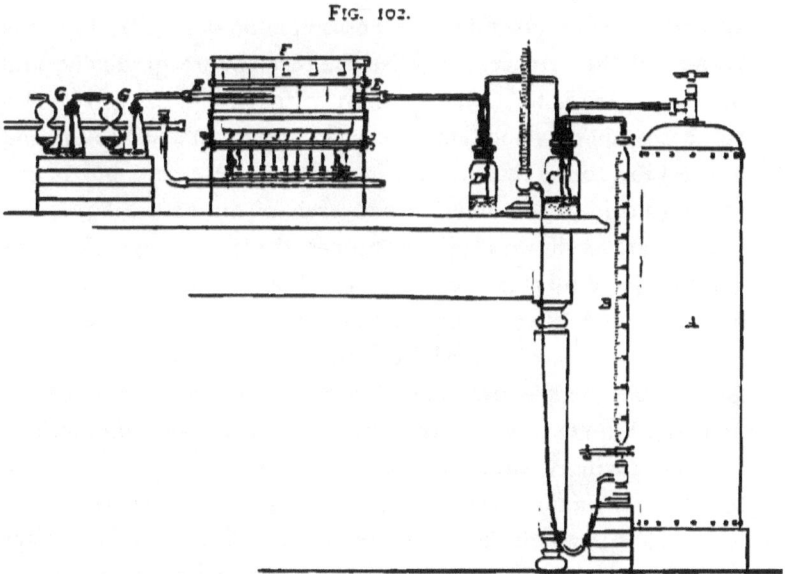

porcelain tube is nearly filled with coarse oxide of copper between loose plugs of asbestos, or with a roll of oxidized copper wire (see page 132). The forward end is connected with two absorption-bottles, G. G. containing caustic baryta solution. These bottles are of such a size that 25 c.c. will fill them, so that the gas in bubbling through forces a little of the solution up into the bulb-tube, thus prolonging the contact. If they are a little too large, the solution of caustic baryta may be diluted, after it is measured in from the pipette, with a little distilled water to·bring it to the proper

Description of the apparatus.
volume. A is a cylinder containing oxygen under pressure, or, if this is not available, a couple of bottles for forcing air through the apparatus may be substituted (such as those shown in Fig. 55, page 128). The cylinder and the burette B are connected, as shown in the sketch (Fig. 102), by means of capillary tubes with the bottle C, containing caustic potassa, 1.27 sp. gr. The bottle C is connected with the bottle D, containing H_2SO_4, and from D a capillary tube passes to the rubber stopper in the end of the por-

Description of the process.
celain tube EE. Start a current of oxygen or air through the apparatus (before attaching the absorption-bottles G, G), light the burners of the furnace, and raise the temperature gradually until the tube is red-hot. Continue the passage of the oxygen until a bottle containing a solution of caustic baryta attached to the end of the tube shows that no CO_2 is given off. Measure out 25 c.c. of the caustic baryta solution into each of the bottles G, G, and attach them as shown in Fig. 102, open the upper stopcock of the burette B, and by means of the 3-way stopcock let water into the burette from the level-tube, so that the gas from the burette is made to bubble very slowly into the bottle C. About three or four bubbles should pass into C from the oxygen cylinder to one from the burette. When the water completely fills the burette and the capillary tube in C, close the upper stopcock of the burette, and continue the passage of the oxygen from A until it is certain that all the gas has been carried through the porcelain tube and the absorption-bottles. In the mean time measure out 25 or 50 c.c. of the caustic baryta solution into a porcelain dish, dilute with water, add a drop of phenolphtalein solution (made by dissolving phenolphtalein in alcohol), and from a burette run in the standard solution of oxalic acid until the pink color of the solution just vanishes. This will give the value of the caustic

baryta solution in terms of the normal oxalic acid solution. When the combustion is finished, detach the absorption-bottles, wash their contents into the dish, add a drop of phenolphtalein solution, and titrate with the oxalic acid solution. The difference between the value of 50 c.c. baryta solution and the value of the 50 c.c. from the absorption-bottles, in terms of the oxalic acid solution, is the number of c.c. of CH_4 in the gas burned at 760 mm. barometric pressure and 0° C. Divide this by the number of c.c. burned, reduced to 760 mm. pressure and 0° C., multiply by 100, and the result is the volume per cent. of CH_4. Add together the percentages obtained of CO_2 (ethylene, C_2H_4), O, CO, H, and CH_4, subtract the sum from 100, and the remainder is the percentage of N by difference.

Calculation of the result.

Determination of N.

An example will illustrate the method of analysis, thus:

EXAMPLE OF ANALYSIS.

Siemens' Producer Gas.

Volume of gas employed, 99.7 c.c.

KHO pipette . . . . . . 93.5 c.c.   Contraction, 6.2 c.c. CO_2 = 6.21 %

Pyrogallol pipette . . . . 93.3 "   "   0.2 "   O = 0.20 "

CuCl   " . . . . 74.0 "   "   19.3 " = 19.36 % CO

Transferred a portion.   From palladium combustion   1.42 " CO (total) = 20.78 "

Remaining in pipette . . . 46.8 "   H   = 11.23 "

= of original gas to . . . 63.24 " $\left[\dfrac{46.8}{74} \times 99.7\right]$ CH_4 = 3.14 "

Admitted air to . . . . . 98.4 "   N   = 58.44 "

                                                              100.00 "

Burned over palladium . . 87.3 "

First contraction . . . . . 11.1 "

KHO pipette . . . . . . 86.4 "

Second contraction . . . . 0.9 " = CO_2 = CO$\left[\dfrac{0.9}{63.24} \times 100\right]$ = 1.42 % CO.

$H = \frac{2}{3}[11.1] - \frac{1}{3}[0.9] = 7.1$ c.c. $\left[\dfrac{7.1}{63.24} \times 100\right]$ = 11.23 % H.

Burned residue over oxide of copper and absorbed CO_2 in caustic baryta solution.

      Thermometer 17° C.   Barometer 745 mm.   745.0 — 14.4 = 730.6

      7 .0086702 × 100 = .86702

      3 .0037158 × 10   = .037158

      0   × 1   = .000000

      6 .0074316 × 0.1 = .00074316

                             .90492116

63.24 c.c. × .90492116 = 57.23 c.c. at 760 mm. and 0° C.

          50 c.c. caustic baryta solution = 48.3 c.c. oxalic acid

    After combustion 50 c.c. "   "   " = 46.5 "   "   "

      Therefore CH_4 in gas burned   = 1.8 "

and $\dfrac{1.8}{57.23} \times 100 = 3.14$ % CH_4.

TABLE I.

Atomic Weights of the Elements used in this Volume.

Name.	Symbol.	At. Wt.	Name.	Symbol.	At. Wt.
Aluminium	Al	27.07	Manganese	Mn	55.00
Antimony	Sb	120.00	Molybdenum	Mo	96.00
Arsenic	As	75.00	Nickel	Ni	58.70
Barium	Ba	137.00	Nitrogen	N	14.03
Bromine	Br	79.95	Oxygen	O	16.00
Calcium	Ca	40.08	Phosphorus	P	30.97
Carbon	C	12.00	Platinum	Pt	194.87
Chlorine	Cl	35.45	Potassium	K	39.11
Chromium	Cr	52.14	Silicon	Si	28.40
Cobalt	Co	59.00	Sodium	Na	23.05
Copper	Cu	63.40	Sulphur	S	32.06
Hydrogen	H	1.007	Tin	Sn	119.00
Iodine	I	126.85	Titanium	Ti	48.00
Iron	Fe	56.00	Tungsten	W	184.00
Lead	Pb	206.95	Vanadium	V	51.37
Magnesium	Mg	24.29	Zinc	Zn	65.27

TABLE II.

Table of Factors.

Found.	Required.	Factor.	Log.
AlPO$_4$............	Al	0.22181	9.3459811–10
Al$_2$O$_3$............	Al	0.53005	9.7243168–10
Sb$_2$O$_4$............	Sb	0.78947	9.8973356–10
Sb$_2$S$_3$............	Sb	0.71390	9.8536374–10
Mg$_2$(NH$_4$)$_2$As$_2$O$_8$ + H$_2$O	As	0.39400	9.5954962–10
Mg$_2$As$_2$O$_7$............	As	0.48297	9.6839202–10
As$_2$S$_3$............	As	0.60931	9.7848383–10
As	FeAs$_2$	1.37333	0.1377749
BaSO$_4$............	S	0.13756	9.1384922–10
	SO$_3$	0.34352	9.5359520–10
CaSO$_4$............	CaO	0.41193	9.6148234–10
	CaCO$_3$	0.73513	9.8663641–10
CaO	CaCO$_3$	1.78459	0.2515385
CO$_2$............	C	0.27273	9.4357329–10
Cr$_2$O$_3$............	Cr	0.68479	9.8355574–10
CoSO$_4$............	Co	0.38050	9.5803547–10
	CoO	0.48370	9.6845761–10
Co	CoO	1.27119	0.1042105
CoO	Co	0.78667	9.8957926–10
Cu	CuO	1.25240	0.0977431
	Cu$_2$S	1.25284	0.0978956
CuO	Cu	0.79849	9.9022695–10
Cu$_2$S	Cu	0.79818	9.9021008–10
Fe$_2$O$_3$............	Fe	0.70000	9.8450980–10
Fe	Fe$_3$O$_4$	1.38095	0.1401779
	FeO	1.28571	0.1091430
PbSO$_4$............	Pb	0.68298	9.8344080–10
	PbO	0.73578	9.8667480–10
	PbS	0.78879	9.8969614–10

TABLE II.—Continued.

Found.	Required.	Factor.	Log.
$Mg_2P_2O_7$	P	0.27836	9.4446068–10
	P_2O_5	0.63788	9.8047390–10
	MgO	0.36212	9.5588525–10
	$MgCO_3$	0.75760	9.8794400–10
Mn_3O_4	Mn	0.72052	9.8576460–10
	MnO	0.93013	9.9685437–10
$Mn_2P_2O_7$	Mn	0.38741	9.5881708–10
	MnO	0.50011	9.6990655–10
MnS	Mn	0.63175	9.8005453–10
	MnO	0.81553	9.9114399–10
$(NH_4)_3 11MoO_3PO_4$	P	0.01630	8.2121876–10
	P_2O_5	0.03735	8.5722906–10
NiO	Ni	0.78581	9.8953176–10
Ni_2S	Ni	0.78549	9.8951407–10
K_2PtCl_6	KCl	0.30696	9.4870818–10
	K_2O	0.19395	9.2876898–10
KCl	K_2CO_3	0.92690	9.9670329–10
NaCl	Na_2O	0.53077	9.7249064–10
	Na_2CO_3	0.90684	9.9575307–10
SiO_2	Si	0.47020	9.6722826–10
S	FeS_2	1.87336	0.2726212
SnO_2	Sn	0.78808	9.8965703–10
TiO_2	Ti	0.60000	9.7781513–10
V_2O_5	V	0.56222	9.7499063–10
WO_3	W	0.79310	9.8993279–10
ZnO	Zn	0.80313	9.9047858–10

TABLE III.

Percentages of P and P_2O_5 for each Milligramme of $Mg_2P_2O_7$ when 10 Grammes of the Sample are used.

Wt. of $Mg_2P_2O_7$.	P.	P_2O_5.	Wt. of $Mg_2P_2O_7$.	P.	P_2O_5.	Wt. of $Mg_2P_2O_7$.	P.	P_2O_5.	Wt of $Mg_2P_2O_7$.	P.	P_2O_5.
1	0.003	0.006	26	0.073	0.166	51	0.142	0.326	76	0.212	0.486
2	0.005	0.013	27	0.075	0.173	52	0.145	0.332	77	0.215	0.492
3	0.008	0.019	28	0.078	0.179	53	0.148	0.339	78	0.218	0.499
4	0.011	0.026	29	0.081	0.185	54	0.151	0.345	79	0.221	0.505
5	0.014	0.032	30	0.084	0.192	55	0.154	0.352	80	0.223	0.512
6	0.017	0.038	31	0.086	0.198	56	0.156	0.358	81	0.226	0.518
7	0.019	0.045	32	0.089	0.204	57	0.159	0.364	82	0.229	0.524
8	0.022	0.051	33	0.092	0.211	58	0.162	0.371	83	0.232	0.531
9	0.025	0.057	34	0.095	0.217	59	0.165	0.377	84	0.235	0.537
10	0.028	0.064	35	0.098	0.224	60	0.167	0.384	85	0.237	0.544
11	0.031	0.070	36	0.101	0.230	61	0.170	0.390	86	0.240	0.550
12	0.033	0.077	37	0.103	0.237	62	0.173	0.396	87	0.243	0.556
13	0.036	0.083	38	0.106	0.243	63	0.176	0.403	88	0.246	0.563
14	0.039	0.089	39	0.109	0.249	64	0.179	0.409	89	0.248	0.569
15	0.042	0.096	40	0.112	0.256	65	0.181	0.416	90	0.251	0.576
16	0.045	0.102	41	0.114	0.262	66	0.184	0.422	91	0.254	0.582
17	0.047	0.108	42	0.117	0.269	67	0.187	0.428	92	0.257	0.588
18	0.050	0.115	43	0.120	0.275	68	0.190	0.434	93	0.259	0.595
19	0.053	0.121	44	0.123	0.281	69	0.193	0.441	94	0.262	0.601
20	0.056	0.128	45	0.126	0.287	70	0.195	0.448	95	0.265	0.607
21	0.059	0.134	46	0.128	0.294	71	0.198	0.454	96	0.268	0.614
22	0.061	0.141	47	0.131	0.300	72	0.201	0.460	97	0.271	0.620
23	0.064	0.147	48	0.134	0.307	73	0.204	0.467	98	0.274	0.627
24	0.067	0.153	49	0.137	0.313	74	0.207	0.473	99	0.276	0.633
25	0.070	0.159	50	0.139	0.319	75	0.209	0.479	100	0.278	0.638

TABLE IV.

Tension of Aqueous Vapor in Millimetres of Mercury from 0° to 34.9° C.

°	Mm.	°	Mm.	°	Mm.	°	Mm.	°	Mm.	°	Mm.	°	Mm.	°	Mm.	°	Mm.	°	Mm.	°	Mm.	°	Mm.	°	Mm.	°	Mm.
0.0	4.600	2.5	5.491	5.0	6.534	7.5	7.751	10.0	9.165	12.5	10.804	15.0	12.699	17.5	14.882	20.0	17.391	22.5	20.265	25.0	23.550	27.5	27.294	30.0	31.548	32.5	36.370
.1	.633	.6	.530	.1	.580	.6	.804	.1	.227	.6	.875	.1	.781	.6	.977	.1	.500	.6	.389	.1	.692	.6	.455	.1	.729	.6	.576
.2	.667	.7	.569	.2	.625	.7	.857	.2	.288	.7	.947	.2	.864	.7	15.072	.2	.608	.7	.514	.2	.834	.7	.617	.2	.911	.7	.783
.3	.700	.8	.608	.3	.671	.8	.910	.3	.350	.8	11.019	.3	.947	.8	.167	.3	.717	.8	.639	.3	.976	.8	.778	.3	32.094	.8	.991
.4	.733	.9	.647	.4	.717	.9	.964	.4	.412	.9	.090	.4	13.029	.9	.262	.4	.826	.9	.763	.4	24.119	.9	.939	.4	.278	.9	37.200
.5	.767	3.0	.687	.5	.763	8.0	8.017	.5	.474	13.0	.162	.5	.112	18.0	.357	.5	.935	23.0	.888	.5	.261	28.0	28.102	.5	.463	33.0	.410
.6	.801	.1	.727	.6	.810	.1	.072	.6	.537	.1	.235	.6	.197	.1	.454	.6	18.047	.1	21.016	.6	.406	.1	.267	.6	.650	.1	.621
.7	.836	.2	.767	.7	.857	.2	.126	.7	.601	.2	.309	.7	.281	.2	.552	.7	.159	.2	.144	.7	.552	.2	.433	.7	.837	.2	.832
.8	.871	.3	.807	.8	.904	.3	.181	.8	.665	.3	.383	.8	.366	.3	.650	.8	.271	.3	.272	.8	.697	.3	.599	.8	33.026	.3	38.045
.9	.905	.4	.848	.9	.951	.4	.236	.9	.728	.4	.456	.9	.451	.4	.747	.9	.383	.4	.400	.9	.842	.4	.765	.9	.215	.4	.258
1.0	.940	.5	.889	6.0	.998	.5	.291	11.0	.792	.5	.530	16.0	.536	.5	.845	21.0	.495	.5	.528	26.0	.988	.5	.931	31.0	.405	.5	.473
.1	.975	.6	.930	.1	7.047	.6	.347	.1	.857	.6	.605	.1	.623	.6	.945	.1	.610	.6	.659	.1	25.138	.6	29.101	.1	.596	.6	.689
.2	5.011	.7	.972	.2	.095	.7	.404	.2	.923	.7	.681	.2	.710	.7	16.045	.2	.724	.7	.790	.2	.288	.7	.271	.2	.787	.7	.906
.3	.047	.8	6.014	.3	.144	.8	.461	.3	.989	.8	.757	.3	.797	.8	.145	.3	.839	.8	.921	.3	.438	.8	.441	.3	.980	.8	39.124
.4	.082	.9	.055	.4	.193	.9	.517	.4	10.054	.9	.832	.4	.885	.9	.246	.4	.954	.9	22.058	.4	.588	.9	.612	.4	34.174	.9	.344
.5	.118	4.0	.097	.5	.242	9.0	.574	.5	.120	14.0	.908	.5	.972	19.0	.346	.5	19.069	24.0	.184	.5	.738	29.0	.782	.5	.368	34.0	.565
.6	.155	.1	.140	.6	.292	.1	.632	.6	.187	.1	.986	.6	14.062	.1	.449	.6	.187	.1	.319	.6	.891	.1	.956	.6	.564	.1	.786
.7	.191	.2	.183	.7	.342	.2	.690	.7	.255	.2	12.064	.7	.151	.2	.552	.7	.305	.2	.453	.7	26.045	.2	30.131	.7	.761	.2	40.007
.8	.228	.3	.226	.8	.392	.3	.748	.8	.322	.3	.142	.8	.241	.3	.655	.8	.423	.3	.588	.8	.198	.3	.305	.8	.959	.3	.230
.9	.265	.4	.270	.9	.442	.4	.807	.9	.389	.4	.220	.9	.331	.4	.758	.9	.541	.4	.723	.9	.351	.4	.479	.9	35.159	.4	.455
2.0	.302	.5	.313	7.0	.492	.5	.865	12.0	.457	.5	.298	17.0	.421	.5	.861	22.0	.659	.5	.858	27.0	.505	.5	.654	32.0	.359	.5	.680
.1	.340	.6	.357	.1	.544	.6	.925	.1	.526	.6	.378	.1	.513	.6	.967	.1	.780	.6	.996	.1	.663	.6	.833	.1	.559	.6	.907
.2	.378	.7	.401	.2	.595	.7	.985	.2	.596	.7	.458	.2	.605	.7	17.073	.2	.901	.7	23.135	.2	.820	.7	31.011	.2	.760	.7	41.135
.3	.416	.8	.445	.3	.647	.8	9.045	.3	.665	.8	.538	.3	.697	.8	.179	.3	20.022	.8	.273	.3	.978	.8	.190	.3	.962	.8	.364

TABLE V.

Table for Reducing Volumes of Gases to the Normal State.

BY PROFESSOR DR. LEO LIEBERMANN.

(From Winkler's "Technical Gas Analysis.")

Instructions for Use.

Suppose the volume of a gas to have been found $= 26.2$ c.c. at 742 mm. barometric pressure, 18° C. temperature, saturated with moisture. In order to reduce it to the normal state (760 mm., 0° C., dry), we proceed as follows:

1st. Look out the degree 18 (columns 1 and 4), and deduct the tension of aqueous vapor given, $= 15.3$ mm., from the observed pressure, $= 742.0$:

$$742.0 - 15.3 = 726.7 \text{ mm.}$$

2d. Now find the volume which 1 vol. of the gas would have at the pressure of 726.7 mm. by looking out seriatim the figures 7, 2, 6, and 7 in column 2 at the temperature 18°, and placing the numerical values, to be found opposite those figures, in the same column, multiplying them seriatim by 100, 10, 1, 0.1; whereupon they are added up, thus:

$$
\begin{array}{llll}
7 & 0.0086408 \times & 100 & = 0.86408 \\
2 & 0.0024688 \times & 10 & = 0.024688 \\
6 & 0.0074064 \times & 1 & = 0.0074064 \\
7 & 0.0085408 \times & 0.1 & = 0.00086408 \\
\hline
& & & 0.89703848
\end{array}
$$

3d. The corrected volume of a cubic centimetre is lastly multiplied by the number of the c.c. previously found; that is, in the present case,

$$0.89703848 \times 26.2 = 23.502 \text{ c.c.}$$

Temperature ° C.	Pressure in millims. mercury.	Volume at 0° and 760 mm.	Tension of aq. vapor in millim. of mercury for ° C.	Temperature ° C.	Pressure in millims. mercury.	Volume at 0° and 760 mm.	Tension of aq. vapor in millim. of mercury for ° C.
0	1	0.0013157		0	6	0.0078946	
0	2	0.0026315		0	7	0.0092104	
0	3	0.0039473		0	8	0.0105262	
0	4	0.0052631		0	9	0.0118420	
0	5	0.0065789	0° = 4.5				

TABLE V.—Continued.

Temperature ° C.	Pressure in millims. mercury.	Volume at 0° and 760 mm.	Tension of aq. vapor in millim. of mercury for ° C.	Temperature ° C.	Pressure in millims. mercury.	Volume at 0° and 760 mm.	Tension of aq. vapor in millim. of mercury for ° C.
1	1	0.0013109		4	1	0.0012965	
1	2	0.0026219		4	2	0.0025930	
1	3	0.0039328		4	3	0.0038895	
1	4	0.0052438		4	4	0.0051860	
1	5	0.0065548	1° = 4.9	4	5	0.0064825	4° = 6.0
1	6	0.0078657		4	6	0.0077790	
1	7	0.0091767		4	7	0.0090755	
1	8	0.0104876		4	8	0.0103720	
1	9	0.0117986		4	9	0.0116685	
2	1	0.0013061		5	1	0.0012916	
2	2	0.0026123		5	2	0.0025833	
2	3	0.0039184		5	3	0.0038750	
2	4	0.0052246		5	4	0.0051667	
2	5	0.0065307	2° = 5.2	5	5	0.0064584	5° = 6.5
2	6	0.0078369		5	6	0.0077501	
2	7	0.0091430		5	7	0.0090418	
2	8	0.0104492		5	8	0.0103335	
2	9	0.0117553		5	9	0.0116252	
3	1	0.0013013		6	1	0.0012868	
3	2	0.0026026		6	2	0.0025737	
3	3	0.0039039		6	3	0.0038606	
3	4	0.0052053		6	4	0.0051474	
3	5	0.0065066	3° = 5.6	6	5	0.0064343	6° = 6.9
3	6	0.0078079		6	6	0.0077212	
3	7	0.0091093		6	7	0.0090080	
3	8	0.0104106		6	8	0.0102949	
3	9	0.0117119		6	9	0.0145818	

TABLE V.—Continued.

Tempera- ture ° C.	Pressure in millims. mercury.	Volume at 0° and 760 mm.	Tension of aq. vapor in millim. of mercury for ° C.	Tempera- ture ° C.	Pressure in millims. mercury.	Volume at 0° and 760 mm.	Tension of aq. vapor in millim. of mercury for ° C.
7	1	0.0012828		10	1	0.0012692	
7	2	0.0025656		10	2	0.0025384	
7	3	0.0038484		10	3	0.0038076	
7	4	0.0051312		10	4	0.0050768	
7	5	0.0064140	7° = 7.4	10	5	0.0063460	10° = 9.1
7	6	0.0076968		10	6	0.0076152	
7	7	0.0089796		10	7	0.0088844	
7	8	0.0102624		10	8	0.0101536	
7	9	0.0115452		10	9	0.0114228	
8	1	0.0012783		11	1	0.0012648	
8	2	0.0025566		11	2	0.0025296	
8	3	0.0038349		11	3	0.0037944	
8	4	0.0051132		11	4	0.0050592	
8	5	0.0063915	8° = 8.0	11	5	0.0063240	11° = 9.7
8	6	0.0076698		11	6	0.0075888	
8	7	0.0089481		11	7	0.0088536	
8	8	0.0102264		11	8	0.0101184	
8	9	0.0115047		11	9	0.0113832	
9	1	0.0012737		12	1	0.0012603	
9	2	0.0025474		12	2	0.0025206	
9	3	0.0038211		12	3	0.0037809	
9	4	0.0050948		12	4	0.0050412	
9	5	0.0063685	9° = 8.5	12	5	0.0063015	12° = 10.4
9	6	0.0076422		12	6	0.0075618	
9	7	0.0089159		12	7	0.0088221	
9	8	0.0101896		12	8	0.0100824	
9	9	0.0114633		12	9	0.0113427	

TABLE V.—Continued.

Tempera-ture ° C.	Pressure in millims. mercury.	Volume at 0° and 760 mm.	Tension of aq. vapor in millim. of mercury for ° C.	Tempera-ture ° C.	Pressure in millims. mercury.	Volume at 0° and 760 mm.	Tension of aq. vapor in millim. of mercury for ° C.
13	1	0.0012559		16	1	0.0012429	
13	2	0.0025118		16	2	0.0024858	
13	3	0.0037677		16	3	0.0037287	
13	4	0.0050236		16	4	0.0049716	
13	5	0.0062795	13° = 11.1	16	5	0.0062145	16° = 13.5
13	6	0.0075354		16	6	0.0074574	
13	7	0.0087913		16	7	0.0087003	
13	8	0.0100472		16	8	0.0099432	
13	9	0.0113031		16	9	0.0111861	
14	1	0.0012516		17	1	0.0012386	
14	2	0.0025032		17	2	0.0024772	
14	3	0.0037548		17	3	0.0037158	
14	4	0.0050064		17	4	0.0049544	
14	5	0.0062580	14° = 11.9	17	5	0.0061930	17° = 14.4
14	6	0.0075096		17	6	0.0074316	
14	7	0.0087612		17	7	0.0086702	
14	8	0.0100128		17	8	0.0099088	
14	9	0.0112644		17	9	0.0111474	
15	1	0.0012472		18	1	0.0012344	
15	2	0.0024944		18	2	0.0024688	
15	3	0.0037416		18	3	0.0037032	
15	4	0.0049888		18	4	0.0049376	
15	5	0.0062360	15° = 12.7	18	5	0.0061720	18° = 15.3
15	6	0.0074832		18	6	0.0074064	
15	7	0.0087304		18	7	0.0086408	
15	8	0.0099776		18	8	0.0098752	
15	9	0.0112248		18	9	0.0111096	

TABLE V.—Continued.

Temperature ° C.	Pressure in millims. mercury.	Volume at 0° and 760 mm.	Tension of aq. vapor in millim. of mercury for ° C.	Temperature ° C.	Pressure in millims. mercury.	Volume at 0° and 760 mm.	Tension of aq. vapor in millim. of mercury for ° C.
19	1	0.0012301		22	1	0.0012176	
19	2	0.0024602		22	2	0.0024352	
19	3	0.0036903		22	3	0.0036528	
19	4	0.0049204		22	4	0.0048704	
19	5	0.0061505	19° = 16.3	22	5	0.0060880	22° = 19.6
19	6	0.0073806		22	6	0.0073056	
19	7	0.0086107		22	7	0.0085232	
19	8	0.0098408		22	8	0.0097408	
19	9	0.0110709		22	9	0.0109584	
20	1	0.0012259		23	1	0.0012135	
20	2	0.0024518		23	2	0.0024270	
20	3	0.0036777		23	3	0.0036405	
20	4	0.0049036		23	4	0.0048540	
20	5	0.0061295	20° = 17.4	23	5	0.0060675	23° = 20.9
20	6	0.0073554		23	6	0.0072810	
20	7	0.0085813		23	7	0.0084945	
20	8	0.0098122		23	8	0.0097080	
20	9	0.0110331		23	9	0.0109215	
21	1	0.0012218		24	1	0.0012094	
21	2	0.0024436		24	2	0.0024188	
21	3	0.0036654		24	3	0.0036282	
21	4	0.0048872		24	4	0.0048376	
21	5	0.0061090	21° = 18.5	24	5	0.0060470	24° = 22.2
21	6	0.0073308		24	6	0.0072564	
21	7	0.0085526		24	7	0.0084658	
21	8	0.0097744		24	8	0.0096752	
21	9	0.0109962		24	9	0.0108846	

TABLE V.—Continued.

Tempera- ture ° C.	Pressure in millims. mercury.	Volume at 0° and 760 mm.	Tension of aq. vapor in millim. of mercury for ° C.	Tempera- ture ° C.	Pressure in millims. mercury.	Volume at 0° and 760 mm.	Tension of aq. vapor in millim. of mercury for ° C.
25	1	0.0012054		28	1	0.0011933	
25	2	0.0024108		28	2	0.0023866	
25	3	0.0036162		28	3	0.0035799	
25	4	0.0048216		28	4	0.0047732	
25	5	0.0060270	25° = 23.5	28	5	0.0059665	28° = 28.1
25	6	0.0072324		28	6	0.0071598	
25	7	0.0084378		28	7	0.0083531	
25	8	0.0096432		28	8	0.0095464	
25	9	0.0108486		28	9	0.0107397	
26	1	0.0012013		29	1	0.0011894	
26	2	0.0024026		29	2	0.0023788	
26	3	0.0036039		29	3	0.0035682	
26	4	0.0048052		29	4	0.0047576	
26	5	0.0060065	26° = 25.0	29	5	0.0059470	29° = 29.8
26	6	0.0072078		29	6	0.0071364	
26	7	0.0084091		29	7	0.0083258	
26	8	0.0096104		29	8	0.0095152	
26	9	0.0108117		29	9	0.0107046	
27	1	0.0011973		30	1	0.0011855	
27	2	0.0023946		30	2	0.0023710	
27	3	0.0035919		30	3	0.0035565	
27	4	0.0047892		30	4	0.0047420	
27	5	0.0059865	27° = 26.5	30	5	0.0059275	30° = 31.6
27	6	0.0071838		30	6	0.0071130	
27	7	0.0083811		30	7	0.0082985	
27	8	0.0095784		30	8	0.0094840	
27	9	0.0107757		30	9	0.0106695	

INDEX.

THE END.

PRINTED BY J. B. LIPPINCOTT COMPANY, PHILADELPHIA.